GINIA

Powhatan

MES

John Hull

A
DURABLE
FIRE

A DURABLE FIRE

VIRGINIA BERNHARD

William Morrow and Company, Inc.
New York

Endpaper illustration, "James Forte at Jamestowne," courtesy A. H. Robbins Company

Library of Congress Cataloging-in-Publication Data

Bernhard, Virginia, 1937–
  A durable fire / Virginia Bernhard.
    p.   cm.
  ISBN 0-688-08900-3
  1. Jamestown (Va.)—History—Fiction.   2. Virginia—History—
Colonial period, ca. 1600–1775—Fiction.   I. Title.
PS3552.E73145D87   1990
813'.54—dc20   89-13011
                                                                                  CIP

Printed in the United States of America

First Edition

1 2 3 4 5 6 7 8 9 10

BOOK DESIGN BY OKSANA KUSHNIR

But true love is a durable fire,
In the mind ever burning,
Never sick, never old, never dead,
From itself never turning.

—Sir Walter Raleigh,
  "Pilgrim to Pilgrim" (1599)

CONTENTS

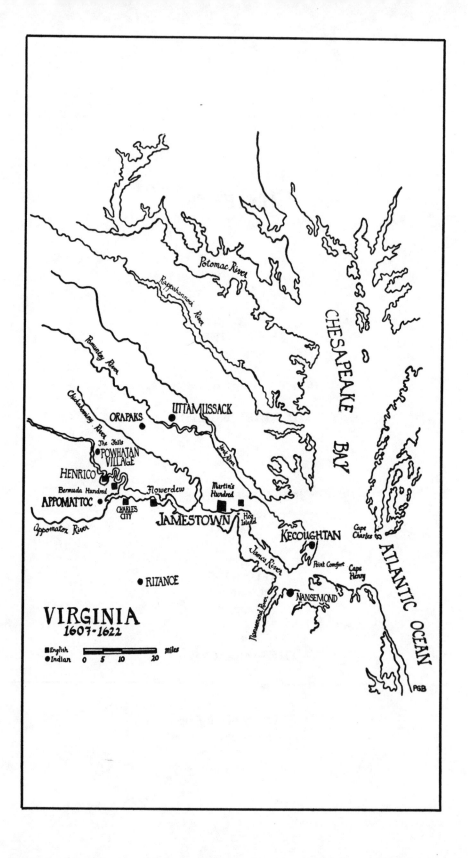

Potomac River

Rappahannock River

CHESAPEAKE BAY

Pamunkey River

Chickahominy River

ORAPAKS

UTTAMUSSACK

The Falls
POWHATAN
VILLAGE

Pamunkey River

HENRICO

Bermuda Hundred

Flowerdew

Martin's
Hundred

APPOMATTOC

CHARLES
CITY

JAMESTOWN

Hog
Island

KECOUGHTAN

Cape
Charles

Appomatox River

James River

Point Comfort

Cape
Henry

ATLANTIC OCEAN

RITANCE

Nansemond River

NANSEMOND

VIRGINIA
1607-1622

■ English
● Indian

0   5 10   20

miles

PGB

AUTHOR'S NOTE

 Long before the *Mayflower* landed at Plymouth, English colonists had sailed across the Atlantic. Some of them, like the 117 men, women, and children who sailed to Roanoke in 1587, disappeared and were never heard of again; others, like 38 of the 104 men and boys who came to Jamestown in 1607, managed to survive. By October 1621, when the Pilgrims bowed their heads over their first Thanksgiving feast in Massachusetts, more than three thousand English settlers had come to Virginia, and some two thousand had died there. Except for a stone monument at Jamestown, those graves today are unmarked, their occupants unknown.

The records of early English settlement in the New World are sketchy. The papers of the Virginia Company from 1606 to 1619, lost in the 1620's, have never been found; the accounts written by the earliest settlers are few and fragmentary; and the Indians, who far outnumbered the English at first, left no written records at all. After nearly four hundred years, the history of early Virginia is a palimpsest with the first tracings still visible and endlessly puzzling to scholars. To this day, no one knows if the Indian chieftain Opechancanough was really carried to Spain in his youth, or what actually happened to the Roanoke colony, or if Pocahontas indeed saved John Smith's life, or why so many people died in Virginia. Readings of the existing evidence change with every generation of historians.

This novel is yet another reading of that evidence. It does not purport to be historical truth, but neither does it deliberately contradict the known facts. *A Durable Fire* is simply the story of what happened, or what might have happened, to the people who settled along the banks of the James River from 1607 to 1622. Most of the characters in this novel are people who actually lived, with the exception of Will Sterling, Meg Worley, and a few minor figures. Their names can be found in the lists of Virginia "planters" in 1607–8, the list of the dead after the Indian attack of 1622, and the census of 1624. In one sense, this novel is a memorial to all the men, women, and children—English and Indian—who lived and died in Virginia so long ago, and about whom nothing is known but their names. The ancient Indian prophecy that "from Chesapeack Bay a Nation should arise which should dissolve and give end" to the empire of the Powhatan is no fiction; the story of what happened to the first English settlers in Virginia, and to the Indians who tried to drive them away, has not been invented. That tangled history is recorded in the documents at the end of this book, and readers may judge for themselves whether truth is stranger than fiction.

I

THE

NATIVES

■

1571–1608

*Wee found the people most gentle,
loving, and faithfull, void of all
guile and treason. . . .*

—*Arthur Barlowe,*
Narrative (1584)

BAHÍA DE SANTA MARIA
(Chesapeake Bay) 1571

On a sun-washed September morning on the north bank of the Pamunkey River, four men tramped toward the Indian village of Uttamussack, their heavy shoes disturbing the primeval carpet of pine needles and dry leaves. Until now, the forest path had known only the soft tread of deerskin moccasins. Three of the men wore the flowing black cassocks of Jesuit priests, and the fourth, taller and darker-skinned than the others, was splendidly attired in a buff jerkin over a shirt of Holland linen and a pair of vermilion trunk hose tied with black ribbon bows. On his head was a soft felt hat with a scarlet plume. He walked a few paces ahead of the others. Above him, in a tall ash tree, a blackbird suddenly began to sing loudly, as if to herald the arrival of the strangers.

"How much farther is it?" Father Segura, vice-provincial of the Jesuits in the Spanish settlement at St. Augustine, Florida, was slightly out of breath.

"The village is just on the other side of that rise in the ground up ahead." Don Luis, Indian convert to Christianity and prized pupil of the Jesuits, gestured with his head, and the plume on his hat waved. Under the jerkin he wore, his heart had begun to pound. Ten years it had been since he had looked upon Uttamussack, the village of his father and his brothers, the village of his boyhood. Ten years since a Spanish galleon had dropped anchor in Chesapeake Bay and Admiral Pedro Menéndez de Avilés had persuaded the fifteen-year-old Ajacanto to visit the land across the sea. Now, at last, he was returning, bearing a strange-sounding name, wearing the clothes of an alien culture, bringing to his people the news of the Christian God. Don Luis began to quicken his steps. The sun was not yet high in the sky; perhaps no one but the women would be stirring in the village. At the top of the gentle slope, he turned and called out to the priests behind him. "There it is! Uttamussack!"

About a hundred yards away, through the trees, was a collection of a dozen large dwellings arranged in a perfect circle around a clearing. The houses varied slightly in size, but were all made of identical materials: saplings set in the ground and bent to form arches, covered with woven straw mats. Inside the circle of houses was a large storehouse, and outside the circle, at some distance from the houses, was a large single structure facing toward the forest. That was the tomb of the werowances: the burial place of the dead chieftains of the river tribes. Don Luis's eyes lingered on the tomb now, as he thought of his father. Would he still be among the living?

"A handsome town. What curious houses!" Father Ortiz, one of the other priests, said amiably. He, like Father Segura, was panting a little. The arduous journey from their mission site on Chesapeake Bay had tired them all.

"My people's houses are not so fine as Spanish houses, but they keep out the summer sun and the winter wind." Don Luis smiled. As they surveyed the village, two young women emerged from the largest of the houses to gather firewood. They wore soft deerskin garments around their waists, but their firm young breasts were bare.

Don Luis, watching them, felt a sudden stirring within him, and glanced sideways at the priests. For ten years, he had lived as a celibate, just like the Jesuit fathers. They told him that subduing desires of the flesh made the spirit strong.

One of the young women, turning around with an armload of cut branches, suddenly dropped them, clutched at her companion's arm, and pointed excitedly to the edge of the woods where Don Luis and the priests were standing. Then, as Don Luis took a step toward them, they ran back to their house. In a moment, three men appeared in the doorway of the house, and the tallest of them stepped forward to meet the visitors. Don Luis, his heart pounding even more, recognized his younger brother Wahunsonacock, now wearing the beaded and feathered headdress of the Powhatan, the chief of all the river tribes. Beside him were Don Luis's other brothers, Opitchapan and Catatough. Doffing his hat and signaling to the priests to stay behind, Don Luis strode across the clearing to meet them. As he neared them, the three stared at him as if he were an apparition, their mouths agape, their eyes unbelieving.

"Ajacanto?"

"Ajacanto!"

"Ajacanto!"

As they called out to him, Don Luis stopped and stood motionless in the clearing while the familiar syllables sounded in his ears like long-forgotten music. He had not heard his Indian name for ten years. "Yes!" he said, "Yes, it is Ajacanto!" He held out his arms to his brothers. They embraced him, each in turn.

"We thought you were dead!"

"We had given you up to the sea long ago!"

"What fine stuff is your coat made of?"

"Look at his hat! What kind of feather is that?"

"Who are those men with you?"

Don Luis, laughing, held up both hands and answered in the Algonquin tongue, "One at a time!" Glancing toward the three priests, he said, "Those men are my spiritual fathers. They have come with me to bring you the word of their God. My God, too." Then he stopped, his face clouded. "To speak of fathers," he began, and then it was his brothers' turn to look solemn. "Where is—"

Wahunsonacock pointed to the tomb at the edge of the clearing. "Our father is there," he said. "We finished mourning his death only seven days ago. He went from us in his sleep."

Don Luis bowed his head. "I am sorry," he said in a low voice. "I am too late."

"You are not too late for this," Wahunsonacock said, touching the headband he wore. "You are the eldest son. You must wear the band of the Powhatan. Now that you are here, I will give it up to you."

"No," Don Luis said slowly. Once he would have seized that symbol of authority and placed it firmly on his own head without a moment's hesitation. It was his by birthright. Now he said, "I did not come back here out of a desire for an earthly kingdom. I came to teach you the way to my Father's kingdom, the kingdom of heaven."

"What do you mean?" His brother Wahunsonacock was offended. "Your father lies there"—he gestured with his head toward the tomb— "and your kingdom lies here, all around you. You are the Powhatan."

"What is this talk of a kingdom of heaven?" Opitchapan, the next-to-youngest brother, asked.

"Are those men your warriors?" Catatough pointed to the priests. "They are not carrying weapons."

"They do not need weapons. They are men of God. Warriors of the Lord Jesus Christ."

Opitchapan and Catatough looked skeptical, and Wahunsonacock's eyes narrowed.

"You are my brother, Ajacanto, who was lost, and I am glad to see you," he said. "But I am not glad to hear your talk. We have our own gods.

The god Okee's image watches over the dead kings, and your own father has just gone to rest among them. If you come here talking of another god, you will make Okee angry, and our father will not rest. Let us talk no more of your Jesus Christ's god. He is not welcome here."

Try as he might, Don Luis could not persuade his brothers to listen to the message of the Gospel. They greeted the priests kindly that first day, and gave them a feast and a dance in honor of his return the next day, but when he tried to tell his people that it was his Christian God who had sent him back to them, they crossed their arms and shook their heads.

"You must be patient," Father Quirós said. "You have just returned, and they are still surprised. Give them time, and the Holy Spirit will soften their hearts." But three days passed, and neither his brothers nor their people changed their minds.

"Put on their clothing," Father Ortiz said. "Put away your Spanish clothes and go among your people dressed as one of them. Let them see that you are still of one heart with them. Then they will listen to you."

And so Don Luis had folded away his Spanish garments and put on a fringed buckskin breechclout and vest and a necklace of shells and tiny beads, but still no one in the village of Uttamussack would listen to him when he spoke of his God.

On the evening of the fourth day, he walked by himself to the edge of the forest. The air was cool but still. Smoke curled in blue-gray spirals from the houses of Uttamussack, and inside them, people made ready for sleep. Don Luis sat down on a log and looked across at the tomb of the dead chiefs. His father was lying there, his body disemboweled, dried, stuffed with beads, and adorned with necklaces and bracelets of copper and pearl. Don Luis had been to see him, had reverently lifted the woven straw mat and touched the bleached deerskin shroud that wrapped his father's body. Nearby, the carved image of the fearsome god Okee glowered with painted eyes. All around, on platforms made of branches lashed together with deer sinews, lay the bodies of other werowances, men who had ruled over the river tribes before his father. Their bodies were all wrapped, like his father's, in white deerskin and covered with straw mats, but their spirits were with Okee in the land beyond the mountains where the sun set. Only chieftains— the werowances—lived after death. Common people rotted like dogs in their shallow graves. Outside the tomb, one of the Indian spirit men paced slowly back and forth. The tomb of the dead chiefs had a spirit man to guard it day and night, to keep out wolves or human enemies who might desecrate the bodies. Inside, the god Okee kept evil spirits at bay. But Okee himself could be evil, could bring death if he chose. The Indians feared him above all other gods. Don Luis had tried to explain to them that his God had died on a cross that death might be vanquished, and even the common people who believed in his God would not die, but they did not believe him. Worse yet, they scoffed at him.

He sighed deeply and watched an owl swoop silently from one pine tree to another. He wished he were like that owl, free, with nothing to think about but hunting and eating and sleeping. All his newfound learning was no good in the wilderness, and he sensed that the Jesuit fathers did not really like his people. As he sat there musing, he felt something touch his shoulder, and a soft voice spoke near his ear.

"Ajacanto, why are you so sad?" It was Nantea, one of the young women he had seen on the first day. She was standing behind him, and when he turned around, his face was a hand's breadth from her deerskin apron. The warm, musky odor of her body filled his nostrils, and the touch of her hand on his bare shoulder awakened feelings the Jesuits had taught him to suppress. Silently, he put his hand over hers, as if to keep it in place. Her hand, under his, was small and soft, but strong. He caressed the ridges of the knuckles, the slender, tapering fingers. Above him, her face was a perfect oval in the fading light.

She bent her head toward him and said, "Ajacanto, you need to have a woman. I was not old enough for you when you went away, but I knew you then. Now I am old enough." Without waiting for him to answer, she leaned over and kissed him lightly on the mouth.

He could not help himself; one touch of her moist rosy lips, and ten years of Jesuit discipline fell away from him like the deerskin garment his feverish fingers flung on the ground. He took her right there, outside in the cool September dusk, lying on the soft earth behind some bushes at the edge of the clearing.

When at last they lay still, locked in each other's arms, he said, "You are right, Nantea, and my Jesuit fathers are wrong."

The next night, Wahunsonacock sent him Nantea's two sisters, and he made love with them, one after the other, as any honored male guest among the river tribes was supposed to do. To refuse one's host's women was considered as rude as refusing his food. The day after that, Don Luis went back to the mission site with the Jesuit fathers to collect the belongings he had left there. This time they walked in cold silence. The priests could barely contain their anger at what he had done.

Back at the mission, Father Segura was determined to make one last effort to convince him of his wrongs: "Don Luis, you have broken the Sixth Commandment. You have let sins of the flesh overtake you, and you have sinned, not with just one woman, but with three! Cast this sin from you, now, and receive the sacrament of penance. I will hear your confession whenever you are ready." Around him, a half-dozen black-robed priests looked on with solemn faces.

Don Luis was furious. Father Segura might have spoken to him privately instead of calling him to account before this grim-faced tribunal.

"No." Don Luis shook his head. Now he would speak his mind to Father Segura. "No, Father, I cannot confess, because I am not sorry for what I have done." He looked the amazed priest squarely in the eye. "I am sorry for you and the others, because my people did not like your God."

Father Segura's heavy black brows drew together in a scowl. Don Luis went on:

"I am grateful for all you have taught me, but I see now that your book learning is not made for the tribes of the forest. I must go back, now, and live among my own people."

"You must not!" Father Segura's voice trembled with ill-concealed rage. "You cannot! After all we have done for you—after all we have taught you, you cannot put away your learning the way you put away your jerkin and trunk hose. You will see, Don Luis. Pray to our heavenly Father, and He will give you guidance. You will feel differently, now that you are away from those savages." Around Father Segura, the other priests smiled sourly and nodded.

Don Luis looked at them and felt his hatred of them growing. It had begun like a little seed, planted by their first condescending smiles at Uttamussack. He could see that these Jesuits were only pretending to be kind; in their hearts, they looked upon his people as ignorant savages. They were looking down on him now, thinking that he was a savage, too. He would soon show them. But first he must go back to Uttamussack. "No, Father, I must go," he said respectfully. Then an idea struck him. "Let me go alone among my people for a while, and speak to their god with them. Give me time with them, so that I may look into my heart and theirs. Then, in a month, I shall return here and tell you whether I shall go or stay."

And so it was agreed, and the next day Don Luis went back through the forest to the village of Uttamussack. But he did not return in a month, as he had promised, nor in two months, nor three. It was February, five months later, when Father Quirós and two other priests came looking for him.

"It has taken me longer than I thought to know my mind," Don Luis said to them apologetically. "But I shall come back to the mission before this moon wanes. You may return and tell Father Segura that I have a plan for the conversion of my people." Then Don Luis and his brothers spread a feast of smoked oysters, roast venison, and Indian bread before the priests and sent them rejoicing on their way.

Two days later, Don Luis and three young Powhatan warriors caught up with the three priests and killed them with a shower of arrows.

Don Luis, wrapped in a bearskin cloak against the cold, surveyed the corpses of the men he had just slain with grim satisfaction. Father Quirós and the two missionary priests he had brought with him lay sprawled on the frozen ground, the arrows that had felled them protruding at various angles from their bodies.

"Now burn them," he said.

"Why? They are already dead." His men were puzzled.

"I want a fire, and I want them burned. Do as I say."

As his warriors set about rubbing sticks and gathering dry leaves and moss to start a fire, Don Luis paced slowly around the dead Spaniards. Killing them had been but the work of a moment; they had offered no resistance at all. Their faces still bore looks of surprise, their eyes wide open, staring at nothing, their mouths agape in silent pleas for mercy. What were they seeing now? Don Luis wondered. Had their souls fled, as the Jesuits had taught him, and were they even now before the throne of God? He laid that thought aside and thought instead of the other priests at the mission downriver. He would show them that his magic was more powerful than theirs, and they would soon fall on their knees before him.

"Take their clothes off." Don Luis sat down to watch with pleasure as his men dragged the three naked, bleeding bodies across the clearing to the fire.

"Why do you want them to be burned?"

"We should leave them to the buzzards."

"How white they are! Like fishes' bellies!"

Lifting the corpses by their hands and feet, Don Luis's men heaved them one by one onto the fire.

"Now gather up their clothes and their bundles. We have other work to do."

"It was work enough to burn them," one of the men grumbled. Don Luis did not answer him, but watched impassively as the flames crept around the bodies and the fire began to smoke. These Jesuits had taught him a useless faith; they had tried to spread an alien religion among his people. In his own land, they were heretics, and he would treat them as they treated heretics in their land. Don Luis had not watched the flames of the Spanish Inquisition for nothing.

Five days later at the tiny mission downriver, Don Luis and his warriors took their tomahawks and split the skulls of Father Segura and the four other priests as they knelt in prayer. Now the Spanish and their God were driven from the land, and Don Luis, who had lived among them for ten years, went back to live among his own people. They did not call him by his old name, Ajacanto, but gave him a new one: Opechancanough, which meant "he whose soul is white." He had lived among foreigners, and in the eyes of his people he was suspect. Even his own brothers did not fully trust him. He had killed the black-robed priests like so many crows; he had burned his buff jerkin and his hat with the scarlet plume; but still the memory of the foreigners hung over the village like some foul miasma. Opechancanough blamed himself for bringing strangers to Uttamussack. There was an ancient prophecy among his people that foreigners in tall ships would some day invade their land; would be driven away twice, but the third time would stay and conquer all the river tribes. Opechancanough, with bitterness and loathing in his heart, vowed that if any other strangers came, they would not live there long.

LONDON
1 September 1607

 "Raleigh tried and failed. The people he sent to Roanoke have been lost these twenty years, and the English have yet to plant a colony on the American continent. This Jamestown venture must not fail." Sir Thomas Smythe, treasurer of the Virginia Company, drew a deep breath and folded his arms across his chest.

Across the table from him, Captain Christopher Newport fingered the empty sleeve of his doublet and frowned. The stump of his left arm was beginning to ache. He had lost that arm to a Spanish cannonball in Cuba eighteen years ago, but the stump still pained him now and then. When he was excited or angry, it throbbed in time with his heartbeats, and for the past hour he had been alternately anxious and furious. Opposite him, seated behind a massive oak table, were twelve men—five councillors and seven of the major stockholders of the Virginia Company. By rights, there should have been fifteen stockholders to make a quorum, but Sir Thomas had decided to hold the meeting anyway, so eager were he and the others to hear Newport's firsthand account of the Company's colony in Virginia. Five months ago, in April, Newport had sailed into the great bay the Indians called Chesapeake and had put ashore a small group of Virginia Company adventurers; last week, after a long and difficult voyage, he had returned to London.

"You say you left a hundred men and four boys there?" Sir Henry Wriothesley, the third Earl of Southampton, pressed his fingertips together and surveyed his well-tended hands as he waited for Newport to answer.

"Aye, my lord. As I said."

"I thought you said there were a hundred and seven." That came from Sir Edwin Sandys, the second son of the Archbishop of York.

"Eustace Clovell and Matthew Fitch died with Indian arrows in them. One of the boys—I forget his name—was killed with a hatchet," Newport answered patiently. "That all happened about a fortnight before I left. God only knows how many are there now."

"And how many Indians are there?" John Ferrar, one of the richest merchants in the Levant Company, repeated an earlier question.

"As I told you before, it's well nigh impossible to number them, sir." Newport tried to mask the exasperation in his voice. "The times we went upriver, we saw twenty here, forty there, scattered about in their towns. Their king, Powhatan, claimed to have a thousand warriors at his beck and call, but I did not see that many. The most I heard of at one time was two hundred. That was when they attacked the fort while we were gone, and Wingfield and Ratcliffe, who were in command, said there were at least that many, and maybe more."

"And yet this Council is to understand that you believe these savages capable of friendship with the English?" Sir Thomas Smythe spoke up.

"I do, my lord. They have a childlike fondness for glass beads and tin whistles. A few cases of trinkets in the right hands could work wonders."

"That is, of course, provided your friend John Smith does not rile them," Henry Wriothesley said with a smirk, and his mention of Smith set off the others.

"That upstart!"

"The man's no upstart; he's a conceited ass, and a hothead to boot."

"He never should have been chosen to be on the Council at Jamestown."

"He's only one of seven, but he's the rotten apple that will spoil the lot."

"It was Gosnold who wanted him. Gosnold knew him from Willoughby, and said he could ride and fight better than any man in Lincoln-shire."

"That may be, but he was lording it over some of the others even before they left, saying he knew better than they how to handle savages, and bragging how he had fought the infidel Turks in hand-to-hand combat."

"He made enemies on the voyage over, and now he's there, and on the Council he'll make more trouble, you mark my words."

"What can you expect of a nobody—a yeoman farmer's son?"

"The fellow has no breeding."

"I don't trust a man who claims he has beheaded three Turks in duels, even if he does have a coat of arms to prove it."

"I don't believe a man who says he was sold into slavery and saved from death by a beautiful princess in Constantinople."

"Captain Newport, you should have hanged him when you had the chance."

"I kept him in irons the whole voyage," Newport said defensively. "I could not very well execute him without evidence of wrongdoing, and when we got to Virginia, all anyone could say was that he had made them angry about this or that, so I saw to it that he was pardoned. If he can but get along with the others, he will be useful to the Company. Smith is not afraid of the Indians, and he's an excellent soldier, whatever else you say about him." Newport began to pace back and forth. "And that is more than I can say for a score or more of the gentlemen's sons you sent to Virginia. Some of them have never done a day's work in their lives, much less killed a man in battle. I pity Captain Smith now, with the likes of them to command!"

"Captain Newport, the Virginia Company Council engaged you to transport its people and goods across the Atlantic, not to give advice about its government." Sir Thomas Smythe spoke evenly, but there was no mis-taking his meaning. "You have sailed a fleet of three ships to Virginia and returned safely, and you have been well paid for your troubles. If you expect to remain in the Company's employ, you will do well to remain silent on affairs that do not concern you."

"Yes, my lord." Through his empty sleeve, Captain Newport rubbed the end of his left arm.

Sir Thomas went on, "Thus far, an investment of nearly a hundred thousand pounds sterling has yielded nothing but some badly hewn clap-boards and a few barrels of sassafras roots." There was a rumble of discon-tent and a good deal of head-shaking from around the table, and Sir Thomas continued, "The investors cannot go long without some kind of return on their shares, and the Crown expects results from Virginia as well. The royal coffers of Spain overflow with the New World's gold and silver, while England's treasury sits virtually empty." He paused and fixed his gaze on Newport. "Let us look truth in the eye. You must remind John Smith and all the others at this place you call Jamestown that they are there to do three things besides plant a colony: find gold, look for the lost Roanoke colonists, and discover a sea route to the Far East. If they cannot do at least one of these things, the Virginia venture's days are numbered."

Around the table, twelve solemn faces registered deep concern. After a dramatic pause, Sir Thomas arranged his features in what might be taken for a smile, and said, "You will return to Jamestown when the necessary provisions can be laid in, and when the second group of persons willing to go out as colonists can be assembled."

"That will be soon, I hope, my lord," Newport said anxiously. "How long do you reckon that will take?"

"Oh, not more than two months, if all goes according to plan."

Christopher Newport, sacker of Spanish towns in Hispaniola and Cuba, survivor of pirate attacks on the Spanish Main, seasoned commander of a dozen Atlantic crossings, thought of the little band of settlers he had left on the banks of a river in Virginia, and shook his head.

"I hope, my lord, that will not be too late for the ones already there."

WEROWOCOMOCO
29 December 1607

 It was a cold winter day, and the smell of roasting venison and turkey drifted deliciously on the clear, sharp air. Powhatan had ordered a feast prepared for a special visitor, and his daughter Pocahontas and her half-sister Matachanna could hardly contain themselves. Three days ago, a messenger from their father's brother Opechancanough had brought news of the capture of one of the Englishmen who had built a fort on the river Powhatan (which they called the James) between Paspahegh and Kecoughtan. This man, said Opechancanough, was the foreigners' leader, their chief werowance, and it was only proper that he be brought before Powhatan Wahunsonacock, the Indian ruler of all the tribes along the Rappahannock, the Potomac, and the Powhatan. Pocahontas and Matachanna had heard tales of these strangers since the time of the dogwood blossoms this past spring, but they had never seen one. Now they were excited as only a twelve-year-old and a six-year-old could be, waiting for the captive to arrive. They were not the only ones. The whole village was astir.

The women anointed themselves with bloodroot dye and oil; the men put on beaded headbands and fastened their quivers of arrows on their backs, and all assembled in Powhatan's great house at dusk. On each side of the door, fifty warriors, each holding a bow with an arrow nocked and ready, solemnly took their places. The rest arranged themselves in ranks around the raised platform that served as both throne and bed for Powhatan. The women stood behind the men, and on either side of Powhatan stood three of the younger women who attended him. To Powhatan's right, in places of honor, sat his half-sister Opossunoquonuske, Queen of the Appamatucks, and his wife Winganuske, the mother of Pocahontas, his favorite daughter. Pocahontas and Matachanna, wearing necklaces of white shell beads like the older girls in their father's retinue, stood behind him. Inside the great domelike house, a large fire crackled festively, and outside, two sentries waited to announce the approach of Opechancanough's warriors with their captive. At last one of the sentries stepped inside and raised his arm, palm extended. Silence fell. In a moment, the deerskin curtain that hung in the doorway parted, and a great "Aaahh!" went up from all those assembled around Powhatan.

The captive Englishman, flanked on either side by a brawny, befeathered Indian, wore a shiny steel helmet and a breastplate. He did not look the least bit afraid. There were at least a hundred Indians near the entrance, and another hundred—fifty men and as many women—standing in ranks around Powhatan, but the prisoner merely glanced at them as he stepped inside. Ignoring the guards on either side of him, he stared straight at Powhatan. Then he planted his feet firmly apart, folded his arms, and waited. For a moment, the only sound in the cavernous chamber was the faint crackling of the fire. Two hundred pairs of eyes were fastened on the Englishman. The visitor was not tall; in fact, he was barely half a head taller than Pocahontas herself. His buff-colored jerkin was stained with mud, and his leggings were torn in several places, but he was an imposing figure, nonetheless.

"Cap-tain John Smith!" announced the guard on his right, and then the one on his left echoed it.

"John Smith!"

The name rang out in the silence, and the visitor acknowledged his name by inclining his head ever so slightly in Powhatan's direction. Then he removed his helmet and held it under his arm. How light his hair is, Pocahontas thought. Sand-colored. And light eyes, too, gray and steady, fastened on her father with a challenging gaze. The mouth above the sand-colored beard was tense now, but Pocahontas tried to imagine how those thin lips would look in a smile. In some curious way, she felt drawn to him; she did not know why.

Powhatan clapped his hands. One of his women brought the visitor a basin of water to wash his hands; another, a bunch of turkey feathers to dry them; still another spread a bearskin rug for him to sit upon. Then, at a nod from Powhatan, a whole roast turkey was brought in. He pulled one of the legs off and then had the remainder of the bird set before Smith. With an exaggerated gesture, Powhatan took a bite of the turkey drumstick, waved it in the air, and indicated to John Smith that he was to do likewise. With a flourish, Smith ripped off the turkey's remaining leg, and, glancing warily around him, began to eat. Then the rest of the food was brought in: haunches of venison, more turkeys, dishes of corn and beans and squash, baskets of Indian bread. The feasting lasted nearly two hours, with neither Powhatan nor Smith taking his eyes long off the other.

They spoke not a word of each other's language, but the mutual suspicion in their looks frightened Pocahontas. She listened as Opechancanough's men told her father that Smith had been captured with some difficulty, and that two other Englishmen with him had been slain. Now Smith was alone, at the mercy of Powhatan, ruler of all the river tribes, emperor of a domain that stretched from the great bay to the foot of the blue mountains. John Smith was only the master of threescore men and boys on a tiny neck of land on a bend of Powhatan's river. Nonetheless, this Englishman seemed to look on Powhatan as his equal, perhaps even his inferior. The two men watched each other warily, and Pocahontas could see that her father was angry at the visitor's lack of deference.

And so, when Pocahontas heard her father order the stones to be brought, her heart froze within her. She knew what that meant, but she had never been allowed to watch. Now two of her father's warriors had John Smith by the elbows, and two others were forcing him to lie face up on the two large flat stones they had dragged to the space in front of the fire. The killing-stones were stained dark with the blood of men who had dared to cross Powhatan. John Smith glared angrily at his captors and at Powhatan, but he did not struggle. This man is brave, Pocahontas thought, but not stupid. What good would it do him to resist, unarmed and alone, in the presence of a king and a hundred warriors? At an order from Powhatan, two more of his men stepped forward. Each of them held a club. They were heavy clubs, made of oak, blunt and wide at one end and carefully tapered to a handle at the other end. They were the killing-clubs, used to crush a man's skull until his face turned to pulp and his brains oozed out on the stones. An awed silence settled over the great chamber as the men with the clubs took their positions.

Stretched out flat on the stones, his arms and legs held fast by four heavily muscled warriors, John Smith closed his eyes and moved his lips silently for a moment. Then, with one last defiant look at Powhatan, he braced himself for what was to come. Slowly, with maddening deliberation, Powhatan raised his arm to give the signal.

"No!" Pocahontas's clear young voice rang out. A shocked murmur rippled through the crowd, and Pocahontas pushed her way to Powhatan's side. He, surprised, turned to look at her, his arm still in the air.

"Opossunoquonuske! Winganuske!" Angrily, he called to his half-sister and to Pocahontas's mother to remove her. But Pocahontas, hardly realizing what she was doing, ducked under her father's arm, eluded the women's outstretched hands, and, running to the stones, flung herself on top of John Smith. The crowd gasped, and Powhatan swore under his breath. Pocahontas, panting, lay with her arms on top of John Smith's arms, and her head next to his, so close that their cheeks touched.

"God be praised!" he whispered, "God be praised!" Against her body, his chest rose and fell.

All eyes were on Powhatan's face, impassive in the flickering firelight. At last his mouth relaxed into something like a rueful smile, and he lowered his arm.

"Very well," he said. "Pocahontas has decided for us." To the guards, he said, "Release him." To John Smith, he said with grudging admiration, "You are a brave man. A good warrior is not afraid of death."

Silently, Pocahontas stood up and, seizing both John Smith's hands in hers, pulled him to his feet. When he had recovered himself, he looked into her eyes and smiled. Then, bending one knee, he took her right hand in both of his and kissed it—a thing no man had ever done to her.

When Opechancanough heard of Pocahontas's rescue of John Smith, he was greatly amused. "Let her be his friend," he told his brother. "She is not yet a woman. Such a friendship can do her no harm, and it can do us a great deal of good. When spring comes, let her go to visit the English at their village as often as she likes. It will put them off their guard."

* * *

And so, in the spring and summer of 1608, Pocahontas visited the English settlement many times. Jamestown was only twelve miles away: half a day's walk through the fragrant forests and a quick canoe crossing of the Pamunkey, the river that ran between Werowocomoco and the Englishmen's fort. Sometimes her father's men went with her, carrying baskets of corn and haunches of venison to trade for copper, knives, and trinkets. Each time she went, John Smith embraced her, feasted with her, and gave her presents: beads, a painted bowl, a small looking glass in a wooden frame. Each time she returned home, her father asked her how the Englishmen fared, if many had died, if any new ones had come. Her father's men spied on the English, but they could not see inside the palisaded fort. Once John Smith captured seven of them lurking about in the woods, and Powhatan sent Pocahontas to ask him for their release.

Smith said, "Only for you, Pocahontas, would I let them go."

Pocahontas was glad. She did not like killing. She knew that her father and her uncle Opechancanough wanted to kill all the English, but for the time being they seemed willing to watch and wait to see how long the English settlement would survive. Many of the newcomers had died the first winter. Of more than a hundred, there were only thirty-eight alive to greet the supply ship when Captain Newport sailed back in the spring. But more settlers came that next autumn, and by the year's end there were more than two hundred English living inside the little log fort on the banks of the river.

The men and boys at Jamestown made much of Pocahontas, and John Smith called her his best friend. He would sit by the hour with her on his knee and talk with her, teaching her English words, having her tell him Indian words for English ones. She taught the boys Indian words, too, when she frolicked with them in the market square of the fort sometimes. There were only two women at Jamestown, and Pocahontas did not like them. They shook their heads at her and said she did not wear enough clothes. She liked the boys. There were four boys near her own age, and they were glad to see her when she came. But it was not their attention she craved, nor that of any of the other men in the fort at Jamestown; it was John Smith's.

He did not seem to realize that she was a woman now. Only this past year she had begun to have the woman sickness with each new moon, and her breasts, bare under the necklaces of shell beads she wore, were firm and rounded. But John Smith did not seem to notice her body, not even when she rubbed herself all over with sweet acorn oil and turned cartwheels in the square with the boys. Round and round they would go, laughing and shouting, and the men would clap their hands and laugh, too, as her fringed doeskin apron flew over her head. She was strong and agile, and she spread her legs wide as she turned.

It was not until the frost moon, after Captain Newport had come back in his ship to visit Jamestown and to bring gifts for Powhatan, that Pocahontas could arrange a way to be alone with John Smith. Smith had come to Werowocomoco to bring Namontack, Powhatan's trusted servant, who had been in England with Newport since the summer. Powhatan had sent him to learn English words and to find out the number of English guns. Besides Namontack, John Smith had brought with him four of his own men: Richard Waldo, who was newly arrived from England, and three others whom Pocahontas knew: Andrew Buckler, Edward Brinton, and a boy named Samuel Collier. They came to see Powhatan, but Powhatan was not there. He had gone to Orapakes, a good two days' journey away, to hunt deer. A runner was sent to tell him of the English visitors, and Namontack, after consulting with Winganuske, whom Powhatan had left in charge of the women during his absence, ordered a side of venison roasted and straw sleeping mats laid for the English guests.

"In England they have beds on sticks, high off the ground, even though they live in houses with floors made of wood," said Namontack. "They have need of many fires, and many covers and clothes to keep them warm in their country. I think that is because their skin is pale. We must make them a big fire here, so they will not feel the cold." Namontack rubbed his bare brown arms and grinned. He had been given a suit of English clothes, but as soon as he reached Werowocomoco, he had taken them off and put them in a basket. Now he wore a buckskin breechclout, moccasins, and a vest made of bear's fur and decorated with bear claws.

"We must give these English some women tonight, to warm them." Winganuske, Pocahontas's mother, spoke up. "Powhatan said we are to see that the English are well treated while they are visitors here. If they have no fear of us, they will be easy to kill later."

"So he thinks," Namontack said. "But he has not seen what I have seen in their land. The English have so many men I could not count them all. And they have many guns. Powhatan must be very careful. I will tell him that when he comes."

"But until he does come, we must entertain them," Winganuske said.

Pocahontas had already welcomed the Englishmen. John Smith had embraced her and kissed her on the forehead, and Samuel Collier had turned a cartwheel in her honor, just to show her he still knew how. "Let us have a love-dance for them," she said suddenly.

Love-dances were usually given on the return of a hunting party or a war party, to celebrate a successful hunt or a victorious battle, but there was no reason one could not be given now, in honor of the English guests. Still, Namontack, Winganuske, and Matachanna looked at her in amazement. Namontack spoke first.

"An excellent idea!"

Before her mother could speak, Pocahontas said, "Matachanna, go tell the women to start mixing the paint and the oil. There is not much time." Matachanna was far too young to dance the love-dance, but she and the other girls her age were allowed to help with the preparations. Now she scampered off excitedly.

"And I shall go and see that someone gathers the leaves." As she spoke, Pocahontas's heart gave an odd little hop of excitement, and she congratulated herself on the success of her plan. But as she went out the door of her mother's house, Winganuske summoned her back.

"Pocahontas," she said slowly, "I know what you are thinking. Powhatan will not like it."

"I am grown up now," Pocahontas answered defiantly. "And I have been more among the English than my father has."

"Ah, but you are still a virgin, Pocahontas, and you are a chief's daughter," Winganuske said solemnly. "I warn you, be careful."

Namontack, listening in silence, nodded his head in agreement.

Pocahontas was anxious to be rid of them both. "I will! I must go now, or we won't have time to get ready."

By the time the sun had slipped halfway down the sky, the fire was laid: A huge pile of wood, carefully arranged to catch fire quickly, waited in the middle of the large, flat clearing between the village and the forest. By the time the sun's edge had touched the tops of the pine trees, the dancers were painting their bodies.

"There are only five white men, and one of them is a boy." Maranas, a daughter of Namontack, spoke as she rubbed her breasts with bloodroot dye. "And there are three times ten of us."

"Then you had better dance well, if you want to be noticed," Matachanna answered, and some of the other girls giggled.

"We'll see which ones they choose," Pocahontas said. She had her own scheme for being chosen.

At last they were ready: thirty lithe young bodies gleaming with oil and painted, some crimson with bloodroot dye, some yellow with tansy-flower stain, some blue with the juices of the indigo plant, each one in a different design. Maranas and some of the others had drawn rings of bright color around their breasts, while another group had wide bands of paint from collarbone to navel, with the same design repeated on their legs from knee to ankle. Pocahontas and some of the younger girls had painted their breasts yellow, in perfect circles. In the centers, their nipples stood out like small pink buds. At their waists, they wore circlets of silk-grass with small aprons of oak leaves front and back, leaving painted buttocks bare, and on their heads, atop their sleek black hair, were crowns of bucks' horns. Each one carried some kind of weapon: Maranas, the leader, had a bow and wore a quiver of arrows at her back, while others had swords, knives, clubs, and spears. Pocahontas carried the small Spanish dagger John Smith had given her last spring, when she began to visit the Englishmen at Jamestown.

"The white men are taking their places. Look!" Maranas pointed to the clearing. John Smith and the others were settling themselves on straw mats some distance from the fire. Around them were the men, women, and children of Werowocomoco, whose voices rose in a pleasant murmur, like the sound of bees.

"It is time!" Maranas said. "Take your places!" At her command, the young women gathered in two circles with their heads close together. The ceremony of the love-dance was about to begin. "Now!" Maranas's low voice sounded above their bowed heads, and the chanting began.

"Ooooh—aaaah—whaaaa!" The voices in one circle rose shrilly in the clear October air. "Aaaah—whaaa—ooooh!" The voices in the other circle answered. Around the fire, the audience fell silent and all eyes were on the trees where the dancers, hidden from view, continued to chant. But the Englishmen, startled by the unfamiliar sounds, leaped to their feet and drew their swords. John Smith and Edward Brinton seized two old men who sat next to them and held them as shields, waiting tensely for whatever might emerge from the forest.

"Look!" Maranas laughed scornfully. "The English are afraid of us!"

"Keep chanting. I'll go tell John Smith," Pocahontas said quickly. Fleet-footed as the buck whose horns she wore, she darted across the clearing. John Smith looked at her painted, nearly naked body in open-mouthed amazement.

"Pocahontas!" he said. "What in—"

She put her fingers on his lips and smiled at him. "Hush," she said. "Sit down. No harm will come to you. It is the love-dance."

"Then what's that hellish noise?"

"That is the hunting call," Pocahontas said. "Sit down and watch." Around them, the men, women, and children of Werowocomoco were nodding and smiling. Smith, Brinton, and the others, looking slightly sheepish, sheathed their swords and sat down again on the mats. Pocahontas was gone as quickly as she had come.

In the grove of pine trees at the edge of the clearing, the chanting continued as she rejoined Maranas and the others. "I have told them there is nothing to fear," she said. "Now we can begin."

At a signal from Maranas, the circles broke apart, and the dancers, each one brandishing her weapon and sounding her own war cry, rushed out of the forest and into the clearing.

"I'll be damned!" said John Smith.

"I don't believe my eyes!" said Edward Brinton, next to him. Around them, Buckler, Waldo, and Collier, joined by the Indian audience, murmured their approval.

They saw thirty pairs of lithe young legs, gleaming with oil, thirty pairs of firm young breasts, elaborately painted, and thirty comely young faces smiling as the dancers arranged themselves in a perfect circle around the fire. Then the dancing began. Maranas went down on one knee, drew an arrow from the quiver at her back, and pretended to shoot it at the fire. Then, with a shout, she leaped high into the air, and then began to stamp her bare feet in a slow rhythm. Next to her, Pocahontas went down on one knee, waved her dagger above her head, leaped, and began to dance in rhythm with Maranas. One by one, each of the others knelt, leaped, shouted, and joined the dance, until all thirty were dancing as one, their feet trampling the soft grass flat, their war cries reverberating in the still air. Then the circle began to move, slowly revolving about the fire, so that some of the dancers were silhouetted while others were highlighted in the rosy glow of the flames. In the dusky light, the antler headdresses seemed to become part of them, curving gracefully above their heads and transforming them into creatures of the forest, savage, supple, and sensual.

Pocahontas, swaying with the rhythm of the dance, brandishing the Spanish dagger above her head, thought joyfully of John Smith. Now he would see that she was no child. This was the love-dance, given only for warriors who had hunted well or fought bravely. It was designed to give them pleasure in their loins and to serve as a prelude to lovemaking. None but unmarried girls could dance the love-dance, and after it, each warrior chose a dancer to spend the night with him. As the circle of dancers revolved, Pocahontas kept her eyes on John Smith.

When the dance ended, the dancers crowded around the bewildered Englishmen, chanting, "Love you not me? Love you not me?"

Namontack, with his newly acquired command of English, whispered a few words in the visitors' ears.

"I cannot believe this!" said Edward Brinton.

"We must all be dreaming!" said Andrew Buckler.

"If this is how savages behave, I'm for savagery!" said Richard Waldo.

"Zounds!" said Samuel Collier.

Only John Smith was silent. Smiling the tenderest of smiles, he held out his arms to Pocahontas as she bowed before him.

WEROWOCOMOCO
10 January 1609

 It was the dead of winter when she saw him again; the wind so cold it froze the tears on her cheeks. He had sailed upriver with forty of his men to trade for corn. The English at Jamestown were desperate for food. Powhatan received them warmly, promising them ten baskets of corn in return for beads and looking glasses. But Pocahontas did not see John Smith at first; Powhatan made Winganuske guard her so she could not leave her house. He had been so angry with her when he found out about the love-dance that he forbade her ever to see John Smith again.

But now, with exaggerated politeness, he invited Smith and his men to come ashore and dine with him. Speaking in his stilted English in a voice that rang out across the village, Powhatan declared that the Indians wanted nothing but peace and friendship.

"If I am your friend, I can eat good meat, lie well, and sleep quietly with my women and children. I can laugh and be merry with you, have copper, hatchets, or what you bring me. If I am your enemy, I will be forced to lie cold in the woods, feed upon acorns and roots, and be so hunted by you that I can neither rest, eat, nor sleep. My tired men must watch, and if a twig but break, everyone will cry, 'There comes Captain Smith.'"

Pocahontas, listening, knew that her father was lying. He had tried without success to persuade Smith and his men to leave their swords and guns aboard their barge, so that he and his men could overpower them. But John Smith had refused to be taken in. He had come ashore with eighteen of his men, heavily armed, and Powhatan was furious.

Leaving the English visitors to warm themselves by the fire in the great lodge, he withdrew to Winganuske's house and ordered Winganuske, two of his younger wives, and Pocahontas and Matachanna and their two younger brothers to gather their belongings and prepare to slip away with him while the Englishmen sat by the fire.

"They think they are clever, but they are not so clever as I am," he said. "We will leave now, and let them wait for me. Later tonight, when they have feasted—they are very hungry, these English, and I will send them roast oysters and venison—their guard will be down, and then my men will kill them with their own weapons." Powhatan's eyes narrowed, and his thin lips stretched themselves into a crooked smile. Then he fastened his gaze on Pocahontas. "I will arrange a special death for John Smith. I have let him live too long." Powhatan's small black eyes glittered. "And without him, the others at Jamestown will die quickly."

Pocahontas lowered her eyes, and said nothing, but her heart began to beat very fast.

As soon as Powhatan's little party had made its way well into the forest, out of sight and earshot of the village of Werowocomoco, he ordered the women to make camp. Silently, dutifully, Pocahontas helped the others assemble her father's sleeping mat and arrange the raccoon-skin covers. He was weary, he said, and wanted to sleep for a while before eating. Then he would go back and watch the Englishmen die. While Winganuske was sweeping the ground to lay the fire, Pocahontas volunteered to search for more kindling. Powhatan was so scornful of his guests that he had not bothered to have anyone keep watch, and the others were occupied with cooking. If she was lucky, they would not miss her. Light-footed as a fawn, she slipped behind a tree in the winter dusk and was gone.

It was no more than a quarter of a mile back to the village, but it seemed to her like twenty. If Powhatan awoke and found her gone, he would know where to look for her, and if he caught her, he would surely have her beaten to death. At last, heart pounding, she crept up to the lodge where the unsuspecting Englishmen were eating. No one was outside, but she could not see who was inside. Since it was bitter cold, the skin curtains of the two windows were fastened shut. She huddled below the window on the far side of the lodge, next to the forest. From here no one in the village could see her. With one trembling finger, she lifted the lower edge of the window covering just enough to peer inside. The feasting had begun, and John Smith was sitting with his back to her, only a few feet away.

"John! John Smith!"

She whispered as loudly as she dared, the words hissing in the still, cold air. Would he recognize her voice? If there were Indians watching him, perhaps he would not dare answer, and then she could do nothing but go away, back to Powhatan, and John Smith would die. She held her breath. Suddenly, he stood up, rubbed his stomach, laughed loudly, and said he had to go outside to relieve himself. Amid a murmur of voices and some laughter, he sauntered slowly to the door. Once outside, he ran to her.

"Pocahontas! Where have—"

As she had done once before, Pocahontas put her fingers against his lips to silence him. But this time her fingers were icy cold. His mouth was soft and warm against them. He reached up and took her hand in both of his. "What is it? Where have you been?" He was whispering, now, and rubbing her fingers to warm them.

"Powhatan is going to kill you." She gasped out the words, her breath still short from running. "His men will take your swords while you are eating. I must go now, or he will know I am here."

Smith pressed her fingers to his mouth and kissed them hard. "God bless you," he said softly. "I have missed you—" he began, but she cut him off.

"I must go!" Her eyes filled with tears. "Good-bye, John Smith!"

"Pocahontas! Wait!" He fumbled inside his jerkin and drew out a small string of sky-blue beads. "Take this to remember me by."

"I cannot! If Powhatan should see it, he would kill me. I must go!" As she ran back through the forest, the tears streamed down her cheeks, and the wind turned them to ice.

Powhatan was waiting for her. He knew without asking where she had been. "You are my favorite daughter," he said coldly. "I cannot kill you, but I can banish you. After what you have done, I do not want to look upon your face."

The next day, Powhatan established a grudging truce with John Smith and sent Pocahontas to live with the Potomacs, far away at the foot of the mountains. She would not see John Smith again for seven long years.

2

THE
STARVING
TIME
∎
1610

This was that time, which still to this day we called the starving time; it were too vile to say, and scarce to be beleeved, what we endured. . . .

—*John Smith,*
Generall Historie (1624)

LATITUDE 30°N, LONGITUDE 60°W,
24 July 1609

 It was nearly noon, but the sun had not come out from behind the clouds. George Yardley, breathing salt air and bracing his feet against the gently rolling deck of the *Sea Venture,* waited impatiently for the ship's boy to turn the glass and call the hour. Across the gray-blue water, the other ships—the *Diamond, Falcon, Blessing, Unity, Lion, Swallow,* and the pinnaces *Virginia* and *Catch*—wallowed in the flagship *Sea Venture*'s wake. They were all bound for Jamestown, carrying settlers and supplies to the Virginia Company's struggling colony. In all, the nine ships carried five hundred people, but the only person George cared about was aboard the *Falcon,* a small vessel sailing just off the *Sea Venture*'s starboard quarter. She was less than half a furlong away this morning, and by squinting, he could make out some figures moving about on her main deck.

One of them was bound to be Temperance, waiting, like him, for noon. George sighed. Why in God's name had he thought it prudent for them to sail on separate vessels? Seven weeks married, and now near that long apart. Temperance had been against it from the beginning. "Mind?" she had said. "Do I *mind* if we sail on different ships? Who in bloody hell thought I'd *not* mind? Surely not you! Some sniveling whoreson of a ship's officer gave you that idea! Damnation! I suppose Sir Thomas Gates wants me out of his way! Damn him, too!" George, amused, had admonished her for swearing.

"Well, who's to hear it but you?" she had said. Even after she saw that he would not be moved, she continued to fume. "I don't want to be looked after by Will Sterling, even if he is your best friend! Hell's bells! I hardly know him! I want to be with you! You may be Thomas Gates's bodyguard, but you're my husband!"

In the end, George had won, and he and Temperance had now been apart for forty-five days and nights. Soon they would have been apart longer than they had been married. Stupid it was, this trying to wave to each other every noontime. But it was better than nothing, and George kept reminding himself that separation was the only sensible course to take at this point. Sir Thomas was testy and demanding, Temperance was high-spirited and outspoken, and George was ambitious and determined to be the best captain of the guards Sir Thomas Gates had ever known. It would never do, George thought, for him to be distracted by the cares of a new-wedded wife when he was supposed to be responsible for the safety of the deputy governor of Virginia and the discipline of twelve soldiers. Besides, knowing Temperance, George feared she might cross verbal swords with Sir Thomas, and there would go his own chances for advancement. But he had not told Temperance that. "Dearest love," he had said, "with us so newly married, there would be no end of crude jests among the men. I'll not have people smirking and joking about wedding and bedding behind our backs. And you know there's no privacy aboard ship, either. Think on that."

There was one other reason he'd kept from Temperance. If, God forbid, the *Sea Venture* should be shipwrecked or set upon by pirates, his first duty would have to be to the man he served as bodyguard, not to the woman he had taken to wife. No, it was better that she should be aboard the *Falcon*. Will would look after her. And every day she came to the *Falcon*'s forecastle at the changing of the noon watch, so that sometimes, at least, the newlyweds could see each other.

Now young Tom Goodwyn, a scrawny urchin off the streets of London who had begged his way into a position as ship's boy on this voyage, turned the *Sea Venture*'s hourglass and called out to George, "Twelve o'clock noon! There she is, Captain Yardley!" The *Falcon* was close by now, and on her foredeck, near the bowsprit, a small figure clad in dark green appeared and began to wave. George, drawing a sigh of relief and pleasure, waved back. The sight of that form, hardly more than a dot in the distance, made his heart turn over, and a curious warm, melting sensation spread through him. Unconsciously, he moistened his lips. He had discovered on their wedding night that his bride, who got her given name from a Puritan mother and her disposition from her pleasure-loving country-squire father, was anything but temperate. She could devour half a capon and still be hungry; she could drink Spanish sherry all night and be only charmingly tipsy; she could make love time and again and never grow tired. George had also discovered that she had a temper, and that those rosy lips could issue forth a stream of profanity that would have shocked the foulest-mouthed sailor in Woolwich. But that was all right; she only swore in private, and he liked spirit in a woman. He could hardly wait for landfall.

"Ah, true love! How's the bridegroom bearing up?" A deep voice boomed, and a hand slapped him on the back. It was Admiral Sir George Somers himself.

"Well, sir," Captain Yardley said with a smile. "Well as one could wish, considering we are apart."

"Sea's so calm today you could almost take the longboat and board the *Falcon* for a visit." Somers squinted at the overcast sky with a practiced eye. "Almost too calm." The July air hung hot and heavy as a blanket around the ships. "If the wind from the southeast doesn't pick up soon, you'll be waving to your lady love longer than you thought."

"How far, do you reckon, are we from landfall?"

Somers laughed his rich, deep laugh. "If I could tell you that, my lad, I could as soon tell you when the world will end! With fair winds, we might make Cape Henry in eight days or so, but unless the wind changes, we might not see the coast of Virginia for another fortnight. We could be dining on moldy ship's biscuit and brackish beer afore we're done." Somers looked up into the rigging at the *Sea Venture*'s great canvas sails, which were barely filled with wind. "Let's take in!" he shouted to the crew. "Let's take in sail! Calling orders to the sailors on the main deck, Somers made his way amidships. "Good lads! Take in the main! Pull her in, and she'll hold fast! Now the mizzen! Trim her up! Good lads!"

Sailors, barefoot and nimble as monkeys, clambered about the rigging high overhead, their loose shirts and trousers flapping like the sails in the light breeze as Somers stood below, calling out to them approvingly. George Yardley, watching that sturdy figure with feet planted wide apart and head thrown back, secretly wished he were in the service of Admiral Somers instead of Sir Thomas Gates. Somers, stocky, grizzled, and jovial, could command the near worship of every man under him. Gates, tall, dark, and spidery, was given to mercurial changes in mood, and would sooner curse than praise. George never approached him without trepidation. Pleasing Sir Thomas, anticipating his commands, satisfying his small whims, demanded constant and undivided attention twenty-four hours a day.

The first few days out, Gates had been violently seasick. He refused to go on deck in the open air lest the crew see him unwell, and after three days, the air in his cabin had reeked with his vomit and sweat. Moaning and swearing, he had demanded that George stay by his side. When at last he was able to totter about on deck, he issued a constant stream of orders:

"Get me a cup of sack."

"Find my buff jerkin."

"See that the breastplates and morions don't rust."

"Have the men drill with their muskets an hour on deck."

Gates was not an easy man to work for, but he paid well. Twenty-four pounds sterling a year, with a promise of a five-pound raise in pay once they got to the New World, was too handsome an offer for the youngest son of a London merchant-tailor to refuse. George, still waving to Temperance, thought fleetingly of his older brothers and congratulated himself. Mixing potions, making corsets, and buying brocade was all right for them, but he wanted far more. Ralph and John and Thomas would live and die in Southwark, a mile from London Bridge, never knowing any other place, never sailing on any water but the Thames. At twenty-one, George had already traveled abroad, fought in a war, and taken a wife, and now he was about to make his fortune in Virginia. There was land there, boundless acres awaiting a man with a sharp eye, a ready wit, and a will to work. Someday he would be rich, and he vowed that someday he would make the name Yardley known in Virginia. And he would have sons to carry it on. Would their first child have Temperance's copper-gold hair, he wondered, or would it be dark like his own? Daydreaming, George did not notice that the wind had changed suddenly, and that the sky to the northeast had turned an ominous iron-gray color.

By the end of the noon watch, at four o'clock in the afternoon, it was nearly too dark to see the sand trickling down in the ship's glass as Tom Goodwyn turned it. To the northeast, huge thunderheads gathered on the horizon obliterated the line between sea and sky, and the wind came in erratic, threatening gusts that tore at the *Sea Venture*'s sails and put four men at the whipstaff in the steerage and four more at the tiller below in the gun room to hold her steady.

"I reckon you'll not see Mistress Yardley for a while, not till this blows over," Goodwyn said to George.

"No." George peered through the darkness on the starboard side, where the *Falcon* had been at noon, but now all he could see were splashes of white foam on the churning water and some light-colored specks that might be sails far in the distance. The wind had scattered the ships, blowing them about like dry leaves. How had this storm come up so quickly?

"She'll weather it fine, sir. You'll see." The boy's cheerfulness irritated George. Why should a London street urchin, never on a ship before in his life, be so cocky in the face of a storm at sea? Didn't he know what could happen? Didn't he know how many ships and men lay rotting at the bottom of the ocean? The wind was already so strong it was nearly impossible to stand upright on deck. Most of the passengers were huddled below, between decks, in their cramped quarters.

Sir Thomas Gates sat in the ship's great cabin, which he shared with Somers and Christopher Newport, the taciturn, one-armed sea captain who had taken the first settlers to Virginia in 1607. Somers and Newport were up on the main deck, keeping an eye on the storm, while Gates was drinking beer to calm his nerves and stomach. He sat in queasy silence, his eyes on the hanging ship's lantern as it swung crazily back and forth from the low ceiling. Ralph Hamor, a twenty-year-old whose father was head of the London Merchant-Tailors' Guild and one of the leading Virginia Company investors, and William Strachey, another investor in this Virginia venture, kept him company. Strachey, a gentle, soft-spoken fellow, had studied law at Gray's Inn in London and aspired to be a writer. He moved in London's literary circles and counted Shakespeare and Jonson among his good friends. But he wore his learning lightly, and in the seven weeks at sea had made it his business to know everyone aboard. He paid gallant compliments to the women, but told them they were none of them as pretty as his wife, Frances, who was expecting their third child and could not sail with him.

"How is it aloft?" Gates, looking pale and sour, asked as George came in. George shook his head in reply, and Gates motioned to him to sit down. "Best have some beer and wait it out." He shoved a pewter tankard toward George and pointed to a cask in the corner.

"Thank you, sir. It's blowing hard. Captain Newport and the admiral are on the main, and they've taken in all the sails except the mizzen." George slapped the smooth wooden mast that grew like a tree trunk through the center of the cabin. "This one's only hoist enough to keep us steady. No sign of the other ships."

"You mean we are alone? The fleet is lost?" Young Ralph Hamor, already pale from the ship's motion, seemed to turn visibly paler. It was his first sea voyage.

"Not lost, pray God," George said. "Just blown off course." He washed those words down with a swig of beer and hoped to God they were true.

"Damn this weather!" said Strachey. "I should have stayed in London. Who in his right mind would trade London for Jamestown? Now I'll likely never get there at all." He drained his tankard and set it down. "I knew I was right not to let Frances come. A ship in a storm is no place for a woman who needs to protect her belly." Strachey smiled, and then suddenly grew solemn. "That reminds me. Did you know John Rolfe's wife is with child? He told me yesterday. She's no more than two months along, but even so, in these rough seas, I'd be worried."

Yardley, the bridegroom; Gates, with a wife and two grown daughters in Devonshire; and Hamor, the bachelor, all nodded in silent agreement. Although John Rolfe, the quiet, shy youngest son of the Rolfes of Heacham Hall, Heacham, Norfolk, kept to himself and did not talk much, they liked him. Rolfe spoke mostly to his buxom blond wife, Gwendolyn, his bride of eleven months, who seldom left his side.

"Bad business, that," Strachey said. "I'd have made her stay home, if she were mine, but they've not been married long, and John couldn't bear to leave her." Strachey clapped George on the shoulder. "Just like Yardley here, and his bride. He's going to be the gladdest man aboard when we cry land, eh, George?"

George would be glad, not only to be once again with Temperance, but to be rid of the ceaseless roll and pitch of the *Sea Venture*. He was a soldier, not a sailor. He had discovered that two years ago when he crossed the Channel to fight the Spanish in the Netherlands. He and half of Gates's company had spent most of that crossing spewing the contents of their stomachs over the ship's rails. At the time, he had attributed it to nerves: At eighteen, that had been his first time on a ship and his first time as a soldier. He had told himself it was not the motion of the ship but the thoughts of being run through with a Spanish sword that made his stomach heave. But on the return crossing, having not only escaped Spanish swords but having distinguished himself on the field of battle and won a promotion to sergeant, he was just as ill as he had been before. He had not felt well this time, either, and now he had Temperance to worry about, besides. She had never been at sea before. At least she had been well enough so far to come on deck and wave.

And Will would look after her. Will Sterling, his best friend since their boyhood days in Southwark, would do anything for him, George knew. Will was, in fact, going to Virginia for him. Will had been alone in the world since his parents had died in the London Plague of 1603, and George had persuaded him to come to Jamestown. He had no stomach for soldiering, he told George, but he could lift a glass with the best of them. It was not that Will was delicate; he was a head taller and a stone heavier than George, but he was gentler. He could play the lute or invent a pun or turn a rhyme with equal ease, and George loved him better than his own brothers.

Will would look after Temperance.

All the same, George wished that Temperance had not dismissed the aged maidservant her parents had given her as part of her dowry. "She's an old dragon," Temperance had said. "I never liked her, and I'm not about to take her to Virginia with me. I can look after myself." Nonetheless, a young woman traveling ought to have a servant to attend her. Joan Pierce, the wife of one of the other men on the *Sea Venture*, was sailing separately on the *Blessing*, but she had her four-year-old daughter and a servant girl with her. George was glad that one of the other female passengers aboard the *Falcon* had struck up a friendship with Temperance. In the few days the fleet had spent provisioning at Falmouth before they sailed, Temperance had met an older woman from Plymouth, with gray hair and a bad scar across one cheek.

Meg Worley, her name was. She was going to Virginia, she said, in hopes of finding what had become of her fiancé. His name was Anthony Gage, and he had sailed to Roanoke with Sir Walter Raleigh's colonists twenty-two years ago and never been heard from again. A hundred and seventeen people had vanished, just like that. Now Meg Worley, with a share in the Virginia Company, was going to see for herself what had happened. She, like Will Sterling, was alone in the world. Not very likely she would find her Anthony Gage, George thought, even though one of the Virginia Company's instructions to its colonists at Jamestown was to search for the lost Roanoke settlers. But Meg Worley was a brave soul, and she would be good company for Temperance.

Shipboard life was hard on women; George could see that aboard the *Sea Venture*. Besides John Rolfe's Gwendolyn, there were 9 other women among the 150 passengers aboard. Four were the wives of other Virginia adventurers, and five were servant girls, all going out to settle in a land they had never seen. The married couples would be glad enough to be on land again, George thought. They had no more privacy than anyone else. All the women slept together in a curtained-off space below the quarterdeck, while their husbands slept below the main with the rest of the men, in hammocks or on pallets in the space allotted, a space that was not quite large enough for a man to stand upright. The only proper cabin was the ship's great cabin, a small chamber on the quarterdeck, high above the stern of the ship. Here Somers and Gates and Newport ate and slept. By rights, George thought, the women ought to have been given that place, but rank, not sex, determined the occupants of a ship's great cabin.

Having females aboard lightened the tedium of shipboard life, but it also contributed to the inevitable stench that rose from the hold of the ship, where two pumps worked day and night to suck up bilge water and the ship's waste: spilled wine and beer, vomit, and urine. The contents of chamber pots went over the nearest ship's rail. Women were not made for sea travel, George thought. Almost every week he had seen one or two of them dumping buckets of bloody water overboard when they had their monthly sickness. They had to wash the clouts they wore then as best they could in pails of seawater and hang them up to dry. No wonder the below-decks areas smelled.

Tonight, as the wind and the rain made the main deck impossible, evening prayers had to be held below decks, with the entire ship's company crowded together, damp and stinking, like mackerel in a barrel. The two Virginia Indians, Namontack and Matchumps, evidencing little faith in the white man's God, stayed at the far edge of the group. Namontack, as Powhatan's trusted lieutenant, had made two voyages to England with

Captain Newport, this last time taking Matchumps, one of Powhatan's young warriors, with him. Now, reasonably fluent in English and conversant with the white men's ways, and dressed in trunk hose and doublets, both were returning home to tell Powhatan all they had learned. Next to them, John Rolfe stood with one arm protectively clasped around his pregnant wife's waist. The Reverend Richard Buck, his thin face pale and sweaty, read from Psalm 46: "God is our refuge and strength, a very present help in trouble."

They did not sing. The air below decks was too foul and humid for a long service. Instead, they said the Lord's Prayer. A hundred and fifty voices rose as one, accompanied by the rhythmic creaking of the ship's frame and the crashing of the waves against it. Before they got to the "Amen," Gwendolyn Rolfe moaned softly and vomited into her hands.

The rain, which blew across the decks in sheets and at times in horizontal walls of water, did not let up. The evening meal was an unsatisfactory cold supper of hardtack—ship's biscuit hard enough to play at bowls with, as Ralph Hamor said—and chunks of pickled beef and cheese. In the brick-lined galley below the forecastle, the sandbox where the cook-fire usually blazed was dark: Captain Newport had ordered Thomas Powell, the ship's cook, to put it out when the wind came up. Fire at sea could be a worse horror than a storm. Outside, night had fallen, and the iron cresset with its pitch-soaked rope wick glowed feebly at the stern of the ship. Starless sky and pitch-black sea blended into a seamless shroud of blackness made more terrifying by the howling wind and driving rain.

Inside, below decks, people settled themselves to get what sleep they could. All but Admiral Somers: He did not plan to close his eyes, he said, until the storm had passed. He was everywhere at once, up on deck encouraging the men at the whipstaff, then down below, overseeing the pumps deep in the hold, then back to the half deck, speaking cheerfully and confidently to the anxious ones about him. In the cramped quarters just below the great cabin, George Yardley bade his men good night, bedded down on his canvas pallet, and said a prayer for Temperance's safety. Then he fell asleep with the thought that all would be well, or if it were not, Admiral Somers would make it so. But just before dawn, George was awakened by a hand on his shoulder and an urgent voice in his ear.

"Captain Yardley, sir!"

George sat up so quickly that he felt giddy. Around him, in the dark, his men lay sleeping soundly. "Who is it? What is it?" His voice sounded fuzzy.

"Come, man, for God's sake, wake up and rouse your men!" It was

Henry Ravens, the first mate, his voice hoarse with fatigue and fear. "We've sprung a leak—a bad one, and we need every able-bodied man aboard to find her! The water's already near a fathom deep above the ballast."

Sleepiness vanished. George was on his feet and fastening his jerkin. "Wake up!" he called to his men, trying to keep the fear out of his voice. "We've sprung a leak! Every man up and wait for me here." Turning to Ravens, he whispered, "I must wake Sir Thomas." He wondered why he was whispering. "Then you tell us what to do." He tried to speak in a normal tone. His chest felt cold and leaden with fright. A bad leak: That could mean they would sink in only a few hours. Pushing thoughts of Temperance from his mind, he made his way to the cabin. Somers and Newport were on deck, but Gates lay snoring in his narrow wooden bunk. For once he did not complain about being aroused. He and George and the other men followed Henry Ravens amidships, lurching and trying to stay upright as the ship tossed violently.

"This way," Ravens said. He was a big man, over six feet tall, with brawny shoulders that nearly filled the narrow passageways of the *Sea Venture*. But it didn't matter what size you were, George thought distractedly, not when the sea had you.

Ravens, grim-faced, handed out candles to every man and set them to work hunting for signs of the leak. The hot tallow from the candle dripped on George's hand, but he hardly felt it. Heart thumping against his ribs, eyes straining in the dimness, legs numb in the cold, knee-deep water, he sloshed along the starboard side of the gunner's room, looking for signs of a leak in the wall above the bins of iron cannonballs. On the other side of the room, Ralph Hamor searched in stricken silence, trying to hold his candle steady in a hand trembling with fright. Suddenly, as the *Sea Venture* rolled deeply to her port side, George saw it: a long thin crack in the oak shell of the ship's interior frame. The caulking had given way, and the heavy three-inch-thick planks had separated from the force of the waves. "Here it is!" he shouted triumphantly. "I've found it!"

In a moment, Admiral Somers and Evan Tubbs, the ship's carpenter, were beside him. "We've got to seal her, but there's no tar nor pitch that can hold underwater," said Tubbs, shaking his head. As he spoke, the *Sea Venture* rolled, again revealing the ominous crack.

Admiral Somers stroked his beard and ran his fingers through his disheveled hair. His hat had long since disappeared overboard. He frowned and pressed his lips together. Suddenly, with a grin, he shouted, "Beef!" Hamor, Yardley, and Tubbs stared at him in wonderment. He read their faces and chuckled. "You heard aright! Beef! Have the men get pieces of ship's beef out of the barrels in the storeroom. Stuff pieces of meat into that crack, and they'll hold till we cry land!" Then he grew solemn. "And if they don't, then no matter. In that case, we shan't be needing them."

George, helping to stuff strings of pickled beef in between the planks of the ship's hull, could not rid himself of the feeling he was having a nightmare. It was an outlandish scene: half a dozen men crouching along the wall, their hands full of meat, tearing the beef into small strips and poking it with desperate care into the crack. One or two of his soldiers crammed pieces of meat into their mouths as they worked, but he did not reprimand them.

But when all of the beef was wedged between the planks, the water continued to seep in. Somers, his mouth set in a taut line, called the hundred and forty men of the *Sea Venture* together in the dark, crowded space below the main deck. "We've got to bail," he said. "If not, we're done for. I want thirty men in the fo'c'sle, forty here in the waist, and thirty down in the bittacle. I mean every man, no matter his rank or station." He glanced fleetingly at Thomas Gates and Christopher Newport, who glared at him. The deputy governor and the seasoned captain, each used to his own command, maintained an uneasy balance of power with the admiral of the fleet. The three had already clashed once or twice on this voyage. "Divide in half and work in shifts," Somers continued. The Indians Namontack and Matchumps, unused to sea travel and still uncertain of their English, did not take their eyes from Somers's face. "Let every man bail or pump one hour and rest one hour until I give the order to stop. I'll be on the main deck, and Captain Newport will be on the fo'c'sle. Go to it, and God help us."

By Wednesday morning, the *Sea Venture* was listing so far to starboard that walking upright on her decks was nearly impossible. At dawn on Thursday, as soon as a dreary daylight gave light enough to see through the rain, the admiral ordered the jettisoning of all extra weight on the starboard side: passengers' trunks and sea chests, butts of beer and wine, cider and vinegar, and finally, the ship's starboard ordnance—the two minions on the quarterdeck.

No guns, no clothes, no food: If they did manage to stay afloat, George thought, how would they survive? Were the *Falcon,* the *Lion,* and all the others jettisoning cargo too? Temperance's trunks, with her dowry linen and her trousseau, might be gone; the silken coverlet she had brought for their bed, and the embroidered lace smocks her mother had given her as well as her green velvet gown, the gown she had been wearing when first he saw her, would rot on the ocean floor.

She had been in the gallery at the Globe Theatre, while he, alone and not wanting to pay for a gallery seat, had stood in the pit to watch *The Merchant of Venice.* In the rows of seats above him he saw John Pory, a fellow Thomas Gates had recently entertained. George lifted a hand in idle greeting, and Pory returned the gesture. With him was a young woman dressed in emerald green, who favored George with a faint smile. She had copper-colored hair and skin as pale as a white rose; wide, dark eyes and a small, mobile mouth. It was such an intelligent, changeable face, now registering eager expectation, now mild impatience, now some amusement, that George continued to watch her. In fact, much of that afternoon's performance of *The Merchant of Venice,* except as it made her laugh or look pensive, was lost upon him. Pory was a fortunate man, he thought, to have such a wife.

And then, at the masked ball George attended that very night, he discovered that she was not Pory's wife but his cousin, and that the family was anxious to arrange a marriage for her. Her father had run through his inheritance to the point of mortgaging the Norfolk manors and he had little to give his youngest daughter for a dowry. "I should like very much to meet her," said George. And thus it was, as the ball commenced, that Thomas Gates presented Captain George Yardley to Mistress Temperance Flowerdew, and John Pory pointed out Captain Yardley to Anthony Flowerdew as a likely prospect for his daughter's hand. She consented to dance the pavane with George. Turning and bowing in the stately rhythm of the dance, he imagined how it would be to feel the curve of her waist unbound by stays, to look into those dark brown eyes in private. And she, amused, seemed to know what he was thinking. Within a fortnight, their marriage banns were posted; within three months, they were husband and wife. It all seemed so long ago.

Dear God, George thought as he moved to take his turn at bailing, would Temperance ever be by his side again? The cold, dark water kept coming, kept coming, no matter how desperately they bailed. Beside him, Thomas Gates hefted the heavy barricadoes full of sloshing saltwater along with everyone else. The deputy governor's thin hair was stuck in strings across his sweaty forehead, and when he stopped to rest, his arms and hands shook uncontrollably with fatigue. Like George's, Gates's were raw and bleeding after the third watch, but George noticed that Gates did not complain. Shoulder to shoulder they bailed and lifted, bailed and lifted, in desperate silence.

Behind the canvas curtain that separated their quarters from the rest of the below-decks space, the women huddled together, weeping and praying. Aloft, Admiral Somers had lashed himself to the mainmast to keep from being swept overboard as he shouted orders to the sailors. He had not eaten or slept in two days. In the great cabin, Christopher Newport recorded the ship's position in the logbook in gloomy silence. By Friday morning, it was clear that the men who had bailed and pumped without ceasing since the second watch on Tuesday could not go on much longer. They had not tasted food in seventy-two hours, and their only drink had been a mouthful or two of beer from the four casks stowed below the quarterdeck. The ship's store of precious fresh water lay deep in the hold under a fathom of dark seawater, as did the barrels of hardtack. Some of these had split under the pressure of the water, and the sodden white ship's biscuits bobbed about like dumplings in the churning fountains brought up by the pumps. Water stood chest deep in the hold, and the men who bailed and worked the pumps there had stripped naked. Their white bodies gleamed eerily in the dark when they climbed out to rest.

Everywhere, from fo'c'sle to poop deck, sleep was an enemy to be fought off. An hour was not long enough for sleep, but an hour was all a man could bail or work the pumps, and so those who had an hour off fell into bunks or hammocks in a half-sleep, drugged with exhaustion, only to be roused again before their eyes had fairly closed. Day and night below decks in the *Sea Venture* had become barely distinguishable; the one lit by a weak gray light from the hatches, the other by a feeble flame in a lantern that swung precariously from a beam. Hell, George thought, could not be any worse than this.

"God's body, I'm weary!" William Strachey, coming to take his hour of rest beside George on the half-deck, rubbed the small of his back. "I say we batten down the hatches, gather amidships, drink up the beer that's left, say a prayer, and be done with bailing! I don't want to go to heaven so tired I can't enjoy it!" He smiled, and his teeth shone white in the dimness. His eyes gleamed white, too. Beard matted, eyes red-rimmed, cheeks sunken, Strachey already resembled a death's head, George thought, and he knew he must look like that, too. For an instant, the thought that Temperance would not see him in such a state cheered him. Then that fleeting remembrance pained him like a sudden knife wound. She would not see him again . . . in any state. Dear God, where was she at this moment?

Forcing his throbbing body to move, George took leave of Strachey with a silent shrug of his shoulders and made his way below. The water pulled at him as he waded through it, and he thought how easy it would be to slip below its surface and let death take him now, instead of waiting. Strachey was right. What was the use? For three days and nights, they had done all that men could do, and still the water poured in. The sea was winning. George wondered idly how long it would take.

* * *

Less than two leagues south-southwest of the *Sea Venture,* the *Falcon,* her mainmast broken in two, wallowed helplessly in the churning waves. Temperance Yardley huddled in a tiny, cramped space below the rainswept decks, swore at the storm, prayed for George, and wished she had never heard of Virginia.

JAMESTOWN, VIRGINIA
17 August 1609

 Sarah Harison was dying. Childbed fever's poisons had distended her belly and hollowed her cheeks, and her blue eyes, sunken and tightly closed, did not open all afternoon. Her bowels had begun to run incessantly in a brown, bloody stream that stained her white shift and soaked into the straw pallet beneath her. Inside the one-room hut where she lay, two flies circled each other drowsily in the still August heat. Beside her, a young woman in a soiled green velvet dress watched them and swore softly. "Damnitall! This is just not right! It's not right for anybody to die like this! Lying on straw, and sweating like a horse! This heat may kill us all." Temperance Yardley, her hair clinging in damp tendrils around her face, her bodice soaked with perspiration, wrung out a cloth in a tin basin of water and laid it on the sick woman's forehead. "And she's not even got a decent bed to die in. There's not a proper bedstead anywhere in this godforsaken place!"

"Not godforsaken, Temperance. And don't swear." Meg Worley spoke placidly, looking up from her scrubbing. She was washing a soiled shift in a wooden bucket.

"Hah! Then show me a sign! Show me some sign of God at Jamestown!" Temperance's voice rose defiantly. "He's not here, not with Sarah, nor with her husband that died at sea, nor with her baby son that was born and died in the same hour!" Her voice quavered. "And not with any of us in this wretched, stinking place!"

"Hush! God is here, and you know it." Meg spoke with quiet assurance. "He is with us. Aren't you and I alive and well? Thank God for that. And it's God who's given us the strength to help her and the others."

"I don't care! I didn't come here to be a nurse!" That much was true. Temperance Flowerdew Yardley, the petted youngest daughter of the Flowerdews of Thickthorne, Hethersett, in Norfolk, in all her nineteen years had never soiled her hands with anything more serious than the birth-sacs of a favorite spaniel's puppies, and she had never emptied a chamber pot in her life. But in the past three weeks she had helped to care for passengers stricken with ship's fever in the foul-smelling quarters of the *Falcon* as it yawed its way into the waters of the Chesapeake with a splintered mainmast, and in the six days she had been ashore she had done little but change filthy straw bedding and feed broth and barley water to the ailing survivors who lay sick and weak, with ashen faces and running bowels, in the tiny thatch-roofed huts inside the log palisade at Jamestown.

Of the 500 people who had sailed from Falmouth on June 8, only 214—188 men, 18 women, and 8 young children—had arrived in Virginia by the middle of August. Thirty people had been lost when the tiny *Catch* was swamped and lost in high seas; 32 of the 110 aboard the *Diamond* and the *Unity* had died, burning hot with the dreaded sweating sickness they called the calenture; dysentery and ship's fever aboard the other ships had claimed the rest. The 150 aboard the *Sea Venture*, 50 on the *Swallow*, and 20 on the tiny *Virginia* were presumed lost in the storm of July 25. By mid-August, five ships—the *Falcon*, the *Blessing*, the *Lion*, the *Unity*, and the *Diamond*—had limped their way up the wide James River to the miserable collection of huts that was Jamestown.

"No, I didn't come here to be a nurse," Temperance said again. "I didn't want to come here at all, and with George gone, the sooner I leave here, the better." She caught her lower lip between her teeth to stifle a sob. She hated people who whined and wept over things they could not help. There was far too much of that at Jamestown already, with a score of new-made widows and widowers among the arrivals.

"Don't give up hope for him yet. I've been hoping to see Anthony Gage these twenty years, and I've not given up." Meg smiled, and the scar across her cheek crinkled at one end. "You mustn't lose heart so soon. Didn't the *Diamond* just come in day before yesterday, when we thought never to see her again? The *Sea Venture* and the *Swallow* and the *Virginia* could be close by." Drying her hands on her skirt, Meg stood up. "I think we ought to turn her on her side," she said.

As they turned the limp form on the pallet, Temperance said, "Even so, if a miracle happens and George does come, he'll not stay. Nobody in his right mind would want to stay in this place! All that fine talk of green forests and crystal streams and wild strawberries was just chaff put out by the Virginia Company. They knew there wasn't a word of it true."

Meg did not answer. The young woman on the pallet stirred and moaned weakly. A fresh dark spot stained the smock that clung between her buttocks, and a few drops of blood and fecal matter dripped through the straw pallet and soaked into the earth floor. Temperance rose to her feet and shook out her dusty skirt. "I'll fetch some water. We'd best wash her again." There was resignation in her tone. Her knees ached from sitting so long, and she moved slowly. There was no need to hurry, she thought. Sarah Harison was going to die anyway, whether she had a wash or not.

Outside, the sun shone hot and painfully bright upon the rows of ragged shelters in the palisade. It had been two years since the English had first set foot on the banks of the wide river they named for their king, but they had yet to build anything better than tiny wattle-and-daub hovels: rude thatch-roofed huts made of woven branches and twigs plastered with mud, and the small log fort perched on the grassy bank of the James had a look of impermanence, of uncertainty. Sixty-six of the 104 men and boys who came in the spring of 1607 had died: salt poisoning and typhoid from the brackish, contaminated river water, malaria from the mosquitoes in the swampy neck of land they settled on, and Indians, hostile from the start, had done their deadly work. But in April of 1608, 120 more settlers had come, and in October another 70. Of all those, 168 were alive to greet the five ships of the Gates expedition.

Captain John Smith, now the president of the governing council in Virginia, was not glad to see the newcomers. All of the ships were short of food, some were full of sick passengers, and three carried men who were his old enemies. John Martin, the grizzled captain of the *Falcon,* Gabriel Archer, the colony's secretary and second in command of the *Blessing,* and John Ratcliffe, a man of indeterminate age and background who was captain of the *Diamond,* had immediately joined forces against Smith with two younger men already at Jamestown: George Percy, the eighth son of the Earl of Northumberland, and Francis West, whose older brother Thomas, Lord de la Warr, had just been appointed governor of Virginia. De la Warr, in poor health, had sent Gates as his deputy. Each of the men at Jamestown had his own reasons for disliking John Smith, and yesterday he had given them another: He had rationed the corn supply and ordered that no more livestock were to be slaughtered for food.

"Any man or woman who kills a hog or chicken from now on will answer to me," he said in his slightly pompous way, and laid his hand on his sword for emphasis. "Butcher the stock now, and we starve before spring." In five days, the famished newcomers had already depleted Jamestown's precious corn supply and devoured fifty of the hogs and as many chickens from the livestock they had brought with them. Now bitter quarrels broke out, with some taking Smith's side and others trying to depose him and make Francis West president. "I am governor until the governor comes," Smith said. "When Thomas Gates arrives, I shall turn over my commission, and not before."

Temperance, making her way slowly along the grassy path that passed for a street, wondered idly how many of the people in the twenty-odd houses inside the palisade would stand with John Smith, and how many with Francis West and the others. She liked Smith well enough, though he had barely even nodded in her direction. Something about him reminded her of George. Smith was short in stature and sturdily built, like George, although his hair was sandy and George's was dark. But like George, he had a deep voice and a blunt manner of speaking, and modesty was not one of his virtues. In a speech to the new arrivals the first day, he had told them that he, John Smith, had once defeated three infidel Turks in single-handed combat, that he had escaped slavery in Constantinople, and that he had twice escaped execution by Wahunsonacock, the wily Indian who was also known as Powhatan, chief of all the neighboring Algonquin tribes.

"I know these savages, and they know me," he said coolly. "And if you do as I say, there is nothing to fear from them."

No wonder, Temperance thought, that men like Francis West and George Percy found it galling to be ordered about by such a man. John Smith, at twenty-nine, was only a few years older than they. But it was he, not they, who had gone among the Indians and feasted with them in their houses, and he, not one of them, who was the beloved of Powhatan's daughter Pocahontas. It was John Smith who had finally established an uneasy peace with the natives of Virginia, and it was John Smith who, after the death of the last surviving Council member, had ruled the little settlement of Jamestown unchallenged. He had made highborn men like West and Percy, who had never turned a hand to manual labor in their lives, work along with the rest at felling trees, chopping wood, and tilling fields.

Trouble was brewing; Temperance could feel it as surely as she felt the tiny stings of the mosquitoes that hovered and hummed everywhere. As she walked, she scratched one arm absently, feeling for the newer and itchier welts. She had already learned not to scratch the old ones; once the skin was broken, they festered. She did not know which she hated more, Virginia's heat or its mosquitoes. Above the high log walls of the palisade, she could see the masts of the five ships, their great canvas sails furled, swaying gently in the light breeze that had sprung up. It carried the faint sound of men's laughter. The ships' crews had not come ashore, but stayed aboard their vessels, drinking, lounging, enjoying the cool river breezes. Most of the sailors had sided with John Smith against the West-Percy faction, and he was spending this afternoon aboard the *Blessing.*

Temperance wished with all her heart that she were aboard one of those ships and bound for England. Somehow she had to get home, and soon. George was lost at sea; she was convinced of that, no matter what anyone said. Will Sterling had done his best to comfort her, but his efforts only made her sadder. Will had stood up with them at their wedding, and his very presence now called up too many painful memories. When he played his lute to console her, it made her want to cry. She had taken to avoiding him whenever she could, and keeping close to Meg.

Meg Worley was old enough to be Temperance's mother, but there was a curiously youthful air about her, as if she were a young girl in a gray wig masquerading as a middle-aged spinster. Temperance had loved her at first sight. When the storm came, and the other women aboard the *Falcon* had wailed in terror with every roll of the ship, Meg merely shrugged her shoulders and said, "If a sparrow cannot fall to the ground without the Almighty's knowledge, surely He would notice a ship sinking." Temperance felt that if the ship did go down, Meg would somehow bob up again, like a cork in a puddle. She was a survivor: The scar across her cheek was testimony to that. She had been a beauty once, with wide gray-green eyes and a small, pale mouth, but now the scar, a jagged ridge from ear to jawbone, was what made people look at her. It was as shocking as a scream. To Temperance, she made light of it. "Some people have hurts that leave scars on the inside," she said. "but God gave me mine on the outside. Someday I'll tell you how I came by it, but not now. Not while we are at sea." But after that, they had been caught up in the business of survival on land. Meg had said nothing more, and Temperance did not have the heart to ask her.

With a little sigh, Temperance drew up a pail of water from the well in the center of the fort and started back. She walked slowly, because she was tired and the water was heavy, but as she walked, her thin kid slipper came down on a rock, and a sharp pain shot through the arch of her foot. "Hell's bells!" she said to herself, and kicked the offending rock out of her path. She needn't have said it to herself; she could have shouted it aloud, and no one would have heard. It was just past midday, and the Jamestown colonists were all at rest, escaping the fierce August sun. Some were in their houses; others were under the trees by the riverbank. Even the men working in the fields and the men building houses took a rest from about ten o'clock to two, and then they went back to work again until sunset. No one but Temperance was abroad. Wearily, she shifted the water pail to her other hand.

Poor Sarah, she thought. Her husband had taken sick and died of the calenture when they were three weeks at sea, and Sarah, big with child, had to watch his body sink beneath the foaming, white-capped waves. Grief brought on labor pains, and she gave birth to a baby boy six weeks too early. The infant, mewing pitifully in the dark, stinking quarters of the *Falcon,* had died almost as soon as it was born. By the time the ship made landfall at Jamestown, Sarah Harison was burning hot with childbed fever and had to be carried ashore. Her husband's older brother, Harmon, who had come to Virginia the year before, had been to see about her every morning and every afternoon.

"It's because of me that she's here," he would say over and over. "It's all my doing. If I hadn't sent for them, my brother and his baby son would be alive, and his wife would not be suffering here so far from home. God help us." For a day or two, Sarah seemed to get better, and then she refused to eat and lay with her face to the wall. Harmon awkwardly stroked her hand when he came, and he told her he would look after her, but she did not acknowledge his presence. Meg bathed her face and told her she would soon be well, but she did not respond. Temperance sat beside her, talking softly of how they were both widows and would soon go back to England together. Once or twice, Sarah had nodded her head weakly and squeezed Temperance's hand, but today she had barely moved.

"Poor soul, she'll be dead before dark." Joan Pierce, the brisk black-haired young woman who shared the house with Meg and Temperance, had taken her four-year-old daughter and her servant girl to stay at another house so that they would not see Sarah's last hours. That was futile, Temperance thought. Death was everywhere at Jamestown, and it would find them, no matter where they hid. Soon little Jane Pierce would have to understand that her father was dead. He, like George Yardley, was lost aboard the *Sea Venture.* Joan Pierce hated Jamestown even more than Temperance did. "There's nothing here but sickness and laziness," she said. "These people have been here two years, and look what they've built for houses. Not one of them has a chimney, and there's not one decent garden in the place. But that's men for you."

Until six days ago, there had been only two women in Jamestown. Last year Thomas Forrest, a country squire from Sussex, had bravely brought his wife, Lucy, and her fourteen-year-old servant girl to live among two hundred men in the wilds of Virginia. The servant, a broad-hipped, sweet-tempered girl named Ann Burras, soon caught the eye of a carpenter named John Laydon. Now Ann Burras was Mistress Laydon, with a husband twice her age. Lucy and Thomas Forrest had not held her to her term of service.

"What do I want with a serving girl in this place?" Lucy had joked. "There's precious little to serve." So Ann Laydon became mistress of her own house at the end of one of Jamestown's three streets. She and Lucy were the only ones at Jamestown who were really glad to see the new arrivals. "Praise to the Almighty!" Lucy said. "Ann and I've seen naught but breeches and beards for a year and a half. What a joy to see some of our own sex besides each other!"

"We did see one other," Ann said. "You forget Pocahontas." She giggled.

"Thank God that little wanton does not come here anymore!" Lucy rolled her eyes heavenward.

"When will we see some Indians?" one of the newcomers wanted to know.

"Not soon, God willing, not anytime soon," Lucy said. "When they come, trouble follows."

Ann and Lucy, the voices of experience, shared what they had learned about life at Jamestown:

"We wash clothes in the river and hang them to dry on trees. But don't go outside the fort alone."

"Indian bread? A child could make it. But it's not much to taste when it's done, since we've no butter nor cheese. We've a nanny goat or two, but what we need is a sweet brown-eyed cow."

"One good thing about this place: When you piss in your pot, you just dump it out on the ground."

Fifteen-year-old Ann was newly pregnant, and she had immediately struck up a close friendship with Martha Scott, the pregnant wife of Peter Scott, a farmer from Cornwall. Lucy, thin as a rail and sharp-witted as an Oxford don, had taken a liking to Joan Pierce. There was a fine pair of shrews, Temperance thought. Both of them were openly scornful of the men's ordering of affairs at Jamestown.

"What does it matter who is governor, with such a pitiful place as this to govern?" said Lucy, but her husband told her to mind her tongue.

Now, as Temperance passed the house that belonged to Francis West, the sound of men's angry voices caused her to walk slower.

"Let him call me a fop-doodle again, and that will be the end of him! Arrogant little bastard! I'll fop-doodle him! God damn me if I take orders from such a man!" That would be Francis West. John Smith ought to be more tactful, Temperance thought. He ought to know that one did not treat a baron's brother like a lackey, or call a gentleman names when he refused to chop wood. But to John Smith, the new arrivals were so many more mouths to feed, so many more bodies to shelter, and he had no patience with those who would not work. Temperance paused, straining to hear more.

"If you know what's good for you, and for us all, you'll not ruffle the cock's feathers. He may not be wellborn, but here in this wilderness he's well connected. Powhatan respects him, and Powhatan commands fifteen hundred Indian warriors." That must be George Percy, Temperance thought. He was the quiet one; West was the boisterous one.

"Smith and his Indian friends don't frighten me," West said. "Savages are fickle creatures. They have turned on Smith before, and might again. Powhatan would have killed him last winter, if it had not been for Pocahontas."

"What if we were to declare you president of the Jamestown Council right now? You are the governor's brother, after all. Gates is only the governor's deputy, and he is lost at sea. What if you took Smith's title away from him?" That deep voice Temperance knew well. It was John Martin, captain of the *Falcon.*

"I don't want to be president," West said petulantly. Then, changing his tone, he went on, "But what about you, Percy? I warrant we could make you president."

"I don't know," Percy said. "I don't know how we could accomplish that. Smith will have served his year come September, but he says he'll not step aside until a proper governor comes."

Then another voice, a flat, nasal tone, joined in. "But suppose something were to . . . happen to our friend Smith?" The voice dropped lower, and Temperance, try as she might, could catch only a few words:

"Grove of laurel trees . . . dark . . . west of the gate . . ." Then they all began to talk at once, and Temperance, unable to make out what they were saying, shrugged and walked on. The last voice she heard could have been John Ratcliffe's. He had only been at Jamestown for one day, but it was rumored that he had disliked John Smith for a long time. He and Smith had both come with the first settlers in 1607, and Ratcliffe had served as president of the Council the year before Smith. There had been some trouble between them then, and Ratcliffe had returned to England. But the day before yesterday, he had brought the storm-damaged *Diamond* into port, laden with sick and dying passengers. Ratcliffe had a rasping, whining voice and a shifting, ratlike gaze. He was aptly named, Temperance thought. Whatever the malcontents were plotting, he and Francis West were at the center of it. West, only twenty-two, was tall and big-boned, and with his brown hair and wide-set brown eyes, he reminded Temperance of a half-grown spaniel: friendly, but rambunctious and apt to cause mischief. He did not seem to her a dangerous man, but Ratcliffe did. Maybe she ought to tell John Smith what she had overheard. But what would she tell him? He was well aware that he had enemies, and she had her own troubles to worry about.

Limping on her bruised foot, she tried to hurry with her pail of water. But too rapid a pace made the water slosh and spill, so she slowed down again. She told herself there was no need to hurry anyway. John Smith was safe aboard the *Blessing* for the moment, and Sarah Harison was going to die in her own filth no matter how often they washed her. And Sarah was not the only one. Maybe they would all die, and Jamestown would be lost like the settlement at Roanoke, never to be heard of again. The Jamestown settlers would die and leave no trace: Their bones would rot and disappear under the soft cover of pine needles and oak leaves that now cushioned their steps. Shifting the heavy pail to her other hand, Temperance plodded on. Futility weighed heavier upon her than the water pail.

For as long as Temperance could remember, her life had been a succession of things to look forward to: a Christmas feast, a new horse to ride, a new gown, a new young man to dance with. As she grew older, there was the fascinating prospect of her own future as the mistress of some man's house and the mother of his children. That was what she had been brought up to be: all the endless hours of embroidery and cookery, of learning how to play the dulcimer and dance the gavotte, had been to fit her for that role, and she could not imagine herself in any other. She used to picture herself as a young matron, elegantly gowned, presiding over a bountiful table and a flawlessly run household, beloved of husband, children, and servants. Nothing in her upbringing had prepared her for surviving in a wilderness three thousand miles from home.

Somehow she must get back to Thickthorne, with its smooth green lawns and its brick house that had stood there a hundred years. She was sick of Jamestown's weeds and wattle and daub, and she longed to see her mother and father. They were the only ones at Thickthorne, now that all the children had gone. Temperance, the youngest, had been the last to leave. Prudence had married a long-faced knight, and Mary a prosperous London merchant; and Stanley had gone off last year to Cambridge. Temperance missed her sisters, but she missed Stanley the most. Tall and rangy with red hair like hers, he was her kindred spirit. His mother wanted him to study for the clergy, but he would have none of that. As a student at Cambridge, he disported himself more often at tavern table than altar rail.

Martha Flowerdew had forced her Puritan faith upon her children with mixed results: Prudence and Mary tried to outdo her in piety, while Stanley and Temperance bowed rebellious heads. Their mother wrote their sins in a small black book, and told them that a love of luxury was the snare of the Devil. When George gave Temperance a gold wedding ring with the words "Be true in heart" engraved upon it, Martha Flowerdew looked down her long nose at it and said that wedding rings were a popish practice. Hot words had followed, but now Temperance would be glad to feel her mother's cool, thin lips upon her forehead, and to take what comfort she could from that stiff-necked embrace. Her father would hold out his arms, and she would run to him, as she had done since she was a little girl. She wished with all her heart that she were standing in the hall at Thickthorne this very moment, with her arms around both her parents.

Reluctantly, with dragging steps, she entered the hut. The stench of the sick woman's bowels filled the small, close space, and Temperance, suddenly nauseated, pressed the back of her hand against her mouth. "Here," she said, setting the pail of water down next to Meg. "Here it is, for all the good it'll do."

Without answering, Meg dipped an already-stained cloth into the water, wrung it out, and began to wash between Sarah Harison's thighs. "It's a pity we haven't any proper cloths to wash her with, nor any decent smock to put on her," she said softly.

"I know," Temperance said. "And there won't be any, either—not till the next supply ship comes, and maybe not even then." They finished bathing Sarah as best they could. As they settled her on her back, she opened her eyes. They were dull and unseeing, Temperance thought sadly, as though death had already taken possession of them. The sick woman's cracked lips moved, and Meg and Temperance bent low over her to catch the words.

"So kind," she whispered, staring straight ahead. "You . . . are so kind." Her tongue, gray-coated, showed between her lips as she tried to shape the word "thanks," but the only sound she made was a soft "thhh . . ." Then her eyes closed, and her mouth fell open. She drew two long, rasping breaths, shuddered slightly, and was still. Meg watched her closely for a moment, and then, wetting her forefinger with her tongue, she held it in front of Sarah Harison's slack mouth. She looked at Temperance and shook her head. She bent low, so that her ear was next to Sarah's mouth, and listened. She shook her head again.

"She's gone."

"Are you certain? So quickly?"

"Death does not tarry long when it comes," Meg said. Gently, she put a hand under Sarah's chin and closed the open mouth. The eyes, already closed, seemed to Temperance to have sunk even deeper in their sockets. The skin was taut and grayish-yellow, and the cheekbones stood out sharply. The thick brown hair, long uncombed, was pulled back from the high forehead, so that the contours of the skull were prominent. What had been a young woman's face was now a death's-head. Temperance, looking at her, began to cry. She had not given way to tears since she arrived, but now loud, racking sobs shook her, and she could not stop them. Meg put her arms around her. "Ah, you've not had a good cry all this time," she said. She stroked Temperance's hair. "Cry it out, and you'll be the better for it."

"No, I'll not be better!" Temperance said, her voice muffled, her face hidden against Meg's shoulder. "Dear God, how I hate this place!"

"Hush," Meg said. "Hush that talk." She spoke tenderly, as though reasoning with a child. "Think on something good. Think how it will be when George comes. Think how he looked when last you saw him."

"I can't," Temperance said. "I can't remember. It was so long ago." But she dried her tears with the back of her hand.

"We'll not be long apart," George had told her, "I promise." That was on June 8. It was now August 17. It had been so long that Temperance, when she thought of him, had difficulty recalling the exact sound of his voice and picturing the shape of his face. The dark blue eyes, so dark they seemed to turn almost black when he was excited, the thick chestnut curls and small, pointed beard were easy enough to remember, but the total configuration of eyes, brows, nose, and mouth, each in its proper relationship to the others, had somehow escaped her memory. His body—thickset and sturdy, with thighs each one nearly as big around as her waist, strong and hard from soldiering—that was not difficult to remember. And his hands—those dear hands, with their short, stubby fingers and powerful wrists—those hands she could still imagine touching her breasts and her privates.

Since she had been at Jamestown, however, Temperance had tried her best not to think of such things. At sea, hoping every dawn that the *Sea Venture* might suddenly appear off the *Falcon*'s port or starboard, she had thought of George constantly. But on land, fearing that every day diminished the chances of seeing him again, she had been overtaken by a curious numbness. Now she felt that if someone were to tell her that George was alive, she would not even have the strength to rejoice. It was no good for Will to say that ships had been lost at sea for longer than this and made port, and it was no good for Meg to tell her not to give up hope. Temperance had begun to feel in her bones that she would never see her husband again.

When Temperance awoke, the sun was in her eyes and someone was calling her name. At first, as usual, she thought it was George.

"Temperance! Temperance!"

As the fog of sleep cleared, she sat up. The voice was not George's, but Will's. Dear Will, who had promised George to look after her, little knowing what that promise would exact from him. Now he was calling to her outside the door.

"I hear you!" She answered softly so as not to disturb Meg, who lay sleeping next to her on a straw pallet. Taking turns, they had kept watch over Sarah Harison's body through the night, and Temperance had only lain down to sleep at dawn. At noon they would bury Sarah in the small, crowded graveyard inside the fort's gate. Isabella Atkins, one of the newly arrived widows, was supposed to be keeping watch, but she had dozed off, and now she slept, leaning against the wall, her head drooping forward on her chest. Temperance did not wake her.

Unfastening the door, she swung it open, and then remembered that she was wearing only a thin white shift. Clutching its folds about her breasts, she peered up at Will. His blond head, gilded by the morning sun behind him, bore a halo like a figure in some religious painting. His gray eyes swept quickly over Temperance, from her tousled hair down to her bare feet, and up again. Any other time, he would have made some jest about her appearance, but now he fastened his clear, steady gaze on her face and spoke with great urgency.

"There's a ship coming in! Just rounding Hog Island! I came as soon as I heard the watch call out."

"Oh, God!" said Temperance, catching her breath. "Let me get dressed. Wait for me." It took only an instant to pull her petticoat over her shift and fasten the fraying velvet bodice and kirtle that were her only other garments. She no longer bothered with busks and busk points; the whalebone stays were uncomfortable in Virginia's heat. As she dressed, Meg awoke and, seeing her haste, sat up.

"What is it?"

"There's a ship coming in. Will's waiting for me outside."

"Praise God!" Meg said. She rose and began to put on her petticoat.

"I'm going on now, with Will," Temperance said. "You'd best wake Isabella before you leave. The dogs might get her"—Temperance glanced at the shrouded body of Sarah Harison—"if nobody watches." Three large mastiffs, good rat-catchers, had been brought as ship's dogs, and now they ran loose, gloriously happy in the wilderness of Jamestown. But one of them had gnawed the toes off a corpse left unguarded the day before yesterday.

Thrusting bare feet hastily into slippers, Temperance took time only to smooth her hair and pin it up under the wire frame of her hood. Married women covered their heads indoors and out, even in the wilds of Virginia. Pulling the door open with one hand and straightening her hood with the other, she stepped out into the sunlight where Will was waiting.

"Hurry," he said. "George won't care if your cap is on crooked." Temperance made a face at him. He grinned and held out his hand to her. Intent on reaching the riverbank, she was not looking into his face and did not see the small involuntary rapture that crossed it as his long fingers closed around hers.

"Did you see the ship yourself? Could you tell anything about it?" Temperance, the daughter of a country squire, would never learn to call a ship by a feminine pronoun.

Will shook his head in the negative. "Too far away yet. Hog Island's a good way off on the horizon, a league or more, and when I saw her, she was barely more than the size of a pea. I could make out her rigging, though, and it looked as if her mainmast was down. She could well be the *Sea Venture.*"

"Or the *Swallow* or some other ship," Temperance said. She could not let herself hope yet. She felt a curious paralysis stealing over her, and she worried that if this incoming ship were, by some miracle, the *Sea Venture,* she would not be able to greet George. "Where have you been?" she could say, but that was all that came to her mind. What would they do after the initial embrace? She could not force her imagination beyond their first kiss.

She and Will hurried across the palisade to the entrance, whose heavy log gates had already been swung open. Like a colony of ants, the inhabitants of the fort were swarming out of their houses and scurrying toward the riverbank. For a wilderness outpost three thousand miles from civilization, the arrival of any contact from the familiar world would be cause for excitement; for beleaguered Jamestown, whose population with the newcomers now numbered 382, the announcement of a ship approaching was enough to bring every able-bodied man, woman, and child to the edge of the broad James River. Everyone who could walk was there, and some of the sick, barely able to move, had dragged themselves from their pallets, anxious not to miss the excitement. Only a dozen or so seriously ill people, and three well ones besides Isabella Atkins watching over dead bodies, did not join the throng on the grassy bank above the pier.

Jamestown had been built for safety from the Indians, on a narrow neck of land not much more than a mile across at its widest part, and the narrowest was narrow enough to be commanded by a blockhouse where no one was allowed to pass in or out without orders from John Smith. For that reason, on this warm summer morning, the inhabitants of the town, if it could be called that, felt safe enough to leave their houses and to venture out to the edge of the river. The James, nearly five miles wide at its bend around Hog Island, east of the fort, narrowed to less than two miles in breadth at Jamestown. Even there, it was still deep enough for oceangoing vessels of up to a hundred tons to navigate, which was the other reason, besides safety, that they had chosen the site on the marshy peninsula. Immediately to the west of Jamestown, the river became narrower and shallower, winding its crooked way far inland, past Powhatan's domain and into the land of the hostile Monacans and Chickahominies.

By the time Will and Temperance reached the riverbank, it was lined with people. As they edged their way forward, someone touched Temperance's sleeve.

"God willing, it's the *Sea Venture,* eh? And soon you'll be reunited with your husband. May you be as blessed as I was when the *Lion* sailed in with my Thomasine aboard!" It was Nathaniel Causey, one of the men who had come to Virginia with Christopher Newport on the first supply ship in January 1608. Until August 1609, he had been without his wife. He was a stout, cheerful fellow, and Temperance liked him. She was not sure how she liked his wife.

Thomasine Causey, as thin as her husband was stout, stood like a shadow by his side. In the August heat, she was fully dressed in a bodice with damask sleeves, stays, and a stomacher, and a velvet kirtle open to show a yellow taffeta petticoat over her farthingale. On her head was a lace cap, and around her neck she wore a starched white ruff. Temperance, looking at Thomasine, wished she had taken time to put on her own farthingale. Without its supports, her skirts dragged the ground. How had Thomasine managed to arrive with a supply of starch, Temperance wondered, let alone her ruffs? Most of the other women, like Temperance, were wearing only their linen shifts open at the throat, with travel-stained bodices and kirtles over bedraggled petticoats, and hoods or lace coifs that looked much the worse for wear.

Only Lucy Forrest and Ann Laydon, who had all the clothes they brought with them last year, were wearing ruffs. They were almost as well turned out as Thomasine. They and the other newly arrived married women all stood beside their husbands, holding on to them as though they were afraid some of the new widows might capture them. Temperance wondered idly how long the Forrests and the Causeys had been married, and why they had no children. She spied Joan Pierce holding her four-year-old Jane tightly by the hand, down almost at the water's edge. They had spent the night at the Forrests' so that Jane would not see Sarah Harison's corpse. Clutching Will by the arm, Temperance pulled him in the direction of the Pierces. "Let us go stand by Joan Pierce," she said. "She and I are the only ones with husbands on the *Sea Venture,* and we may as well stand together."

Joan was squinting against the morning sun, shading her eyes with one freckled hand, trying to see the ship. Her wedding ring, a thin circlet of gold, glimmered in the sunlight.

"Can you tell anything yet?" Temperance asked her.

"No." Joan's voice was taut as a fiddle string. She did not even glance at Temperance; she seemed scarcely to breathe, so intent was she on seeing the approaching ship.

"My father may be coming on that ship," said little Jane. She smiled up at Temperance and Will, and began to dance up and down, her black curls bobbing.

"Jane, come stand by me, and let your mother see what she can see." Meg, slightly out of breath, came down the sloping bank and took Jane by the hand. With her other hand, she gave Temperance a pat on the shoulder. "This may be the one," she said.

Temperance nodded silently. Too excited to speak, she stood still as a statue, unaware that her fingers were digging into Will Sterling's arm. He would have been the last to tell her.

The ship was now drawing nearly close enough to identify, and Temperance's heart began to race. Its mainmast was broken; that was why it sailed so slowly. No mainmast, she thought; maybe no George, either. He could have been swept overboard in the storm; he could have died of ship's fever. Temperance let her imagination run rampant. What if Joan Pierce's husband raced ashore and took his wife in his arms, while she had to stand there looking on, bereft? She pictured the Pierces, their faces full of pity, watching her. But as she and Will shielded their eyes against the glint of the sun on the water, Temperance heard John Martin's voice.

"She's the *Swallow,* I'll be bound. See that patched foresail? I remember it. And she's too small to be the *Sea Venture.* But maybe she's got word of the *Venture.* "

But she did not. John Smith, waiting at the end of the pier, called out as soon as the *Swallow* was within shouting distance: "What news of the

Sea Venture? The *Virginia?"* The *Virginia,* the smallest vessel of the fleet, had nearly been forgotten.

"Don't know!" the *Swallow*'s captain called back. "No sign of them!" Slowly, Temperance relaxed her grip on Will's arm. He put his hand over hers and looked down at her apprehensively, as though he expected a fit of weeping.

"Damn," she said softly. Her shoulders sagged. The numbness she had felt earlier returned. Expectation or disappointment, it was all the same: There was nothing left inside her to produce emotion. She felt fragile and empty, like a broken eggshell. But she did not cry. She looked at Joan Pierce standing motionless and silent in the murmuring crowd. Joan was not crying, either, but her small daughter suddenly squeezed both fists against her eyes, bowed her head, and began to wail. The thin, sorrowful cry cut through the conversations around it and left silence in its wake. Meg knelt beside the child, trying to comfort her. Her mother distractedly stroked the little girl's dark hair and looked out at the river as though she still expected the *Sea Venture* to appear at any moment. Then she looked at Temperance.

"I wonder," she said dully. "I wonder if there's any cause to hope now."

"I don't know," Temperance said. She saw her own grief mirrored in the other woman's eyes. "I don't know," she said again, "but how can we mourn for them if we don't know they're dead?"

As the crippled *Swallow* cast her lines ashore, a great cheer went up from all assembled. On her main deck, her gaunt, sunburned passengers and crew shouted and waved. Soon eager hands ashore began helping the first passengers to debark. After eleven weeks at sea, some had to be carried: The calenture had found its way aboard the *Swallow,* as it had the *Unity.* Of the fifty passengers who had set out from Plymouth in June, twenty-one had died at sea and eight others—five men, three women, and one young boy—arrived too ill to stand. As for the rest, some walked with help, and all were near to starving. Some fell on the sun-warmed grassy bank and lay sobbing weakly, overcome with joy at being on land. Around them, the residents of Jamestown murmured to each other as the crowd began to disperse.

"More sick ones—who's going to nurse them?"

"There's not enough corn for us, let alone them."

"Where will they all sleep? We've no more beds."

As the *Swallow*'s weary passengers made their way up the path to the palisade, Meg gripped Temperance by the elbow.

"What's the matter?" Temperance, lost in her own grief and disappointment, did not much care what was the matter with anybody but herself.

"See that man?" Meg pointed with a trembling hand. "See that gray-haired one there with the cane? I know him!"

"What do you mean, you know him?" Will, overhearing, joined in. "Who is he?"

"That is the man who was master of the *Brave* when I sailed on her twenty years ago!" Meg's voice quavered. "His hair's gone gray, but I know his face! Facy, his name was—Arthur Facy. I could never forget that face. He helped me when I—when my face was cut." The man she pointed to walked with a slight limp, leaning on a cane. He seemed to be alone. He spoke casually to some of the *Swallow*'s passengers as they passed him, but he did not seem to belong to any of them.

"Captain Facy!" As the man approached, Meg called out to him, and he started at the sound of his name. "Captain Facy," she called out again, "Arthur Facy! Over here!" Then, as he turned in her direction, Meg ran toward him. He stood stock still, staring at her.

"How do you know my name?" He narrowed his eyes and looked perplexed for a moment, and then a smile broke over his face. "Great God! It can't be, but it is! I know you! I'd know that pretty face anywhere!" His eyes lingered briefly on her scar. "You were aboard the *Brave* when the Frenchmen tried to take her!" He held out both hands, and Meg clasped them joyfully in her own.

"Captain Facy! What brings you here to Virginia?"

"I could ask the same of you," he said with a grin. Worley, your name was, Meg Worley. Is that still your name?" Meg nodded, and he lifted her hands and brushed his lips against them. "What a strange trick of fate this is! What brings me here is a long story, and you must have one, too. Let me get my bearings here, and then you and I, Mistress Worley, must have a talk." Gallantly, he drew her arm through his, and they walked together to the palisade.

"Meg seems to have found a friend," Will said with a smile. Then, seeing Temperance's dispirited look, he grew solemn again. Temperance was not looking at him or Meg or Captain Facy, but at John Smith. Smith was on the pier, conferring with the *Swallow*'s captain and first mate. They were obviously arguing about something. Watching them, Temperance suddenly remembered the conversation she had heard the day before. Sarah's death and the *Swallow*'s arrival had driven it from her mind, but now it all came back. If she warned John Smith of some plot against him, he might be so grateful he would give her first chance at passage back to England. The six ships now riding at anchor in the James River had been waiting for the *Sea Venture*, but now that the *Swallow* had brought no news of their flagship, there was no reason for the other ships to tarry at Jamestown. They would be leaving soon, and when they sailed, Temperance meant to be aboard one of them.

"I have to see Captain Smith," she said abruptly. Will and the others looked at her with surprise.

"What is it?" They spoke almost in unison.

"What do you want with him?" Will asked gently.

"I have something to tell him—and something to ask him." Temperance spoke sharply. Didn't he think she could have business with John Smith on her own if she chose? She turned on her heel and, with a swirl of her skirts, walked boldly onto the pier. "Captain Smith!" At the sound of his name, he turned around and saw her. Before he could speak, Temperance continued, "Captain Smith, if you please, I must speak to you— privately." She heard her own voice and marveled at her forwardness. "I have reason to believe you are in some danger," Temperance went on hurriedly, "and I—I have a favor to ask of you."

Smith looked at her kindly, and with some curiosity. "Very well, but let us not talk here." He glanced around him with a slight frown. "Will you meet me at my house? I'll be along in a trice."

Will was waiting for Temperance at the head of the pier. "What do you want with John Smith?" His voice, gentle, indulgent, irritated her.

"That's my affair," she snapped. She felt like lashing out at someone. Will drew back as though she had struck him. Then, suddenly remorseful, she said, "Oh, Will, I didn't mean to be rude. It's just—I don't know—I'm not myself."

"We're none of us ourselves," he said quietly. "After all this, how could we be?" He looked long and searchingly into her face, and then he said, "If there is aught you need, Temperance, or something I can do, you know I—"

"No," she said sharply. They walked in silence for a moment, and then Temperance said grudgingly, "But you can come along with me to John Smith's house, if you like." When they reached the small thatch-roofed structure that served the president of the Council of Jamestown for a residence, Temperance stopped so suddenly that Will nearly ran into her. Seizing him by the arm, she pointed at the doorway of Smith's house. Standing in that doorway, framed by the rough-hewn beams, was an Indian.

His long black hair was pulled back into a topknot wrapped tightly at the top of his head and adorned with small white shells. The rest of his head was shaved and glistened, like his tawny skin, with bear grease and sweat. He wore a breechclout of soft deerskin, fringed and decorated with the same kind of small white shells that he wore in his hair. He was tall and well muscled, and his powerful-looking body nearly filled the small door to Smith's house. What held Temperance's gaze in horrid fascination, however, was not his body or his attire, but his choice of ornament: from the lobe of his right ear hung a large dead rat. Suspended by a thin piece of deerskin, the animal hung by its long pinkish tail, and its head rested on the Indian's shoulder. Its brownish fur was matted, and it was quite stiff.

Temperance shuddered. She had heard that some of the Pamunkey tribe wore small live grass snakes tied to their ears, but dead rats had never been mentioned. The Indian had caught sight of Temperance and Will watching him, and he smiled. It was a chilling smile, a slight elongation of closed lips and a sidelong glance of small dark eyes. The dangling rat, with its matted empty eyesockets and its snout showing a gleam of needle-sharp white teeth, seemed to smile, too.

"Ah, Tanx-Powhatan!" John Smith, having conducted his business with Captain Moore of the *Swallow* and given what instructions he could for the housing and feeding of the damaged ship's crew and passengers, came up behind Temperance and Will. "And Mistress Yardley and Master—" Smith clapped a hand to his forehead. "Master—Sterling, isn't it?" Will nodded, and John Smith smiled. "You must forgive my poor memory. But I find learning near two hundred names and faces in one week is more than I can do. To what do I owe the honor of this visit?"

"I—I wanted to speak with you about a matter of importance," Temperance said. "I overheard something that may mean danger to you."

Smith caught her meaning at once. He made a quizzical face, raising his eyebrows and pursing his lips. "Aha," he said. "I shall be interested to hear that. Come inside—but first I must hear what Tanx-Powhatan has to say." Taking Temperance and Will each by the elbow, he steered them past the Indian. To him, Smith said something that sounded like "Nettopew, nettopew," and pointed to Temperance and Will. "That means 'friends,' " he said. "I've told him you are friends." Smith motioned them to take seats on two rough-hewn joint stools next to a table in the dirt-floored room. "Please take a seat. If you'll excuse me, I must speak first with Tanx-Powhatan. He brings me news of some crucial business at Powhatan Village."

With that, Smith turned to the Indian and began to speak rapidly and fluently in the liquid-sounding, guttural syllables of the Algonquin dialect used by the Chesapeake tribes. Tanx-Powhatan, his dark eyes wide open now, replied at some length, and then there followed a series of short exchanges between the two, as though they were cementing the terms of an agreement. Then they clasped hands, and Tanx-Powhatan, inclining his head almost imperceptibly in the direction of Temperance and Will, took his leave, exiting silently as a cat. John Smith watched him thoughtfully for a moment or two, and then turned his attention to Temperance.

"That was the chief Powhatan's son. He brought me good news. With all these newcomers, we are in desperate need of more dwellings, and Powhatan Village has fifty or more tight, dry houses and near two hundred acres of cleared land. I proposed to strike a bargain with his father, and he brings news that old Powhatan has agreed to my terms. He sells our people his village, and we protect his people from their enemies, the Monacans!" Smith leaned forward and clapped both hands on his knees in a gesture of satisfaction and enthusiasm. "All it will take will be a portion of copper now, and a bushel of corn from every house once a year!" He rubbed his hands together in boyish glee. "That will see us all sheltered and able to plant on cleared land come spring." He smiled at Temperance, who smiled back. "Now, Mistress Yardley. I am sorry the *Swallow* was not the *Sea Venture,* for all our sakes as well as yours. But she may come in yet." He sighed and looked out the window. "Now let me hear your tale of danger." He leaned back in his chair and folded his arms across his chest.

Temperance, sitting very straight on her joint stool, began to speak. "Yesterday afternoon during the rest time, I had to fetch water for Sarah Harison—she died before sundown—and as I was coming back from the well, I overheard some of the men talking about you."

"Aha!" Smith unfolded his arms and leaned forward.

"They were at Francis West's house. I know one of the voices was Captain Martin's, because I was aboard the *Falcon,* and I think maybe the others were John Ratcliffe and either Gabriel Archer or George Percy—I couldn't tell." As Temperance recounted the scrap of conversation she had overheard, Smith listened intently, his eyes never leaving her face. When she had finished, he stood up and began to pace back and forth in the tiny room.

"What you heard does not surprise me," he said slowly. "West and Archer and Ratcliffe started trying to turn others against me as soon as they set foot on dry land. They are up to something, and what you say of yesterday afternoon explains what happened last night."

"What?" Will, who had been watching Temperance, spoke for the first time.

"Someone shot an arrow at me as I was coming back from dining aboard the *Blessing,*" Smith said tersely. "It was dark, and so little moon I could not see who did the deed. The culprit fled into the woods just behind the fort. The arrow missed me by this much." Smith pressed his thumb and forefinger together in an eloquent gesture. "There has been no sign of Indian troubles or any unfriendly Indians about these parts in over a fortnight. I have no doubt it was one of our own, trying to prick me with an Indian arrow, so they could report to the Virginia Company that poor John Smith had been unfortunately slain by the savages. Then they could put Francis West or George Percy—those highborn ones—in my place as president of the Council." Smith's voice was scornful. He stopped pacing and smiled grimly at Temperance. "I thank you, Mistress Yardley, for this information. It confirms what I have long suspected, and it puts me on my guard. They will no doubt try again. I am much obliged to you." He sat down again and placed his hands flat on the table. "You have told me of the danger; now what was the favor you had to ask?"

"I want to go home—back to England," Temperance said simply.

John Smith threw back his head and laughed. "My dear lady, so do all the others! Who in his right mind would want to stay here? If I let you go, I'd have to let three hundred others take passage, and then what would become of the poor Virginia Company's investment?" Smith's tone grew solemn. "And what would become of England's future in the New World? This colony is all we have, and it must endure." He spoke the last words softly, almost prayerfully, his eyes on the forest outside.

"But I thought—since my husband is lost—I might be able to find space aboard the *Swallow* or one of the other ships when they sail for home," Temperance said. "I am a widow now, you know, and there is no reason for me to stay here."

"Maybe so, maybe not so. What if you left, and the *Sea Venture* arrived? What would I tell George Yardley?"

"That is unlikely, and you know it!" Temperance's voice had an edge of anger in it. "I don't want to hear any more what if's! I want to go back to England, and you are the only person in Virginia who can see to it!"

"I am sorry," Smith said gently. "Perhaps it can be arranged later, but not now. There are too many others. Think of poor Gabriel Morgan, with his wife and child that came on the *Unity* both dead last week of the fever. God knows, he wants to go home. And what of Mistress Joan Pierce? Her husband was aboard the *Sea Venture,* too, you know, and she has a child with her. I could name you dozens of others, and all of them with as much reason to leave Virginia as you." Smith looked Temperance in the eye, and so compelling was his gaze that she could not turn from it. "It is not just that I want to see this settlement succeed," he went on. "But in our present state we cannot provision even one ship to cross the Atlantic, let alone seven. There is not enough food for the captains and crews, and they will do well to get back by themselves, without any passengers. The captains would not take you aboard, even if I gave you permission to sail." He spoke kindly enough, but Temperance felt suddenly weak, as though he had struck her. She lowered her head and studied her lap. Will reached out and put his hand over hers.

"I see," she said, almost in a whisper.

"Now," John Smith continued, obviously relieved to see that she was not going to become hysterical, "speaking of provisions, I think we shall shortly have enough food to see us all in better spirits. I am this day making plans to disperse the colonists—the men, that is—to other places, to hunt and forage for themselves. With the new people from the *Swallow,* we have over four hundred souls to take care of, with food enough for half that number. But if some can fend for themselves this fall, that will ease the burden on the storehouse this winter. I'm sending John Martin and George Percy with a hundred and twenty men down to Nansemond, about ten leagues from here, where the Nansemond River joins the James. Then I shall send about forty more down to Point Comfort. There's plenty of oysters there, and sturgeon as long as a man is tall. I've seen them myself. And then I shall send Francis West"—he pronounced the name with a hostile hiss—"and a hundred and twenty more upriver to the Falls near Powhatan Village." He put the tips of his fingers together and examined them thoughtfully. "West will be close to Powhatan that way, and Powhatan will . . . watch out for him." The flicker of a satisfied smile lighted his face as he spoke the last words. Then he looked at Will. "Master Sterling, you are a good man, in good health, from the looks of you, and one, I think, to be trusted. I'd like you to go with Francis West and those men to the Falls. Be ready to leave tomorrow morning."

Will's hand was resting on Temperance's, and she felt his fingers stiffen. The incongruity of Will Sterling, glove-maker, lute player, in a wilderness with Francis West and Powhatan's Indians, almost made her smile. He must be having the same thought. And John Smith, true to form, had ordered, not asked.

"Now you must excuse me," Smith said. "I have not yet announced these plans to the others, and there is much to be done. Martin and West and Archer and Percy are coming here for a council at noon. And you have to bury Sarah Harison. God rest her and go with you." He rose to his feet, and the interview was ended.

Temperance, seeing him two months later, was to wish that God had been a little more with Captain John Smith.

POWHATAN VILLAGE
2 September 1609

In the firelight, drops of sweat on Francis West's forehead glistened like the glass beads he had traded to the Indians earlier that day. Opposite him, seated cross-legged on a wooden platform, was Wahunsonacock, known as Powhatan, the ruler of all the river tribes. On West's right, Nathaniel Causey, and on his left, Will Sterling, sat watching West and Powhatan apprehensively. It was a cool fall evening, but all three Englishmen were perspiring. Powhatan was not sweating but smiling; his small black eyes squinting, his strong white teeth shining.

"I wish to God we had an interpreter," West said through his teeth. "Smith told me Tom Savage would be here."

"That makes me uneasy," Causey said under his breath. "That puts us at Powhatan's mercy, with no one to intercede for us."

Will, awed by his first contact with the Indians, spoke hesitantly. "These are savages, but it's plain to see they are not fools. They may not need an interpreter."

John Smith, dispatching Francis West and 120 men to the Falls according to his agreement with Powhatan, had promised that young Tom Savage, a twelve-year-old English boy he had left among the Indians to learn their language, would be there to serve as interpreter. But Powhatan had not brought the boy with him. When West inquired after young Savage, the wily old chief only smiled and shook his head. "Not here," he said in English. "He is at Werowocomoco."

Now Powhatan smiled again and spoke to them. "You may call me Wahunsonacock," he said amiably, striking his breast with majestic slowness. "I am the Powhatan, but I am Wahunsonacock."

"What the devil does that mean?" Nathaniel Causey whispered in West's ear. On West's other side, Will leaned closer to hear the answer.

West, whose eyes had not left Powhatan's face, spoke in as normal a tone as he could manage. "That is his real name. He wants us to call him

Wahunsonacock." As he pronounced the name, West smiled and nodded toward its owner. "For God's sake," he continued in an even voice, "don't whisper in my ear. Smile."

The three Englishmen grinned nervously at their host. Powhatan, enjoying their discomfort, gazed at his guests with a mixture of amusement and contempt.

Will, who had never seen Powhatan before, felt only reluctant admiration. This was no ignorant savage. Shrewd native intelligence, cunning, and cruelty looked out of this man's eyes. One would not want him for a foe, Will thought, and perhaps not for a friend, either. Wahunsonacock was a tall, well-muscled man, perhaps sixty or older, to judge by his graying hair. The hair was pulled into a single topknot and bound with a strip of beaten copper. In his ears, dangling from each of three large holes in the lobes, were smaller copper ornaments. He wore a single magnificent garment, a robe made of wild turkey feathers so artfully fashioned that nothing could be seen of the material underneath. Will, the glove-maker, appreciated its workmanship.

Powhatan lounged on a rug made of raccoon skins, and at each side of his platform stood two Indian women, waiting to serve his food. The women wore soft deerskin garments around their hips, but their breasts, painted with bloodroot in circles of red, were uncovered. In their ears and around their necks were ornaments made of tiny shells and bones. Though Will did not know it, their necklaces, and the fact that their breasts were painted in concentric circles, proclaimed the fact that they had borne children. Young girls who had not yet carried a child wore necklaces of large white beads, not shells. One of the women wore a headband made of patterned beadwork; the other, a plain deerskin band with one blue glass bead dangling from it.

"Opossunoquonuske!" Powhatan pointed to the woman wearing the blue bead. She was a young woman, but tall and big-boned, with a piercing gaze. At the mention of her name, she turned the corners of her mouth upward and inclined her head slightly in the direction of the three English visitors. Her dark eyes, flashing her hatred, met theirs boldly for a brief moment, and then she lowered her gaze.

"Smith told me she might be here," West said. "She is an important personage, Powhatan's cousin, or half-sister, or some such. She's the Queen of the Appamatucks, and comes to visit him now and then. Her husband has two hundred warriors, and we are to pay court to her."

"Winganuske!" With a wave of his hand, Powhatan indicated the woman with the beaded headband. The mother of Pocahontas nodded and smiled shyly at the Englishmen.

"Tanx-Powhatan!" Powhatan pointed to his right, where his eldest son lounged on a platform similar to his father's but lacking the raccoon rug. Tanx-Powhatan, who had barely acknowledged the visitors' presence, was resplendent in an intricately beaded deerskin vest. Around his waist was a belt made of snakeskin, and in that belt was a small pearl-handled Spanish dagger, which he fingered idly from time to time.

"I don't like to think how he came by that knife," Causey whispered.

Will was still looking at Powhatan, but out of the corner of his eye he caught a glimpse of Causey's florid, frightened face. What business, Will thought, did a country squire and a glove-maker and a baron's younger brother have sitting here with these half-naked savages? Savages they were; there was no question about that, yet there was a dignity and a presence about them that he had never imagined.

On Powhatan's left was his chief adviser, an Indian priest named Basamuck. He was a small, thin man of uncertain age, his scrawny, wrinkled neck adorned with a long necklace of beads and bird claws. Atop his head was a headdress made of twelve snakeskins, stuffed with grass and tied together at their necks, so that their heads formed a kind of topknot, which was encircled by a ring of blue-jay feathers. The long, scaly bodies of the snakes dangled around his face and shoulders like grotesque locks of hair. The snakes partially obscured his face, but his dark eyes darted from the Englishmen to Powhatan and back again with an expression of malevolent glee.

The three Englishmen had come to Powhatan on John Smith's instructions, to announce their arrival at the Falls and to bring gifts: two strings of blue glass beads for Powhatan (on an earlier visit, Smith had told the Indian chief that these beads were very precious because they were the color of the sky, and that in Europe they were worn only by kings and their families). This time there were also clear glass beads and tin whistles for him to bestow on his subordinates. Powhatan had thanked them for these gifts and invited them to dine with him.

But for all the ceremonial courtesy, he could not hide his hatred of the English, nor they their fear of Indians.

"Friends," West said, pointing to himself, to Causey, to Will, and then to Powhatan, "We are your friends, friends of John Smith." The name drew knowing grins and nods of approval from the Indians.

Then Powhatan clapped his hands sharply three times, and in came a procession of women carrying the feast: huge wooden platters of baked sturgeon, dishes of wild duck with persimmons, bowls of beans and squash, and baskets of Indian bread made with corn.

"This is his thanks for our promise to protect him and his people from the Monacans, is it?" The aroma of the roast meat filled the room, and Causey unconsciously licked his lips as he spoke.

West nodded. "Smith arranged this. That is why he wanted us to visit Powhatan at once. It is to cement the agreement."

"It's a fine cement," Will said.

With great ceremony, Powhatan dipped his hands into a bowl of water presented to him by Opossunoquonuske, and dried them on a bunch of feathers held by Winganuske. Then he motioned for his guests to begin eating. Attended by Opossunoquonuske, Winganuske, and the three other women who had brought the food, Powhatan, Tanx-Powhatan, Basamuck, and the three Englishmen ate in an uneasy silence broken only by the crunching of small bones and the smacking of lips. When they had eaten their fill, the water bowl and feathers were again brought to Powhatan, who washed his hands, while his English guests had no choice but to wipe theirs on doublets and breeches already heavily encrusted with grime. Powhatan, drying his hands fastidiously, smiled at his guests with feigned innocence.

Conversation, with the visitors unable to use more than a handful of words in their host's language, was kept to a minimum, but, thanks to John Smith, both sides knew the purpose of this visit, and few words were needed. The Englishmen West had brought to the Falls would make a camp there and then move to Powhatan Village as soon as the Indians vacated it.

When the food had been cleared away and the uneaten portions of bread and meat hung in baskets from the ceiling, Powhatan clapped his hands again, and through the door came two young men, one carrying a piece of cane with holes in it, the other, a pair of gourd rattles. Their headdresses were the heads and spread wings of large black crows, fastened so that the beaks pointed downward toward the wearers' noses. They sat down and began to play their instruments, first softly, then faster and louder.

Will, the lute player, found himself mesmerized by the wild, sweet notes of the primitive flute and the staccato rhythm of the rattles. As the music grew louder, a procession of young women entered. First one, then another, and another, all swaying with the music until there were ten of them standing in a row before Powhatan.

Nathaniel Causey drew in his breath deeply and let it out slowly. "What's this?" he asked softly.

"Is this our dessert? Some sweetmeats?" Will grinned. The young women, who kept their eyes downcast, were all dressed alike in soft tan deerskin garments that covered them from waist to knee. Their thick black hair, unbound, hung down their backs. Above the waist, their only adornments were necklaces of large white beads. Ten faces and ten pairs of breasts, painted crimson with bloodroot and oil, gleamed in the firelight.

"Smith told me they might give us women," Francis West whispered under the sounds of the Indian gourds and flute. "Old Powhatan likes to display his property." With a knowing look, he nudged Will. "You ought to see his favorite daughter. She used to come to Jamestown sometimes, but he keeps her away from the English now. Her name is Pocahontas."

West's voice, low as it was, did not go unheard by the Indians. At the mention of his daughter's name, Powhatan's eyes narrowed and Basamuck frowned. Then Powhatan, as if remembering the business at hand, waved expansively toward the row of young women and smiled broadly.

"I think he means for us to choose our bedfellows," West said.

"Good Lord, man!" Causey's voice was hoarse. "I never bargained on this! I can't do it—what will Thomasine say?"

On the other side of West, Will studied the young women in rapt silence. "Indian maidens covered with bear grease," he had once called them. These were certainly not the ones he had pictured when he joked about them with George Yardley. He thought of George, and then he thought of Temperance. His jaw tightened, his lips pressed themselves together, and with great effort he forced himself to concentrate on the swaying creatures in front of him.

"Yes, you can, Nat, and you will," West said through his teeth. "They'll think us rude if you don't."

"Think on it as good English diplomacy," Will said. "I'll go first." He pointed to one of the young women on the far end from him. Powhatan called out her name, something musical-sounding like "Co-Yala," and she stepped forward and dropped to her knees in front of Will. She had soft tawny skin and small, firm breasts, and large black eyes that glanced shyly at him as she knelt. Her hands were clasped in front of her, and in that posture her arms pushed her breasts together, making their cleavage deeper and making his breath come faster. Her skin, bronzed by nature and tinted with bloodroot dye, made him think of plums, rosy brown and ripe in the summer sun. Dear God, how long it had been since he had had a woman! He leaned forward and took Co-Yala's clasped hands in his.

"You are very pretty, Co-Yala," he said, speaking very slowly, as if he could thus make her understand him. She raised her eyes, smiled, and squeezed his hands. Her fingers were warm and soft. Will raised them to his lips. As her arms moved upward, he could see the small tufts of black hair in her armpits, and he could smell the faint scent of her body—a sweet, female perfume that made him draw in his breath and press his mouth hard against her hands. As he did so, he imagined them to be another pair of hands, pale and slightly freckled from the Virginia sun.

Powhatan, Tanx-Powhatan, and the medicine man Basamuck were all grinning at him. He felt lightheaded, intoxicated, although the Indians had given them nothing but water to drink. He was vaguely aware that Causey and West had also chosen women and taken them by the hand. Powhatan was nodding and pointing toward the far end of the spacious chamber, where some piles of straw mats and furs were placed against the wall. At the same time, Opossunoquonuske, attended by one of the younger women, made a regal departure.

Prompted by Powhatan, Will rose to his feet, took Co-Yala by the hand, and led her out of the firelight to the sleeping area. There, in the dark, he quickly forgot Powhatan, and Basamuck, and even Causey and West. He was vaguely aware that Powhatan had taken Winganuske to his couch, and that Tanx-Powhatan and Basamuck, like West and Causey, had chosen partners from the young women paraded before them. Once or twice, he heard Causey's voice uttering deep groans of pleasure, and he wondered idly if Thomasine ever caused him to make such sounds. But Co-Yala left Will little time for wondering. When at last she spread her legs for him, the pleasure was so intense, and the climax so sweet after the long months of forced celibacy, that he sobbed aloud. He came twice, in rapid, blissful succession. Then he closed his eyes and imagined that the black hair he stroked was copper-colored; that the tawny breasts he kissed were pink and white.

When he was spent, Co-Yala used her hands and mouth to make him come again, and when he was tired, she sat astride him, moving her hips in rhythms of maddening sensation until he could stand no more. At last he fell into a deep sleep, all thoughts of Temperance Yardley erased from his mind. When he woke at dawn, Co-Yala was gone. When he went with Nathaniel Causey and Francis West to take leave of Powhatan, with many expressions of thanks, Will felt dazed, as if they were all actors in a dream.

And when he and Causey and West, paddling their canoe downstream to rejoin the men at the Falls, found themselves the target of a volley of arrows from Powhatan's warriors, he could hardly believe they were real.

NANSEMOND
6 September 1609

"Fire!" On command, the four long-barreled muskets spoke almost as one, their staccato reports shattering the forest stillness. Fifty yards away, the elaborately painted Indian shield splintered into pitiful, jagged fragments. A frightened murmuring arose from the crowd of Indians—men, women, and children—who had been watching.

"There!" Captain John Martin grinned at the four men who had just fired. "These heathens don't know the fear of the Almighty, but they can damn well learn the fear of English guns! Well done, men!" On either side of the marksmen, arranged in two even rows, stood the rest of the 120 men who had come to Nansemond under Martin's and Percy's command. Opposite them, at the edge of the forest clearing, was their Indian audience: the 107 inhabitants of the Indian village of Nansemond, nearly thirty miles downriver from Jamestown. "That will teach them not to refuse us corn when we ask for it. Now, Master Percy," Martin said to his co-captain, "post your men around that storehouse and around the chief's house, to let them know we mean to stay here."

"Aye. That's a good tactic." George Percy touched his helmet and turned on his heel. He had fought in the Dutch wars, and he had been in Virginia for two years this past April, but the Indians still made him nervous. He wished he had John Smith's bravado around them. He and Smith were exactly the same age, twenty-nine, but Smith seemed wise beyond his years, and his arrogance knew no limits. Percy hated him, and Smith knew it. That was why Percy thought Smith had sent him and John Martin to Nansemond where the Indians were known to be treacherous. Smith would be glad if something happened to them; an unfortunate incident would rid him of his enemies, and, if many of the men were killed, there would be more food for Smith's people at Jamestown. Oh, Smith was a shrewd one, all right.

Across the clearing, in majestic, wounded silence, stood the Indian chief Wanaton, attended by his medicine man and a dozen of his warriors. As Percy and his soldiers moved to carry out Martin's orders, Wanaton and his retinue came forward and placed themselves squarely in front of Captain Martin.

"Marrapough," said the chief. He stood still as a statue, his arms folded across his chest, his turkey-feather headdress waving gently in the breeze. His eyes, hard and glittering, traveled slowly from John Martin's shining steel helmet and breastplate to his thick leather boots, and back to the helmet again. Wanaton's eyes were the eyes of a reptile sizing up a prey that is too large for it. These strangers had come here asking for food, when he barely had enough corn to feed his own people. Now, firing their weapons, they had shamed him before the entire village. *Marrapough* was the word for "enemies." He hoped these white men knew it. If not, he would soon find a way to show them.

"Not *marrapough,"* Martin said in a firm voice. He had been at Nansemond with John Smith two years ago, and he knew a little of the Indian language, but not enough to communicate with any degree of ease.

"Not *marrapough,"* he said again, shaking his head. "No." With elaborate gestures and broad smiles, John Martin, who had once argued the law at London's Inner Temple, tried to make the Indian chief understand that all the English wanted was one meal, and one night's lodging. Wanaton, unmoving, impassive, watched him. When Martin had done his best, the chief, arms still folded, turned his back on the English officer and stalked away without uttering a word. His warriors and his medicine man followed him silently, some of them casting hostile looks over their shoulders at the white men.

"I don't think he understands." Edward Brinton, a stonemason from Colchester who was now a seasoned Indian fighter, spoke in an undertone to his commanding officer.

"Damnit!" Martin's voice, tired and angry, was louder than he meant it to be, and the Indians across the clearing turned to look at him. "What are we to do but this? I can't move a hundred and twenty men nearly thirty miles and then make them fish for their victuals, can I? And make them sleep on the cold, damp ground when there are snug, dry houses—straw thatch though they be—to shelter them. Smith told me these savages were our friends, and they would welcome us." He shrugged his shoulders wearily and turned to Brinton. "Go tell your men to start boiling that corn in the storehouse. We'll eat and then bed down as soon as we've finished. The chief's house will hold at least forty men, and the storehouse will do for the rest."

"Aye, sir." Brinton went back to his men, and John Martin sat down in front of the doorway to Chief Wanaton's spacious house, which was now surrounded by a dozen soldiers in armor, with pikes at the ready. Across the clearing from him, Captain Percy and his men had taken possession of the Indian village's storehouse. Wanaton and his attendants watched them with grim faces. The rest of the Nansemond Indians had disappeared inside the houses that stood in a half-circle opposite the chief's house. A chilly September wind picked up a handful of leaves and swirled them about on the bare earth of the clearing. Martin was glad he and his men would have roofs over their heads tonight. These Indian houses, with their high, curved roofs and thick walls of bundled straw, were snug shelters, and there were fur rugs and plenty of straw mats for them to sleep on in Chief Wanaton's house. Tomorrow, he thought wearily, he and his men would have to move again, to start building their own shelters and erecting a palisade some distance downriver.

In the meantime, it felt good to rest. Next April he would be fifty years old, and his bones were feeling their age. He might well die here in this godforsaken wilderness, for all he knew, but he did not care. He had not cared what happened to him for the past two years, since his only son had died of the bloody flux at Jamestown that first awful summer of 1607. Young John would be twenty-one now, if he had lived. His grave, marked only by a rough wooden cross with his name scratched on it, was one of the earliest ones in the burying ground at Jamestown. Now the land, a thousand choice acres on the James River that the father had hoped to pass on to his only heir, lay empty, with not so much as a straw hut erected on it. That was the way the world was, Martin thought. Men's plans and God's were often at cross purposes. Now the only family he had was the men under his command. He would try to do his best for them.

Moved by that thought, he got to his feet again. They must be on their guard, sleeping among these savages. Wanaton and his company had at last gone inside one of the houses across the clearing, and Martin hoped he had seen the last of them until morning. As for the night, he felt none too confident about their situation, but, he told himself, they had given the Indians some beads when they arrived, and Wanaton would soon see that they did not intend to take permanent possession of his house and storehouse.

"We'll post a watch at sundown," he said with forced cheer to Captain Percy. "Eight men, one at each corner of the house and the storehouse, with changes until dawn. But we've given these savages a show, and I doubt we'll hear from them."

Martin was right, Percy thought afterward. So silently, so swiftly, did Wanaton's warriors cut the throats of the eight sentries on the pre-dawn watch, that not one of them had time to make a sound.

UTTAMUSSACK
18 September 1609

 "Twenty-seven killed at the Falls, thirty dead at Nansemond." Opechancanough smiled through a cloud of tobacco smoke at his brothers, Wahunsonacock, Opitchapan, and Catatough. "That is enough for now." Opechancanough was pleased. The ancient prophecy would not come true after all. It had originated among the river tribes long ago, a prophecy born at their first sight of a galleon's sails on the horizon. Three times, the prophecy foretold, strange ships would enter the great Bay of Chesapeake and pale-skinned strangers would come ashore. Twice the river tribes would drive them away, but the third time the strangers would triumph and found a nation that would arise and conquer the empire of the Powhatan. But now the English downriver, like Father Segura and the Jesuit priests so long ago, and like the settlers at Roanoke more recently, would soon be dead, all of them. The forests would ring no more with the alien sounds of ax and saw; the streams would flow clear, unsullied by the foreigners' offal.

"It should have been thirty at the Falls," Wahunsonacock said regretfully, "but three got away." He shook his head. "That is my fault. I gulled them with food and women, as you said, and they suspected nothing. But I did not gauge the swiftness of the current as they departed, and our arrows hit only one of them. They flung themselves flat in their canoe and escaped."

"Do not trouble yourself over those three," Opechancanough said. "Their turn will come. You did well, my brother. When they came seeking revenge, you took twenty-seven of their men and lost none of yours."

Wahunsonacock brightened. "That is so. Wanaton lost six in taking thirty English at Nansemond. And I did get some swords." Lovingly, he caressed the ornate silver hilt of the sword at his side. He had presented a similar weapon to each of his brothers. "Besides these, we have sixteen plain swords and as many warm cloaks from the English." Wahunsonacock tore off a piece of tobacco leaf.

"You have done very well," Opechancanough said. "I myself could not be a better Powhatan."

"How many English are left outside their fort?" Catatough, the youngest of the brothers, spoke with a slight impediment. He was slow of speech and slower still of wit.

"There are still near a hundred at the Falls with Francis West. But they may be useful where they are. John Smith made West swear he would not turn against us anymore, and pledged him to protect us from the Monacans, as we had agreed in the beginning."

"But there are ninety left with Martin and Percy at Nansemond," Opitchapan said.

"And forty at the mouth of the river where it runs into the sea," Opechancanough said. "You forgot them."

"Too many," Wahunsonacock said, lighting his tobacco leaf with a glowing twig from the fire and inhaling the smoke. "Far too many."

"Wait and see, my brother, wait and see." Opechancanough ran his fingers down the gleaming blade of one of the foreigner's swords. "When Nemattonow returns from hunting with the Pamunkeys, I shall set him to watch the English for us."

"That will be good. Your son can stalk the English the way he stalks deer. Not even the sparrows start at his step. He moves through the woods like a shadow." Opitchapan, lame in one leg since birth, spoke wistfully.

Opechancanough smiled at the compliment to Nemattonow, his only surviving son. Long ago, Nantea had given him three sons, but two of them had died of the sickness of red spots, a pestilence brought by the Roanoke colonists that swept through village after village along the coast, killing hundreds of adults and children alike. Nemattonow, his youngest son, his pride and joy, famed as the best warrior and hunter among the river people, was all Opechancanough had left. The loss of his sons still pained him, and he renewed his vow that no foreigners should live long in his land.

"Watching these English is not enough," Wahunsonacock said. "I say we should make a plan to destroy their fort now."

"Be patient," Opechancanough said. "Winter is coming. Hunger and cold will do our work for us. The English are poor hunters, and they have yet to plant enough corn to see them through a winter. Soon they will come to trade their trinkets for food, but this winter we will not give them any They will crawl inside their earthen houses and die before spring."

"What about John Smith?" Catatough asked. His brows were knit with his effort to follow the conversation.

"John Smith may not live to fight again," Wahunsonacock said. He shook his head sorrowfully. He had developed a grudging admiration for his rival. Had Pocahontas not flung herself at John Smith, Wahunsonacock might have adopted him into the tribe. But Pocahontas had to be disciplined, and her father told himself he did not want his daughter sleeping with a foreigner.

"He has the courage of a hawk, but he is badly wounded. I saw the fire aboard his ship myself, and I saw how it burned him as he leaped into the river. His clothes were all in flames. When his men pulled him out of the water, he was very near death. They said it was his gunpowder bag that caught fire." Wahunsonacock inhaled the fragrant smoke from his tobacco leaf, exhaled, and squinted at his brothers through a fine blue haze. "I say Francis West tried to kill him."

"Why?"

"Smith made him stay at the Falls. They had hot words. West said he wanted to go back to England, and Smith said he could not."

Opechancanough smiled. "If these English begin to quarrel among themselves, they may kill each other and save us the trouble."

"And you sent Basamuck to Jamestown with John Smith?" Opitchapan looked puzzled.

"Yes," Wahunsonacock said defensively. "The sailors of his boat did not know what to do for him, so great was his pain, so I sent Basamuck to work a spirit cure on him. If he does not heal Smith's wounds, at least he will come back and tell us how it goes inside the fort at Jamestown."

"Again, well done, my brother," Opechancanough said approvingly.

But Wahunsonacock, whose heart ached for his banished daughter, and who wished that John Smith could have been his son, not his enemy, was silent.

JAMESTOWN
19 September 1609

No one seemed to know how it had happened. Some whispered that Francis West, who blamed Smith for inciting the Indians against him at the Falls, had bribed one of Smith's own men to do it. Some said John Ratcliffe had planned it from the beginning, while others thought that John Martin and George Percy, just returned with the survivors of Nansemond, were at the bottom of it. One thing was certain: John Smith, drifting in and out of delirium, with his right side hideously burned, was in no condition to make accusations.

"He is not long for this world, I fear." Thomas Wotton, the surgeon, shook his head at the oozing raw flesh on Smith's hip and thigh. "The best cure for a gunpowder burn is onion juice. I have known it to heal a wound sometimes, though never one as bad as this. But we can try."

Wotton's wife, Esther, who had arrived on the *Swallow,* found a patch of wild onions near the palisade gate, and Temperance, Meg, Thomasine, Lucy, and a handful of other women took turns peeling the onions and pounding them with mortar and pestle. It made their arms ache, and their eyes water.

"We've enough to cry over as it is," Lucy said wryly, "without these onion tears."

Typhoid, which they called "the burning fever," and dysentery, "the bloody flux," were raging through Jamestown, and thirty-eight people had died since August. John Smith was not the only one who lay near death; there were a dozen others.

One of them was Arthur Facy, Meg's sea captain who had sailed on the *Swallow.* He had lost his wife and two sons to smallpox in England, and now he was slowly wasting away with typhoid in Virginia.

"How is Captain Facy this morning?" Thomasine Causey, stirring a pot of squirrel and chicken bones simmering to make broth, looked up at Meg.

"No better," Meg said wearily, "and neither is Captain Smith."

"What are we coming to?" Thomasine said, shaking her head slowly. "John Smith nearly dead, and most of the men gone, and the Indians turned against us." She sighed. "And then there is the fever. I worry day and night about Nat being up at the Falls and getting shot full of Indian arrows, but if he were here, I would worry about him getting the fever. I worry about getting it myself, as it is, but somebody has to nurse the ones that can't nurse themselves."

"At least the men at the Falls don't have it. The ones that brought Captain Smith back said there was no sign of the sickness up there. We can thank God for that," Meg said.

Temperance, who was peeling onions, sniffled loudly.

"What's the matter, Temperance?" Thomasine's bright, birdlike eyes fastened on her.

"Nothing!" Temperance answered crossly. Thomasine's endless chatter irritated her.

"Well, that's a blessing. I wish I could say 'nothing.' But I worry. It's my nature. At home, my sisters never worried, but I did. My mother would say to me, 'Thomasine, you are a worrier,' and she spoke the truth." Thomasine laid down the wooden spoon she had been using and shook her head. "But then I didn't know what worry was." She gazed out over the palisade wall and sighed. "If John Smith dies, who will rescue us from this miserable place?"

"He may recover." That was Meg, ever optimistic.

"And he may damn well not!" Temperance said. "Then what's to become of us?"

On the other side of the palisade, Captains Percy and Martin took council with Captain Ratcliffe and Gabriel Archer, the colony's secretary.

"Smith must go," Ratcliffe said in his thin, nasal voice. "We have kept that arseworm in our midst far too long. Look what happened at Nansemond and at the Falls. Let him live, and he'll turn all the Indians against us."

Percy, weak and sweating from the onset of a malaria attack, looked uneasy. "God's blood, man! What are you proposing?"

"I don't like the sound of this," Martin said. "After all, the man's near dead now."

"Ah, but what if he recovers? Then where are we? Use your heads."

"I want no truck with murder," Percy said nervously.

"You'll have none," Ratcliffe said. "Leave that to me." He laughed grimly. "Master John Smith, like a cat, seems to have nine lives. But there is more than one way to skin a cat."

"What about that Indian? What about Basamuck?" Archer spoke up. "He never leaves Smith's side."

"And he will never leave this palisade, either," Ratcliffe said coolly.

"Let murder in, and law and order will vanish." That was Martin, the lawyer.

Ratcliffe grinned. "We are in a wilderness three thousand miles away from law," he said. "And order, friend, is what we make it."

At first light the next morning, when Thomasine and Esther went to dress John Smith's wounds, they found him raving incoherently about Ratcliffe and a pistol that misfired in the night. The Indian, Basamuck, had disappeared. The women did not know what to make of these things, and when they reported them to Ratcliffe, he told them the Indian had left of his own accord, and advised them to pay no attention to a sick man's ramblings.

But late that afternoon, John Smith's delirium left him. He opened his eyes, looked up at Edward Brinton, who had been assigned to watch him, and spoke in a voice so weak Brinton could barely hear it.

"Someone is trying to kill me. Ratcliffe . . . Basamuck knows. . . ." His voice trailed off, and he closed his eyes. Brinton bent over him. "What? What does Basamuck know? Where is he?"

Smith rolled his head from side to side in pain and frustration. With great effort, he spoke again. "Can't stay here. Get me aboard the *Falcon* before night."

Brinton sent for Robert Nelson, the master of the *Falcon,* who brought six sturdy sailors with him. Slowly and gently, they hoisted Smith's bed onto their shoulders and carried him aboard the *Falcon,* easing the bed down in the center of the ship's great cabin.

There he lay for a week, seeing no one but Thomas Wotton, whose surgical skills could not ease his pain.

"He has given up," Wotton said. "As soon as he can stand the voyage, he aims to sail for England, but I don't know if he'll live to see Plymouth Sound again."

On October 9, on John Smith's orders, the *Falcon,* along with the *Blessing,* the *Lion,* the *Unity,* and the *Diamond,* set sail. As Smith had predicted, the ships' captains refused to take any other passengers except some unruly urchins who had been sent out by the Virginia Company. These boys they took for only one reason: Twenty-two of the seventy crew members had died since these five ships had arrived at Jamestown in August, and the boys would make themselves useful at sea—or else. With them, there would be a full complement of crew for every ship, even though there would be a shortage of bread. There was not enough grain at Jamestown to provision the vessels properly for an eight-week Atlantic crossing, and malnutrition would sail with them. The captains and crews were jubilant at leaving, nonetheless. They waved and cheered as their ships' sails filled with wind on that crisp October morning, and their cheerful farewells rang out over the waters of the broad James River until they were around the bend of Hog Island and out of sight.

The little band of settlers who watched them leave were not so cheerful. They knew there would be no more ships until January at the earliest. What they did not know was that long before spring came, hunger would become as deadly an enemy as the Indians.

JAMESTOWN
Autumn 1609

 By October's end, the frosts, which had painted oak and ash and laurel leaves in colors of flame, had begun to strip the branches. On the ground, a thick covering of dead leaves announced every footstep with a loud, dry rustle. With John Smith gone, fears of a surprise Indian attack mounted with every day that passed. After dark, the noise of a prowling dog or a scuttling squirrel outside the palisade could banish sleep for the night. It was not just the Indians that frightened them; it was the wilderness itself. No matter that the forest harbored deer and quail, squirrels and rabbits; hunters used to England's neatly hedged fields and peaceful wooded parks feared to venture far into Virginia's wilds.

They feared it even more after what happened when Gabriel Archer and some of the men went down to Nansemond. On October 26, George Percy, who had acted as president since John Smith's departure, dispatched Archer on a mission. Archer, a plump, cheerful fellow, volunteered to take a dozen men in a small boat nearly thirty miles downriver, where he hoped they could find the remainder of the men whom Percy and Martin had left there in September. The two groups would then join forces and persuade the Indians at Kecoughtan to trade for corn. Archer and his men, all protected by buff coats, breastplates, and steel helmets, sailed away one bright morning, full of good spirits.

None came back alive.

At dawn on the last day of October, All Hallow's Eve, the bodies of fifteen men were discovered outside the palisade at Jamestown. They were neatly arranged in a row with their arms outstretched, hands touching each other, and throats cut. The dead men's eyes were open, and their mouths had been grotesquely stuffed with Indian bread. The corpses made such a grisly tableau that some who saw them vomited. Others merely swore at the barbarity of the Indians. Gabriel Archer was not among the dead; but he and the twelve men he had taken to join these men of Martin's were never heard from again. The fact that the Indians had taken such pains to transport the bodies from Nansemond all the way back to Jamestown and arrange them so carefully was far more terrifying than the deaths themselves. The river tribes knew that the English had not enough corn to last the winter, and the grim humor of the mouths stuffed with bread was all too clear.

The next day, President Percy called a special meeting. "Because of the Indians, no one is to leave this palisade from now on, starting today. The gate will be bolted, but the watch will continue as usual, with two men on each lookout, changing every four hours."

"What do you mean, no one outside? What about the hogs and chickens on Hog Island?" John Laydon, sitting beside his pregnant wife, spoke up. "We've got to eat!"

"There's close to five hundred hogs over there!" Harmon Harison said angrily.

"We cannot risk it now," Percy said. "We can eat the ones we have left inside the fort, and leave the others be."

This pronouncement was met with a sullen chorus: "Leave them for the savages, you mean!"

"But who is brave enough to go and get them, after what happened yesterday?"

"Those damned savages would catch us before we could catch the hogs."

"What good are half a dozen hogs to feed two hundred people all winter?" Thomas Wotton shook his head. "And what about the sick? They can't live on corn alone." Wotton's wife, Esther, was now among them.

"Who is to portion out the meat? There is not enough to go around, and some of us need it more than others." Peter Scott stood up. On the bench beside him, his pregnant wife, Martha, sat with lowered head, shyly twisting her hands in her lap.

"That," Percy said, "will be a matter for the Council to decide. Certainly Mistress Scott and Mistress Laydon have special needs to consider."

With Nathaniel Causey and Francis West still at the Falls, and Gabriel Archer dead, the only members of the Council present besides Percy were Martin and Ratcliffe. Now Martin looked troubled, while Ratcliffe smiled his oily smile at Peter Scott's pretty wife. "And from now on," Percy continued, "since we can no longer depend on the Indians for corn, what we have will be rationed: There will be half a can of meal a day for each person. At that rate, we should be able to make it last for three months."

The colonists in the meetinghouse began to mutter.

"What happens then?"

"What if the supply ship doesn't come in January?"

"We can't live on a handful of cornmeal a day!"

"Damnation! I'd as soon have an arrow in my back as have starvation staring me in the face!" Lucy Forrest, with an angry flounce of her skirts, stood up and stalked out of the meetinghouse.

"Mistress Forrest!" Percy shouted after her. "We are not adjourned, and you are not free to go." His voice trembled with ill-concealed rage.

"If her husband were here, she'd not act that way," John Martin said with a sneer.

"Women without men are bound to make trouble."

"She didn't send Thomas Forrest off to the Falls—you men did!" Joan Pierce arose and faced the Council in a fury. "And some of us are alone through no fault of our own! You men mind your tongues!"

Tempers were short these days. Even the soft-spoken were sharp, and those with a cantankerous nature, like Joan Pierce, were as easily provoked as hornets.

"Please!" Percy said, "Please, for God's sake, let us have order here!" A sullen silence settled over the crowd. "We shall do the best we can."

Martha Scott and Ann Laydon did get their share of the meat when the hogs were butchered, but there was more grumbling about the division of the rest of the shares. In the storehouse, the pile of canvas bags filled with Indian corn and a little English wheat and barley grew ever smaller. Because the few remaining chickens could not forage for food outside the palisade, they, along with the handful of hogs, were soon killed and consumed. Thus the food supply John Smith had tried to conserve to see Jamestown through the winter was all gone by the end of November. Then, on Percy's orders, the six mares and one stallion were also slaughtered. "We cannot afford to feed horses when we cannot feed ourselves," said Percy. Every edible part of the animals, including the hides, was eaten.

Meanwhile, outside the palisade, Indian storehouses were soon hung with haunches from Hog Island, and Powhatan and his brothers dined royally and often on roast English pork.

After the arrival of the pinnace *Virginia*'s sixteen passengers at summer's end, there had been 427 English men, women, and children in the entire colony; now, as winter approached, diseases and Indians had reduced their number to 215. One hundred thirteen of them lived within the walls of the Jamestown palisade: Sixty-eight men, sixteen boys, twenty-two women, and seven girls had survived the summer sickness. There were still forty men at Point Comfort under the command of Captain James Davis, and sixty-two remained with Francis West at the Falls, but the Indians had woven a net of terror between them and Jamestown.

Unless a miracle happened, the people inside the palisade would run out of food by the end of February. In mid-November, when the stallion—the last of the meat supply—was killed, Percy, Martin, and Ratcliffe asked for volunteers to make one last attempt to get corn from the Indians. To the group assembled in the meetinghouse, Ratcliffe spoke with a great show of confidence. "We can sail the *Virginia* upriver," he said, "and offer Powhatan the rest of the blue beads and the two copper pots we have left. I say if we stay aboard the ship and keep our muskets primed, we should have nothing to fear." To Martin and Percy, Ratcliffe said privately, "We may as well die outside this fort as in it."

Every able-bodied man and boy in the fort volunteered, including Peter Scott, whose wife begged him not to go. "But I must go," he told her. "They need me. If we don't show a brave front to those savages, we are lost, and if we don't make them give us corn, you know what will happen." She wept, but he went, along with forty-seven others. The only men who did not go were President Percy, who now stayed in his house most of the time, shivering with the chills of malaria; Captain Martin, his second in command, and the men who were too weakened by fever or dysentery to undertake such a mission. After all, Percy reminded them, someone had to stay and protect the fort.

While Ratcliffe and the men were gone, life went on as best it could inside the confines of the palisade. Lucy Forrest and Ann Laydon, who had spent the previous year devising ways to vary the Jamestown diet, showed the other women how to make what was left of the grain palatable. They pounded the corn with mortar and pestle and boiled it into a porridgelike substance; they mixed it with hog fat and with acorn oil when the hog fat was gone; when acorn oil grew scarce, they mixed it with water and baked it into rocklike bread. Augmented by chestnuts, boiled acorns, and an occasional luckless squirrel that ventured inside the palisade, corn was all there was.

"If it's all there's likely to be," Lucy said, "we had better learn to like it." Sleeves pushed up to her elbows, hair falling down from her cap, she spoke one afternoon as she and Meg and Temperance pounded corn. Three stone pestles on the hard dry kernels made a rasping counterpoint to her voice. "I never thought to be doing such drudge-work in Virginia. Thomas and I thought Virginia would make us rich." She laughed, but her laughter had no humor in it. "Now Virginia may make me a widow, instead."

"Don't borrow trouble," Meg said gently. "The men at the Falls were well when John Smith left them, and may still be."

"I might as well be a widow, I miss Thomas so!" Lucy punctuated her speech with vigorous pestle strokes. "In our whole lives, we've never been apart this long. We've not been apart since we were children. Our families had houses right next to each other, and we saw each other every day of our lives. It was only natural we should marry. We were both the youngest children, and Thomas would get no land of his own, and so we came to Virginia." She stopped grinding and looked at Temperance. "I wish I were as brave as you are. How do you bear it?"

Temperance shrugged and did not answer. Her sense of loss was nestled deep inside her like some sleeping animal, and she did not like to disturb it with talk.

"Anyhow," Lucy said, changing the subject, "at least there are some other women now for the men to ogle. Two females among a hundred or so men is just not what the Almighty intended. They used to make eyes at Ann and me like rutting sheep!" She laughed to herself. "Ann winked back at one of them, and now look at her! If Martha Scott is not brought to bed first, Ann may have the first English child born at Jamestown. She's already had the first English wedding. Reverend Hunt married them last December, just a few weeks before he died."

Since Hunt's death, the little flock at Jamestown had had to do without a spiritual shepherd, but they still gathered faithfully in the meetinghouse for prayers morning and night and a makeshift service on Sundays. There, sitting in the rough-hewn cedar pews, they prayed to the God who had sent them to such a desolate place. Edward Brinton led the prayers. He had volunteered when Hunt died, and the others, relieved to be told what to do, dutifully flocked to hear him at ten every morning and four every afternoon. There was, after all, little else they had to do now. Brinton's sonorous voice, rumbling through the Lord's Prayer and reading the Psalms, filled part of the vast emptiness of their days. In his spare time, which was more than ample now that he could not work outside the palisade, Edward Brinton carved tombstones out of wood, fashioning in walnut or ash what he was used to shaping in marble. Wood was quicker than stone, but even then he had not been able to keep up with the number of dead.

Row upon row of wooden markers had nearly filled the allotted space near the meetinghouse, and there were always a dozen or so bare new mounds. Soon the graveyard would be larger than the space for the living.

They could not bury outside the palisade for fear that the savages would desecrate the graves, but Temperance wished the burying ground were not so prominent. Before she came to Jamestown, she had seen only one death, her grandmother's, at close hand. But that, at the end of a long life, in a curtained bed in a high-ceilinged chamber at Thickthorne, with a small phalanx of servants to make death presentable, had seemed peaceful and proper. Since the morning she had set foot on the deck of the *Falcon* to sail for Virginia, Temperance had seen so many deaths she could not remember them all. She did not want to remember them. They had been mostly young men and women, and their deaths had been neither peaceful nor proper. Some of them would never leave her memory, and some still haunted her sleep, even now.

There was the fellow Martin's men had brought back on a litter from Nansemond, with seventeen Indian arrows in him, and one all the way through him, so that he had to lie on his side on the floor of his hut. They had not known what to do for him except to keep him drunk on the little aqua vitae they had left in the storehouse, and work a few of the arrows loose. It was God's will, people said, that his wife and child had died of the fever in the summer, and did not have to look upon him. He lived that way for seven days. But soon his wounds began to fester, and toward the end they had to wave laurel branches over him day and night to keep the flies and gnats off. He never complained, but his eyes, sad and knowing, like the soft brown eyes of a dying stag, kept coming back in Temperance's dreams.

Sarah Harison she would never forget: Sarah's had been her first deathwatch at Jamestown. Since then, she had grown used to the procedures: closing the eyes and sometimes the mouth, wiping the face. Then, a practice distasteful but necessary: stripping the body of wearable clothing that could be washed in the river and worn by the living. Those who laid the dead to rest got first chance at their clothes. Meg had acquired a fine warm cloak, and Temperance had come by a bright crimson stammel gown that way. The color of the gown clashed with her hair, but the gown was warm, and she wore it often.

At least, with the coming of colder weather, there was not such haste to bury the dead. For a while, at the end of summer and the first warm days of Indian summer, there were hardly enough well men to dig the graves. Some bodies reached the last stages of decomposition before they could be laid away, and the smell of death hung like a foul miasma over the palisade.

The corpses were buried without coffins, and the shovelfuls of earth fell on them with soft plops as the graves were filled in. Then, at the end, there would be a scraping and a shaping of the loose soil into a mound.

For the thirty-two men killed on the expedition upriver, however, there would be no Jamestown burials. On November 17, sixteen of the forty-eight who had set out so bravely in the pinnace *Virginia* sailed her back, bringing a tale of horror with them: Powhatan had given them a surprisingly cordial welcome, and had even allowed two of his younger children, a girl named Matachanna and her brother Munto, to come aboard their ship, but then, when the children went ashore, so did many of the English, and Powhatan's Indians surprised and killed all they could reach, including Captain Ratcliffe.

"Ratcliffe! Good God, what a fool!" President Percy began to pace back and forth, pounding one pale white fist into the palm of the other hand. "What a fool! He should have taken those children hostage, and then he could have forced Powhatan to terms! And I told him not to let his men leave the ship! Good God, what a fool!"

"But Captain Ratcliffe didn't know," Peter Scott said, and some of the other survivors murmured agreement. "It appeared as though the savages were glad to see us. They came out to greet the ship, and they invited us to sup with them in their houses. We were hungry, and we did." Scott paused. Beside him, his wife, Martha, stroked his arm, and he went on. "They invited the captain, too, and he went in good faith. God knows, he paid for his mistake. Nobody should have to die the way he did!" Scott's voice broke, and he could not go on.

"Powhatan tied him to a tree and made us watch while his women scraped Ratcliffe to death with mussel shells!" John Laydon blurted it out all at once.

"Those savage bitches scraped him right down to his bones," Thomas Wotton said. "He was nothing but ribs and thigh and leg bones. Powhatan made us watch it all."

With that last sortie for food went the last hopes for surviving the winter without starvation. Desperation, unspoken, turned to incessant petty squabbles: Whose turn was it to go for firewood? Who stole a bag of oatmeal from the storehouse? Who slept at guard duty? Complaints and accusations flew as thick as the snowflakes that swirled into the palisade in late November. It was only a light snow, and it melted by noon, but it carried the ominous reminder that soon bitter cold would be added to hunger at Jamestown.

The cold weather gave the settlers, who had begun to think only of satisfying their gnawing hunger, another physical need: warmth. Gaunt and hollow-eyed, they spent their waking hours crouched beside their fires, warming first their faces, then their backsides, and then repeating the process. At least, Meg had remarked to Temperance, they did not have to be cold all the time as well as hungry. The stacks of logs that were to have framed new houses now furnished fuel for existing ones. With only eighty people now remaining, they could tear down the empty houses for firewood as well.

The dwelling that Temperance and Meg shared with Joan Pierce, her daughter, Jane, and her serving girl, Phyllis, was a small house, as were all the three dozen houses inside the fort. Temperance thought with some amusement that their whole house would barely have filled one end of the great hall at Thickthorne. But its thatched roof and framed earthen walls, hung with straw mats inside and covered with bark outside, made it fairly snug, and with a fire in the middle of its one room (Jamestown's first builders had learned that from the Indians) and deerskins stretched over its one tiny window, it kept the cold at bay. Inside the house were two wooden bedsteads, three straw pallets with blankets, a carved wooden chest, three joint stools, and two iron pots. Here the four women and the little girl slept and woke and slept again, washing and dressing, cooking and eating, as the fall days became shorter and darker.

Between prayers in the morning and afternoon lay a stretch of daylight hours that was impossible to fill. One could rise, dress, grind what little corn there was, gather acorns and boil them, eat, tend the sick, attend a burial, and still the day would have empty spaces. There were needles at James-town, but nothing to sew or any thread to sew it with; there were some books, but except for Lucy Forrest's volumes of Latin poetry, they were mainly fragments of religious tracts saved from the fire that had destroyed the late Reverend Hunt's library the previous winter.

To Temperance, unaccustomed to either boredom or squalor, life at Jamestown was paralyzing: She felt as if some invisible weight were pressing down upon her, making her move slower and slower, so that one day she could stop moving altogether and just lie on her pallet until she stopped breathing. With food so short, there was small chance of living until spring anyway.

BERMUDA
26 November 1609

 No one will ever find us here. Ever.

George Yardley had been telling himself that for four months. Four months, and never a sign of a ship or a sail on the horizon. What did it matter, he thought, that they feasted on wild hogs and melons and turtle meat? What did it matter that they basked in sunshine in a place where blue waters washed upon fine pink sands? All around this island paradise lay jagged underwater reefs, rims of coral and rock so treacherous that no mariners dared come close. Well they were named the Devil's Islands, George thought.

Had the crippled *Sea Venture* not lodged between two rocks, she would have been dashed to splinters. But she had stuck fast, and had remained intact long enough for her weary crew and passengers to salvage a good part of her rigging and stores. With hurried trips to and fro in her longboat, all the 140 men and 10 women had got safely ashore, after they had thought never to set foot on dry land again. Many had thrown themselves facedown in the sand, arms spread wide, as if to embrace the very earth itself.

And that first night, how they had feasted! Large, fat fish, unused to humankind, had swum up to them as they waded ashore, as though begging to be caught. And plump seabirds the size of partridges had settled on their heads and shoulders. That sweet white flesh of fish and fowl, roasted over hastily built fires on the beach, had tasted like food from the gods. Seven weeks and five days they had been at sea, and for the last three days had subsisted on waterlogged ship's biscuits. At sunset the Reverend Buck had gathered them all for evening prayers, and for once there was no grumbling about attendance. In loud, grateful voices that rose as one in the soft summer dusk, the survivors of the wreck of the *Sea Venture* gave thanks for their deliverance.

That had been July 28. It was now November 26. Scattered near the grassy shore, like handfuls of pebbles flung on a beach, were eighteen thatch-roofed huts built of cedar limbs and palmetto leaves. Nestled on a small, level space close to the sea but protected from wind was a garden whose neat rows had been planted with good English seeds once meant for Virginia's soil: cabbages, radishes, turnips, and peas. There was a storehouse, and near it was a saltworks where two large iron kettles salvaged from the *Sea Venture* were kept constantly boiling brine, making salt to preserve the fish they caught in such abundance, and to cure the flesh meat of the wild hogs they hunted. Oh, they had settled in, George thought, as though they would stay there forever.

At first they had thought to leave soon. By the end of August, they had built a deck on the *Sea Venture*'s longboat and fitted it with sails, and sent it with Henry Ravens, the ship's pilot, and six men aboard to make for Virginia. Somers and Newport calculated that the craft could sail to the mainland colony and back to Bermuda in a month. During September and October, lookouts on Bermuda's shore had strained their eyes in the daytime and tended huge beacon fires at night, awaiting the returning longboat, but by November, hope had died.

Now, on a sunny autumn morning, George glumly followed Sir Thomas Gates down to the shore, where the castaways' best hopes of deliverance now lay: They had begun to build their own ship. But she was a small vessel, only forty feet from stem to stern, probably no more than seventy tons, and she could not possibly carry all of the passengers and crew who had set out aboard the three-hundred-ton *Sea Venture*. And even if they were able to finish her, using the makeshift materials they had, there was no assurance she would be seaworthy enough to stand a long voyage.

"Thank God for Frobisher," Gates said cheerfully as they walked down to inspect the progress of the building. Richard Frobisher, born at Gravesend, where the River Thames winds its way to the sea, was a shipwright by trade. Thus, when he found himself stranded on an island, he had lost no time in setting to work to get off again. On August 28, one month to the day after coming ashore, and the same day the refitted longboat had set sail for Virginia, Frobisher had supervised the laying of a keel, and now, on this bright blue November morning, he was proudly overseeing the first planking of his ship's frame.

As George and Sir Thomas approached, the screeching of saws, the scraping of planes, and the pounding of hammers blended in a cacophony that nearly drowned their voices. "What would we have done without Frobisher?" Gates shouted to George above the din.

Frobisher, a barrel-chested man with a broad face and a grin that seemed even broader, hailed them. "Come and see! We're just starting to plank her. The frame was finished yesterday." Around him, two dozen men, including four carpenters, two joiners, a cooper, and a cordwainer, scurried back and forth, clambering inside and outside the skeleton of the ship's frame, cutting and carrying and fitting cedar planks over the stout oak ribs. Nearby, two master sawyers and three hastily trained apprentices labored at cutting planks by hand. Bermuda's cedar trees supplied what the salvaged oak timbers from the *Sea Venture* could not furnish in the way of lumber, and precious barrels of pitch, tar, and nails rescued from the wreck would make possible the construction of a fair-sized vessel on the sandy shore of an island two thousand miles from the nearest shipyard.

The most exacting part of the work had been completed: the laying of keel, floor timbers, and keelson, all bolted together with thick tree nails cut from oak timbers; then the laying of long, narrow wooden ribbands stem to stern to shape the frame; then cutting, fitting, and scarfing together the scores of wooden futtocks to fashion the curved ribs. Now the remaining work would take just as long, if not longer: the planking of her frame, inside and out, the building of decks, rails, cabins, galleries, hatchways, gratings, ports; the seating of mainmast, mizzenmast, foremast, and bowsprit; the rigging of stays, backstays, shrouds, ratlines, guys, halyards, martinets, braces, bowlines, and the like, not to mention the cutting and sewing of sails.

All that work would certainly keep a large number of men occupied all winter and well into the spring, George thought. That was just as well. After the *Sea Venture*'s survivors had built their houses, there was little to do on these Bermuda islands except hunt, fish, or take one's ease. The weather was so pleasant and the living so easy that there was already talk among some of the colonists of settling there permanently and not going to Virginia at all. They had snug houses and plenty to eat, and a minister to look after their spiritual needs; why undertake yet another perilous voyage to a colony where, as one of them put it, "nothing but wretchedness and labor" awaited them? The longer they remained on the islands, the harder it would be to leave.

"You and your men have done good work. That is plain to see," Sir Thomas said.

"We'll stop afore noon, though, so as to be ready for the wedding," Frobisher said with another grin.

At midday that day, Bermuda celebrated its first wedding. Thomas Powell, the *Sea Venture*'s cook, and Elizabeth Persons, one of the five serving maids in the company, exchanged nuptial vows when the sun stood high overhead, and the afternoon was devoted to dancing and feasting in their honor, just as if they had been married in a village church in England.

But for George Yardley and William Pierce, both grieving for the wives they had given up to the sea, the festivities had a hollow ring. The two of them sat unsmiling through the wedding ceremony and parted company afterward, too sad even to commiserate with each other. They had done that to excess already.

As soon as the service ended, George wandered away from the festive crowd to sit on a rock and be by himself. All around him was merriment; all inside him was gloom. Dear God, how he missed Temperance! Watching Thomas Powell kiss his bride had made him almost ill with longing. He tried to remember how Temperance's mouth felt on his. He could almost taste the salty-sweet flavor of her skin, feel the silky softness of parts of her that no man but himself had touched. He tried to call up the sound of her voice, clear and pure to him as the plucked strings of a lute, and her laughter, the dearest music in the world. If only he had not insisted that she sail on the *Falcon,* he thought over and over, she would be here beside him now, and he would not care if they ever left Bermuda. At first his physical longing for her had been a comfort to him, had held out hope. Now, mingled with grief, it pained him like a fresh wound.

As he had done so many times, he gazed sadly out to sea. The water here on the north shore was calm and clear, with very little surf. It was hard to imagine that same sea raging, tossing ships about like toys. Temperance had met her death out there somewhere, he thought, and so had Joan Pierce and all the others. God in His unfathomable mercy had chosen to save only the *Sea Venture.*

"Come, old man, this is no time for reverie!" A hand fell lightly on George's shoulder. William Strachey had come up behind him, walking silently on the sand. George shook his head slowly from side to side, his eyes on the horizon. "Come now," Strachey said gently, "I know you miss her. God knows, I miss Frances and the child she's carrying. I've two sons already, and God willing, I might have another by now. But I'd be just as glad of a daughter. I miss them all. And our friend Pierce misses his Joan and his little Jane, but brooding never did a man any good. Come and help toast the newlyweds." He gave George's shoulder an affectionate shake. "Thomas Powell's grinning is like to split his face in two, and Elizabeth has not taken her eyes from her true love's face since they said 'I do.' It will do you good to see someone that happy. And besides," he added, "Jane Wright is asking where you are."

George turned around, half in anger, to face his friend. "She'd better be asking where her master is instead! Lovesick wench!"

"Ah, I thought I'd set you off with that," Strachey said, laughing his quiet laugh. "Can she help it if she fancies the youngest and handsomest officer among us? And you never even favor her with a glance."

"Nor will I," George said sharply. "She would do better to stay close to her mistress and tend to her needs, instead of cosseting every single man among us. Margaret Whittingham is wasting away with grief day by day, the longer Thomas is gone, while Jane runs after every cock between two legs." He poked the sand savagely with a stick he had picked up. "God knows, with a hundred and thirty-odd men, and now only four single women since Elizabeth has joined the married ones, Jane had better watch herself."

Jane Wright, plump and black-haired, with breasts as round and tempting as melons, was the twenty-year-old serving maid to the Whittinghams. Her master, Thomas Whittingham, had been aboard the longboat that had set out for Virginia. He was the Virginia Company's merchant, and he felt it was his duty to get to Jamestown as soon as possible, to let them know that the rest of the fleet and all their long-awaited supplies were at the bottom of the Atlantic. Now his wife was inconsolable in her grief.

"We'd all better watch ourselves," Strachey said with a sigh. "Too many men, too long without women."

"Too long on these damned islands," George said through his teeth. "Sending that longboat was our only hope, and now she's lost. To say nothing of five sailors and Whittingham and Ravens."

"Henry Ravens was a fine ship's pilot. You may be giving them up too soon. Virginia is a good hundred and thirty leagues from here, as they reckoned it, and they might have had contrary winds." Strachey, as always, was optimistic.

"Contrary winds! Contrary enough to keep them gone since the first of September? Do you realize how long that is?" George refused to be cheerful. "If the wind is right, you can sail from England to America in eight weeks!"

"Well, longer voyages have happened, you know," Strachey said. "Maybe they got to Virginia, and are waiting till a larger ship—a supply ship—comes there, so they can sail it back here."

"Damnit, *we* were the supply ship! There will be no other supply ship from the Company to Jamestown till they find out we didn't get there! You forget that right now not a soul on God's green earth knows where we are—except the poor men in that longboat, and they're lost at sea like all the rest!" George's exasperated voice would have risen to a shout, except that he ran short of breath toward the end. He looked up at Strachey, who towered above him by a hand's breadth, and almost wished they would come to blows. Maybe physical contact would make him feel better.

But Strachey only laughed his quiet, dry laugh again and shook him by the shoulder. "Ah, George! I was only trying to make you feel better. Maybe I have." He grinned. "Anger is better than melancholy, so they say. Come, before we are missed. Let's go drink a toast to the newlyweds."

And so the two of them went back among the others, with John Rolfe and his Gwendolyn, whose waist was growing thick with their first child, due to be born sometime in February; with Sir Thomas Gates, whose title, deputy governor of Virginia, was so much empty air here; with Christopher Newport, who longed for a ship of his own to command, and with Sir George Somers, whose unquenchable good spirits never left him. With the bride and groom, they all feasted on the island's delicacies: roasted haunches of wild hog, great succulent chunks of turtle meat dripping with sweet oil, boiled crabs, baked rockfish, cooked palmetto heads, mulberries, and baked prickly pears, all washed down with a passable wine made from fermented cedar berries.

George, watching Thomas Powell kiss his bride, and seeing John Rolfe lay a loving, protective hand on his pregnant wife's belly, took a long drink of cedar-berry wine. Sir Thomas Gates would have to do without him tonight.

He was going to get very, very drunk.

JAMESTOWN
27 November 1609

 The monotony of life inside the palisade was broken suddenly one chilly afternoon just before prayers, with shouts from the north lookout tower of the palisade. John Laydon, on guard duty that day, had sighted three large canoes approaching from upriver: Francis West and the survivors of the company he had taken to the Falls in August were returning. Doors hung ajar and pots on fires simmered untended as every able-bodied soul inside the palisade gathered at the main gate. President Percy, too weak to walk, was carried out on a litter to welcome the returning adventurers. The heavy log gates swung open, and in came the company, straggling up from the riverbank, with Francis West, gaunt and grinning, at their head. Behind him were 60 ragged, weary-looking men, all that remained of the 120 who had set out with him four months ago.

There were joyous cries of welcome, and suddenly the swarm of men broke apart as the handful of husbands ran to their wives. Here and there were couples locked in delirious embraces, kissing hungrily and unabashedly. Thomas and Lucy Forrest clung to each other as if they meant never to part. Temperance saw Nathaniel Causey, shaggy-bearded and much reduced in girth, enfold Thomasine in a bear hug that lifted her high off the ground. Men without wives clapped each other on the back and embraced those who had remained at Jamestown. But there were others—men like Richard Pace, who learned that his wife had died of the flux a fortnight after he left. Their eager faces turned to masks of sorrow, they sought each other out and stood together with sagging shoulders and bowed heads, trying to comprehend their losses, seeking solace in their shared grief.

Amid these scenes of joy and mourning, Temperance searched anxiously for Will Sterling. Fear lay cold in her stomach as she scanned the faces of the crowd, unable to find him. Nearly everyone had come through the gates except a little knot of latecomers just now making their way from the boats. They approached slowly; they were the sick and the wounded. Some of them were supporting others, and two or three hobbled on makeshift crutches. One of them was Will.

Temperance barely recognized him. The blond hair that used to shine in the sun was matted and filthy, with a beard to match; the strong shoulders were stooped, and the long, easy stride was now a series of heartrending hops as he made his way with the aid of a stick, not touching one leg to the ground. That leg was wrapped from ankle to calf in what appeared to be one large dirty rag. Gathering her skirts, Temperance began to run toward him, waving.

"Will! Oh, Will! What has happened to you?"

He heard her and stopped where he was, transfixed, a weary smile on his face. "Temperance! Thank God you're still here!" He held out his free arm to her and pulled her against him in an awkward embrace. "Dear God, I'm glad to see you!" His voice was hoarse, and Temperance could feel his whole body trembling. She stood on tiptoe to kiss him on the cheek, and then slipped her shoulders under his free arm to support him.

"Here. Lean on me," she said. "What's the matter with your leg?"

"It got in the path of a Monacan arrow. It ought to have healed by now, but it hasn't." He tried to speak of it lightly, but the arm around

Temperance's neck was hot with fever, and as he spoke, he faltered, and would have fallen if she had not held him up.

"Then we must get you well," she said, trying to match the lightness of his tone. "Look, there's Meg, hunting for us."

"Just let me stop a minute, and I'll be all right," Will said. It was a cold day, but there were beads of sweat on his forehead, and he was breathing heavily.

"Ah, Will!" Meg reached them and stood in front of Will, looking him up and down with a practiced eye. "You need some nursing, that's plain to see. And some dressing, I trow." Her eyes were on the dirt-encrusted, bloodstained wrapping on his leg.

"Oh, I'll be well enough, now I'm here," he said with a faint smile. "A little rest will put me right. Haven't had much of that of late." But he could barely walk, even with Temperance on one side and Meg on the other, and they had to stop every few paces for him to get his breath. When at last they reached the house, he collapsed gratefully onto a straw pallet and lay there, shivering.

"Let us have a look at this leg," Meg said briskly. "It wants a proper washing and dressing." She knelt beside him and began to undo the bandage around his calf.

"Ahh! Easy, woman! I thought nurses were supposed to be gentle." Will closed his eyes and clenched his teeth in pain. The wound was a jagged, festering hole in the fleshy part of his calf, and red streaks from it extended upward toward his thigh. Meg looked at them and shook her head.

"Hand me the knife," she said to Temperance, who looked startled. "These hose have got to be cut away, and this wound cleaned and poulticed. See the poison?" She pointed to the angry red streaks around the wound. Over Will's protests, they unfastened his jerkin, cut away his trunk hose, and stripped him naked.

"You ought not to be doing this," he said weakly, with his face turned to the wall in embarrassment. "What if somebody comes? Where are the others—Joan Pierce, and Jane, and their girl?"

"Hush!" Temperance said. "We'll tell them to wait outside till we've dressed your leg."

"It's not . . . proper," Will said. "I shouldn't be here, in with you women."

"Be quiet and lie still," Temperance said. Will tried to put his hand over his privates, but Temperance, bathing his thigh, pushed it away. "I'm a married woman, you know."

He did not answer.

"You've nothing we haven't seen before," Meg said cheerfully. But to Temperance, when Will had at last dropped into a feverish doze, she spoke grimly. "Poke up the fire. We've work to do this night. I've seen wounds like this before, and this is a bad one. We'll try hot poultices to draw out the poison, and cardinal flower juice for his fever, and see what we can do."

All that long night and into the next day and the following night, they worked over him, keeping warm compresses on his left side from ankle to waist, and giving him sips of the bitter juice of the cardinal flower. Joan Pierce sat up with Meg and Temperance, helping, while her daughter and servant girl slept.

In the morning, little Jane looked at Will with large, solemn eyes. "Is he going to die?" she asked. It was a matter-of-fact question. She had seen so many deaths since summer that she now took them for granted. But she was concerned for Will. He had played his lute for her aboard the *Falcon*.

"No," her mother said, "but you must be quiet, so he can get well. Now go with Phyllis, and she'll take you out to play."

Later on that day, Francis West looked in to see how Will was, but Will, half-delirious with fever, did not know him. "He's a brave fellow," West said. "A brave fellow. I'd not be here if it weren't for Will Sterling." He paused as though about to tell them a story, but then he smiled and pulled his cloak about him.

"That's a tale I'll save for us to tell you when he's well."

When he's well. Bone-weary, Temperance sat watching him the second night while the others slept. He had showed little sign of improvement, and as Temperance turned the hourglass over and over, she began to fear the worst. Sleeping fitfully, sweating with fever and then shaking with chills, he had not recognized anyone for the past twenty-four hours. Toward dawn, he slept more peacefully. Temperance kept her eyes fixed on his face, as if by watching closely, she could ward off death. Will's face was familiar enough to her, but now she studied it anew, as if it were the face of a stranger. In its way, it was a handsome face. The deep-set gray eyes were tightly closed, their lashes, dark for one so blond, rested against fair cheeks reddened by weather and fever. The lips, half-parted, were as full and delicately formed as a woman's. It was a sensitive, expressive face, which belonged in a scholar's rooms at Oxford, Temperance thought, or in some great house in London, not in a miserable dirt-floored hut in a wilderness. Will was out of place here. He, like herself, had come only to please George, and now George was gone and they were here. George, who loved soldiering, would have relished confrontations with the savages and forays into the wilds. But Will, pacific by nature, had not shirked his duty. Those strong, slender hands, now lying motionless and weak outside the rug that covered him, had carried weapons, had dealt out death. Temperance, moved to a tenderness that surprised her, leaned over him and took both his hands in hers. He did not stir, and she put each hand in turn to her lips and kissed it. So dear, she thought, so dear. Please, God, let him live.

He moaned suddenly, and flung one hand sideways off the pallet. When Temperance put her hand on his forehead, he opened his eyes and looked at her. It was a blank stare at first, and then, slowly, a glimmer of recognition and a trace of a smile. "Temperance," he whispered. "Dearest, darling Temperance. I love you." Then he closed his eyes again and fell into a deep, peaceful sleep. When morning came, he awoke, asked for food, and demanded a pair of breeches.

JAMESTOWN
10 December 1609

 As soon as he could walk unaided, Will went one cold gray morning to see Francis West. When he came back to the house, it was nearly dinnertime. Temperance and Meg were preparing their ration of thin corn mush and a handful of boiled acorns when he came in. Will's eyes were bright with excitement, and he looked better, Temperance thought, than he had looked in weeks.

"I must talk to you two alone," he said mysteriously. "Where are the others?"

Almost before he finished asking, Joan, little Jane, and Phyllis burst in, their thin faces pink with the cold air. They had been out looking for acorns. The child, her dark eyes shining, held out both small, full hands. "Look! See how many we found! We can eat these tomorrow." The search for food was still like a game to her.

"Good, Janey," Meg said. "Put them in the basket over there."

"I think we found all there was," Phyllis said gloomily. She wiped her nose on her sleeve. Even when she was not weeping about something, which happened often, her nose ran, and she sniffled constantly. Her face was lightly pitted with smallpox scars, and her hair, poking untidily from under her cap, was greasy and straw-colored. In temperament and appearance, a more unattractive servant girl could not be imagined, but she worked willingly at the most menial of chores, emptying the chamber pot, washing the shifts and shirts, and sweeping the earth floor of the house with a broom made of twigs and straw. Besides that, she was fiercely devoted to little Jane.

"I'll go for more wood now. We'll need some before dark." With that, Will stepped outside again and was gone. Meg and Temperance looked at each other, wondering what was on his mind.

Joan, pulling off her cloak, sat down on a stool close to the fire and warmed her hands. "I'd give anything for one pair of good warm gloves," she said wistfully. "I used to have three or four. If Will had any thread, he could make us some gloves out of deerskin." She rubbed her hands. "We'd better boil those acorns long enough to make some oil, and keep some back for our hands and faces in this cold."

"Joan, what don't you think of?" Temperance said with a smile.

"Well, we may not have full stomachs, but we need not have cracked skin." Joan peered into the pot that hung over the fire. "Where's the ladle? This mush is about to scorch." Meg and Temperance, distracted by Will's mysterious air, had forgotten to watch the pot. But Joan, with her brisk, efficient ways, never forgot anything. "Phyllis, come here and stir this, and pour a little more water in it," she said.

When Will came back with the wood, they ate. The six of them—Temperance, Meg, Joan, Jane, Phyllis, and Will—sat down cross-legged, Indian-style, on straw mats near the fire, eating off wooden trenchers with their fingers. Spoons were scarce in Jamestown. Spoons were a link with civilization, and the people who had them treasured their pewter utensils as though they were made of gold.

Meg, wiping her mouth with the back of her hand, and that hand on her already soiled skirt, said ruefully, "I wonder if I remember how to eat with a spoon. I'm not sure I can do it anymore."

"If God didn't mean for us to eat with our hands, then why did he give us fingers?" said Will, licking his thumb. "Isn't that right, Jane?"

The child, her face smeared with bits of corn mush, giggled.

"I used to have a silver spoon," Temperance said wistfully, "and a little silver porringer with a gadrooned handle."

"Let us not talk about 'used to,' " Joan said.

"I forgot," Temperance said, chastened. "I'm sorry."

In the late afternoon, after four o'clock prayers in the meetinghouse, Will took Temperance and Meg each by the elbow, and whispered in their ears, "Don't go back to the house. Come walk with me, so we can talk."

There was not much room for walking inside the half-acre enclosure of the palisade, but people who wanted to stretch their legs had worn a path just inside the perimeters of the triangle formed by the log walls. Now Will steered Temperance and Meg toward the path, drawing their arms through his and strolling as aimlessly as if they had been on a promenade along the Strand in London.

Will glanced quickly around to make certain no one else was within hearing distance. "How would you like a voyage to England?"

"I've no heart for jesting, Will!" Temperance snapped. "You might as well ask how we'd like a voyage to the moon!"

Will, watching her closely, raised his eyebrows. "Would I say it if it weren't so? You misjudge me, my lady." He spoke lightly, and kicked at a pebble in the path. "Don't you want me to tell you what I know?"

"Don't tease us," Meg said.

"I am not teasing," Will replied. "I swear it. Sit down." He pointed to a wooden box that held the cannonballs for the south bulwark of the fort, and Temperance and Meg obediently sat down on it. Will put his hands behind his back and began to pace up and down in front of them. His eyes, all the time he had been talking, had not left Temperance's face. "Francis West is going to make for England, and he'll take us with him if we want to go."

Temperance looked at him unbelievingly. "What?"

Will, now relishing both her attention and her bewilderment, paused and grinned. "I said," he began again, slowly and patiently, as though explaining something to a child, "Francis West is sailing for England, and he will take us if we want to go."

"How can he?"

"Why is he going?"

"How soon?"

Will stopped his pacing. "Tomorrow night, if all goes well." He spoke in a low voice and glanced around him again. "He's got command of the *Swallow,* and her captain, Thomas Moore, has agreed to sail her."

"But how can they leave? How will Percy let them go?" Meg looked skeptical.

"Aye, that's the thing," Will said. "Percy himself has ordered this. He wants West to take twenty or thirty men with him upriver in the *Swallow* to try and barter for corn from the Potomack Indians above the Falls. They don't like Powhatan, and Percy thinks they might give us food just to spite the chief. If we don't get some more corn, we are like to die anyway, so he must have thought the risk of lives was worth it."

"Well, how does going up beyond the Falls get Francis West to England?" Temperance said impatiently.

"Well," said Will, his voice lilting, gently mimicking her, "Francis West has a plan, you see. If he does get some grain from the Potomacks, he'll bring it back here and leave it ashore in the dark of night, and then the *Swallow* will make for England before anyone realizes she's gone. West says he's had his fill of Virginia, and he wants to reach London before his brother sails for Jamestown, to tell him to resign his commission as governor of this place before it's too late. He—"

Meg interrupted. "But why would he take extra passengers? Francis West is not exactly known for doing good deeds."

"Ah, that is another story," Will said. "He'll take me, and anyone else I want with me, because he owes me a debt. I saved his life when we were at the Falls." Will gazed into the distance, his eyes on the pine trees outside the palisade. "I kept us both from being treated like poor George Cassen."

"What do you mean?"

"What happened?"

"A great many things happened at the Falls that are not common knowledge," Will said slowly. "Even Cassen's brothers don't know how he died." Hugh Cassen, age fourteen, and his brother Roland, seventeen, had sailed aboard the *Lion* to join their older brother, who had been in Virginia since 1608.

"Nobody knows about what happened to Cassen but West and me. We saw it."

"Will, for God's sake! Just tell us what happened," Temperance said impatiently.

Will, seeing her displeasure, frowned slightly. "Well, one day West decided he would take some beads and looking glasses to truck with the Indians left at Powhatan Village. He thought they might give us venison. So he took Cassen and me with him, and left Nat Causey in command. As it happened, the Indians were not disposed to part with any of their venison. They did invite us to eat with them and show them our trinkets, which we did. Then, all of a sudden, without warning, they took hold of us. We didn't even have time to reach our guns. They took us out and tied us to three pine trees at the edge of the clearing. They were laughing and singing all the while. Powhatan was not there, but his man Basamuck was, and Basamuck made it clear this was to show the rest of the English what would happen to them if they tried to live on Powhatan's land." Will rubbed a hand across his face and drew a deep breath. "First they built a big fire, and then they danced around all three of us. Then—God knows why—they began with Cassen. They took their tomahawks and chopped his fingers off, one by one, and threw them into the fire. Then they cut off the stumps of his hands at his wrists, and threw his hands into the fire, too." Will paused. "Then they scalped him, and cut out his tongue, and then they began to . . . skin his face."

"Oh, no!"

"Oh, Will!"

Will went on talking as if he did not hear Temperance and Meg. "Cassen was right strong, and he cursed them at first." Will shook his head mournfully. "Sometimes, in the night, I dream about him, and I can still hear the sounds he made, and the sounds of the Indians laughing. He took a long, long time to die. Six of those demons danced around him, poking at him with their spears, but he stayed conscious until four of them stuck their knives into him all at once and pulled out his bowels."

In the fading light of the winter afternoon, Temperance and Meg sat still and silent as statues.

Then, after a moment, Will said softly, "God was watching out for West and me, I suppose. Poor Cassen took so long to die that the Indians were weary. They set two of their braves to guard us, and the rest of them went off to their houses for the night."

"Then what did you do?"

"How did you get away?"

"Well, we hadn't much hope at first, but we knew we had all night. We looked at each other and didn't talk much, and after a while our two guards fell asleep. They had bound me last, in a hurry, and the deerskin thongs they used were not pulled very tight. I began to try and work one hand free. It took a long time, and it took off some skin, but at last I did it."

"Then what did you do?" Temperance said. "Don't be so slow in the telling!"

"With my one hand free, I could reach inside my jerkin and get a little mirror I had put there earlier, while we were showing our trinkets to the Indians. My other hand was still bound to the tree, you see. I broke the mirror against the tree trunk and then cut my other hand free. I cut West free, and then we crept up on our two snoring sentries, and we grabbed them and cut their throats with the two little pieces of looking glass. Then we made off through the woods as fast as we could in the dark, and we got back to our fort before daylight. West said he'd never have got away but for me, and then and there he said he owed me a favor that I could collect when we reached Jamestown again."

Meg leaned over and gently took hold of Will's arm. "You are a brave man, Will Sterling," she said. "I never knew you were so brave."

"Why didn't you tell us about all that before?" Temperance said.

Will shrugged. "We didn't even tell the men at the Falls. We thought it would only frighten them, or make them take some foolhardy revenge on the Indians, and so we just told them that Cassen was killed, and we escaped." He bent over Temperance and Meg, putting a hand on each of their shoulders, and looked into their faces. "And because we did escape, Francis West will take me to England. Now, do you want to go, or not?"

"You know my answer," Temperance said without a pause. "God must have heard my prayers after all."

"Meg?"

Meg smiled and shook her head. "I am beholden to you for asking me," she said softly, "but I am not leaving Virginia." She held up a warning hand against their protests. "I know I am foolish, but I—I can't go yet." She paused, looking over the wall at the gathering darkness.

"Oh, Meg! Hell's bells!" Temperance's voice rose in exasperation. "You know they're not going to find anybody from Roanoke. By now, surely, if anyone from Roanoke were alive, they'd have made themselves known. Jamestown has been here for two years, remember?"

"I know," Meg said. "But I have to stay until I'm certain there's no hope at all." Then she brightened. "And if I stay on, who knows? Maybe in seven years I'll take my fifty acres of the headright claim that's due me for coming, and I'll settle right here." Meg glanced at Will, and then leaned over to embrace Temperance. "But you two—you know you must go. There is nothing for you here."

Late the next night, Temperance, with a small bundle of clothing and a pounding heart, slipped out of the silent house with Will. Joan and Jane and Phyllis lay fast asleep, and Meg was not there. She had gone to the Laydons' house to help Ann nurse John, who had taken deathly ill with the bloody flux.

"This way will be better," Will had told her. "You can truthfully say you didn't see us leave."

The night was clear, but bitter cold. Temperance was grateful for the heavy serge cloak Meg had made her wear. It was the one that Esther Wotton had given to Meg, and the latter had insisted on giving it to Temperance. "Someone else will die and leave me another," Meg had said with a smile. "You'll need it more than I will."

Now Temperance drew the cloak close about her as she and Will set out across the open space between the three rows of houses that faced each other inside the palisade. The December moon, nearly full, cast a pale light on the two silent figures. With his free hand (he, too, carried a small bundle) Will took hold of Temperance's hand. The two of them were as cold as corpses, Temperance thought distractedly, realizing that Will was as nervous as she. If they happened to be discovered leaving, George Percy would surely lock them up as an example to the others, and the *Swallow* would sail without them. Temperance suddenly stopped and pulled back on Will's hand.

"It's too bright!" she hissed. "Someone's bound to see us crossing to the gate!" The main gate was brightly lit now by moonlight. The palisade had been built with rounded watchtowers at each of its three corners, and the gate facing the river was midway between the two platforms on the southeast side. Anyone nearing it would be plainly visible from the lookout posts.

All at once, Temperance was furious with Will for not having spelled out to her the details of their escape, and with herself for not asking. Maybe he hadn't even thought about this part, she thought. He was given to daydreaming, to thinking up verses, to making up tunes, not to planning escapes. Will stopped and looked down at her.

"Don't worry," he said evenly. "At midnight, when the watch changes, I'll take over for Richard Pace there." He jerked his head in the direction of the south platform. "He knows, but he'll not tell."

Temperance refused to be mollified. "And who's in the other post—the north one? What about him?"

"Ah, that'll be Phetiplace Close, if all goes as planned. And you know he's so shortsighted he'll not notice us even if he does look this way." Phetiplace Close, a gangling, nearsighted schoolmaster from Sudbury, had been pressed into watch duty because he was one of the few able-bodied males left in the compound. Twenty men had gone with Francis West aboard the *Swallow,* and a dozen others lay sick. Will and Temperance approached the south platform, their feet crunching loudly on the dry leaves and twigs.

"Ho, Richard!" Will called softly from below the lookout post.

"That you, Will Sterling?" Pace's deep voice answered back. Without waiting for an answer, he clambered down the rough ladder to the ground. He and Will clapped their hands on each other's shoulders. "Good luck to you," Richard Pace said. "God be with you both." He bowed to Temperance. "I hope you have a safe voyage, my lady."

"Thank you," Temperance said through chattering teeth. She was beginning to tremble violently from the cold, and Will put his arm around her.

"Many thanks, Richard. I'll send you a barrel of ale from Plymouth."

Pace grinned, his teeth glinting white in the moonlight. "Good," he said. "I'll be on the lookout for it by the next supply ship."

"Take care of yourself," Will said.

"You, too—both of you." Then Richard Pace was gone, striding across the open space without looking back. Will climbed nimbly up onto the lookout platform and peered through the darkness in the direction of the river.

"No sign of them yet," he said. "Here. Let me give you a hand up. There's plenty of room up here, out of the wind." The wind, in fact, had just begun to blow, and it whipped Temperance's skirts against her legs as she climbed up the ladder. The platform was a sort of large, rounded box with slits made to serve as gun ports in case of attack. But if guns could go out, wind could come in, and the watch fire burning in a small iron brazier did little more than cast a flickering light in the cold. To the southeast, toward the river, Temperance could barely make out the line of trees near the log pier. Beyond them was the James, broad and beckoning in the moonlight, a highway to home. But there was no ship anywhere to be seen.

Will settled himself on the tall sentry's stool and took a deep breath. "So far, so good," he said. "Are you too cold? I'm sorry we haven't a bigger fire."

Though her teeth were still chattering, Temperance shook her head. "I'll be fine when they come. How long do you reckon it will be?"

"Not long." Will kept his gaze on the river. "They have to be here in time to unload the grain, if they got any, and to make away before dawn, so it has to be soon."

Temperance huddled down in a corner, pulling her cloak about her, and leaned her head against the rough planks. Will kept watch, alternately squinting out into the moonlight, and pacing nervously back and forth in the cramped space.

"You'll be tired before we ever get aboard," Temperance said.

"I'm just anxious to be gone from here," Will said. "Look out there. Squalid little huts, and scores of hungry people inside them. We're away from this place just in time. Before winter is over, the food will run out, and these people will starve."

"Oh, Will! Surely not!"

"Surely yes," he said grimly. "I've seen the supply of grain in that storehouse, and so have you. Even if they ration it to a handful for every person per day, it won't last past January." Will shook his head slowly. "Thank God we are leaving here. I hate to think what it will be like in a few more weeks."

Temperance shivered. She had been doing that ever since they had left the house, and try as she might, she could not stop for more than a few minutes. She felt as if a giant clock spring were wound up inside her, and every muscle in her body was pulled taut. Now Will's casual talk of starvation and death sent a curiously heavy sensation through her, as though premonitions of doom carried physical weight.

"Will, we should have made Meg come with us, and we should have taken Joan and Jane and Phyllis. Why didn't we? Why didn't we just make them come?" Temperance choked back a sob. "We can't leave them to die!"

Will stopped pacing. He turned to Temperance, seized her by the shoulders and, forcing her to look at him, gave her a gentle shake. "Hush! Meg wouldn't come, remember? She knows what may happen as well as anyone, but she wants to stay. She's a brave person, Meg is, and you know it. And if there are any survivors at Jamestown, one of them will be Joan Pierce, and she'll see to Jane and Phyllis." Will's face was close to Temperance's, and she could feel his breath on her cheek.

"Oh, Will!" Temperance buried her face in the rough material of his jerkin and began to cry, her sobs muffled against his shoulder. Will put his arms around her. He had never done that before, and for a moment the two of them clung together in silence.

"It will all come right," Will whispered, his mouth close to her hair, his voice curiously tender. "And we'll be all right. I promise you."

Temperance raised her head and sniffled. "You promised George, too, and look what happened! You didn't know how hard it would be, looking after me, did you?" She felt his body stiffen, and then he dropped his arms and stepped backward awkwardly.

"No," he said abruptly, "I never knew."

"No matter. If I ever get back to Thickthorne, I'll make amends to you," Temperance said. "You must come and stay for a long visit." With a small pang of guilt, she realized she had never given a thought to what Will would do on returning to England. "What will you do when we get home?" The word *home* hung in the air, a hollow syllable that had nearly lost its meaning for her, she thought suddenly, and perhaps for him, too. He had turned his back on her and was gazing out toward the river. For a long moment, he did not answer.

"Go back to London and make gloves, I suppose," he said at last. "If I still remember how."

"Then you can make some for me," Temperance said lightly. "I'll be your first buyer. I'll need some good soft riding gloves right away, and some fancy ones later. I'll have to make a list." She heard her own voice saying these words and felt detached from it, as if some other person were making this silly chatter. She rattled on. "I'll go home to Thickthorne for a while, and then I'll come to London and see you, if you'd like me to," she said.

"You do that," he said absently.

Temperance fell silent, and Will resumed his pacing. The fire in the brazier was nearly out, and the sky outside was growing paler. Each of them was vaguely aware that midnight had long since come and gone, and there was no sign of the *Swallow*. Temperance tried to curl up in a corner of the lookout enclosure, but she could not sit still. Will, restless and silent, continued to walk back and forth. The wind had died down, and his footsteps on the wood floor of the lookout station sounded loud in the stillness. At last Temperance could stand it no longer. Rising to her feet, she shook out her skirts. Reaching out, she seized him by the elbow, forcing him to stand still.

"Will, they—they're not coming, are they?" She spoke in a small, hesitant whisper, hating to put into words what they both knew was the truth. Will drew a long, deep breath and stared out at the pale sky and the river, as if by concentration he might make the *Swallow* suddenly heave into view.

"It doesn't look like it," he said slowly. "It's too close to daylight now, anyway. Something must have happened. I don't know." His broad shoulders sagged, and then suddenly he struck the wall with his fist. "Goddamnit!" He leaned his forehead against the wall, and hit the rough planks again with his fist. "Goddamnitall!" He leaned against the wall, his head and both hands pressed against it. His shoulders rose and fell with his hard breathing. Even in the dim light, Temperance could see blood on the knuckles of the hand that had hit the wall. Timidly, she touched that hand with one finger.

"Let me alone!" He snatched his hand away.

"Oh, hell's bells!" Temperance backed away from him and stumbled, encumbered by her cloak. "What good is standing there hitting the wall? You—you—" She paused for want of a word biting enough to call him, but could not think of one. "Don't you think I'm as disappointed as you? Francis West is not going to come for us, and there's damned little we can do about it, isn't there? I don't know about you, but I'm going back to the house and go to sleep. There's plenty of sleep to be had at Jamestown, even if there's nothing else!" Out of breath, she choked out the last words and started to climb down the ladder.

Will caught her by the arm. There was a look of bewilderment on his face. "Temperance Yardley, you are a wonder." His eyes sought hers, and the two stared at each other, both breathing hard. Then he let go her arm and stepped backward. "Look at you," he said softly. "You are the bravest person I have ever known. Any other woman would have been awash in tears by now. But here you are, putting me to shame." He bowed his head. "You ought to go back before the next watch comes and finds you here. I'll have to stay till then, but you go ahead. Here, let me hand you down." He climbed down the ladder, and held up outstretched arms to her. When she was within his reach, he put both hands around her waist and swung her lightly to the ground.

Temperance had never realized how strong Will was. George could lift her, but not so effortlessly. "Thank you, Will," she said softly. "Thank you . . . for trying. It's not your fault they didn't come." She reached up and put her hand on his cheek. "I'll see you at the house." Pulling her cloak about her, she turned back toward the place she had hoped never to see again. Dawn was showing grayish-pink over the ash and laurel trees by the river as she reached the house. There she found Meg, just returning from her night's nursing of John Laydon, and in a little while, when Will came, the three of them lay down and slept like stones until midmorning.

While they slept, the *Swallow* sailed past Jamestown just at dawn, headed downriver for the open sea. Only Peter Scott and Harmon Harison, standing watch on the south side, saw her pass, and there was nothing they could do to stop her.

JAMESTOWN
12 December 1609

 It was four o'clock in the afternoon, time for prayers. But the people who came into the meetinghouse were restless and noisy, swarming in little groups like bees in a field of clover. As latecomers appeared, the groups rearranged themselves, their voices blending, filling the cavernous space of the meetinghouse with a loud, excited hum. President Percy, a pale scarecrow in clothes now much too large for his fever-wasted frame, stood talking with Edward Brinton near the pulpit. Both looked grim, and they put their heads close together as though to keep their words to themselves.

As soon as the company had taken their seats, Brinton raised his hands for silence. When it fell, however, he did not speak. He gazed for a moment over the heads of those assembled, and then, lowering his head, he began the Lord's Prayer in a loud, deep voice that commanded them to follow. When they had said "Amen," Percy rose from his seat and stepped forward.

"I have this day some unwelcome news," he began. His voice was slightly hoarse, and, despite the chill air inside the meetinghouse, two spots of red appeared on his cheeks. "Last night two of our number—Hugh and Roland Cassen—broke into the storehouse and stole two bags of corn."

"Those poor boys!" Lucy Forrest, sitting next to Temperance, whispered in her ear. "You know the Indians killed their brother up at the Falls."

"I know," Temperance said.

Percy, raising his voice slightly, continued, "But Richard Pace, coming back from his watch, saw them." All eyes turned to Pace, sitting on the end of a bench in front. He kept his eyes on the floor, perhaps not knowing whether the others would see him as a benefactor or as an informer. "Pace came to me," Percy went on, "knowing how short our food supply is, and fearing evil would come of their action." He paused as if to gather his strength. "The officers of the watch found the boys with the corn and arrested them. Today a Council hearing was held, and a punishment laid down." Percy pressed his lips into a thin line and looked at Nathaniel Causey and John Martin, the only surviving Council members. Then he looked grimly over the heads of the crowd in the meetinghouse.

"For the stealing of goods rightfully belonging to the Virginia Company, and for committing an act so harmful to the public good, and as an example to others, Hugh and Roland Cassen, residents of this settlement of Jamestown, in His Majesty's colony of Virginia, will be hanged by the neck until dead at dawn tomorrow."

"Hugh Cassen is only fourteen!"

"If their brother were alive, this would not have happened!"

"Hanging boys! What have we come to?"

Percy, wiping his forehead with the back of one bony hand, held up the other hand for quiet. "We all know that our food supply is short. While we may not have a proper diet here, I intend we shall have order. We shall not—we cannot—behave like savages. We are His Majesty's subjects, and we shall conduct ourselves as such, no matter what happens."

Percy paused again. "I also regret to report that Captain Francis West, who took twenty men in the *Swallow* to barter with the Indians above the Falls, did not get any corn. Instead, he and his men apparently set sail for England. Harmon Harison and Peter Scott saw the *Swallow* pass by at dawn this morning." There was a louder murmur this time. Percy, eyeing the restive crowd, held up both hands for silence, and then continued, "Since we now have no hope of any corn at all from the Indians, we must husband our remaining grain supply with great care, so that we can last the winter. Any man, woman, or child who takes one grain more than the one-half can per day, or any person who tries to steal from the common store, will be hanged."

UTTAMUSSACK
20 December 1609

Opechancanough leaned forward on his fur-covered couch and took a rib of roast pork from the platter in front of him. He was grateful to the English for bringing so many hogs with them. At first his people had been reluctant to taste hog's flesh, but they soon found the sweet white meat a delicious change from venison and turkey, and the river tribes had had a surfeit of it this winter. Opechancanough had not dined so well so often since he had lived among the Jesuits in Seville, more than forty years ago. Now his only son was older than he had been when he had gone by the name of Don Luis and said his prayers to the Christians' God. Opechancanough almost wished that Nemattonow, now twenty-eight, could sail the Atlantic and see the strange lands across the ocean as he himself had done. Instead, the strangers had come here, and Nemattonow, unbeknown to them, was their closest observer.

"Tell me again about their numbers," Opechancanough said to his son, who reclined on a couch next to his. "How many at the place near Kecoughtan—the place they call Point Comfort?"

Smacking his lips and laying down a well-gnawed rib bone, Nemattonow reached for another and said, "Still the same. About forty. They are not sick, like the ones upriver. They have no corn, but they have plenty of hogs and crabs to eat."

"Do they hunt outside their fort?"

Nemattonow shook his head. "No. They are afraid. They post their men to watch from the platforms of their fort day and night, and they do not go far from it."

Opechancanough smiled. "Sooner or later, they will have to. But there is no need to watch them so closely during the cold weather. What about the numbers at the other fort?"

"They are still dying as fast as May flies, as they have done since John Smith left."

"He was a good man," Opechancanough said thoughtfully. "A brave man. Even my brother admired him—until Pocahontas became too fond of him. That was unfortunate. It was just as well he had to leave. But tell me about those who are still at Jamestown."

"The sixty who were at the Falls have come back, but that many more have died. I think there are no more than eighty alive. There are so many new mounds of earth in their burying place that I cannot count them all." Nemattonow paused. "And now they have built a tree with one branch and a rope on it. What do they do with that?"

Opechancanough smiled broadly this time. "Does the rope have a loop in it like this?" He traced an oval in the air, and Nemattonow nodded. "Ah!" Opechancanough said. "Then they have built a gallows."

"What is that?"

"It is a way they have to kill each other. They can hang a man from it and break his neck."

"I see." Nemattonow spoke quickly. "Then they must be quarreling among themselves."

Opechancanough smiled again. "That means they have begun to fight over food. They will soon starve, and the ones who survive may kill each other off. All we have to do is watch and wait."

"What if they go downriver and join the others?"

"They are too few, and too frightened. They fear us more than they fear hunger. The ones at Jamestown will stay where they are and die, and the ones near Kecoughtan can be killed off when warm weather comes." With a firebrand, Opechancanough lit the end of a tobacco leaf and sniffed it contentedly. "The prophecy is wrong," he said.

"What do you mean?"

Opechancanough squinted at his son through a fine blue haze of tobacco smoke. "When I was no older than you, I heard the prophecy from the oldest man in our village. He was much older than my father, and he told it to me after I had killed the Spanish priests who tried to live on the banks of the river. He said that Okee and our other gods did not like foreigners with strange gods. Okee had told him the strangers would come ashore three times. The first two times, we would be able to kill them, but the third time, they would kill us and take our land. He was wrong."

"I see that these Englishmen living on the river are going to die, but how does that make the prophecy wrong?" Nemattonow looked puzzled. "We burned that whole village of English from Roanoke two winters ago. They would be the first strangers, and these would be the second, wouldn't they?"

"No, no. You have forgotten the Spanish priests. That was long before you were born. They were the first. And the ones from Roanoke were the second." Opechancanough blew a cloud of tobacco smoke into the air.

"These English are the third group, and we will be rid of them by spring. In the meantime, keep the watch at Jamestown, and tell your men to shoot anyone who tries to leave the fort."

JAMESTOWN
20 December 1609

On good days, they found a few acorns to boil with their corn; on the other days, they just ate it plain, scraping every tiny morsel from their trenchers and then licking the wood surface clean with their tongues. Temperance, trying not to think of food, had begun to dream about it, instead. In one recurring dream, she and George were guests in some great hall, richly hung with tapestries and lit with hundreds of tapers. A procession of liveried footmen brought in huge pewter chargers laden with saddles of roast mutton and whole roast pigs with raisins for eyes and apples in their mouths. There were flaming puddings and flagons of sack and muscadine wine, all for George and herself alone. In the dream, they feasted until they could hold no more, and then they made love on the banquet table.

Not only was the diet at Jamestown sparse; it was unbearably monotonous. Everyone grubbed for edible roots until the earth inside the palisade walls resembled a badly plowed field. Acorns became scarcer and scarcer, and soon even the squirrels learned that there was no food to be had in the fort. One day Thomasine Causey made a thick paste of the starch she had brought with her to stiffen her ruff collars, and ate the gluey mixture. "It'll do me more good inside than out," she said. "What a fool I was, to think I'd be wearing pleated and starched ruffs in the middle of a forest!"

Peter Scott killed a snake once, but Martha could not stomach it. In their craving for meat, people scoured the fort for toads, lizards, rats—any living creature whose flesh could be boiled or roasted, but the hunting was largely unsuccessful, and the craving grew worse.

Most people—there were now only eighty-three left—spent their aimless days huddled beside their fires, waiting for time to pass. Meg, Temperance, and Will now had a house to themselves: Joan Pierce, Jane, and Phyllis had taken the house next door. "We can't help being hungry," Joan said, "but there is no need to be crowded." Malnutrition made them all pale and listless. Winter's chill had lessened the attacks of malarial fevers, but it brought racking coughs and agues in their place. The weaker ones went quickly: Maria Cadway, the frail wife of a farmer from Cornwall, developed a terrible rattle in her chest, struggled for breath for three days, and then died in her sleep, her hands folded across her breast.

Jeremy Deale, a joiner's apprentice from Salisbury, ravaged by chronic dysentery and unable to digest his meager ration of boiled corn, parceled it out to others until he was too weak to move. Then he wrapped himself in a blanket and expired.

John Laydon, already emaciated by his earlier bout with the bloody flux, grew thinner as his young wife's belly grew rounder. The baby was due in March, three months away. John, with his carpenter's skills, had long since fashioned a birthing chair, its sturdy arms shaped to Ann's hands, its high seat open and rounded so that a midwife's hands could catch the newborn easily.

Jamestown's only other pregnancy was about to come to term: Martha Scott was entering her ninth month.

"Ann Laydon's got enough flesh on her bones to see her through," Joan Pierce said, "but poor little Martha! I just don't know. God help her. God help us all." To Temperance and Meg, Joan said, "We may not have our men with us, but at least we don't have to worry about *that*. I can think of nothing worse than birthing a child in this place."

One day, when Margery Easton, the wife of a shoemaker from Bristol, died of pneumonia, Meg came back from helping to lay her out, carrying a small, cloth-wrapped bundle. Undoing it before Will and Temperance, she held up the bundle's contents: a pair of black kidskin slippers, worn paper-thin and shapeless. "Look!" She waved them jubilantly in the air. "Look what I got! They were hers—Margery's—and I took them before anyone else saw me."

"What on earth for? They're worn out, and anyway, they look too small to fit either of us," Temperance said crossly. Meg's perpetual cheerfulness had begun to irritate her. She had begun to feel tired all the time, even early in the morning after a long night's sleep. Her very bones ached, and her skin was beginning to hang in little folds under her neck and on the underside of her forearms. She looked at Will and Meg, and found she could not remember how they had looked before hunger had hollowed their cheeks and stretched their skin too tightly over forehead and cheekbones. We all look like skeletons, she thought, and here is Meg crowing over a pair of shoes.

"What is it about a pair of slippers that excites you so?" Will spoke languidly, not bothering to lift his head from the pallet where he had lain all afternoon. He seldom got up these days, except to bring in more firewood. They seemed to need more fire, the thinner they got.

Meg held one slipper up to the light and rubbed its kidskin top between two fingers. "Ah, that's good and soft," she said happily. "That was once on a nice fat kid, and he'll have left some flavor of himself inside it." Taking a knife, she began to hack at the shoe, cutting the leather into small pieces.

"What are you doing?" Temperance's voice rose shrilly.

"She's taken leave of her senses," Will said calmly, but he sat up to watch.

Meg grinned at them and shook her head. "You two sillies," she said. "What would you do if it weren't for me? We are about to have something to eat with that hateful . . . boiled . . . mush." She punctuated the last sentence with short knife strokes.

"I can't believe this," Temperance said. "Meg, have you lost your reason? We can't eat *shoes!*"

"I'm willing to try," Will said, looking with interest at the small, neat strips of kidskin Meg was laying out on a wooden trencher. "After all, we do eat meat, don't we? And that skin was once next to some flesh, wasn't it?"

"Some people ate Percy's horse's skin when it died. Some got the flesh, and others got the skin," Meg said. "Why can't we have kidskin for ourselves? No one need know about it."

"I doubt if anyone would want to know," Temperance said disgustedly.

Meg was busily putting the strips she had cut into their one iron pot to boil. "Plenty of water and a nice slow fire," she said, rubbing her hands in anticipation.

Two hours later, the contents of the pot were fished out, covered with salt, and arranged on a trencher. They bore a very, very slight resemblance to thin, blackened pieces of meat. Will took one, held it up in midair for a moment, and then put it into his mouth. "I think the thing is to chew a good while, and then down it in one swallow," he said with his mouth full. Meg followed his example, and Temperance reluctantly did likewise. All three chewed in silence, watching each other. At last Will swallowed noisily and reached for another piece. "Not quite the flavor of good roast beef," he said thoughtfully, "but all things considered, not bad. Not bad." He and Meg laughed. Temperance did not laugh. Watching them eat, squatting around the fire like savages, licking their fingers and smacking their lips, their eyes gleaming, their thin hands like claws clutching their trenchers, she was suddenly seized by nausea. The strip of kidskin she had been chewing stuck in her throat, and she doubled over in a fit of violent, uncontrollable retching.

"Oh, Temperance!"

'Poor dear!"

Will and Meg were beside her in an instant, Meg holding her head and Will putting a hesitant hand on her back.

"Sorry!" she gasped as soon as she could speak. "Sorry! Didn't mean to spoil your feast!" Then stomach cramps, sharp as knives, cut off speech, and Temperance doubled up again.

"Here," Meg said tenderly, "let me bathe your face." But Temperance flung one arm over her face and curled up into an unyielding ball. "No," she said in a weak, muffled voice. "No. Never mind. Just leave me alone." Catching a glimpse of the two gaunt faces leaning over her, she burst into sobs of helpless rage. "Leave me alone! Just let me die! We're all going to die soon enough anyway!"

"Hush." Meg's voice was firm, without emotion. "You must not say such things. You are just tired. It'll be better come morning."

"Oh, Temperance," Will said softly. He touched her shoulder timidly. "I'm sorry. Fine work of looking after you I'm doing. I'll go fishing tomorrow. You need some real meat—not kidskin." Temperance, curled up like a small child, her arm still over her face, did not respond. Will removed his hand from her shoulder.

"You'll not go fishing," Meg said. "Not if you're in your right mind, you won't. It's too cold, in the first place, and too dangerous, in the second." She was right, as usual, and the next morning proved it.

* * *

At daylight, a young sailor named Elias Crookdeck disobeyed Percy's orders and climbed over the palisade wall. Nathaniel Causey and Edward Brinton, on watch that morning, saw him and called out to him, but he ignored them and ran into the trees behind the fort, shouting that he was going to catch a squirrel. He came staggering out of the woods almost as soon as he went in, an Indian arrow protruding from his side. He fell but managed to crawl back to the main gate before he died, and his final hemorrhage stained the snow there bright red. They laid him out just inside the gate while a grave was readied, and as word spread, an uneven procession of curious spectators filed past young Crookdeck's body.

This killing was the first sign they had had from their Indian neighbors since the murders of Ratcliffe and his men. The arrow was still stuck in Crookdeck's rib cage, but the point had gone in sideways, so that his back lay flat against the ground. There was very little blood now from the arrow wound, and one might almost believe that this young man had fallen asleep with a make-believe arrow affixed to his jerkin. Most of the blood had come from his mouth, and a thin red line had trickled from the corner of his mouth to his ear. The eyes were closed; the thin, boyish face in repose brought a stifled sob or two from Ann Laydon and Thomasine Causey, the first women who came to see.

They met Thomas Wotton, who looked impassively upon the corpse and said, "Damned savages! They'll kill us all, one by one!" He turned to go back to his house. "I'd as soon be next. Now Esther's dead and gone, there's nothing holding me here."

After Crookdeck's burial, President Percy announced that the night watch would be doubled, in case this killing portended a larger Indian attack. Thomas Wotton and Richard Pace volunteered.

Late that night, sometime after midnight, Temperance, who had felt unwell and had slept most of the day, awoke suddenly. She had been dreaming again of Thickthorne and its great hall tables laden with food. This time it had been haunches of roast venison and jugged hare, and the aroma of roasting meat she had smelled in her sleep was so strong and so real it had awakened her. She lay very still in the dark, depressed, as always, to wake up and realize that she was in Jamestown, hungry, widowed, and three thousand miles from home. But this time, part of her dream had not vanished: The rich aroma of roasting meat was in the air yet.

Temperance opened her eyes in the dark, sniffed, and sat bolt upright. She had not mistaken it; the smell of cooked meat hung so heavily in the air that she wondered why it had not awakened Will and Meg. They were both sound asleep, and Will was snoring softly. Temperance sat wide-eyed in the darkness, sniffing the air and wondering if she could be hallucinating. Hunger could play tricks with one's senses; she knew that. The aroma seemed to drift in from outside, wafting its way around the edges of the deerskin that stretched across the window. There was no question about it: Fresh meat—hot, succulent, savory meat—was being cooked somewhere close by. Drawing the scent into her nostrils made Temperance's mouth tingle. She could almost taste the meat. The aroma reminded her of roast pork, but there was a slightly sweeter odor. She could not quite identify it, much less determine why it was present at Jamestown. Puzzled, but not wanting to wake the others, she lay drowsing until dawn, when the wind had blown away all but a faint trace of the smell. Then she fell into a fitful sleep.

In a house on the other side of the palisade, six people—a woman and five men—buried something in a corner of the earth floor, and then they, too, fell asleep. Their stomachs were blessedly full, their hands and faces still greasy from the forbidden flesh they had consumed.

When Will and Meg awoke the next morning, Temperance told them about the smell, but they refused to believe her.

"Imagination's a powerful thing," Meg said, "and hunger makes it stronger. I've been dreaming of a room full of fresh-baked loaves of bread and crocks of butter and honey two nights in a row."

"I wouldn't mind a dream or two like that myself," Will said. "I've only been dreaming of being at sea lately, and I'm as hungry aboard that ship in my sleep as I am when I'm awake. That's not fair, somehow." He grinned, but only with his mouth. His eyes, since the night he and Temperance had tried to leave Jamestown, had a look of infinite sadness about them.

"Well, you can say what you like," Temperance said with a flounce. "I know what I smelled, and I know it was no dream. There was fresh roast meat somewhere in Jamestown last night."

When Will went to fetch water, he came back with a puzzled frown on his face.

"Something is wrong at the Laydons'," he said, setting down the water pail near the door. "As I was passing their house, George Percy and Nat Causey were going in, and on my way back from the well, they were coming out, and they had the Laydons with them. They were holding John up between them, and Ann was screaming at them like a shrew—something about their not being the only ones. She was calling out names—Richard Pace, Thomas Wotton, and some others I didn't catch. Percy was taking them to his house for some reason, and it can't be a good one."

Later, when everyone gathered for morning prayer, Thomasine Causey, her emaciated face glowing with excitement, was talking to a small group clustered at the back of the meetinghouse.

"Ah," Will said, "now we'll find out something."

Thomasine hailed them frantically. "Have you heard what happened last night?"

"No," Meg said patiently, "how could we have?"

But Thomasine did not wait for an answer. "You know that young fellow the Indians shot yesterday morning? Crookdeck? I don't understand it—I was there when they laid him out yesterday, and he was just skin and bones." She shook her head sadly. "He was fat when he went up to the Falls. He was up there, you know, with Francis West and the others. Such a sweet-faced boy." Thomasine shook her head again and sighed.

"What happened, Thomasine? Get on with it and tell us what happened." Peter Scott and Martha, heavy in the last month of her pregnancy, joined the group. As Peter spoke, he put his arm protectively around his wife. Martha wore a perpetually frightened look these days.

"Well, you know," Thomasine said, "Thomas Wotton was in charge of the burial duty yesterday. I don't think he has been quite right since Esther died. That was hard on him, being a surgeon, and her dying like that, and his not being able to help her."

"Thomasine, for heaven's sake! We all know about Thomas and Esther; that was months ago! What happened last night?" This time it was Isabella Atkins who spoke up. She lived in the house next to the Wottons. Since Esther's death, Thomas had shared his house with Richard Pace.

Thomasine, relishing being the center of attention for once, was not to be hurried. "Well!" She rolled her eyes heavenward and sighed deeply. "Thomas Wotton and Richard Pace went to the burial ground late last night, when it was good and dark, and dug up Elias Crookdeck's body, and took it to the Laydons' house—John, you know, has been so sick and weak for such a long time— Then they took that poor boy's body, and they washed it, and they chopped off his arms and his legs, and they roasted them and ate them!" The last words were spoken in a rush, as though they were too distasteful for Thomasine to keep in her mouth.

For a long moment, no one said a word. Martha Scott hid her face against her Peter's shoulder and shuddered.

"God help us." Phetiplace Close, the schoolmaster, spoke in a quiet voice.

"Isn't it terrible?" Thomasine, her pale eyes darting from one face to another, twisted her hands in the folds of her skirt. "It is so terrible that no one knows what to do about it. Nat is in there right now, meeting with George Percy and John Martin, trying to think what to do. They're the only Council members left, but none of them knows what to do."

"How did they find them out?" Meg asked.

"Whoever was standing watch at the south tower after midnight— Andrew Buckler and Edward Brinton, I think it was—saw that the Laydons had a big fire going for so late at night, and they smelled something cooking. They went and woke up Percy, and they went to investigate. When they went to the house, the smell was very strong, and in one corner of the floor they could see something had just been buried. That was where they had buried the . . . bones." Thomasine shuddered. "There. I've told you all I know. It's too awful for words. I think it'll be the end of us."

At that moment, Edward Brinton, looking grim, arrived late for morning prayers, and without a word to anyone, he strode up to the pulpit, bowed his head, and began the Lord's Prayer. By the time they had reached "For thine is the kingdom, and the power, and the glory," Percy, Martin, and Causey filed in and took their places beneath the pulpit.

At the "Amen," Percy, his thin frame trembling with emotion, ascended the pulpit and faced the crowd. For a moment, he gazed over their heads, as if summoning some power of eloquence, and then he began to speak in a voice shaking with suppressed anger. "Last night, as most of us slept, a terrible deed was done." He paused, but the pause was needless: Seventy pairs of eyes were on him, seventy pairs of ears were anxiously attuned to his every syllable. "Some of our number, forswearing propriety, morality, and humanity, did desecrate a grave, and did in secret, in the dead of night, dig up and cook and eat the flesh of Elias Crookdeck."

A great gasp, almost in unison, arose from the assembly, and then an agitated murmuring filled the air.

Percy held up both hands for silence. "I tell you this to quell false rumors. The truth is bad enough, but falsehoods could make it worse. The guilty parties have been apprehended, and are in jail to await trial." Percy swayed slightly. "It will be a fair trial," he said, his voice rising. "I promise you that." Gathering his strength, he went on, "We shall not all descend to savagery here, though the savages themselves would like to destroy us, though the wilderness close in about us, though nature itself conspire against us. We shall see that the laws of England exist even at Jamestown, and that justice is done. We cannot do otherwise."

There was talk of little else in the Jamestown palisade that day, and for the three days following, as the trials of Ann and John Laydon, Thomas Wotton, Richard Pace, and John Short, a cousin of Pace's, and Tom Dalton, a butcher, dragged on. Was Wotton, who had suggested they dig up young Crookdeck's body while it was still fresh, guiltier than the others? Were Richard Pace and John Short, who had helped in the actual digging and preparing, and Tom Dalton, who had used his butcher's skills in the cutting, deserving of harsher punishment than the Laydons, who merely joined in the eating?

After prayers on the third day, Will and Temperance and Meg stopped at the Causeys' house, along with Andrew Buckler, who had discovered the crime, and Phetiplace Close and Joan Pierce.

"If Percy hanged those poor Cassen boys just for stealing two bags of corn," Andrew said, "what punishment can he devise for stealing a body out of a grave?"

"But stealing from the storehouse harmed us all," Phetiplace Close said thoughtfully. "That was an act against the public good. But what did stealing a dead body deprive us of? That's the question, is it not?"

"No." Nathaniel Causey, whose girth and good spirits were both much diminished these days, spoke up.

"The question is, is it wrong to eat human flesh? Are we become like the savages? I say the culprits ought to be burned. Roasted, like they roasted poor young Crookdeck."

Thomasine, who never disagreed with a word her husband uttered, nodded her head and folded her arms. "It would serve them right," she said.

"But how heinous a crime is hunger?" Phetiplace said softly. "What kind of sin is it to want to stay alive?"

"John Laydon has never got his strength back since he had that fever," Meg said. "And Thomas Wotton's his good friend. Suppose Wotton did what he did not for himself, but for John Laydon to have some meat to nourish him? And for Ann, and that unborn child?"

"I'll wager not one of them that feasted that night regrets it," Temperance said. "They may be sorry for their punishment, but not their deed. I smelled the cooking, and I thought I was dreaming. It smelled like—like good roast pork." The others looked at her, aghast. "I swear it did. And I don't much blame them. What good was Elias Crookdeck in his grave?"

Will stared at her openmouthed, as though he were seeing her for the first time. "Temperance Yardley, mind your words. You know you'd never do that—not eat human flesh."

Temperance looked him in the eye. "I might," she said. "I wouldn't eat the flesh of someone who had been sick, but someone young and healthy, like Crookdeck, who had just been shot—that might be different."

Isabella Atkins disagreed. "It might be, but I—I don't know. I don't think I could do it, ever." But there was a hint of uncertainty in her voice.

"How long do you think we can live on half a can of corn a day?" Temperance said. "Even if more people die, as they surely will before spring, there's not enough grain in that storehouse to see us through, no matter how much Percy preaches to us to have courage. What we need is fresh meat, not courage!"

In the end, Thomas Wotton, who signed himself "Thomas Wotton, Gent." because of his two hundred acres in Essex, was sentenced to a fortnight in solitary confinement to meditate on his crime, and then to chop wood for all the households without able-bodied men. Ann and John Laydon, because of John's feeble health and Ann's pregnancy, were sentenced to confinement in their own house for ten days, and Ann was ordered to help grind meal for those too sick or weak to grind their own. Richard Pace, John Short, and Tom Dalton were sentenced to stand double watches for a month. In addition, all six were to stand before the entire assembly at prayers and publicly acknowledge their wrongdoing.

President Percy, announcing these sentences, defended them on the grounds that "with public repentance and labor for the public good, these persons shall serve as reminders to others. Dead, they would soon be forgotten. And," he added, "thus they will be of use. There are graves enough at Jamestown, as it is."

JAMESTOWN
5 January 1610

 Two weeks after the Elias Crookdeck incident, Gabriel Morgan, standing watch, shot and killed an Indian who was skulking in a grove of trees outside the palisade. Within the hour, hunger-crazed colonists had dragged the body inside, built a huge fire, and set up the roasting spits. Eating the flesh of a heathen savage, they said, was no worse than eating the flesh of a horse, which they had done months ago. There was not enough of the Indian for everyone, but not everyone wanted to share in the feast. A few held back, and a few others, unused to the richness (it had, after all, been a fat Indian) vomited almost as soon as they ate.

Three days later, Peter Scott cut his wife and unborn child into pieces and salted them in a chest in his house.

When George Percy heard what Scott had done, his eyes glittered, and he drew back his lips in a snarl like a beast of prey. "Savagery! I'll not have it! We're all about to turn to savages!" He pounded his fist weakly on the table in front of him. "We cannot stand this! We will have order! We cannot act like animals! We are Englishmen, not cannibals!" He paused briefly for breath, and continued, "If this gets back to London, the Virginia Company—and the Virginia colony—are doomed! Doomed!" He was shouting now. "First Elias Crookdeck, and then that Indian—but at least *they* were already dead! But this! But this—my God!" Percy put his head in his hands. "To kill one's wife and eat her!" He held his head with both hands, as though it might split.

It was Meg, with her calm, soothing voice, the voice she used to quiet the fevered ravings of the sick, who spoke up that day in the meetinghouse. "But we don't know that he killed her. He says she died in her sleep."

Percy lifted his head. "What do you mean, he didn't kill her? How, pray tell, did she get cut into pieces and put into that chest?" Percy pounded both fists hard on the edge of the pulpit.

"There were no witnesses! We have only his word, and what's that worth, if he's out of his mind?"

Percy leaned back, stretching both arms out, hands palm down, bracing himself. "I say he killed her and salted her flesh, intending to eat it and save his own wretched self from starvation!" A sudden recollection made him pause.

"I saw him—two or three days ago—throwing something in the river. He was outside the palisade, against orders. I called to him then, and he pretended not to hear me. But I saw him. I'll make him tell."

"But the man is not himself." Will, who had found the grisly evidence inside a chest in the Scotts' house, shook his head sadly. "Poor Peter Scott is not in his right mind."

"No matter!" Percy said.

And so Peter Scott, weeping softly, was locked up alone in the small building they used for a jail. It had no windows, a dirt floor, and no furniture. They left him in solitary confinement for two long January days, with no light and no fire. Will observed wryly that they could hardly have reduced his food any further; it was already starvation fare.

On the third day, before a gathering of horrified colonists, Percy ordered Scott to be brought outside and suspended by his thumbs from the branch of an oak tree near the main gate.

"Pull him up higher!"

President Percy, barely recovered from his bout with fever and leaning heavily on a cane, gave the order. Richard Pace and Andrew Buckler hauled on the ropes until Scott's body jerked upward. His hair, matted and unkempt, partly concealed his face, and his body dangled limply, like a broken puppet.

"Now, Master Scott, you will please to answer the questions put to you, if you want to be let down from there," Percy said. Then he cleared his throat. "Do you, Peter Scott, own an ax?"

There was a weak, barely discernible nod from the silent, suspended figure.

"Do you also possess a knife with a blade of five inches?"

Another nod.

"Did you have a bag of salt among your provisions last week?"

A nod.

"And where is that salt now? What did you do with that salt?"

The suspended figure did not answer.

With a flourish of his cloak, Percy moved closer to his victim, so that he was looking directly up at Scott's face. "Did you, Peter Scott, murder your wife, Martha, and cut up and salt her body?"

The lowered head now shook slowly from side to side in the negative.

Percy pounded his cane on the ground and swore under his breath. "Pull him up higher!" He raised his head and looked around at the crowd. "Weight his feet! Go get two sacks, and put rocks in them, and tie them to his feet! We'll see how he likes that!"

The crowd murmured uneasily.

At Percy's command, Pace and Buckler tied the sacks to Scott's ankles. Then they took hold of the ropes that suspended him, and pulled. It was a primitive engine of torture they had rigged: rawhide thongs fastened to Scott's thumbs were tied to heavier ropes, which had been thrown over a high limb of the oak tree, and fastened to a lower branch to hold the weight of his body. Readjusting the ropes caused his suspended body to jerk in midair. The sudden movement and the added weight wrung from him a muffled cry of pain, the first sound he had uttered. The crowd of awed spectators murmured again, and then fell silent as Percy held up his hand for quiet. Standing under Scott, whose feet now dangled about half a yard off the ground, Percy began again:

"Do you, Peter Scott, own an ax?"

After a quarter of an hour of this relentless repetition, Peter Scott was in such agony that he could not even nod. He was nearly unconscious, and at the end of the last question, "Did you, Peter Scott, murder your wife?", his head fell forward onto his chest. A jubilant George Percy interpreted that movement as a nod of assent. "Let him down! Let him down and take him away!" Percy, waving his cane in the air, was almost dancing with triumph.

The trial, held the next day, was brief. Percy, Martin, and Causey sat as judges, and Peter Scott, who had not uttered a word since he was put in jail, was sentenced to be burned at the stake for the murder of his wife and child.

"Hanging is too merciful," Percy said. "The world must see that the colony of Virginia is not a savage wilderness, and that criminals here are punished for their crimes."

At midday on January 10, 1610, the execution of Peter Scott, age twenty-four, commenced. The day was bitter cold and gray, with a weak winter sun that hid itself behind the clouds, as though reluctant to witness the proceedings. President Percy had insisted on what he called a proper ceremony to accompany this event, and so, at a few minutes before noon, two rows of people were lined up to make an avenue from the jail to the center of the palisade where the pyre had been constructed. Percy had not had many people to work with: Of the 122 people at Jamestown after Francis West's and the *Swallow*'s departure, there were now only 81 left, and half of those were ill. But everyone who could walk turned out for this occasion. Most people had seen hangings aplenty in England, but burnings were rare.

As the prisoner emerged from the jail, a murmur traveled down the rows of spectators, like a ripple in a stream. John Short began to beat a mournful cadence on his drum, and Edward Brinton stepped forward to escort Scott to his place of execution. Scott glanced around him at the people, and then looked up at the sky and down at the ground, as if to make certain of his own place in this scene. His face was impassive, and his eyes, as he passed through the crowd, were dull, staring straight ahead. His mouth was set in a straight line, and the muscles of his jaw and neck worked like taut cords under his pale skin. He walked slowly, but with a firm step. His feet were bare, and he wore only a coarse homespun shirt and a pair of brown serge breeches.

"He must be cold," someone said, and another answered, "But not for long."

Near the pyre, a huge pile of tree limbs and smaller branches taller than a man's head, stood Richard Pace and Tom Dalton, and between them was an iron pot containing the fire. An occasional tongue of flame licked over the pot's rim when the wind blew. Thomas Wotton and Harmon Harison stood holding the ropes that would bind Peter Scott to the stake. President Percy, with a flourish of his crimson cloak, stepped forward to meet Scott.

"Here in the colony of Virginia, in Jamestown, at noon on the tenth day of January in the year of our Lord 1610, you, Peter Scott, are soon to pass out of this life to heaven or to hell. As a sign before God and man that you have made your peace with your Creator, let us all here assembled recite together the Lord's Prayer."

As Percy spoke, Edward Brinton waved one arm in an expansive, beckoning gesture, motioning to the crowd to move in close, as if inviting them to join in the awfulness of what was about to happen.

Heads bowed, eyes downcast, the crowd obeyed. Their combined voices rose as one solemn, rumbling chorus, rising and falling in the still, cold air.

When the "Amen" had reverberated in the silence, Percy spoke again. "Have you, Master Scott, any last words you wish to speak to us, who are assembled here?" Percy leaned heavily on his cane, and his voice was weak. His sallow face showed the strain of the past few days, and the rings under his eyes were larger and darker. It was clear that Peter Scott had not been the only sufferer during the past four days.

The condemned man suddenly raised his head and looked over the faces of the crowd. Then, gazing over their heads, he spoke in a firm, clear voice:

"Before God Almighty, I did not kill her. May God have mercy on us all."

Scattered whispers ran through the crowd. Percy swayed slightly and steadied himself with his cane. With a wave of his hand, he signaled to Wotton and Harison. They stepped forward, each taking one of Scott's arms, and climbed with him to the top of the pyre, where they bound him fast. Round and round they passed the pitch-soaked ropes, until he was encircled from head to foot. He stared straight ahead of him, but when Pace and Dalton came forward to start the fire, he looked at them. As Wotton and Harison climbed down, the other two men knelt and dumped the burning chunks of wood from their pot onto the pile of kindling.

With a faint crackling sound and a curl of smoke, the kindling caught fire. Atop the pyre, Scott saw it, bowed his head, and closed his eyes. Some of the women began to sob softly. The men who had lined up to form the two rows where Peter Scott had walked his last few steps now broke apart. People milled about quietly, aimlessly, not wanting to stand still, but not wanting to leave, either. They arranged themselves in little clusters, their heads close together, whispering, weeping, waiting, watching in horrid fascination as the bright yellow tongues of fire licked upward and outward. Soon there would be a ring of flame encircling the pyre.

Scott was waiting, too.

The fire, fanned by a capricious wind, burned higher, and the smoke grew thicker. Scott coughed several times. Then, as the assembled crowd watched in breathless horror, the fire reached him. It licked at his bare feet, and he moved his head from side to side and bit his lip until a thin red trickle of blood ran down his chin. For what seemed like a long time, he made no sound as the flames scorched his feet. Finally, he raised his head and gave one great wrenching, anguished cry. In the cold air, the sound seemed to hang suspended, echoing, resonating, pulsating long after Scott's head had dropped on his chest and he had lost consciousness.

Gradually, the crowd began to drift away, talking in hushed tones. The day was bitter cold, and, despite the heat given off by the huge pyre's flames, no one cared to stay beside it. Having seen what they came to see, they went away to their own fires in their own houses.

They could go home and shut out the terrible scene in the center of the palisade, but they could not escape the smell. The odor of burned human flesh, the sickly-sweet smell of charred skin, inner organs, fat, and gristle, hung like a greasy pall over the entire palisade long after sunset. There were many who could not stomach their ration of ground corn that evening, and others who went to sleep with cloths over their faces in a futile attempt to escape the lingering, sickening odor.

"I'll warrant Percy's justice has had its effect," Will said thoughtfully as he lay down to sleep. "It will be a long time before anybody can think about eating human flesh after today."

"Poor Peter," Meg said drowsily. "And poor Martha, and poor child. Perhaps they are together in heaven this very moment."

"They are a sight better off than the rest of us, wherever they are," Temperance said.

BERMUDA
12 January 1610

Nearly 1,000 leagues to the east lay England; 150 leagues to the west lay the unknown land of Virginia. George Yardley, standing midnight watch on the north shore of Bermuda, wondered idly if he would ever see either coast. He hugged himself, shivered, and threw another cedar log on the fire. It was hard to keep a fire going when the wind came up. In the time he spent on watch at the point, he had started building a windbreak, but it was not yet high enough to offer much protection. Bermuda's winds, so warm and fragrant in the summertime, had turned chilly and capricious as winter came. One day the sun would shine and little soft breezes would blow, and the next day biting winds could whip the sea into whitecaps and send the waves crashing far up on the shore, as though wind and water were hungry for the land. On those days, people huddled inside their houses and tried not to go out at all. No one in Bermuda had any winter clothing; all that had been jettisoned in the July storm.

But someone had to stand watch, wind or no wind, and George volunteered oftener than most. Somehow he liked being alone up at the point. The lookout was a spot chosen by Gates and Somers after they had sailed around the entire island group. A tip of land farthest to the northeast, it was higher ground than the south shore, ideally suited to see and be seen by any ships passing to the north. They kept a watch there day and night, but no ships came. In the daytime, George's eyes would ache from constant squinting at the horizon, where the two shades of blue, sky and sea, came together in a long line never broken by the appearance of a ship's sail. But at night, in the starry blackness, keeping watch was easier. The tiniest gleam of a single ship's lantern would be visible for miles, as would the small watch fire kept burning on the point. Someone sailing by might see that light a long way off. But if that someone happened to be Spanish or French, what defense, George wondered, could a few Englishmen with no cannons put up? The *Sea Venture*'s guns lay on the ocean floor, and Bermuda's little settlement was at the mercy of any unfriendly visitors who might happen by. But if all went well, the *Sea Venture*'s company would soon be leaving the island.

The longboat they had sent forth when they arrived was lost, but the seventy-ton pinnace that Richard Frobisher had begun in August was now half finished, and Christopher Newport would be her master. She was not large enough to hold 143 people, so Admiral Somers, with the help of two carpenters he commandeered from Frobisher's work force, had begun the construction of a vessel half the size of the first. Somers himself did not shirk hard labor, and every day but Sunday he could be seen wielding ax or saw alongside his men, cutting the planks for his pinnace. She was to be called the *Patience,* and the larger ship would be christened the *Deliverance.* Reverend Buck had already begun to make tiresome use of those names in his sermons. Come spring, everyone said, they would be ready to set sail for Virginia. Lately the people on the island talked of little else.

That was another reason George took more than his share of watches. He was sick of hearing the Rolfes and the Powells and all the others telling each other what they would do when they got to Virginia. His grief had not lightened with the passage of time; instead, self-pity had fastened itself like a weight around his heart. At the Powells' wedding feast, he had tried to wash it away with cedar-berry wine, and succeeded so well that Strachey and Rolfe had had to carry him to his quarters. The next day he had felt terrible, not so much from the aftereffects of the wine as from the ignominy of his own weakness.

Now he had another reason to grieve for Temperance: Gwendolyn Rolfe had given birth to a baby girl, a tiny, pink, mewing creature who made George's heart turn over when he looked at her. John Rolfe, beaming with fatherly pride, had taken him to see this baby when she was only a day old. "She is the first child born on this island," he said. "We are going to name her Bermuda, in honor of it."

"I see," George said. But what he saw was Temperance's face the last time they had made love, and what he thought was that he would never look on any child of theirs.

Now he sat looking out to sea, poking the watch fire occasionally and turning the glass to mark the passage of time. Suddenly, he heard a noise and leaped to his feet, his hand on his sword. A faint crackling of dry leaves and twigs told him that someone was on the other side of the small grove of cedar trees just behind him. In the flickering light of his watch fire, he could see nothing but the trees. "Who's there?" he called out sharply, although he was sure whoever was there was someone he knew.

"It's Jane, sir." The soft female voice startled George. "Jane Wright."

What on earth was she doing up here at the lookout point in the middle of the night? He could see her now, a shadowy form approaching him in the dim light of the fire. She was carrying a jug. Annoyed at having his reverie interrupted, but curious about why she had come, he tried to speak gently. "Why, Jane! What brings you up here so late? It's well after midnight. Is anything wrong?"

"Oh, no, sir, nothing's wrong." She was close enough now that George could see her face, and she was smiling shyly. "It's a cold night, and I—I just thought you might like something to warm your insides." She held out the jug. "I brought you some wassail. We made it with wild plums instead of apples, but it tastes good. See if you don't think so." She thrust the jug toward him with both hands. As she did so, the shawl she wore slipped off her shoulders. Actually, it was not a proper shawl, but a piece of a petticoat she had torn in two. The other women had done likewise to ward off the winter's chill, and it gave them a curiously ragamuffin appearance. As Jane's wrap fell to the ground behind her, it revealed her plump white arms and her breasts. The laces of her kirtle had broken, so that she could not fasten it all the way up, and her breasts, covered only by a thin white smock, were unconfined. She smiled at George in the firelight, and her teeth showed white and even. George took the jug, and in doing so, his fingers brushed against hers. The touch went through him like a warm wave, up his arm, and down his chest to his loins. His fingers were chilled by the cool night air, but hers were warm. The thought suddenly struck him that he had not touched a woman's flesh since he and Temperance had parted. Lifting the jug to his lips, he drank deeply, and then wiped his mouth with the back of his hand. Jane stood motionless in front of him, her hands clasped in front of her, her eyes on his face, waiting expectantly for him to speak.

"It's very good," he said stiffly. "Very good, indeed. It was kind of you to think of me." Part of him wanted her to leave, but another part had become suddenly insistent. Jane took the jug, but she made no move to go.

"You look lonesome, Master George," she said softly, setting the jug on the ground. "I've been watching you a long time, and you always look lonesome." She took a step closer to him and put her hands lightly on his shoulders, palms flat. She was almost his equal in height, and her face was very close to his. Her breath in his nostrils was warm and sweet, smelling faintly of wassail. She must have drunk some before she came, he thought. The taste of it must still be on her lips.

And then, without quite knowing what he did, George kissed her. Her arms went round him in an instant. She kissed him back, making little darting, caressing movements with her tongue, quick and light as a hummingbird. With a muffled moan of pleasure and surrender, George pressed his mouth hard to her mouth, his body against hers. He could feel himself growing hard under his codpiece as it pushed against her skirts. He closed his eyes and thought, why not? But then inside his eyelids he saw a dear, familiar image: a delicate face with great brown eyes under a mass of coppery-gold hair. Reaching behind him for Jane's wrists, he pulled her arms away from him roughly and stepped backward at the same time, so that she would have lost her balance if he had not kept hold of her.

"What is it?" she said. "What's wrong?" It was dark, but not too dark for George to see the hurt in her eyes.

"Nothing," he said. He was breathing as though he had been running. "I—I'm sorry. I let myself go, and I shouldn't have. I'm sorry."

"Why?" Jane was bewildered. "What harm would a little lovemaking do, if you felt like it? I thought you might want some, and . . . they said you would. Now I've made a botch of things."

"Who said I would? What do you mean?"

Jane shook her head slowly from side to side, keeping a wounded silence.

"Jane, what are you talking about?" George's voice was rough with anger, and Jane did not answer. Then, realizing that he had frightened her, he tried again. "Jane, you can tell me." He tried to speak gently. "Nobody will know what happened here between you and me, but I want to know what you are saying. Did someone send you here?"

She nodded in silent assent.

"Who?"

"Master Strachey and Sir Thomas. They said you needed cheering up, and I should come to you up here. They said it wasn't good for you to be sad all the time. But now I see you don't want me, so I'll go." With a stifled sob, she started down the path, but George caught her arm.

"No—wait," he said. "Don't go. I didn't mean to be angry. I was just surprised. I didn't know anyone thought I was . . . in need of help."

"Oh, maybe you are, Master George, and you just don't know it. I've watched you ever since we came here, and you do look sad. I know you miss your wife, but it's not good to mourn too long."

Jane's cap had slipped to one side, and some wisps of her black hair curled rather bewitchingly around her face. Here she was, giving herself to him, and he was turning her away. And what would Strachey and Gates think of him now?

"I know it's not good, Jane, but I can't help it. You—you needn't go yet. You could just stay and . . . talk for a bit, if you like."

"Oh, yes!" her manner was shy, but eager. "Yes, Master George, I'd be pleased to."

George was touched. This young woman, like him, had been stranded on an island in the middle of nowhere, and like him, she must be lonely. They had both been cast up, like flotsam and jetsam, with no ties to anything or anyone ashore. Except for Thomas Gates, George had not consciously tried to please anyone but himself for a long time. Now he motioned toward a small bench by the watch fire. "Sit down, Jane Wright, and keep me company a while." And just for her, he smiled.

JAMESTOWN
12 January 1610

Two days after Peter Scott's execution, it snowed. At daylight, when the inhabitants of the houses inside the palisade began to stir, they looked out on a landscape of magical white, and a fine powdery fall of snow was still sifting down. The ragged thatched roofs of the huts, the bare ground, and the blackened pile of ashes and charred wood in the center of the palisade were wondrously transformed, their ugliness hidden by a coverlet of soft, shimmering white. Rough shapes were smoothed, jagged edges were softened, uneven places were leveled, and all was pure, unsullied whiteness except for the pale blue shadows cast by the trees as the sun rose higher. It was as if Nature had tried to conceal the grisly reality that was Jamestown.

But famine refused to be masked, and that very day the new-fallen snow was sullied by the dragging of two dead bodies to an empty hut in a corner of the palisade. A servant girl and her widowed mistress had lain down and died together in the night. Their poor thin bodies were not heavy, but the men assigned to burial were too weak to carry them, much less to bury them, even if the ground had not been frozen. And so they dragged the bodies, and laid them to rest, swaddling them in old cloaks, in the empty hut. A half-dozen other bodies were already there, along with the chest containing Martha Scott's remains. They would keep until warmer weather, when the ground thawed.

This winter, said those who should know, was colder than the previous ones. But with the clothing salvaged from those who had died, everyone in the palisade could dress warmly. In fact, most now had at least two or three changes of clothing, but their malnourishment was so great, and the wind from the river so icy, that everyone wore all the clothing he or she possessed. Bony legs were encased in several pairs of stockings and trunk hose; necks were wrapped with more stockings or with pieces of woolen petticoats; emaciated bodies were turned out in layers of shirts and jerkins and doublets, bodices and kirtles and gowns and petticoats, that gave them all an oddly comical air, like so many well-padded scarecrows.

Some people still made a vain effort to keep up appearances. Thomasine Causey wore a high pearl-and-gold comb in her thin mouse-colored hair. Above her sallow, sunken cheeks, the comb gave her an incongruously festive look, far out of keeping with her dismal surroundings. Temperance, who no longer bothered to dress her own hair, thought Thomasine affected, and said as much.

"I don't think Thomasine Causey is silly, as you so charitably put it," Will said, eyeing Temperance's mass of unkempt curls. "That pearl comb is her flag of courage. I warrant that every time she puts it in her hair, she thinks of happier times when she wore it, and then she thinks of better times to come. And if they do come, she'll be ready for them, while the rest of us may be no better than savages." Will stroked his matted, untrimmed beard, and grinned a rueful grin at Temperance. "No," he said. "The savages at least pluck their beards and tie their hair. We'll be worse than savages."

"Well, who's to care?" Temperance said irritably. Meg had gone out, and the two of them were alone by the fire. "We shall all be dead soon enough, so what does it matter? You yourself told me that, long ago, that night we tried to leave with Francis West, remember?"

For a long moment, Will was silent. "Yes," he said quietly, "I remember."

Temperance turned her back to him. Talking tired her. Everyone was tired these days; they were like sleepwalkers, shuffling over to the storehouse to get their meager handfuls of corn, sitting endless hours before their fires, doing nothing now but waiting for death. Only a few, like the Forrests and the Causeys, and Edward Brinton, and Meg, seemed not to lose heart. Meg was never too tired to tend the sick, and many of them asked for her. There were more sick people now, as the months of malnutrition took their toll. Many were simply too weak to care for themselves. The dirt floors of many huts stank of urine and feces, and it was too cold, and too much trouble, to carry and heat water for washing. The sick who could not move about developed festering bed sores. But Meg and a few others did what homely tasks could be done for them, and Edward still offered prayers morning and night for all who were able to come to the meetinghouse.

Temperance moved closer to the fire, her one source of pleasure, and hugged her skinny knees. Will was stretched out on his straw pallet behind her. As the warmth from the fire crept over her, Temperance gave an involuntary shiver. Heat and cold were almost the only sensations that her body responded to these days. Then she felt a light touch on her shoulder.

"Are you cold?" Will, leaning on one elbow, reached over and patted her awkwardly. "Shall I get some more wood?"

"No."

She had started at his touch. Close as they were in daily contact, Will almost never touched her. Now he got up, stretched, and stood behind her, looking into the fire.

"Oh, Temperance!" he said softly. "What do you suppose will be the end of us? There will be an end, you know, and it will be right here, most likely in this very house."

Temperance, watching the stump of a log turn to embers, nodded slowly and did not answer. Will dropped to his knees beside her, his eyes on the fire. The two of them sat there in a curiously companionable silence for a while.

Then, turning to look at Temperance, Will said, "Don't be sad. It grieves me so to see you sad." With one finger, he touched the hollow of her cheek and traced the sharp, bony line of her jaw. As he did so, the loose white sleeve of his shirt fell back, exposing his thin wrist and forearm. The sight of that arm, all bone and sinew and so little flesh, with the blue veins standing out in bas-relief against the pale skin, suddenly constricted Temperance's throat so that she could not speak. Those arms and hands, once so strong and supple, had made music for her on a lute on her wedding day, had steadied her in seasickness aboard the *Falcon,* had gathered acorns to keep her from starving at Jamestown. Now the arms were wasted, wraith-like, the hands knobby.

Gently, she took Will's hand in both her own and looked at it. She caressed each of the bony knuckles and touched each of the short, ragged fingernails. Then she bent her head over the hand and held it to her lips. As she did, she blinked, and her tears fell on Will's wrist. He drew a long, shuddering breath. Then, almost without thinking, Temperance turned his hand over, palm up, and kissed the inside of his wrist. She could feel his pulse beating against her mouth. With his free hand, Will pulled her close, and with a stifled sob, let his head fall against her shoulder. She put her arms around him and they clung to each other silently, rocking gently back and forth in front of the fire.

"Oh, Will, dearest Will!" she whispered. "Life has played false with us, somehow." She wanted to comfort him, but she also wanted something else, and the suddenness of the feelings took her by surprise. The sensations in her breasts and her privates had nothing to do with pity.

Then, Will, his face still hidden in the soft folds of her shift, spoke in a voice so low she could barely hear it. "Oh, God, Temperance! God forgive me, but I love you! I do love you so!"

Temperance put her hands on his shoulders and pushed him away from her, but she did not let go of him. Her eyes met his, and then, taking Will's face between her hands, she kissed him full on the mouth. For a few seconds, he seemed passive, taken by surprise, but at last he began to kiss back, tentatively at first, then harder and harder. When she felt his tongue, Temperance opened her mouth and tightened her arms around him. With a small choked, joyous sound, he began to kiss her anew, so hungrily that they had to stop for breath, weak and trembling from the unaccustomed exertion. For a moment, the only sounds in the house were the crackling of the fire and the soft, labored rasping of their own breaths.

"When is Meg coming back?" Will's voice, close to Temperance's ear, was deep and musical, suffused with a new intimacy.

"Suppertime," Temperance answered. With one hand, she began to untie the laces of his doublet. Wordlessly, with rapturous haste and trembling fingers, they began to loosen each other's clothing, pushing aside shift and shirt to kiss, inch by inch, the skin they had always kept hidden from each other. Throat, collarbone, shoulders, breasts, were covered with kisses until, in the chilly room, the warm breath from their own nostrils on newly moistened skin made them shiver. With one hand, Will reached for a rug and pulled it over them. Then the kissing was resumed.

At last, Will's voice, with tender urgency, whispered, "Now?"

"Yes, oh, yes! Now!" Temperance pulled him toward her, and he made his entry with one smooth, quick thrust. For a moment, they lay perfectly still, two frail, thin bodies gathering their strength. Then, slowly, almost reverently, Will began to move. Temperance locked her legs around his hips and moved with him.

When they were finished, he dropped his head onto her shoulder and sighed. It was a great heaving sigh, as though it were releasing half a year's store of pent-up feelings. They held each other close for a long time, drawing blessed warmth from the fire and from each other. It was Will who broke the silence.

"Dear God, Temperance," he said, "what have we done? You are a married woman, and the wife of my best friend."

After that day, they discovered that guilt, like hunger, was inescapable.

But when they told Meg what they had done, she merely smiled and said, "I know."

"What do you mean, you know?" Temperance said.

Meg looked at her, and then at Will, like a mother with two naughty children. "I mean," she said, "that a body with half a grain of sense could see Will was smitten with you. I saw that long ago, aboard the *Falcon.*"

Will's eyes widened, and he looked ashamed.

"And when he came back with that hurt leg, and you sat anursing him night and day, I saw that, too."

Temperance looked surprised.

"I knew there was something in your heart for him then, whether you knew it or no." Meg smiled. "You've no cause to fret now. I shan't tell a soul." She gave each of them a congratulatory embrace. "And I shall leave you alone whenever you like."

"You don't think we are . . . doing wrong?" Will asked.

"And if you are?" Meg said slowly. "In this place, and in this awful time, what does it matter? Who will care?" She shrugged. "We none of us have much time left, unless a miracle happens."

"No one ever imagined we'd come to this." As he spoke, Will looked at Temperance and suddenly realized his words had a double meaning.

She smiled.

LONDON
2 February 1610

 As the carriage turned into Fenchurch Street, the snow, which had been drifting down a few desultory flakes at a time, began to fall in earnest, and the driver could hardly see his way. Inside the carriage, a pale-looking man swathed in a heavy woolen cloak shivered and peered out at the swirling snowflakes. He did not relish the visit he was about to pay, but it had to be done.

"Philpot Lane!" the driver called out, and under his hands the pair of matched chestnut geldings reluctantly slowed their pace. Beside him, a footman in green and gold livery swung down from his seat and called out to the passenger.

"Here you are, sir! This house right here's the one you want. Sir Thomas Smythe's."

"I know," said the passenger, without much enthusiasm. Seizing his cane, he descended slowly and awkwardly from the carriage. His right side still pained him, and he walked upright with great difficulty. He was grateful to the Earl of Bedford for lending him his carriage. Lifting the ornate brass knocker, he let it fall sharply on the heavy oak panel of the door. Almost instantly, the door swung open and a serving man ushered him inside.

"Are you expected, sire?"

"Yes," said the visitor wearily.

"Whom shall I say is calling?"

"Captain John Smith."

"Very good, sire. I shall tell Sir Thomas that you are here. He has been expecting you."

If Smith's side had not been so painful, he would have paced up and down the richly figured Turkey carpet in Sir Thomas Smythe's entrance hall. Instead, he stood still, leaning on his cane and waiting. Under his trunk hose on his right side was a bandage, and under that was a patch of oozing raw flesh the size of a man's two hands. His gunpowder burn had begun to fester in the ten weeks he had spent at sea, and now the skin refused to grow back over the wound. Until a few days ago, he had been unable to bear anything touching it, and since his return from Virginia in December he had been a half-naked invalid at the country house of his friend, Edward Seymour, the Earl of Bedford. But after the Virginia Company had convened for its Hilary Term meeting on January 15, John Smith knew that he must make an effort, pain or no, to see Sir Thomas, the Company's treasurer, and explain to him in person what had happened in Virginia. Smith had, of course, sent a letter addressed to the entire Council, but pen and paper was too weak a weapon to combat the ill will and disillusion he knew were rife within the "Company of Adventurers and Planters in Virginia."

"Ah, Captain Smith! How are you?" Sir Thomas strode into the hall, his wine-colored velvet robe sweeping behind him.

"Not so well as I'd like, or as I'd hoped to be by now," Smith said. He planned to proceed cautiously, not knowing what conflicting reports had reached the man who stood smiling before him. Thomas Smythe, treasurer of the Virginia Company, member of the Haberdashers' and Skinners'

Companies, the Levant Company, and at one time governor of the Muscovy Company, was also a member of one of the richest merchant families in all of England. His elegant house in Philpot Lane, not far from the tall spires of the Church of St. Margaret's Pattens, had become the headquarters of the Virginia Company. It was here that the Company's broadsides instructed all interested "workmen of whatever craft they may be, blacksmiths, carpenters, coopers, shipwrights, turners and such as know how to plant vineyards, hunters, fishermen, and all who work in any kind of metal, men who make bricks, architects, bakers, weavers, shoemakers, sawyers and those who spin wool and all others, men as well as women, who have any occupation, who wish to go out" to Virginia, to come and have their names entered on the list and receive instructions about their work for the Company and their eventual share in the division of land. Those who did not wish to go to Virginia themselves could buy a share of the joint-stock issue for twelve pounds sterling. Then, as the Virginia Company fervently hoped, the new colony's future earnings would provide them all with handsome profits.

"Come into the library," Sir Thomas said. When he and Smith were inside, he closed the large double doors carefully and turned the brass lock. "Now," he said, "we can talk undisturbed—and not be overheard. I have read your letter, but I want to hear what happened in your own words."

And so, for the next hour, John Smith told him of what had transpired in Virginia, of the discord and factions, of the troubles with the Indians, of the plots against his life.

"I have read Archer's and Ratcliffe's letters," Sir Thomas said, tapping his fingers thoughtfully on the polished surface of the table in front of him. "Archer says you sided with the sailors and refused to surrender your commission as president; Ratcliffe says you were high-handed, and—how did he put it? You 'were sent home to answer some misdemeanors.'" From the tone of voice, Smith could not tell what his host was thinking. Suddenly, Sir Thomas looked up and smiled. "And I say Archer's a rumormonger and Ratcliffe's a bastard. Have some aqua vitae."

Relief, like a warm, welcome bath, washed over John Smith. His frail, ravaged body straightened slightly; his awful wound felt as if someone had spread a healing balm over it. He was not, then, out of favor with the Virginia Company Council. He knew he was not at fault; he had followed his own best judgment and had written in his own defense, but he was, after all, only the son of a yeoman farmer in Willoughby, Lincolnshire, and the men he dealt with were the sons of old, distinguished families. Francis West and his brother Thomas, Virginia's future governor, were first cousins twice removed to the late Queen of England, and John Smith had made an implacable enemy of Francis.

Thomas West, Lord de La Warr, was scheduled to sail soon with a massive relief expedition for the beleaguered Virginia colony: over a thousand colonists and ample supplies for them and the survivors at Jamestown. But he would be sailing without Captain John Smith, whose gunpowder wound would keep him out of commission for as much as a year. Even now, after four months, the slightest exertion exhausted him; the smallest movement of his right leg pained him. For the time being, at least, Smith knew that he would have to be relegated to another, lesser role in the affairs of the colony so dear to his heart.

"What will you do now?" Sir Thomas asked as the two sipped their liquor.

Smith studied the liquid in his cup. "I don't know," he said.

"No man in England knows more about Virginia than you do," Sir Thomas said. "Why don't you write something? God knows, the Company needs all the help it can get. A book with the truth set down would be very useful indeed."

Sir Thomas was deeply worried about the fate of the Virginia Company, Smith knew. Already, there had been sharp differences of opinion between the stockholders who were anxious for a quick return on their investments, the group championed by Sir Edwin Sandys, son of the Archbishop of York, and those like Smythe and his wealthy friends, who could afford to wait. It was obvious by now that the land along the James River was not going to yield gold or silver or any other source of windfall profits. Iron and glass were possibilities, as were pitch, tar, and ship's masts from the forests, and the fertile soil might produce some staple crop. But all of these would take time. There would be no quick return from Virginia. The news of the missing *Sea Venture* and the troubles at Jamestown had spread, and now, with the loss of the *Unity* and the *Diamond* on the return voyage, many of the subscribers in the joint-stock venture had simply withdrawn their payments. With four out of the nine ships of the Gates expedition lost, and nothing aboard the returning vessels to sell for profit, many investors simply lost heart.

"This enterprise owes a great deal to you," Sir Thomas went on. "And now that we have the new charter this year, there could be a further need of you. How is your wound?"

Smith hated to reply, but the answer was all too obvious. "Slow to heal." He shrugged. "The surgeons I have seen tell me it will take a long time—too long, perhaps."

"That is a pity." Sir Thomas frowned. "Lord de la Warr is supposed to leave before the summer, and he will have absolute authority over all Virginia." He set his drink aside. "Fate—or Providence, if you like—plays a cruel game. I must tell you something, Captain Smith." Without waiting for an acknowledgment, he continued, "Inside the black box that went down with the *Sea Venture* was a copy of your new commission as an officer under Deputy Governor Gates. You were to be second in the military command—second only to Admiral Somers, and that only because a captain cannot outrank an admiral. You were to be senior officer in command of the land defenses of all Virginia. But now—" Sir Thomas held out both hands, palms up. "I am sorry, truly sorry. Perhaps this fledgling Virginia Company can someday make you a proper recompense. In the meantime, think of writing."

"I shall," John Smith said. Setting down the history of the Virginia colony, he thought, might ease both the pain of his wound and the ache in his heart. He felt old and tired and, of late, very lonely. His time in Virginia had been the best time of his life, and his fondest memories lay there. He vowed to return as soon as he could, and he wondered how changed he would find the colony when he did return. But by that time, he thought, Pocahontas would no doubt have taken a husband.

JAMESTOWN
February 1610

 As the weeks passed, Temperance marveled at the intensity of her newfound feelings for Will. She had only to look at his face, its fine bones chiseled by malnutrition, and his eyes, lit by a wondrous gentleness, to feel the same curious passion she had felt when he had first touched her cheek that afternoon before the fire. Was this love? she wondered. It was different from anything she had felt for George, and yet she knew she had loved George. Could she love two men at once, in different ways? Had she come to love Will Sterling unawares, or was this strange intensity of feeling an effect of malnutrition? Mystics, she had once read, fasted in order to achieve great spiritual awareness; perhaps her feelings for Will were merely an accidental consequence of starvation. But whatever they were, they were real enough, and she could not help herself.

Even before Will had awakened her passion, Temperance had laid her memories of George to rest. In her mind's eye, images of their brief time together had begun to fade like threads in a tapestry exposed to strong light. George had been so different from Will. That, she thought, was probably the reason the two of them had become best friends: the attraction of opposites. George was energetic, ambitious, practical; Will was languid, pensive, given to daydreaming. George was seemingly self-assured, sometimes arrogant; Will wore about him an air of vulnerability, as though a word could wound him as surely as a sword. But Will opened himself to her, while Temperance felt there would always be a part of George he would hold in reserve. Even when they made love, George never quite let go. He always seemed to be positioning himself for advancement, calculating the next move. That was why he had insisted that Temperance not sail with him on the *Sea Venture,* she knew, and she had never quite forgiven him for it.

"I just wish to God that George had not made me promise to look after you," Will said suddenly one evening. He had been playing his lute for Temperance, strumming catches neither of them could recall the words to, picking out jig tunes to make her laugh, when all at once he laid the lute aside and turned solemn.

Temperance looked at him in surprise. "How long is it since the *Sea Venture* was lost at sea?"

"Six months. God knows, I've kept count," Will answered moodily.

"And how likely is it the *Sea Venture* will be found?"

"I don't know," Will said. "But I know that George Yardley is my best friend, closer than a brother, and I have . . . betrayed him."

"*Was,*" Temperance said softly. "*Was* your best friend. Will, you know, and I know, that George is dead." She kissed Will lightly on the mouth. "And you and I are alive."

"But—"

"Hush! Listen to me! You and I are three thousand miles from home, starving to death in a godforsaken wilderness. And God, if He is here, knows we are only doing what He meant for a man and a woman to do. He cannot begrudge us that, can He?"

After that day, they did not mention George.

They did try to preserve a facade of propriety, making love only when Meg was spending the night tending the sick, which she did now with an obvious regularity that went unacknowledged, by unspoken agreement among the three of them. Temperance and Will did not mention hunger, either, though it was as constant as their love.

There were now only seventy-six people in all of Jamestown. Of the married couples, only three, the Causeys, the Forrests, and the Laydons, had survived. Ann Laydon's abdomen, swollen in her eighth month of pregnancy, was the only rounded part of her body; her arms and legs were pitifully thin. When people gathered in the meetinghouse for morning and evening prayers, their voices echoed eerily in the empty spaces of a structure meant to hold three hundred. When they said the Lord's Prayer, "Give us this day our daily bread" sounded like a cruel jest. In an empty house in one corner of the palisade, the bodies of the dead, awaiting burial when the ground thawed, continued to accumulate, while in the storehouse the supply of grain grew ever smaller. There was now a bitter irony in this state of affairs: the more deaths, the more food for the living. Rationing had turned into a grim lottery. Who would survive? It was an unspoken, ever-present question as the days slipped drearily past.

When March came, Temperance discovered that she was carrying Will's child.

At first she had not been certain.

"It may be just because you are so thin that your time did not come," Meg said the first month, when Temperance did not use any of the makeshift clouts she and Meg had made to wear during their monthly cycles. They had lost the supply they brought from England when their trunks were jettisoned in the storm, and at Jamestown they had had to make new ones from petticoats and shifts left in the wardrobes of the dead. Now, in the bottom of a chest, there was a pile of cloth strips that they wore and washed, wore and washed, each time the moon waxed and waned.

But as Temperance's second month came and went, the certainty of her condition settled upon her with a great foreboding. She was convinced that neither she nor the child growing within her would survive. That grim thought came to her anew every morning when she awoke, and its persistence made her think that God was punishing her for living in sin with Will.

"When are you going to tell him?" Meg said one afternoon. She stood gazing out the window at Will as he left to gather firewood.

Temperance, who had been listlessly stirring a pot of gruel, looked up, startled. "Tell him what?"

"About the baby. Don't you think he should know?"

"Oh, Meg!" Temperance looked down and put both hands on her abdomen as if to flatten it. "Does it show?"

Meg threw back her head and laughed. "No, you silly goose, you're not showing. But how long do you think to keep it from Will?"

Temperance sighed and sat down on a joint stool. "Oh, God help me, Meg!" She bent forward and put her head in her hands. Meg knelt and put her arms around Temperance. That silent embrace spoke of the fears that neither of them wanted to put into words.

It remained for Will to do that, the moment that Temperance told him. "You cannot give birth on a handful of boiled corn a day."

"There is Ann Laydon," Temperance said hopefully. "She's like to be brought to bed soon, and she seems strong enough."

"But Ann Laydon had enough to eat at first, and she had more flesh on her than you to start with. No," Will said, "we must think on this."

The news that Temperance was carrying his child had given Will an unexpected vitality, as though some age-old instinct had suddenly endowed him with new strength. Thin though he was, there was a new lightness in his step, a new authority in his voice, and a new tenderness in his touch. He almost made Temperance forget her fears.

The next morning he said, "If we could get downriver, somehow, to Point Comfort, we could stay there until the spring supply comes. There is bound to be food there, with only forty men at the fort."

"But we cannot get downriver. You know that." Temperance spoke softly, wistfully, knowing full well that what he proposed was impossible.

"We must contrive a way. I want my child born alive, and I want you to . . . be well." He took her hand in both of his, and kissed it reverently.

"But, Will, no one is allowed outside these walls. The gates are bolted shut. You know that, and you know Percy's orders. He'd never let us leave."

"And I'd never let him stop me. Percy be damned," Will said quietly. "That man has lost heart as well as health, and it's his fault we're in this condition. If John Smith had been here this winter, things would have been far different."

"Maybe so," Temperance said, "but John Smith is not here, and we have no choice but to stay here. Besides," she said, "we don't even know if the men at Point Comfort are still there. If they are, why have we not heard from them in all this time?" Temperance was skeptical. "Maybe they hailed the *Swallow* and left for England with Francis West."

Will shook his head. "West would never have taken them. There would have been too many for the *Swallow*. I trow they are still there, and they have food. There are bound to be fish and crabs, and gulls and geese and ducks near the Point." Will spoke with mounting excitement. "We've not heard from the men there because they have no need of us. Why would they come upriver in the midst of winter? Percy is too fainthearted to go to them, but we can." Rubbing his hands together, Will began to pace around the cramped room. Temperance and Meg looked at each other in apprehensive silence. "Well, my ladies, has the cat got both your tongues?"

It was Meg who spoke first. "If what you say is true about Point Comfort, then why hasn't Percy sent someone to bring back food for us when people are dying here for want of nourishment?"

"Ah, but that's the thing! Dying, indeed, for want of spirit! Because George Percy could not come to terms with the Indians, we ran short of food, and because we ran out of food, we turned into a flock of sheep. All this time we thought we could do nothing but wait for spring and pray for a supply ship, when we should have been thinking of ways to get round the Indians and fend for ourselves." Will turned suddenly, knelt in front of Temperance, and took both her hands in his. "Dear God, Temperance! If it had not been for you—for this—I'd have been like all the others, a damned stupid fool, minding George Percy and waiting for death!"

"And if we should get out," Temperance said, "how would we get to Point Comfort?"

"There are two dugout canoes by the main gate. One of them will do us nicely."

Will unfolded his long legs and stood up, as if he meant to leave then and there. "I'll contrive to take a midnight watch." He began to pace back and forth, and the two women watched him, mesmerized. "And whoever watches with me will have to be silenced, somehow."

"Henbane," Meg said suddenly.

"What?"

"Henbane leaves. They make one sleep. What if we were to make a good strong tea of henbane leaves, and bring it to you at the watch? Whoever is with you would not be able to keep his eyes open, I promise you."

"Meg, you are a wonder!"

"No, a fool, more likely," she said with a wry smile. "But what have we to lose by trying?"

That night, after they had banked the fire and gone to bed, Temperance could not sleep. The three of them slept close together for warmth, and she tried not to disturb Will, on her right side, and Meg, on her left. But her head was spinning, and her heart was pounding, as hope and fear went round and round. She tried to imagine herself safe at Point Comfort, giving birth, with Will and Meg there to help her. But instead, she kept imagining the escape from the palisade and the journey downriver.

At last her restlessness woke Will, who put one arm around her from behind, and said groggily, "What's the matter, love?"

Her answer was one word, whispered in the dark.

"Indians."

THE JAMES RIVER
5 March 1610

 "Indians!" Temperance's voice rose as her heart sank. The first arrow whistled harmlessly over their heads, but the next one struck the wooden prow of the canoe with an ominous *thunk.*

"Get down! Flat!" Will flung himself sideways and backward, falling against Temperance, who had been sitting in the midsection of the canoe, and forcing her down. At the same instant, Meg, who had been paddling from the stern, leaned forward, so that the three of them were wedged into the wide middle section of the canoe, their faces close together, their bodies rigid with fear. The canoe, no longer controlled by their paddles, veered crazily in the swift current. For a moment or two, there was no sound except their own frightened breathing, and then the solid *thunk* again as another arrow hit the canoe amidships. "Damn!" Will's voice was an angry whisper. "Don't move. Just lie still."

Temperance gripped Will's arm. From where she lay, she could not see his face. Her heart was pounding so wildly that she was sure the Indians could hear it. A few inches away from her was Meg's face, frozen in terror. Her eyes met Temperance's, and they gazed at each other like two hunted creatures. A third arrow hit, ricocheting into the bottom of the boat with a harmless clatter. Its shaft was a reed with a hickory foreshaft; its head, a deadly sharp splinter of bone.

"Be still!" Will's voice was a barely audible whisper. The canoe, un-manned, suddenly caught the current and spun around, pointing the prow back toward Jamestown. At the same time, the stern was pointed toward the shoreline, less than a hundred yards distant, and the craft began to move backward. The river, it seemed, was about to deliver them into the hands of their enemies. Will had deliberately tried to stay close to the northern shore of the James until they could get past Hog Island, three miles to the east, where the river would be at its narrowest and swiftest. They could have hugged the south shore, but to reach it would have meant paddling cross-wise against the current for nearly five miles, crossing the James at one of its widest points. Will had grown up on the banks of the Thames River and knew something of boats, but neither Temperance nor Meg had ever held an oar, and he could not manage a ten-foot canoe unaided.

Now they were drifting toward death.

"There is no help for it—we have got to paddle," Will said through his teeth. "Otherwise we'll drift right to shore. I'll take the stern and steer; Meg, you take the prow; Temperance, you stay here and use your paddle just like Meg. You'll both put in and stroke on this side when I give the word. Don't sit up till you have your hand on your paddle, and then keep as low as you can." Without waiting for an answer, he said, "We'll go when I count three, and God help us. Ready?"

"Ready!"

"Ready!"

"One, two, *three!* Go to it!" Will's voice rose to a shout as all three scrambled madly to their positions, paddles clutched in cold-numbed fingers. "Pull! Pull! We've got to turn!" The icy water seemed to drag against their paddles, resisting at every stroke, and for an awful moment the canoe was dead in the water, not forty feet from the shore, where now six Paspahegh warriors were dancing about and shouting with anticipation as they fitted new arrows to their bows.

"Keep your head down and hunch over. Don't look at them." Will's voice was cool and steady, and he pulled with long, powerful strokes that moved them slowly but surely toward the opposite shore, nearly three miles distant. One after the other, the Indians on the sandy riverbank drew back their bows, and then one after the other, the arrows came. Two hit the water off the canoe's prow; two hit with the now-familiar *thunk* in its gunwales; one went into the water in the canoe's wake.

The last arrow hit Meg.

"Aaah!" It was a cry of surprise and anger as she put her hand to where the pain was, between her neck and shoulder. Her paddle fell into the current and floated quickly out of reach.

"Meg!" Temperance's voice rang out shrilly over the water.

"Leave her be!" Will said sharply. "If you quit paddling now, we'll all be hit! Hold fast, Meg! We'll get you ashore."

Meg had slumped sideways. The arrow in her neck was now perpendicular, its shaft pointing toward the sky. A dark red stain was beginning to seep through her heavy gray cloak.

"Oh, God! Meg! Meg! Can you hear me? Oh, dear God! Sweet Meg!" Temperance began to babble and sob hysterically, and her paddle hung motionless in the water.

"Temperance!" Will's voice cut through her panic. "Temperance! Put your paddle in the water and pull! Now on the starboard side—the right side! For God's sake—for Meg's sake—pull!"

Will had never stopped paddling, and his long, powerful strokes alone were gradually carrying them farther and farther from the Indians on the riverbank. The canoe, made in the Indian fashion by hollowing and shaping a single tree trunk, was slender but heavy. It took all of Temperance's strength to pull her paddle against the crosscurrent, but fear gave her renewed energy, and behind her was the reassuring sound of Will's voice.

"Just a few more yards, and they can't reach us! Keep it up! A little more, and they can't hit us!" The Indians ashore had realized that, and at last, with a few parting shouts, they put down their bows.

Meg had not made a sound.

"Hold fast, Meg," Will said. "If you can hear me, hold fast. We'll be ashore soon." But the river was carrying them downstream almost as swiftly as they were moving forward. Unless they could make more headway, they would drift broadside into the swift currents at Hog Island, where the risk of capsizing would be great. "Temperance, pull as hard as you can. We've got to reach the shore before Hog Island. Pull!"

"Oh, Will! She can't be dead! She mustn't be dead!" Temperance was still sobbing, but she was paddling steadily.

"She's probably just fainted," Will said, but there was little assurance in his tone. "We'll get her ashore and see."

For nearly a quarter of an hour, they paddled in desperate silence.

Across the brownish-gray expanse of water, they could see the outlines of the pine trees on the western shore of Hog Island. Behind them, two miles to the northwest, lay Jamestown, its position marked by the smoke of early morning fires. It was about two hours past daybreak. Will's plan had been to set out just before dawn in order to round Hog Island, where the river made a sharp right-angle turn, by daylight. Then, for the rest of the fifty miles to Point Comfort, they would travel by night, hugging the shore, and sleep by day to avoid being seen by the Indians. But the Paspaheghs, whose village was the nearest one to Jamestown, had happened to spy the canoe as the sun came up.

"See that tallest grove of trees?" Will said at last. "That will give us cover. Head for it, and we'll beach the canoe right there."

Temperance obeyed silently, and in a few more minutes, she felt the blessed firmness of the sandy riverbank scrape against the canoe. The sudden change in movement caused Meg to stir. She moaned softly, and put one hand around the shaft of the arrow.

"No, no, Meg," Will said gently. "Don't touch it. Leave it alone till we get you ashore, and we'll take care of it." To Temperance, he said, "Go spread a cloak to put her on, and make her a pillow. We need to keep her warm."

Temperance did as she was told. Thank God, she thought, at least they had plenty of clothing with them. Since they had planned to make no fires, they had bundled themselves in layers of all the clothes they possessed. Now Temperance began to tear one of her linen shifts for bandages.

The arrow was imbedded in the large muscles midway between neck and shoulder.

"The first thing we have to do is get it out," Will said. "Thank God it's not deep in, but I wish we had some liquor to give her. It's going to bleed more when I pull the head out, so you'd better get something now to staunch the flow."

Temperance obeyed him silently, like a sleepwalker.

"You hold her shoulder and head steady, and I'll work the arrow," he said. Bending low over Meg, he spoke softly but firmly into her ear. "Meg, can you hear me?"

She stirred again and murmured something they could not catch.

"We're going to take the arrow out, Meg, and it's going to hurt some, but then it'll be over."

The wound was an ugly one after the arrowhead was removed: a large, jagged tear in the flesh of Meg's shoulder. And it had bled profusely. Will and Temperance bound it tightly with strips of soft white Holland linen, and then they made a pallet for Meg and covered her with two heavy blankets. By the time they had finished, the sun had driven away the mist from the river, and the sky was a bright, cloudless blue.

"We'll be safe here for now," Will said. "The Paspaheghs won't bother crossing the river. They were just after us for sport."

They rested until late afternoon, nestled close against Meg to keep her warm. She was now fully conscious and anxious to be off again.

"How long do you think it will take to make Point Comfort now?" Temperance sat up and stretched her aching arms.

"A longer time than if I could help you paddle," Meg said weakly. "I hate being a dead weight."

"You're not dead, thank God," Will said, grinning at her, "and in our present condition, none of us is much of a weight. Don't waste your strength worrying. I reckon to make the north shore again in maybe an hour, and with any luck we can get a good ways downriver before daybreak." He did not say that with any luck the Kecoughtans, whose village they must pass, would not see them. He prayed that his memory of John Smith's map of the river and the bay was accurate, and that there were no more Indian towns close by.

"One more night's travel should put us right," he said with forced cheerfulness, "and then, please God, we'll breakfast on—what do you think—boiled crabs? Cold boiled duck? Baked sturgeon? Captain Davis and his men will give us their best, you can be sure."

"Meanwhile, have some bread," Temperance said. Knowing they could not build any fires on the way for fear of revealing their presence to the Indians, they had brought a meager ration of hard cakes made of ground corn and water. None of them was really hungry; their nerves were stretched too taut for eating. But they made Meg swallow a small portion.

"Tomorrow I'll try to catch us a fish," Will said. "It will be raw, but at least it can soften this stuff." He spoke the last sentence with difficulty, having bitten off a chunk of corn cake.

At last, with Meg tucked into the canoe, wrapped as warmly as they could manage, her head on the small bundle of their extra clothing, they shoved off into the cold, swirling waters of the James. The sun had already dropped behind the pines and oaks to the west, leaving only a pale pinkish glow to light their way.

"Once we are free of the shallows, we have got to paddle for dear life while we're close to the north shore, because if we don't get back across now, we'll end up in the mouth of the Nansemond River," Will said. He did not say that there the James grew much wider and deeper as it neared the Bay of Chesapeake, and that a heavily laden dugout canoe could easily be swept out into the bay itself. Not only that, but the Chesepian Indians, who lived on the south shore near Cape Henry, might not welcome visitors. Apprehension lay on him like a lead weight. What in God's name had possessed him, to think that he could take two women, one of them two months with child—and the other one now wounded and helpless—through a wilderness inhabited by hostile Indians, and down a river whose treacherous turns and currents he had never traveled? The weather was against them as well. If by some miracle nothing else threatened them, they stood in peril of freezing to death.

But then, watching Temperance in the bow of the canoe, Will felt a wave of affection and admiration for her that warmed him almost as pleasantly as a fire. She was wearing so many clothes she resembled a shapeless bundle, and her hair was hidden beneath a wool hat and an old green shawl she had wrapped around her neck, but he knew her form and face by heart, and he marveled at the force of his love for her. Weak as he was, passion stirred within him as he watched that small, determined figure moving rhythmically forward and backward, paddling just as he told her to. His own shoulders had already begun to ache; what must hers feel like? But she had not uttered one word of complaint.

As soon as they neared the north shoreline, he said, "Ease a bit, Temperance. I'll keep us on course, and you need to rest yourself." She turned to look at him, and his heart gave an odd little hop.

"How was that?" she said. It was so dark he could not see her face, but he could feel that she was smiling. "Another day of this, and I'll be as good as . . . as an Indian."

"I love you," he said.

As the moon came up, they were able to keep a fairly steady course close to the riverbank, and as the moon began to set, just before daybreak, they put in to shore. Cold and exhaustion were beginning to tell. It took every ounce of strength Will had to lift Meg out of the canoe, and for an awful moment he thought that his numbed legs would give way and he would drop her in the icy shallows. She had not complained, either, though he knew from experience how her wound must be paining her. As gently as he could, he laid her on the pallet Temperance had made.

"How much—how much longer is it?" Meg asked. "Can you tell?"

Her eyes, in the pale light of early morning, were two large dark holes. Will touched her cheek, and drew his hand away in fright. Her skin was as icy and waxy as a dead person's. Of course, he thought. It was the cold. He and Temperance had been warmed by their own body heat from the exertions of paddling, but Meg had lain virtually motionless in near-freezing temperatures for nearly half a day. Indians or no Indians, Meg had to have a fire.

"Oh, not long," Will said with false optimism. "We must get you warm first, and then we'll set off again and be there soon." He hoped he was not lying. To Temperance, he spoke in a low, worried voice: "Go lie down beside her, and warm her as best you can. I'll look for some wood to build a fire. She's got to have something to warm her."

Temperance's eyes widened. "But what about the Indians? Won't they see the smoke?"

"Not if God is on our side," Will said. "If we don't make a fire, Meg could die of the cold. She hasn't enough blood in her."

With the wood gathered, Will rubbed his hands together, blew on his cold-numbed fingers, and knelt to start the fire. He prayed the spark would catch. The wind from the river was icy; the wood was damp. But he had been lucky to find some dry kindling underneath a fallen tree trunk, and at last, as he spun the small, pointed stick in the hole in the wooden block, a spark did catch, and it fell on a piece of moss, turning it to a golden, glowing thread. Will's breath on it was as light as a baby's breath, and the glow spread to another strand, and then to the end of a twig. An ember dropped to a dry leaf, and the leaf began to burn. The flame spread with maddening slowness, until at last there was a small, bright fire, crackling merrily and giving forth blessed warmth.

It also gave off a plume of gray smoke.

Will, watching the smoke, said wearily, "As soon as we've eaten and rested a little, I think we had best leave. We have sent out a signal that can be seen a good ways off. We'll be safer on the water." They kept the fire long enough to ease the bone-chilling cold in their hands and feet, and to heat some of the murky river water that Temperance had strained through a piece of linen. With bits of camomile from the small store of dried herbs she and Meg had brought with them, she made a fine warm tea, and parceled out the rest of the corn cakes.

"Ah, that will give us the strength to make Point Comfort in no time," Will said as he handed his empty cup to Temperance.

He was wrong.

The pale winter sun was high overhead by the time they pushed off, but the wind was knife-sharp, slashing at faces, making ears ache; the air was so cold it was painful to breathe.

"Meg, you have got to keep awake. If you doze off in this cold, you're done for," Will said, a trace of grim humor in his voice. "And keep wiggling your fingers and toes."

"I will," she said in a small, tired voice. "You two just paddle. Don't worry about me." But they did worry, and twice in the first two hours they put in to shore in order to rub her hands and feet and help her to sit up and move about, to keep the cold at bay. By Will's reckoning, they were about halfway to Point Comfort by midafternoon. The James was wider now, nearly four miles across, and as nearly as he could remember, it stayed that way until just before Point Comfort, where the uneven coast of both shores narrowed its width to just under two miles. They were now near enough to the bay for its tides to slow the river's current, which meant they would travel slower and have to paddle harder against incoming tides. They would also have to travel past the mouth of the Nansemond River, past the land of the hostile Nansemond Indians, where so many of John Martin's men had been killed last September. It would be best to pass Nansemond under cover of darkness, Will thought. But to do that meant that he and Temperance would have to keep paddling the rest of the daylight hours and into the night as well, and they had not slept since the day before. But better to die of cold on the river than in a bonfire in an Indian camp, he thought wearily. And if they put in from time to time to walk about and rest themselves, they might just make it. But at dusk, a cold rain began to fall. In an hour, it had turned to sleet. Like a hail of bullets, the tiny ice pellets rattled against the wooden sides of the canoe.

"Damn!" It was the first word Temperance had spoken in over an hour. "Damnit to hell," she said, without much emotion.

"Temperance, you oughtn't to swear," Meg said. "We ought to be praying."

"Well, you can pray, if you like, while I swear, but I don't think God is listening to either one of us," Temperance said. "Where is He when we need Him?"

"He's here," Meg said. "Aren't we still alive? We must not lose heart."

"I'm not losing heart; I'm losing strength," Temperance said. "Will, can we rest again? Just for a moment? If I can rest my arms just for a little while, I can keep on." She was breathing heavily, and as she spoke, her words came in puffs of steam that hovered and then disappeared in the icy air.

"See that little inlet up ahead, on the port side?" Will said. "Pull for it. We'll stop there. Maybe, with any luck, the sleet will stop, too." He spoke slowly. His lips, his face, his very brain, were numb. His fingers and toes had long since lost feeling; fatigue was the only sensation that kept him aware of his shoulders and arms. If he felt like this, what must Temperance feel? And Meg? And did it matter anymore? He would stop, and then he would keep them going again, for as long as it was humanly possible, but he was fast losing hope of making Point Comfort.

The sleet on the bank grated loudly, like pebbles, against the keel of the canoe as they came ashore, while the sleet that was falling stung their faces.

"Let us take shelter under those pines over there," Will said. "Meg, can you walk if we help you?"

"I think so. I need to move about. My legs are numb," she said gamely. She drew in her breath sharply as Will slipped his arm under her wounded shoulder, but she did not complain. With him on one side and Temperance on the other, half-carrying, half-dragging her, they reached the trees and leaned, all three still entwined, against the largest tree trunk. The ground was too icy to sit upon, and their aching legs needed the stimulation of standing. They clung to each other for a moment in silence. "If you didn't have me," Meg said, "you could go on, and maybe get there. As it is, I'm no use but extra weight in that canoe. And there's the baby to think of. You could leave me here. Nobody'd miss me, and I—I'm so cold already, it wouldn't be long."

"Meg Worley, if you didn't have a wounded shoulder, I'd give you a good shake for talking like that," Will said quietly.

"Damnation, Meg! That's the stupidest thing I've ever heard of! Don't be a goose!" Temperance tightened her arm around Meg's waist.

"Come on," Will said. "We can be there by first light in the morning."

Before dawn, the sleet had turned to snow.

POINT COMFORT
9 March 1610

 Gabriel Morgan, the sentry on watch on the south side of the fort at Point Comfort, stamped his feet and hugged himself. It was late in the season for ice and snow, and four hours of this weather was more than a man ought to take, he thought as he turned the hourglass. Another turn, and he would be drinking hot plum wine and warming his aching fingers and toes over a good roaring fire. He was glad John Smith had sent him down to this fort. Last August, when the *Unity* had arrived with the news that his wife and six-year-old son had died of ship's fever, he had thought his life was over. He had sworn that there was nothing for him in Virginia, but he was wrong. Time had begun to heal his sorrow, and it had not been a bad winter. Forty men in a fairly snug fort, with plenty of fish and crabs, an occasional rabbit or squirrel or duck, and the hogs they had brought down from Hog Island, had had nothing but boredom to complain of. The Indians, perhaps wishing to avoid the cold winds that blew constantly around the point, had apparently retreated to their winter villages by late November. Standing watch had become an unexciting chore.

Gabriel decided he would round his side of the palisade once more, and signal to Richard Waldo, his companion at watch on the north side, that all was well. As he peered through the flurries of falling snow, looking toward the point of land where the James River met the Bay of Chesapeake, he thought he saw something move in a small grove of pine trees between the fort and the shore. Seizing his matchlock musket, he propped its long barrel on the edge of the lookout tower's wall, made sure the match was burning in case he needed to fire, and waited. Blinking the snowflakes off his eyelashes, he saw now that the moving object was the figure of a man—not an Indian, but a tall man heavily clad and stumbling through the snow like someone drunk. As Gabriel watched, the man staggered once, twice, and then fell face forward in the snow. Leaning his musket against the wall, Gabriel Morgan ran along the platform to the north corner and called to his fellow sentry. "Waldo! Come see! There's a man fallen down by the shore!"

"What if it's the Indians laying a trap for us?" Waldo asked warily.

"Not likely in this cold. No, near as I could tell, this is some Englishman. Maybe some of them at Jamestown. What he's doing here, I don't know, but we'd best bring him in before he freezes." Together they slid back the heavy wooden bolt of the palisade gate and hurried outside, their boots sinking at every step in the new-fallen snow. "God Almighty! Look how thin he is. He looks like a skeleton!" Gabriel said as they turned the man over.

"Is he dead?" Waldo asked.

"No, he's breathing, see? I think he's just fainted. Let's get him inside. He won't be heavy." Morgan motioned for Waldo to take the man's feet, while he slipped his arms under the shoulders. "This fellow needs a fire, and something warm inside him," Gabriel said as they laid their burden down inside the gate. "We'd better rouse Captain Davis."

As he spoke, the man on the ground stirred. "The women," he murmured weakly. "Get the women . . . in the canoe . . . cold. So cold." Then he lost consciousness again.

"What's he saying?" Waldo's voice was incredulous. "What women?"

"I don't know," Gabriel said, "but we'd better look to it. You go and rouse the captain and bring some help, and I'll go see what this fellow's talking about. And hurry, man, hurry!"

Following the unknown visitor's tracks through the snow, Morgan found the beached canoe, and in it, what appeared at first to be a pile of clothing that the snow had already coated with white. He lifted a cloak, and then stood looking down for a moment, dumbfounded. Two women, unconscious and barely breathing, their arms around each other, were lying in the bottom of the canoe.

He ran back to the palisade as fast as he could through the snow, shouting all the way.

POINT COMFORT
19 May 1610

"Temperance, I swear you are getting fat." Will eyed her thickened waist and her abdomen, rounded by four months of pregnancy. "I don't believe that's a baby; it's just boiled crabs and roast pork." He spoke teasingly, leaning over to caress the bulge at her middle. She had given up wearing bodice stays and stomacher, and the laces of her kirtle were tied high up, almost under her breasts, instead of at her waist. Petticoats would no longer fasten, and she wore only a white smock under the open bodice and skirt.

"You'll see when the time comes," she said, looking down. "If I'm showing this much now, what will I look like in five more months?"

Will laughed. "It's a good thing Captain Davis married us as soon as he did, Mistress Sterling."

"That's a boy, for sure," Meg said. "And a good-sized one, like his father."

She smiled at Will, who, like Temperance, had filled out in the two and a half months since their arrival at Point Comfort. Recovered at last from the wound in her shoulder, Meg herself had begun to put on weight.

Captain James Davis and the other men at the fort had outdone themselves in providing food for their unexpected guests. Rich hot broth at first, when all three had been too weak and malnourished to digest much else; then boiled crabs, baked rockfish, roast goose and duck, and thick slabs of sizzling pork, cakes made from Indian corn, and, with the coming of warmer weather, tender young greens—wild mustard and sallet—gathered in the forest. Later, there would be mulberries and blackberries and plums.

The fragile white blossoms of the wild plum trees were just beginning to open, and memories of the nightmarish winter at Jamestown were fading. As springtime bloomed, Temperance and Meg and Will tried not to think of the plight of those they had left behind.

Then, on May 20, George Percy arrived. Recovered from his malaria, he had found the strength to drift downriver in a dugout canoe like the one

Will and Temperance and Meg had used. He had surprised the noon watch and come ashore, his long nose quivering with outrage to see the well-nourished condition of the men at the fort and the three fugitives from Jamestown. "What in God's holy name did you think to do here, when we are starving at Jamestown?" He had railed and raged, and nothing Captain Davis or the others could say would assuage his anger. "You feed crabmeat to your hogs, while we fight over a few kernels of corn! Were it not for a few wild mushrooms and spring greens, we'd be dead! God in heaven, Davis, did you never think to come and see what was happening at Jamestown? And you, Master Sterling, and Mistress Yardley, I mean, *Sterling*"—he corrected himself with a sneer—"and Mistress Worley! You three who left against orders! Thought just to save yourselves, didn't you?" He would not be mollified, though Captain Davis tried to explain that Point Comfort's crabs could not feed all of Jamestown. "No! You thought to feed yourselves fat this winter and all of you set sail for England without us, didn't you?" Without pausing for breath, he continued, "Well, Captain Davis, I intend to commandeer one of your pinnaces and enough men to sail her, and head upriver at once. I'll bring half my poor Jamestown people down here, and then I'll go back for the rest!"

"But you don't mean to abandon Jamestown?" Captain Davis said. "Not leave our only town to the savages, surely?"

"Towns and forts can be built with ease," Percy said dramatically, "but men's lives, once lost, cannot be so easily recovered."

"As you wish, President Percy." Captain James Davis bowed before his superior, and gave orders for the *Virginia* to be made ready to sail the next day.

"Let us go for a walk," Will said that next morning after he and Temperance had finished eating. They had dined comfortably on corn mush and boiled pork, and now the warm May morning beckoned them out of doors. "It looks a bit like rain, but not for a while yet. We can walk down to the shore and back by that time."

Outside, a gentle breeze carried the fragrance of pine needles mixed with the sweet, spicy smell of wild plum blossoms in a grove just east of the fort. There had been no sign of Indians on the point since winter, but Will wore a long-barreled French pistol tucked in his belt just the same. No one went outside the fort unarmed.

When they reached the shore, Temperance took off her shoes and went barefoot in the soft sand.

"If my boots weren't so hard to get off and on, I'd do that very thing,"

Will said, amused. "But you'd best put them on again. Look at the sky behind you."

The morning sky, which had only suggested rain, now declared it ominously. The sun had disappeared, and a line of black clouds was moving inland toward Point Comfort from Cape Charles and Cape Henry, the two points of land that marked the entrance to Chesapeake Bay. The wind from the bay whipped Temperance's loose white smock against her body, revealing her swelling breasts and her rounded abdomen, and billowing the edges of her green kirtle behind her like a ship's sail. She had pulled off her cap and unfastened her hair, and it streamed behind her like a red-gold banner. Will thought she had never been more beautiful.

As he watched her, silhouetted against the sea and sky, something on the far horizon caught his eye. Squinting, he could just make out two infinitesimal dots on the line where water met air. They were almost centered between Cape Henry and Cape Charles.

"Temperance," he said, his voice trembling with excitement, "look out there! I see two ships!" Taking her by the shoulders, he turned her toward the entrance to the bay and pointed. "Look out there. Do you see what I see?"

"God in heaven! Maybe it's the spring supply! Let's go tell the others!"

"No. Wait and see if they are really entering the bay. They could be Spanish ships just passing by, and we ought not to raise a false alarm. Come sit down, and I'll help you put your shoes on."

But the two dots on the horizon gradually grew larger and larger, and it was clear they were moving into the bay itself.

"It has to be the supply," Will said happily. "Let us go tell Captain Davis to make ready." In an hour, the two ships had reached the entrance to the bay, but they were still too far away to identify. Captain Davis ordered his men to prepare to fire the fort's cannon when the vessels entered the bay. Then every man was to don his armor and have his weapon—pike or musket—at the ready.

"If they are Spanish, and we fire the cannon, they'll think twice about coming ashore, knowing we are armed and waiting. We won't be caught unawares," he said. By noon the two ships, a large pinnace and a smaller one half its size, had furled their sails and dropped anchor off the point. They were unquestionably English: From the top mast of the larger vessel fluttered the red-and-white Cross of St. George. On shore, the entire company of forty men at Point Comfort, Captain Davis, President Percy, and Will, Temperance, and Meg were all assembled outside the main gate, waiting to see who the visitors were, hoping the rain would hold off a little longer.

"Those are both pinnaces. Neither of them is big enough to be a supply ship," Captain Davis said, squinting through his spyglass. "But they are English, that's plain enough, and heavily freighted. Look how low in the water they draw. I can see people all over their decks, fore and aft." As Davis spoke, thunder rolled threateningly in the distance. The sky had grown unnaturally dark, and the bay was filled with white-capped waves.

"This is going to be a hard blow," Gabriel Morgan, who was Davis's lieutenant, said anxiously. "They may decide to hold off and wait to come ashore till it passes." But they did not. The small assembly at the fort watched in growing excitement as sailors on the larger of the two pinnaces made ready the longboat that trailed at its stern, and as six men clambered down into it and took up their oars. At last, four other figures climbed down into the boat, and it began to move slowly through the choppy waters of the bay. As the boat drew near the shore, it was possible to see that the four passengers were persons of some importance: One of them wore a brigantine ornamented with silver studs; two others had blued and gilded breastplates; the last, a shiny black corselet. All of them wore the ornately decorated steel helmets of military officers.

"Go down." Davis motioned to four of his men. "Help them ashore and make fast their boat." He drew himself up, straightened his helmet, and, with one hand on his sword, struck a dignified pose at the head of the path leading to the water. As the commanding officer at Point Comfort, he would let the visitors come to him. Soon the four men from the boat were climbing the steep path to where Davis and the assembled crowd awaited them. Temperance and Will, by virtue of having been the first to see the ships, stood to one side of Captain Davis and his officers, with Meg just behind them.

"Who do you suppose it is?" Temperance said. Holding Will's hand, she was so excited she could hardly keep still. These people were not bringing supplies, but they would bring news of England, perhaps of Norfolk, of home.

"I don't know, love, but we'll soon find out," Will said indulgently, grinning down at her. He was as excited as she.

From the top of the path, it was impossible to see the visitors' faces under the steel brims of their helmets. The two in the blue-and-gilt breastplates led the way, followed by the one wearing the silver-studded brigantine. He was the tallest. Behind him, the one in the black corselet, slightly shorter and stockier than the rest, walked quickly to keep pace.

Something about that walk caught Temperance's attention: a certain determined set of the shoulders, a hint of a swagger—her heart turned over, and her fingers tightened around Will's hand.

"What is it?" he said.

But Temperance, her eyes on the approaching visitors, did not hear him. Every ounce of her being was concentrated on her recognition of that figure in the black steel corselet and helmet. When at last he raised his head so she could see his face, she caught her breath so sharply that it hurt, and she felt she might suffocate. That face, the sea in the background, the grassy path in the foreground, all swam before her eyes.

The man in the black helmet was George Yardley.

Temperance was vaguely aware that Will's fingers suddenly gripped hers like a vise. "Good God," he said. His lips did not move, and his voice was so low that no one but Temperance heard it. "Good God."

No, Temperance thought wildly, God is not good. Not now. Frozen in disbelief, she and Will stood as if turned to stone, waiting. Soon George could not help but see them. For the moment, however, his eyes were on the man in front of him, who was now being presented to Captain Davis and President Percy as Sir Thomas Gates, the long-lost deputy governor of the Virginia colony. The men with him were Admiral Sir George Somers, and Captain Christopher Newport, and all were engaged in telling how they had survived for the past ten months on the island of Bermuda, and had built their two small ships—the *Deliverance* and the *Patience*—mostly from the wreckage of the *Sea Venture.* There was much laughter and slapping of backs, and at last the group began to walk toward the rest of the waiting crowd. It was then that George, glancing over the expectant faces, spied Temperance.

At first disbelief, then amazement, and finally a dawning of transcendent, unutterable joy were by turns reflected in his face. "Temperance! Temperance! Oh, dear God! Temperance!" George began to run toward her, his soldier's bandolier rattling against his armor, his sword clanking at his side. "It is you! I can't believe it's you! Oh, Temperance, thank God! How did—" George stopped not ten feet from her. His eyes were on her thickened waist, her rounded abdomen. Amid the hubbub of voices, his sudden silence was louder and more painful than any words he could have spoken. It hung between him and Temperance like an invisible curtain, and for a long, long moment, neither dared to pierce it. George took a halting step closer. His eyes, which had not left Temperance's figure, now traveled slowly, reluctantly to her face, and then he saw Will, standing behind her. He looked from one to the other with an expression of desperate pleading, as though begging them for a word of denial, a phrase or two that would restore all to rightful order and return the three of them to their proper places.

"Oh, George," Temperance said at last. "We . . . thought you were dead."

"I wish I were," he said numbly, his eyes on her protruding abdomen. "I wish to God I were."

"No," Will said. "It is I who should wish that."

"You!" Never had grief and rage mingled so in one word, one single syllable. "I ought to call you out and kill you myself, but—" Here George glanced again at Temperance and then continued, his voice shaking with cold fury, "But that would leave your child a fatherless bastard, wouldn't it?"

His words struck Temperance like blows. Her head was spinning, her ears were ringing, and she felt faint. "Oh, George—" She longed to answer him with something that would ease their pain, but she could not. Never, never in her life had she been in a situation so sadly irrevocable, so awful that words had no power over it. She swayed slightly, and Will put his arm around her.

Behind George, Sir Thomas Gates, Captain Davis, and the others had tactfully moved some distance away during his meeting with Temperance, and now they were walking rapidly toward the main building at the fort. Meg had also separated herself from them. A few large drops of rain spattered down. The rainstorm, which had threatened all morning, chose midday for its arrival. A jagged streak of lightning danced in the sky over Cape Henry; a clap of thunder boomed and seemed to roll across the bay; and then the rain, cold sheets of water driven by the wind, reached the shore. At the top of the grassy bank, George, Temperance, and Will stood very still. The rain splashed and dripped off the rim of George's helmet and washed, like tears, across the faces of Temperance and Will. For a long moment, no one moved. Then, slowly, silently, like sleepwalkers, the three began to make their way toward shelter. Below them, the *Deliverance* and the *Patience* were straining at anchor in the churning waters of Chesapeake Bay.

3

INDIAN SUMMERS

■

1610–1614

*The Salvages be nott Soe Simple as
many Imagin. . . .*

—*George Percy,*
'Trewe Relacyon" (1612)

JAMESTOWN
26 May 1610

"Oh, God, our heavenly father, help us to be of good heart and strong faith, as we find all things in this land so contrary to our expectations." The Reverend Richard Buck's words echoed hollowly in the meetinghouse. In the front row, George Yardley bowed his head even lower and closed his eyes tightly. So contrary to our expectations. So contrary, he thought numbly. Inside his eyelids, the image of Temperance, her belly large with Will's child, kept reappearing, no matter how hard he tried to blot it out.

Reverend Buck continued, "As we find nothing but misery and misgovernment here, give us wisdom to find the right course, and the courage to pursue it. Help us to trust in Thy divine providence in this time of trouble. In Jesus' name, Amen."

They had found conditions at Jamestown even worse than Percy had described them. Only sixty people—forty-three men and boys, seventeen women and girls—were now alive. About forty of them, all who were well enough to walk, had come down to the water's edge to greet the *Patience* and the *Deliverance* two days ago. A pitiful gathering of gaunt, hollow-eyed scarecrows, they had clapped their hands and shouted at the sight of the ships.

"Thank God Almighty!"

"Providence has preserved us!"

"Food! Decent food! They're bound to have some!"

"What have you got to eat?"

The people on the shore crowded close to the water's edge, as though they would leap aboard the ships and search out the food. On the main deck of the *Deliverance,* Deputy Governor Gates, President Percy, and Captain Newport held a grim-faced conference, and then sent for Admiral Somers from the *Patience.* Expecting to find a flourishing settlement at Jamestown, the voyagers from Bermuda had brought barely enough provisions to last the journey, and most of that was now consumed.

"We cannot feed these people!"

Gates was furious with Percy, whose obsequious apologies for conditions in the colony had enraged him and irritated even the cheerful Somers.

"With our hundred and forty, that's two hundred mouths to feed. And you've got no corn in your storehouse, and none planted." Somers began to pace up and down.

"I've told you, we couldn't plant," Percy said defensively. "The Indians would have killed every man outside the palisade. And even if there had been no Indians, we had no able-bodied men, none well enough to plow and sow."

"There is no excuse for this," Newport said. "No excuse."

"There is only one thing to be done," Somers said in a conciliatory tone. "I'll go back to Bermuda and freight the *Deliverance* with hogs and turtles and garden stock. There's food aplenty there."

"But you might not get back in time," Newport said. "These people need food right now."

"We need to weigh this matter carefully," Gates said. "Let us go ashore, and then decide." But it was not easy to reach an agreement. Percy and the other surviving Council members, John Martin and Nathaniel Causey, were for moving down to Point Comfort; Gates and Somers and Newport wanted to make for England with what meager supplies remained.

As the prayer service was ending, Thomas Gates spoke in a low voice to George. "Come with us afterward. Somers and Newport and I are going to inspect the whole palisade, to take a final account of what's here—food, weapons, and so on—and then decide what to do. We'll get nowhere with Percy and the others in our way."

George nodded. He was grateful for something to do. During the prayer service, he had moved his lips and heard his own voice among all the others, but he did not feel any better for having prayed. Since the day of his arrival in Virginia, he had not really felt anything. A terrible deadness of body and spirit had settled on him, and he was unable to think beyond the immediate moment. Gates and Somers and the others had been especially kind to him, but their pity only made his pain worse.

William Strachey had something more practical to offer. "You can have the marriage dissolved," he said, "and then you must try to forget her. I know it's nigh impossible for you to think of that now, but you must. You're a young man, with plenty of time to start over. Fate has played you a cruel trick, that's all."

But George did not want to start over. He wanted Temperance, and if he could not have her, he wished her dead. So many people had died since this ill-starred venture began, he thought, why couldn't she and Will have been among them? Or better still, perhaps, if he himself had been among them. Then he would not have had to witness William Pierce's joyous reunion with his wife and daughter. At least he had been able to leave Temperance and Will behind at Point Comfort. "From this time on," he had said to Temperance, "you are dead to me. And you, too," he said to Will. "I shall never speak your names again, nor come where you are." But as long as he remained in Virginia as the captain of the deputy governor's guards, there was that risk. Temperance and Will intended to stay at Point Comfort, but if Gates decided to abandon the colony and leave for England, they would have to sail with all the others. If that should happen, he would ask Gates to see that Temperance and Will were not aboard the same ship with him. In the meantime, he would do his best to serve Deputy Governor Gates well. His work, his hope for advancement, were all he had left, and there was plenty of work to be done at Jamestown.

Outside the meetinghouse, the warm May sun shone on a scene that would have been better left in darkness: the once-neat triangle of houses had great gaps in it where houses had been pulled down, dismantled for firewood by people too weak or sick or frightened to cut wood outside the fort. At the ends of these snaggletoothed, desolate rows of houses, the pits they had dug for human waste lay uncovered and stinking under clouds of flies. The flimsy twig fences that once enclosed garden plots had fallen down; ground that last year held herbs and vegetables and even a few flowers here and there had all gone to weeds. Some of the grass was as high as a man's waist.

And in the storehouse, Percy's rationing and the sadly reduced population of the fort had left four remaining bags of grain.

"Great God! That's starvation fare, for sure!" Admiral Somers, peering into the gloomy, vacant interior of the storehouse, swore under his breath. "We've got to get some victuals here, somehow!"

"I know," Gates said. "They've got next to nothing, and not even any nets to fish with. The damned fools let them all rot."

Christopher Newport, who had brought the first supply of colonists to Virginia in 1607, kept silent and merely shook his head sorrowfully. "John Smith is a hothead, but he would never have let things come to this. Virginia lost a good man the day he left."

"It's the damnedest thing I ever witnessed," Somers said angrily. "Percy and the others must bear the blame for what has happened here. I'd like to hold a martial court for the lot of them!"

"No," Gates said thoughtfully. "For the Virginia Company's sake we cannot afford that. But we need to make our own judgment of what must be done, independently of them. I am governor now, and we can ignore George Percy. I told him and the others we would take counsel with them later, in their houses."

"Such houses as they are," Somers said.

George, walking behind Gates and Somers, wondered which house had belonged to Temperance and Will. As he strolled along, he tried to imagine their conversations, their kisses, their couplings. He failed to answer when Gates spoke to him.

"Yardley!" The raspy voice was impatient at having to repeat itself. "Yardley!"

"Aye, sir!" George came to, suddenly. "Sorry, sir! What is it?"

"Go back to the ships. Take some of your men with you, and have them count up just exactly how much food and what kind is there. Every bag of peas, every barrel of pork, and so on aboard both vessels. You may report to me at noon, in front of the meetinghouse."

"Aye, sir."

The *Deliverance* and the *Patience* between them had, by the most accurate and careful count that Captain Yardley and his men could muster, no more than ten days' provisions. And so the deliberations began again in earnest, with Gates and Somers and Newport in favor of abandoning the colony, and Percy and Martin and Causey for moving downriver and living on crabs and sturgeon until the next planting season. But the 140 Bermuda refugees, weary of deprivation and having no settled place, wanted to make for England at once.

The sixty Jamestown survivors were divided in their opinions, some feeling that they had invested so much suffering in this venture they wanted to stay no matter what, and some, mainly the sick, wanting to set sail for England immediately.

One of the sick was Tom Dalton, the butcher, who had managed to survive the Starving Time only to lose his mind. He had gone violently mad in March, and had been tied to a post in a house at the far end of the palisade for three months. But on the fourth day after the Gates expedition arrived, Tom Dalton broke out of the house where he had been confined and ran naked into the center of the palisade during the midday rest time.

"There is no God!" he shouted hoarsely, and people poked their heads out of their houses to see who it was. When the Jamestown settlers saw, they merely shook their heads.

"There is no God! He has left us here to starve!" Dalton shook a bony fist at the sky. "There is no God, or He would not have left us to starve! We have prayed, and He has not heard us!" The noonday sun beat down on Dalton's pale, thin body, and he stood like a grotesque statue in the center of the palisade until John Short came to fetch him. But Dalton would not be moved, and finally Short had to promise him a walk to look for food outside the palisade. They went out the gate and turned north toward the woods behind the fort, but at dark they had not come back. The next morning a search party ventured out to look for them, and found them about two hundred yards from the fort. Both had been slain by Indian arrows.

WEROWOCOMOCO
1 June 1610

 "I shot two of them in the woods outside the fort yesterday, and one of them was naked as a baby. His penis was the size of a baby's, too—no bigger than that." Nemattonow waggled the first two joints of his index finger contemptuously. "Do all Englishmen have so little between their legs? Is that why they wear so many garments, to cover their shame?" Opechancanough's son laughed at his own wit.

"No. And if I were you, I would not make fun of the Englishmen's parts," Opechancanough said quietly. Nemattonow, twenty-nine this year, had yet to get a woman with child. He was strong and well featured, but no woman had ever carried his seed. Opechancanough had a passionate longing for a grandchild.

Nemattonow chose to ignore his father's barb. "The English who came upriver in the two ships seem uncertain whether they will go or stay," he said. "They do not live inside the fort, but stay mostly on their ships "

"That may mean they wish to depart soon." Wahunsonacock, who had invited Opechancanough and Nemattonow to his lodge to discuss the arrival of the newcomers, spoke thoughtfully. "Maybe the others will go with them. What do you think, my brother?"

Opechancanough finished anointing his arms with bear grease, and handed the earthen pot to Nemattonow, who began to grease himself. The oily stuff kept off the May flies and mosquitoes that swarmed along the river. "I think that we should watch and be patient a little longer." Turning to his son, Opechancanough continued, "Do not waste any more arrows on the English at Jamestown until we see what they intend to do."

"But now that the days are long and the weather is warm, I can guard the fort easily. With one or two good men, I could keep the Englishmen trapped inside their walls like raccoons." Nemattonow rubbed his hands in gleeful anticipation. He was in a good mood, no matter what his father said. He knew that he was the best hunter of all the men in his father's tribe, and perhaps in his uncle's as well. He had recently brought down not one, but two of the great white swans that flew north from the Chesapeake every spring. He had caught them, one after the other, in midflight with two well-placed arrows—a thing no one had ever done before. He had saved their magnificent wings, and was fashioning a headdress and a cape of swan feathers.

"There is no need to watch the Jamestown fort so closely," Opechancanough said. "They cannot stay long without food. What little corn they had stored must be all gone by now. I think they will leave before the next new moon."

"Then you have no need of me now," Nemattanow said. "If you do not wish me to watch over the English for a while, may I go?"

"Why? Will you not stay and eat with us?" Wahunsonacock asked. Winganuske and Matachanna have roasted fish and smoked oysters all morning."

"Thank you," Nemattonow said, "but I have . . . things to do."

"When shall I see you again?" Opechancanough looked vaguely distressed.

"By the next new moon, when you say the English will leave," Nemattonow said respectfully. "If they are not gone then, I shall come and do with them whatever you wish. Until then, I shall be at Paspahegh."

"Paspahegh?" Opechancanough was puzzled.

"I have friends there. They expect me." With that, Nemattonow bowed to his father and his uncle, and strode off through the forest toward the river.

"He will not reach Paspahegh until well after dark," Wahunsonacock said. "Perhaps I should have asked him to stay here until tomorrow. He is a fine young man." He smiled at Opechancanough.

"So is Tanx-Powhatan. Your son has two wives, and he will soon have a family," Opechancanough said wistfully.

"But then there are my younger ones," Wahunsonacock said. "I hope that Munto and Wintako will grow up to be as good with their bows and arrows as Nemattonow."

"Yes," Opechancanough said absently.

"We can only hope our children live up to our expectations: good hunters, good mothers, what more can one ask of sons and daughters?" Wahunsonacock paused, and, receiving no reply, went on, "You should be proud of your son. When is he going to give you a grandson?"

"I don't know. He has no women," Opechancanough said. "He is all I have, but I do not always know what is in his mind."

"Nor do I, in Pocahontas's mind," Wahunsonacock said sadly.

"What do you hear from her in the village of the Potomacs?"

"Nothing. She has sworn she will not speak to me as long as she lives." Opechancanough did not comment.

"I did wrong, sending her so far away."

"You did what you believed was right," Opechancanough said at last. "Give her time. She will change her mind."

"I hope so. But Opossunoquonuske hears from her cousin Iapazeus that Pocahontas has renounced me." Wahunsonacock sighed deeply. "Opossunoquonuske brought her three little ones here when she came, and to see them made me sad. Two handsome boys, five and four years old, and a girl just turned two. And their father dead, killed by the English. Opossunoquonuske vows she will have revenge. I do not blame her. She says our killing one Englishman here, one Englishman there is not enough for her. I agree."

"Tell her to wait," Opechancanough said softly. "Tell her she must be patient."

But Wahunsonacock, gazing at the cloud-flecked June sky, was not listening. "Her little girl has hair braided the way Pocahontas's used to be," he said. He looked at his brother and shook his head. "If these English had not come, Pocahontas would not have been banished, and Opossunoquonuske's children would have a father. And if those other English had not come, our firstborn children and many others would not have died of white men's diseases, and you and I would have many grandchildren. I say it is time to strike."

JAMESTOWN
6 June 1610

In twenty iron pots, chunks of brine-soaked pork from the *Sea Venture*'s stores boiled and bubbled in their own savory juices; among the ashes of a dozen fires, cakes made with the last of Jamestown's corn were baking. To the sixty survivors of the Starving Time, as they had begun to call it, the mere aroma of meat cooking was enough to make them weep for joy. To the 140 new arrivals from Bermuda, weary from two weeks at sea in the cramped quarters of the *Patience* and the *Deliverance,* this communal meal that Sir Thomas Gates had ordered was a welcome respite between voyages.

Tomorrow at dawn they would set sail for England and leave Jamestown to the Indians. Deputy Governor Gates, after much deliberation with Admiral Somers and Captain Newport, had decided the only course open to them was to abandon the colony and make for Newfoundland, where the summer fishing fleet would be in, and where they might provision their ships or find passage back to England. To cheer the voyagers from Bermuda and to nourish the nearly-starved residents of Jamestown, Gates and Somers had decided to share part of their remaining provisions in as decent a feast as the women could prepare.

There were now twenty-two women at Jamestown, the ten who had come from Bermuda, and the twelve who had managed to live through the winter inside the palisade. Of those, only six—Thomasine Causey, Lucy Forrest, Ann Laydon, Isabella Atkins, Joan Pierce, and Phyllis Murphy—were able to help the newcomers with the preparation of the last dinner they would eat at Jamestown. The others, suffering from malnutrition, fever, or chronic dysentery, would have to have their food brought to them, and one or two would have to be fed.

One other female at Jamestown had to be fed, but not because she was sick: The Laydons' ten-week-old daughter Virginia suckled hungrily at her mother's breast. Ann Laydon sat nursing her on a bench, watching the other women cook. On this warm June day, they had built all the fires together outside, in the center of the palisade, partly to celebrate this meal and partly so that the cooks could be together.

Lucy Forrest, godmother to the Laydons' infant, sat down beside Ann and caressed the baby's tiny head as she nursed. "She grows bigger by the minute, I swear," Lucy said. "Thank God she's healthy. That was a miracle, that you carried her nine months and delivered her safe."

Ann, who had turned sixteen the day after her daughter was born, smiled and shifted little Virginia to her other breast. "I reckon it was," she said. Her happiness showed in her face.

"Same as it was a miracle that Joan and her husband found each other again, alive and well," Thomasine said. She glanced about her to see who was listening before she spoke again. "I don't see how fate could be so cruel to Temperance and George. They say that when he arrived and saw her with Will, he went off and sat on a rock by himself for a whole day, looking out at the bay and not speaking a word."

Nearby, Jane Wright bent over a fire to turn corn cakes and said nothing. She had tried to comfort Captain Yardley that day he saw his wife at Point Comfort, but he had spoken sharply to her and sent her away.

"George was so taken with our baby." Gwendolyn Rolfe, who had buried her newborn daughter in Bermuda, looked wistfully at little Virginia Laydon, now asleep in her cradle. Tenderly, she touched the baby's cheek, and when the tiny pink mouth opened and yawned, Gwendolyn lowered her head and began to sob.

"When our baby died, George Yardley put white lilies all over her grave. Such a tiny mound of earth it was."

Lucy put her arms around Gwendolyn. "Don't cry. At least you had her for a little while, and you'll have others. I've been married for three years, and I don't even have one to mourn."

"That is just as well, Lucy," Thomasine said. "We'd not want children born in this godforsaken place if we could help it. I, for one, can hardly wait to get aboard that ship in the morning."

Shortly after sunrise the next morning, Sir Thomas Gates gave final instructions to George Yardley. "You and I will be the last aboard. I want to make certain those damned fools don't try to set fire to this place as they leave." Gates spat the words through clenched teeth. The abandonment of Jamestown had drawn to the surface all the festering ill will among present and former leaders, and every decision brought forth bitter arguments. Percy and Martin had stoutly maintained that the palisade and all its buildings should be razed when the colonists departed.

"Why give these damned savages the pleasure of taking over a town? That is exactly what they will do, the moment we are gone. I know them," Percy said.

"And if they don't take it, the Spanish will. You are leaving a stout fort and three well-armed cannons to our enemies," said Martin.

"No," Gates had said with a sneer, "I am leaving it for others with cooler heads and stouter hearts to plant an English colony." Now, with a flourish of the cloak he still affected, refusing to believe that a Virginia June was different from an English June, the deputy governor positioned himself at the palisade gate with his captain and a dozen soldiers at his side. Then he nodded to George, who signaled Corporal Timothy Dowse, the drummer, to begin playing. Dowse, nineteen, stood ramrod-straight, looking very solemn, and began to beat a smart tattoo on his snare drum. That was the sign to begin boarding the ships.

Past Dowse and Gates and George and the soldiers, in a long, straggling line, came the survivors of the English settlement at Jamestown, carrying bundles of clothing, lugging chests and boxes. Then came the ones who could not carry anything, but who had to be carried themselves. There were nineteen people, thirteen men and six women, who had to be helped aboard, many of them too ill to walk even the short distance from their beds to the pier. There the *Virginia* and the *Deliverance* rode at anchor, ready to sail. Most of the Bermuda settlers, who had declined to reside in the squalor of the fort, were already aboard. Awaiting the Jamestown colonists were the two smaller pinnaces, the *Patience* and the *Discovery*. In all, two hundred people and all their meager possessions would be stowed aboard these four vessels.

Once under way, they would sail downriver, stopping at Point Comfort to collect Captain Davis and his men at the fort there, and then, wind and tides permitting, they would set their course northward along the coast. If all went according to plan, they would make Newfoundland before their scant food supply ran out. There, with the summer fishing season about to start, they could expect to meet some English vessels. Some of the Jamestown and Bermuda survivors could get passage home aboard them, and the rest could rummage and provision the *Deliverance* and the *Virginia,* and set sail for England before the summer ended.

"I was the first Englishwoman to set foot on this land," said Lucy Forrest, setting down the large wooden box she was carrying, "and I'll be the last one to leave. That's only fitting." With a flounce of her skirts, she sat down on her box and folded her arms. They were thin arms, so thin that the gold bracelet on one wrist slid all the way to her elbow when she raised her arm.

"Lucy, we should get aboard and get out of the way, I think." Her husband, Thomas, his large, bony frame wrapped in a blanket and shaking with an attack of the fever he had had since April, stopped beside her.

"No," she said resolutely. "No, I want to be the last. Ann Laydon's already aboard the *Virginia* with John and the baby, or I'd get her to wait with me. She and I were here from the first, and we ought to be here at the last. I want to tell my children that, if I ever have any."

Thomas Forrest, too ill and weak to argue with her, sat down beside his wife.

Past them went the rest of the Jamestown survivors, among them Thomasine and Nathaniel Causey, carrying between them a large brass-bound chest with all the clothing Thomasine had refused to leave behind, and Edward Brinton, being carried with difficulty by Richard Pace and Harmon Harison on a makeshift litter. A four-day spell of dysentery had left Jamestown's stonemason and erstwhile minister too weak to walk. Then came a handful of *Sea Venture* survivors, many of whom had been complaining loudly that they would prefer to return to Bermuda. John and Gwendolyn Rolfe walked arm in arm, Gwendolyn looking pale and leaning heavily on her husband. "John, do you know it will be a year tomorrow since we left England? We keep sailing, and sailing, and never staying anywhere," she said wistfully. "I want to go home."

There were many like Gwendolyn Rolfe who had had enough of colonizing, but there were a few who still kept a cheerful face. Young Ralph Hamor, who had had more adventure than he had ever dreamed of when he sailed out of Falmouth last year, stepped smartly along, eager for more. Thomas and Elizabeth Powell, who had celebrated their wedding in Bermuda, looked happy to be leaving Virginia.

Then George Percy and John Martin marched stiffly past, looking neither right nor left.

"You will regret what you've done this day, Thomas Gates!" Percy, on reaching the pier, hurled the words back at Gates in the manner of one pronouncing a curse. Gates did not respond.

"Burying the cannons is not enough." John Martin, like Percy a veteran of the Indian wars, spoke with grim conviction as he climbed aboard the *Discovery.*

"These savages are clever enough to dig them up and learn to use them somehow, and with Jamestown left standing, they have a ready-made fortress to guard the river."

Gates had ordered the fort's three cannons buried in the soft earth just inside the gate. As soon as everyone was safely aboard and the four small ships were hauling up their anchors, he instructed Captain Yardley to have his men aboard the *Deliverance* fire a parting volley.

"Matches alight! One end will do." George watched with satisfaction as six of his men prepared their long matchlock muskets. With coals brought up from the ship's galley, each man lighted one end of the saltpeter-soaked cord he used as a match to ignite his powder.

"Pieces charged!" Mechanically, George called out the orders and smiled as the men deftly manipulated their bandoliers, their bullet pouches, and their ramrods. He had trained them well in the long months of enforced idleness in Bermuda, and there was not a man in his company who lacked speed and proficiency in the use of matchlock, pike, and sword.

"Pieces primed!" Powder was poured into flash pans, and six pan covers snapped shut in staccato succession.

"Matches at the ready!"

"Fire!" As the shots shattered the summer morning's peace, Sir Thomas Gates clapped George on the shoulder.

"Well done, and well rid. Now come below and have a beer." Gratefully, George obeyed. He did not care if he ever saw the Virginia coastline again.

By nightfall, they had made Hog Island; and by the next morning, they made Mulberry Island, near Nansemond. There they were forced to drop anchor and wait for the tide to turn.

With their sails neatly furled and their tall masts swaying gently against the clouds, the four ships looked like some species of giant spiked sea turtles floating lazily together in the sun. It was quiet aboard the ships, and many of the passengers, wearied by their early morning leave-taking, had lain down to rest or doze. There was nothing to do until dark, when the tide turned and they could move on downriver to the sea. They would stop briefly to pick up the men with Captain Davis at Point Comfort, and then chart their course for Newfoundland. Above them, a few curious gulls from Chesapeake Bay flapped about, and some came to rest in the ships' riggings.

It was William Strachey, lounging about on the fo'c'sle of the *Deliverance*, who first sighted the longboat.

"A ship! There's a ship!"

Strachey's shout roused a couple of crew members who had been taking their ease in the shadow of the great cabin. It also roused Thomas Gates, who bounded out of his quarters as if he had been shot out by a cannon. "The devil you say! Where?" Gates clambered up the ladder to where Strachey and the two sailors were now standing and pointing. The approaching vessel was barely more than a speck on the horizon, where the wide James River opened even wider to empty into the Chesapeake Bay. At such a distance, the vessel was impossible to identify.

"What do you think she might be?" Strachey asked. "Someone from Point Comfort?" Next to him, George Yardley prayed silently that the ship had nothing to do with Point Comfort: Temperance and Will would not be sailing on the same ship with him, he had already seen to that with Gates, but he did not want to see them at all, if he could help it.

"Damned if I know who it is," Gates said. "With out luck, she'll be some Spaniard out for plunder."

"Well, that's no matter," Strachey said wryly. "We've got naught for her to plunder."

"All the same, it won't hurt to take some precautions," Gates said. "Yardley, have the gunners stand ready."

By this time, some of the people on the *Patience* had also sighted the approaching vessel, and their shouts, ringing out across the water, alerted the *Discovery* and the *Virginia*. For the next hour, all was commotion and speculation, as they watched the ship coming toward them. Muskets were hastily primed, swords buckled on.

"All we need is a fight with a Spaniard."

"Who else could it be?"

"What if it's a supply ship from the Company?"

"They think we've got plenty of supplies. Why would they send one?"

"Maybe it's a Dutchman."

But at last they could see that it was neither a galleon nor a pinnace, but a smaller craft, a longboat with a single spritsail. In her bow, her commanding officer began waving both arms and shouting.

"I come from Lord de la Warr! Is Sir Thomas Gates aboard?"

"Good God!" Aboard the *Deliverance*, Thomas Gates was thunder-struck. "I don't believe it! De la Warr!"

Around him and on the decks of the other three ships arose a hubbub of voices that filled the air like the humming of beehives suddenly disturbed. At last the longboat was close enough to throw a line and make fast, and her commander, one Edward Bruster, captain of Lord de la Warr's guards, came aboard the *Deliverance*. Presenting himself before Deputy Governor Gates, he saluted smartly, and, panting a little from the exertion of climbing aboard, said, "I bring you word from the governor, my Lord. He is here with men and supplies for Jamestown." He held out a canvas-wrapped packet.

With trembling fingers, Gates undid the parcel and extracted a paper, which he scanned with remarkable speed, and then, folding it carefully, tucked it inside his jerkin and looked around him at a sea of anxious faces. "Lord de la Warr is at Point Comfort with near two hundred men and a year's supplies. He sends word we are to hold fast to Jamestown." But Gates's last words were drowned by the cheer that went up at the words "a year's supplies."

"A year's supplies!" The words were repeated, echoing across the water from ship to ship.

"A year's supplies!"

"God be praised!"

"It's a miracle, plain and clear!"

"A year's supplies! They'll have beer!"

"And cheese!"

"And barley, and honey!"

"Thank God we did not burn the fort," said Deputy Governor Gates.

And so, the wind being favorable, they made their way upriver, not down, and were back at Jamestown by nightfall.

Edward Bruster sailed his longboat back to Point Comfort, and two days later, on June 10, Lord de la Warr's three ships dropped anchor at Jamestown. The new governor came ashore, fell to his knees, and, before the assembled company, bowed his head in a long silent prayer. A solemn, frail-looking man with thinning brown hair, Thomas West, Lord de la Warr, looked much older than his thirty-three years. Deputy Governor Gates met him with an honor guard at the south gate. William Strachey, chosen by Gates to carry his colors, bowed low before Lord de la Warr and, with a flourish, let fall the deputy governor's silken banner at the new governor's feet. Thus was the transfer of power effected.

By June 12, Lord de la Warr had moved his supplies into the storehouse, appointed a council, and set up a military command. Thomas Gates was now Lieutenant General Gates, and George Yardley, captain of the lieutenant general's company, now had fifty men under him. Under the firm hand of the twelfth Baron de la Warr, regular meals, orderly government, and a measure of hope returned to Jamestown. All the able-bodied men were set to work rebuilding the fallen-down houses, repairing the palisade gates, mending fishing nets and weirs, and beginning a glassworks and an ironworks. Besides that, two new forts, to be called Fort Henry and Fort Charles after the former and present Princes of Wales, were to be built downriver. It was too late to plant corn, but there was grain enough in the storehouse to feed four hundred people for a year, and Admiral Somers in the *Patience* and Captain Samuel Argall in the *Discovery* set out for Bermuda in mid-June to bring back a cargo of hogs and turtles. Everything was in good order except the Indians.

WARRASKOYACK (Blunt Point) 6 July 1610

Humphrey Blunt had volunteered. As his cries split the air of the calm afternoon, that was the only consolation Lieutenant General Gates and Captain Yardley had.

Approaching Point Comfort in the pinnace *Discovery,* they had found the fort's longboat broken free from its moorings. "Let me go after it," Blunt had said. "I can take the little canoe and catch her, tie her line round my waist, and tow her back in a trice." Small and agile, he had been a waterman on the Thames River when he was twelve.

Now the Indians had him.

A sudden and contrary wind had blown his canoe and the longboat against the sandy riverbank on the Nansemond side, and before he could push off, there was a wild, gleeful shouting from the woods, and nine Indians wearing the heads of bears and foxes ran out. Two of the tallest ones took Humphrey Blunt by the arms and dragged him out of the canoe. On the deck of the ship, Thomas Gates, George Yardley, and the rest of the men could do nothing but watch in horror.

Gates, his knuckles white on the hilt of his sword, cursed himself for letting Blunt go. There was nothing they could do now. By the time they could load and fire a round from the ship's demi-culverins, poor Blunt would be dead and the Indians long gone.

"Shall I order the men to fire, sir?" George asked.

"No. No point wasting powder and shot." Gates pounded both fists helplessly on the *Discovery*'s gunwale. "Save it for later," he said through his teeth.

On the shore, Humphrey Blunt struggled briefly with his captors, but they were too powerful and too many. They dragged him, shouting and swearing, to the edge of the woods and tied him to a tall pine tree. Then, using hatchets traded to them by the English, they began the systematic dismembering of Blunt's body. Grinning, the two warriors who had captured him took hold of his right thumb and his left thumb and, with swift clean strokes, severed both from his hands.

Only then, when he realized what they were about to do, did Blunt begin to scream. His cries, torn from his throat as his parts were torn from his body, rent the air with chilling, sickening repetition. Around him, the Indians began to dance, each one holding up a bloody part of Humphrey Blunt.

"Up anchor!" Thomas Gates said in a choked voice. "We can do nothing here, nothing for him! God rest his soul! Let's get under way." Silently, the men aboard the *Discovery* trimmed her sails and set her course for Point Comfort.

In the clearing in the woods, the Indians, who had chopped off Blunt's fingers, one by one, and then his toes, and then his arms and legs, joint by joint, continued to dance until the Englishmen's ship was out of sight. In a few minutes, all that remained of Humphrey Blunt was a pile of bloody parts in a heap upon the soft green grass. His severed head, with its thick blond hair, they carried away in a deerskin bag.

"Last winter the English cut off the head of Opossunoquonuske's husband," one of the Indians said. "Now we have one of theirs."

POINT COMFORT
8 July 1610

 "Goddamnit, man, you're about to kill the wrong Indians!" Will Sterling, his face white with anger, set his tankard of wine down so hard that some of the dark red liquid spilled over the edge. Across the table from him, George Yardley watched the stain seep into the wooden surface and said nothing. "God knows, I did not mean to come here," Will said in a quieter voice. "But I know those Indians at Kecoughtan, and they are not the ones who killed Humphrey Blunt. Their werowance is Tanx-Powhatan, Powhatan's eldest son, and he is upriver visiting his father. They would never act without him." Will tried to look George in the eye, but the latter turned away. "I know these Indians, and you don't, George. Spilling the wrong blood will not avenge Humphrey Blunt's death, but it will bring Powhatan and his son and all the river tribes down on you. You must make Sir Thomas call off this attack."

"Will, you never did have any stomach for fighting." George's tone had a sarcastic edge. "You should leave that to proper soldiers. I am the captain of Lieutenant General Gates's company, and I take orders from him, not you. I think you had better go now." George set his own tankard down next to Will's, got up from the table, and strode across the room to the window, standing with his back to his visitor. George's stomach was churning and his head had begun to pound. The sight of Will, that fair hair, that familiar face, so dear to him for as long as he could remember, had aroused in him a strange, powerful mingling of murderous intent and deep sadness. He had managed to preserve a cold civility in front of Corporal Dowse when he brought the wine, but it was no good. The men knew. Every soldier in George's company knew that Temperance was his wife. Now, by coming to his quarters, Will had forced him to play a charade in front of his men.

"I am sorry, George." There was quiet resignation in Will's voice. He, too, rose from the table. "I am sorry . . . for everything."

"Pah!" George did not turn around.

"Words cannot help what has happened to you and me, George. You know, and God knows, that neither you nor I nor Temperance meant for this to happen. Believe me, I've anguished over this as much as you."

"Anguish, indeed!" With a snarl, George turned on Will, facing him like an animal about to attack. "You and your pretty ways with words! Anguish! You father a bastard on my wife, and you say you feel anguish!" George's eyes narrowed. His jaw was set, his lips a thin line, his face a map of pain and rage.

"I didn't mean it to sound that way," Will said helplessly. "God help me, George, I've prayed, I've wept, I've tried every waking moment since that day you first came ashore to think what is the right thing to do. And so has Temperance."

"Don't mention her name to me! Not ever, ever again! I don't want to hear it! Not from your lips!"

"It was not her fault," Will said. "Blame me, not her."

"She was a married woman, and she committed adultery." George's voice dropped to a whisper. "She made me a cuckold!" The last word was spat out like poison.

"No!"

"Yes!"

"You're wrong! She'd never have done it, not if it hadn't been for me! I made her pity me, and we—we both thought you were dead, George. Can you not see that?"

"Oh, and that makes it right, does it?"

"No."

They confronted each other in angry silence, each of them breathing heavily, as though he had been running.

"You must not blame Temperance for my sin," Will said softly. "I coveted her, George. I broke the Sixth Commandment. I broke it in my heart the day you married her."

George's eyes widened. "What?"

Will put both hands palm down on the table and leaned on it. "I fell in love with Temperance the day you said your wedding vows. Then, when I thought you were lost at sea, I began to think maybe she could be mine. For a long time, I prayed and prayed, George, but she loved you. I think she still loves you. But last winter we thought we were going to die, and she came to me in despair, not love. I took her in a moment of weakness." Will put his head in his hands.

"It was my fault, George, all my fault!"

All my fault. The words rang in George's ears. A fleeting memory carried him back to Horseshoe Court in Southwark, where two small boys, one fair-haired and one dark, were playing. The fair-haired one had broken the dark-haired one's wooden sword, and he was holding out the two jagged pieces, saying, "It's my fault, George, my fault."

"No, Will. Temperance was a married woman, and I'd not even been gone a year. She could have waited." George almost choked on the last words, and for one terrible moment he thought Will would see him unmanned by tears. *She could have waited.* Dear God, he thought, if only she had. With her at his side, he would be the envy of all his men. Instead, she had made him an object of pity.

"Damnit, George, she didn't know! This has grieved her beyond measure. You must know that. And in her condition—"

"Her condition is none of my concern! What do you expect me to do—forgive you both and be godfather to your bastard?"

Will recoiled as though George had struck him across the face. "No." His lips shaped the word, but no sound emerged. Then, in a whisper, he repeated the word. "No, George, no."

George had turned his back again, and stood looking out the window, his hand resting idly on the hilt of his sword. Will watched him for a minute or two in silence, waiting for him to speak, but he did not. At last, moving quietly, as if not to disturb him, Will turned and walked out the door.

When Will had gone, George suddenly drew his sword, drove it deep into the wattle-and-daub wall of the guardhouse, and leaned against it, sobbing.

THE FALLS, JAMES RIVER
August 1610

"Lord de la Warr wants the Queen burned at the stake."

Captain James Davis, reporting to Lieutenant General George Percy, looked at him with bloodshot eyes. Both men were battle-stained and bone-weary, and neither had slept for more than forty-eight hours.

"Great God! Doesn't he think we've done enough killing for today?" Percy leaned his elbows on the gunwale of the pinnace *Discovery* and put his head in his hands. "I can't do it." He closed his eyes. *Burning at the stake.* In his mind, he saw again the burning of Peter Scott last winter; in his nostrils was the smell of charred human flesh. What did this wilderness do to men, that they did such things to each other?

"We have to do it. He has ordered it." Davis, his nerves still taut from battle, began to pace up and down the deck. From time to time, he glanced nervously at the door to the great cabin, where Thomas West, Lord de la Warr, governor general of Virginia, lay shivering with ague. West had sailed upriver hoping the higher ground and clearer air near the Falls would improve his health. He had not set foot ashore in two weeks, but he had followed Percy's engagement with the Indians and continued to give orders.

"I won't do it!" Percy pounded his fist on the gunwale. "I'm sick to my stomach from killing! I gave in to those bloodthirsty bastards when they wanted to kill the children, and that was enough! God Almighty!" Percy held his head as though it might come apart. He could not get the children out of his mind. There had been three of them—two little boys, no more than four or five years old, and a little girl younger than that. Handsome, they were, with their smooth brown skin and their Indian-black hair. They had been playing, naked in the hot August sun, just outside their house when the attack came. The moment they saw the soldiers, their large dark eyes grew round with fear, and they skittered inside the house like frightened squirrels. When the soldiers threw them into the river, they clung to the men's arms like small wild creatures, scratching and screaming. They had thrashed and splashed about when they hit the water, and so, for sport, three of the soldiers took out their pistols and shot at them. At such close range, the shells blew away parts of the children's skulls, and some of their brain matter came out in the water.

"There's three that won't grow up to make trouble!" one of the soldiers had said.

"That'll teach them a lesson!" said another.

"We got the girl, too. Even these savages' females are treacherous!" said a third.

"That will serve her mother right for tricking English soldiers! Savage bitch!"

Percy had thought to take these children and their mother back to Jamestown, where De la Warr would probably hold them as hostages to make the Paspaheghs do his bidding. But then, through the Indian interpreter Kempes, Captain Percy had learned that the mother was not a Paspahegh at all.

She was Opossunoquonuske, half-sister to Powhatan, and Queen of Appamatuck, a Nansemond settlement further upriver toward Powhatan Village. Kempes said that her husband, the King of the Appamatucks, had been beheaded by Englishmen who came upriver in a ship last winter. That would have been Francis West and the *Swallow,* Percy thought. Last week, Opossonoquonuske had enticed fourteen of George Yardley's soldiers into her house for a feast, and had them slaughtered.

Now she must die.

It must have been her scornful, haughty bearing that offended Lord de la Warr. When Percy led her aboard the *Discovery,* she had refused to bow before the governor, or even to acknowledge his presence. She was a curiously strong woman, this Queen of Appamatuck. She had seen her husband slain by the Englishmen; she had been forced to watch as English soldiers murdered her children, but she did not weep. She only stared, her dark eyes full of grief and rage, her face set as if chiseled in stone. When the killing of her two sons and daughter was over, she had ripped the beads from around her neck and taken the feather ornament from her hair and dropped them overboard. The necklace sank; the blue and white feather headdress floated over the spot where her children's bodies had disappeared. Only Percy's intervention had prevented the men from killing her in the same manner as her children.

"I cannot kill her now," Percy said wearily.

"You must. The governor has ordered it done. You have no choice." Davis continued to pace.

"God's blood, man!" Percy spoke savagely. "Did I have a choice not to lead two companies to avenge the deaths of Yardley's men and all the others this summer? Did I have a choice not to order the burning of the burial house at Uttamussack, or the destruction of the village at Appamatuck, with all its women and children, too? This goddamned wilderness chooses for me, and I'm sick of it!"

"I know," said Davis quietly. He stopped pacing and put his hand on Percy's shoulder. "This place has done its damage to us all. Look at poor George Yardley."

"Indeed!" Percy raised his head.

"There's as fine a soldier as you'd ever see, turned into a cowardly cuckold. I heard he couldn't stomach the killing at Kecoughtan when they avenged Humphrey Blunt's death, and that was why Gates took him back to England."

"Yardley's no coward," Davis said quickly. "I was with him at Kecoughtan. He fought like a demon. It was seeing Will Sterling and his wife that made him ill. How would you like to see your wife's belly big with another man's child, and that man your best friend? Yardley's better off in England, where he can forget."

"It's a bad business, that," Percy said. "A queer trick of fate."

"Yardley was not himself at Paspahegh. If he had been, he'd never have let his men go into the Queen's house."

"Well, he did let them go in, and she killed them," Percy said sharply. "And so we had to go and avenge their deaths, and now we have to kill the Queen." He sighed. "Take her ashore, into the woods. I don't want to see or hear anything. Put her to the sword, or shoot her, whichever you prefer. Better take a couple of men with you, in case she fights you. She's a spirited one."

"And the lord governor's orders about the burning?"

"I'll answer for that. Just get rid of her."

JAMESTOWN
8 September 1610

"Ask him what Powhatan says now."

Thomas West, Lord de la Warr, spoke in a low voice to Kempes, his Indian interpreter. Kempes had learned his first English words from John Smith, and the rest from Thomas Savage when the latter was living at Powhatan Village. That was nearly two years ago. Now Kempes was trying his best to help these new Englishmen understand his own people.

He spoke in the Algonquin tongue to Nakinto, the tall young warrior from Powhatan Village, and then listened to the reply. Reluctantly, Kempes turned to Lord de la Warr. "He says Powhatan wishes you English to come no more to his village. Powhatan wishes you to go from this land. If you do not go, you must stay at Jamestown. If you come again to Powhatan Village, he will say to his people to kill your people."

"Damnation!" De la Warr, still racked by ague, had been leaning on a stout ash cudgel. Now he raised it in the air and drove it into the soft earth. He was trembling with rage. In front of him, the Indian Nakinto and his companion, a younger and slighter-built brave named Okewan, stood with their arms folded across their chests, silent and impassive.

"Tell him," De la Warr said to Kempes, "tell him Powhatan must give back what is ours. He has taken near two hundred swords from us, and axes and poleaxes and chisels and hoes, and he has taken some of our people prisoner."

Kempes spoke again with Nakinto. "Powhatan says—" he began hesitantly, knowing what he said would only add to the Englishman's anger. "Powhatan says, because you have taken his land, he has taken your weapons and iron things. If you give him a coach and three horses, such as the great men in your country have, he will give you the iron things back."

De la Warr pounded his cudgel again and turned to Captain John Martin. "You see what comes of trying to civilize these damned savages? Now that scoundrel wants a coach and three horses!"

"At least he didn't ask for a coach-and-four." Martin grinned.

"There is nought for humor in this!" De la Warr snapped. He lowered his head and leaned with both hands on his cudgel. Around him, his own officers, in front of him, the interpreter, Kempes, and the Indian emissaries, Nakinto and Okewan, all waited with rapt attention for him to speak. At last De la Warr raised his head. "Powhatan has been the cause of all our troubles," he said slowly. "We have lost too many good men because of him. Now we shall send him a message he can understand." Turning to Captain Martin, he said, "Take your broadsword and cut off this one's right hand." He jerked his head toward the Indian Okewan.

Martin's mouth dropped open in disbelief, and he put his hand on the hilt of his sword, not to draw it, but to keep it firmly in its place. "My lord! You cannot mean that! These two have come here in good faith!"

"Savages have no faith!" De la Warr said. "Words do no good with them. Blood is the language they understand!"

"But—"

"But me no buts! I gave you an order! Will you carry it out, or not?"

"Aye, sir." Sadly, Martin turned to his men. "Buckler and Brinton, when I say 'now,' take him by the arms and march him to that stump over there. Pace and Morgan, you take the big fellow by the arms and hold him. We'll try to make this quick."

Nakinto and Okewan shifted their feet and looked uneasily at each other and at Kempes. They did not understand the words, but they knew something was about to happen. Kempes knew all too well, but it would do no good to try to warn them, even if he dared. What could three Indians do, surrounded by a dozen Englishmen with swords and pistols? And if he did give warning, the English would be so angry they might kill him. So he kept silent, his eyes on the ground.

"Now!"

In an instant, Okewan's right arm was on the tree stump, Martin's sword was lifted high above it, and with one single flashing stroke, brought downward.

"Aaahh!"

Blood spurted, and Okewan's right hand, cleanly severed at the wrist-bone, hung at the edge of the tree stump and then fell on the grass.

"Aaaaah!" The first cry had been pain; the second, pure rage. Okewan crouched over the tree stump, his left hand clutching his right forearm just above the bleeding wrist joint. His eyes fastened first on Lord de la Warr, then on Captain Martin, with an expression of such pain and hatred that the soldiers surrounding them instinctively moved closer together. Richard

Pace and Gabriel Morgan, holding the Indian Nakinto, tightened their grip on his arms.

"*Sawwehone! Maskapow! Maskapow!*" Nakinto made the words into a cry of hideous rage.

"What is he saying, Kempes?" De la Warr, who had observed the amputation with great satisfaction, now crossed the clearing and stood directly in front of Nakinto.

"He says you shed Okewan's blood; you are *Maskapow,* the worst of enemies."

De la Warr shrugged. "Tell him we will do worse than this, if Powhatan and his people trouble us again." De la Warr looked into Nakinto's eyes. "We shall send this one back with a message to his master." De la Warr walked over to the tree stump. With his cane, he poked at Okewan's severed right hand as it lay on the bloodstained grass. "Tell him he is to take this hand back to Powhatan, and say that unless Powhatan returns our weapons and tools, and sends back our men he holds prisoners within three days, we will kill his man here." He waved his cane toward Okewan.

But the next day, Okewan, whose wound had never stopped bleeding, was dead.

The third day came and went, and there was no response from Powhatan.

POWHATAN VILLAGE
20 September 1610

 As the sunrise silvered the tops of the pine trees, Maranas, the daughter of Namontack, said a prayer to Okee. She had been lying awake in the dark for a long time, tossing and turning on her straw mat, grieving for Okewan. Never again would she lie with him, never again would he sing to her, never again would they laugh together. His right hand lay drying on a platform for the dead, but his body she would never see again. When Nemattonow had brought the word of Okewan's death yesterday, she had gone to the platform where she herself had placed his poor severed hand, and she had kissed that hand to bid Okewan farewell. The flies had ceased to buzz around it, and the skin of it was already stiff and leathery. Something inside Maranas felt as shriveled and lifeless as that desiccated flesh, and her hatred for the English burned anew.

It was the English who had taken her father. Namontack had gone away with Captain Newport in his ship two years ago, but this past spring, when Newport came back, he sent word that Namontack had died on an island called Bermuda. Maranas had nothing except her father's war shield to remember him by. He had taken his bow and his quiver full of arrows with him, but the English had assured him their land was a peaceful place, and he would have no need for his shield. She did not even know how he died, or where he was buried.

Now the English had killed Okewan. They had buried him near their fort, Nemattonow told her. He had seen them throw Okewan's body into a shallow pit, and when they had finished replacing the earth over him, some of them had stamped their feet in a joyful dance on the newly made grave. The burial place was not marked, but Nemattonow had described its location near two laurel trees by the south gate. Someday, when the English were gone, Maranas thought, she would go and see Okewan's grave for herself.

She asked Okee to guide her beloved's spirit on its journey to the Land of the Dead, and then she rose and made ready to attend Powhatan and his brothers. He had sent for them the day Nakinto brought Okewan's hand back to Powhatan Village.

It was a bright, cool morning, so sunny and pleasant that the men spread their mats outside under the trees. The four brothers, Opitchapan, with his lame leg, Catatough, Opechancanough, and Wahunsonacock sat facing each other and Tanx-Powhatan, Wahunsonacock's eldest son. Nemattonow, who had brought the news of Okewan's death from Jamestown, had departed as quickly as he had come.

"When the summer began, you said the English would be gone by the next new moon," Wahunsonacock said to Opechancanough. "That was four moons ago."

"And look how many are still here!" Catatough broke in. "Too many for me to count!"

"When the English sailed away from Jamestown, you said we were rid of them," Opitchapan said accusingly. "And when they sailed back again with two new ships, you said they would not stay long because they had no food. But look what happened! More came, and they all stayed!"

"We should have struck them down while they were weak and hungry and few in number," Wahunsonacock said.

"How could I know that Lord de la Warr would come with near two hundred men?" Opechancanough spoke angrily. "Even the English at Jamestown did not know that!"

"Now they have food as well," Catatough said. "Nemattonow told me their storehouse is full of grain."

"We must move against them soon," Wahunsonacock said. "Before cold weather comes, we must strike a deathblow to Jamestown."

"That will not be as easy as you seem to think, my brother," Opechancanough said slowly. "Nemattonow's lookouts tell him the new governor brought a hundred suits of armor and many more guns with him. If we attacked the fort at Jamestown, our arrows would be just so many useless reeds."

"The killings at Kecoughtan must not go unavenged," Tanx-Powhatan said, "no matter what it costs."

"And the deaths of Opossunoquonuske and her three little ones cry out for swift vengeance," Wahunsonacock said softly.

"And the spirits of all the rest who died at Appamatuck," Opitchapan said.

"And Manato, the husband of Opossunoquonuske, before that," said Catatough.

"And are we to let the burning of the House of the Dead at Uttamussack go unpunished?" Tanx-Powhatan asked. He looked at his father and his three uncles, one after the other. "Do you not hear the spirit of your father—my grandfather—calling you to punish those who profaned the sacred ground and destroyed his resting place?"

"I hear him. I hear them all." Opechancanough folded his arms across his chest. "And I hear you, my brothers, and you, Tanx-Powhatan, my brother's son. But I do not want to see any more of our people's blood shed. When we move against the English, we must move with a large force, and we must move quickly. Against their cannons and muskets, surprise is our only hope. That will take careful planning."

Wahunsonacock shook his head, and the others looked displeased at Opechancanough's words. "Hear me, brother," Wahunsonacock said. "There are no more than three hundred English at Jamestown, and some of them are always sick. There are less than a hundred at their forts downriver. I say we send six hundred warriors against Jamestown tomorrow, and against the forts the day after tomorrow. Why wait?"

"I have told you why!" Opechancanough unfolded his arms and leaned forward. "They are so fearful of us they keep lookouts day and night, and they would give the alarm long before we could surprise them. We cannot storm their log walls with arrows and spears, or even with the English swords we have. And once they put on armor, they are like shellfish, hard to kill. They will fire their cannons into our midst, and they will fire their muskets over the walls at us. Then they will send their men to burn our villages and our cornfields in retaliation."

"Then what do you propose to do?" Wahunsonacock was angry.

"I propose to take counsel with every werowance in every village in the kingdom of the Powhatan," Opechancanough said slowly. "I propose to have fifteen hundred warriors strike at one moment, all up and down the river, and leave not one Englishman alive."

The others looked at him in amazement.

"You are asking the impossible!"

"How would you do it?"

"What about their guns?"

"We would take them by surprise. We would offer peace, and then, when they are off their guard, send our men among them, and kill them with their own weapons."

"You dream of something that cannot be."

"It would take too long, even if you could arrange such an attack. The longer we wait, the more English may come."

"It is the only way," Opechancanough said quietly.

"It is not my way," Wahunsonacock said. "I am the Powhatan, and I say the deaths of my half-sister and her children, and the death of Okewan and the destruction of my father's burial ground, call for swift vengeance."

Maranas, who had come with a basket of newly baked bread, smiled as she heard Wahunsonacock's words. Silently, she set the basket down and left, feeling strangely comforted.

Two days later, Powhatan sent a force of five hundred warriors against the fort at Jamestown. Arrows fell on the ground like rain, but only twenty Englishmen died.

The day after that, a hundred Englishmen in full armor sailed down to Nansemond and burned the entire village and all the surrounding corn-fields.

It was just as Opechancanough had said.

POINT COMFORT
30 September 1610

All day, the wind from the sea had been so light that hardly a pine needle stirred. It was warm for so late in September, and the air inside the huts at the fort held the heat of late afternoon. Most of the men, except for those on watch, had gone down to the shore, where it was cooler. A few of them stayed within the compound, resting on the grass and drinking plum wine, their voices rising and falling in the soft twilight like the sounds of a flock of bass-throated doves. Now and then, a line or two of conversation could be heard distinctly.

"No moon tonight, and not even many stars."

"We'll have rain before the night's done. You can feel it."

"I hope I don't feel any Indian arrows this night. What if they try here what they did at Jamestown?"

"Let us hope they do not choose tonight, at least, for Mistress Temperance's sake."

"How long has it been, now?"

"Since early morning, Sterling said."

In a small house near the gate of the fort, some distance from the other houses, Temperance was struggling to give birth. The pains had begun before dawn; it was now an hour past sundown.

"Will, you ought not to be here. This is women's work. I've told you that." Meg wrung out another cloth and placed it on Temperance's forehead.

"This is my work," Will said in a low, worried voice. "God knows, I'm the one who did this to her. I'll not leave her now."

Temperance's fingers closed weakly around his, and her body went suddenly rigid with pain as another contraction came.

"Keep your knees up, Temperance! That's it. Come on, now, just push a little.

"Hold on, love. Hold on to me."

The sounds of the voices floated to Temperance on a sea of pain. They seemed far away, but she could feel hands holding her legs, and someone was still holding her hand. Someone else in the room was making a noise, a dreadful, harsh cry like some injured animal. It hurt her ears, but most of the hurt was in her body: a terrible, cramping weight was pushing against her privates with a pressure so intense that soon she must burst. The pain was like a great fist that closed about her lower abdomen, holding and twisting tighter, tighter each time. The fist was squeezing the strength, the very life, from her. She wished it would take her and be done with her. But the fist refused to be satisfied. With fiendish cunning, it only let her rest a blessed moment or two, and then it seized her again, each time harder than before.

Now the loud crying noise had stopped, and the only sound was her own labored breathing. She could not seem to get enough air, though she drew in great rasping gulps of it. She had to be ready for the pain when it came again. It was her enemy, and for a while she had fought it. But that had been so long ago, and now, as she grew weaker, she felt that it was winning.

"Temperance, can you hear me?" That was Will's voice. She did not open her eyes, but she tried to squeeze his hand.

"Temperance, listen." That was Meg's voice. "Temperance, listen to me."

Why was Meg so insistent? Temperance wanted her to be quiet. Why didn't they just leave her alone?

"We've got to rouse her. She's got to push to bring this baby."

That was fine for Meg to say. Let her try pushing for a while. Temperance turned her head away from the sound of that voice.

"Oh, God! Oh, Temperance, what have I done to you?"

Will's voice was close to her ear, and he was almost sobbing. Why was he sad? She did not want him to be sad. She tried to squeeze his hand again, but she had to get ready for the pain. The fist was taking hold of her once more. She arched her back and screamed as it closed. They held her, but they were no help. Nothing was any help. Not even God. She could not ask Him for help, because He was punishing her with this pain.

"I don't believe she can do this lying down. But she's too weak now for the birthing chair. Her labor has gone on too long."

That was Meg again. She was whispering, but Temperance could hear her. She felt the fist loosening its grip, and she wanted to rest. She wanted to tell them she could not sit up, and to leave her alone, but she was too tired. One of them was bathing her face, and one of them was trying to move her. She did not want to be moved. She had to lie in wait for the pain.

"What if—what if I held her?" That was Will.

"That would not be right, somehow. I don't know. You oughtn't even to be in here. Why don't you wait outside, and let me see what I can do to help her?"

"Don't be stupid! There are no other women here, and this is my child she's birthing!"

Why were they arguing? Temperance rolled her head from side to side, as if to make them stop.

"Temperance, can you hear me?" Will's voice was in her ear again. "Temperance, dearest love, listen to me. I'm going to lift you up, and when the pain comes again, I'll hold you tight, and you push down when Meg tells you." Temperance tried to say no, but his arms were already underneath her shoulders. "That's it. That's good."

Temperance opened her eyes ever so slightly, and saw Meg crouched in front of her. Then Will, kneeling behind her, lifted her up, his arms encircling her body just below her breasts. He kissed her cheek, and tucked his chin firmly against her shoulder. At the same time, Meg pushed her knees up and held them steady, so that Temperance was in a squatting position, with Will keeping her upright and bearing her weight.

"There."

She wanted to tell Will to lay her down, but she had no strength left. She had lain flat on the straw mat for so many hours that the sudden change to an upright position made her dizzy and nauseated, and she could not speak. Will and Meg were holding her, but her body was so drenched with sweat she felt she might slip from their grasp. It was hot in the room, and dark. Even when she opened her eyes, all she could see were shadows in the flickering light of a pine torch. Hell must be like this, she thought. God was giving her a foretaste of what she would pay for her sins with Will.

The pain was taking hold of her again.

"Oh, God!"

"Push, Temperance! Bear down!"

"Come on, love, listen to Meg. Push. I'll hold you."

"Ooohh!" The cry was torn from Temperance's throat as the tissues in her birth canal tore, but the labor pain was so intense she could not feel the tear. Something warm was trickling between her legs.

"Oh, that was a good one. I can feel the baby's head now. Come on, Temperance, just a few more."

This time the pain was playing tricks. Just when Temperance thought it was leaving, it came again, harder than ever. Soon her body would burst, and it would be over.

"Aaaahh!"

"Push!"

"Come on!"

"More, Temperance, more! You've got to push!"

The voices sounded dim and far away. The fist of pain was squeezing so hard her very bones seemed about to splinter, and it would not let go. It was pushing down with a great weight, and she could not get her breath.

"Come on, Temperance." Will's voice was so tender, so pleading. Poor Will.

"Bear down. Just a little more."

"Here it comes—here it . . . is!" That was Meg's voice.

Something had happened to the pain. Relief was so sweet and sudden that Temperance began to weep in great, gasping sobs.

"It's all right, love. It's all over." Will, cradling her in his arms, laid her down again on the pallet. She was grateful they were done with her.

There was a new sound in the room: a small, angry, wailing sound. Temperance made an effort to open her eyes. Meg was holding the baby upside down, by its feet.

"It's a boy, Will! I knew it would be! A fine, beautiful boy!"

"Thank God! Oh, thank God! Temperance, can you hear? It's a boy!" Will's voice was trembling. He sounded near to tears himself.

"Here, see for yourself, while I cut the cord." Meg laid the baby facedown on Temperance's abdomen. He wailed and wriggled, seeking comfort, seeking warmth outside her body. With both hands, Temperance caressed his head and felt his strong little back and his arms and legs, still wet from birth. She longed to hold him close in her arms, to cuddle him, but she was so tired, so very tired. Then she felt Will's big hands taking hold of hers, and Meg took the baby.

"Oh, Temperance!" Will kissed her hands, and then her cheek, and then her mouth. "What a wonder he is! What a fine boy! What a dear, brave love you are!"

Temperance put up one hand to touch his face. "I'm glad," she whispered. "So glad." She smiled. She wanted to thank him, and thank Meg, too, but a great drowsiness was stealing over her, and she could not think of the right words. She squeezed Will's hand, and then she closed her eyes again and slept.

In her sleep, she tossed and moaned, dreaming of a baby with George Yardley's face.

LONDON
30 October 1610

"Strachey's letter to you must never see the light of day. If it does, we are done for." Sir Thomas Smythe smiled ruefully at his wife. "We may be done for anyway."

Lady Sara Smythe replaced the pages she had been reading in the small lap desk, closed the inlaid wooden lid, and turned the tiny brass lock. Then she set the desk aside and stood up. "If the Virginia Company fails, my love, it will not be because of you. No man could have done more, and worried more, than you have." Crossing to where her husband sat, she placed both hands lightly on his shoulders and kissed his forehead. "I worry about your worrying. I know when you rise at night and pace up and down. The Virginia Company is making circles under your eyes."

"Well it might."

On September 14, the *Blessing* and the *Rye* had arrived from Virginia, bearing Deputy Governor Sir Thomas Gates, Captain Christopher Newport, and their companies of guards. They brought with them the astounding news of the *Sea Venture*'s miraculous deliverance from the storm, but they also brought the first pitiful stories of the Starving Time at Jamestown and the unrelenting hostility of the Indians.

Now Sir Thomas took one of his wife's hands and held it against his cheek and smiled ruefully. "I cannot help but worry." He looked at his wife's locked desk. "A 'True Reportory' indeed! If William Strachey's account of what has really happened in Virginia were to be published now, it would ruin us. We need thirty thousand pounds sterling to keep that colony alive, and with the disastrous returns on investments thus far, we'll be hard pressed to raise it, as things stand. Who would put his money into a venture that so far has lost four ships and five hundred souls?"

The treasurer of the Virginia Company pounded his clenched fist slowly on the arm of his chair as he spoke. Until last month, the Company's Council had hoped against hope that part of the original *Sea Venture* expedition might turn up; that the three-hundred-ton flagship itself was not lost; that some small return on that expensive undertaking might be realized. Then, when the truth was learned, there had been deep consultation and deeper division over what course to take in the face of such devastating losses. At the Michaelmas Quarter session of the entire Company, many investors were for recalling Lord de la Warr and the survivors of Jamestown and abandoning the entire project.

But others, convinced by Deputy Governor Gates's report on his return that Virginia was "one of the goodliest countries under the sun," voted to supply the struggling colony anew, with more settlers and more provisions. The Virginia Company's members were also moved by a letter from Governor de la Warr declaring his determination to sacrifice himself and all he had for the success of the Virginia plantation. His younger brother Francis, who had sailed home last spring in the *Swallow,* was aiming to return to Virginia as well. And so the Virginia Company voted to open a new joint-stock subscription in November. Individual shares would go for seventy-five pounds sterling, payable at twenty-five pounds per annum for three years.

"Well," Lady Sara said, "things worthwhile are seldom easy. You yourself have always said that." She grew pensive and gazed into the fire. "But this enterprise has such a strange story, with so many providential happenings in it, with the *Sea Venture* being lost in the tempest, and all its people saved in the Bermudas, and then Lord de la Warr arriving in Virginia just in time to turn back the ships from Jamestown. You must believe that divine Providence has a hand in all this," she said softly.

"I do, Sara, I do." Sir Thomas kissed his wife's hand. "I only hope enough others are of like mind." He was silent for a moment, and then, as if he were talking to himself, he said, "We'll not make the same mistakes again. Two smaller supply groups instead of one big one. Gates will go again, and Thomas Dale. Dale is a damned fine soldier; that's why they want him in the Netherlands. But the States General will give him a leave of absence, and we'll make him Marshal Dale in Virginia. If any man can subdue the savages of Virginia, it is Thomas Dale. Then Gates will have time to put his affairs in order here and follow Dale before next year is out. I understand that Gates has promised to obtain a decree of divorce for the captain of his guards, a fellow named Yardley, before he returns to Virginia."

"And then what?"

Sir Thomas looked at his wife in some perplexity. "What do you mean, 'Then what'?"

"I mean, what will all this effort in Virginia yield? At first it was to be gold and pearls and a waterway to the riches of the East, and then it was to be glass and iron and ship's masts and such. What will it be this time?" Lady Sara was infinitely more practical than her husband. She smiled at him and said, "You must remember, dear heart, that not all the stockholders can afford to wait years and years for their profits the way you and Southampton and Warwick and the others can."

Ignoring the slightly teasing tone of his wife's voice, Smythe rose, crossed the library, and rummaged in his desk. "Here, if you are so curious, listen to this! We know what sorts of things Virginia can produce, and, believe me, there is good money in them." Flourishing a piece of paper, he began to enumerate: "Sassafras roots, worth fifty pounds sterling the ton; bayberries, twelve pounds the ton; sarsaparilla, two hundred pounds; turpentine, eighteen pounds—not to mention pitch and tar, and beaver and otter skins, and silk grass, and sturgeon caviar, and—"

Lady Sara held up both hands in mock protest. "No more, no more," she said with a laugh. "I see riches pouring in."

"You are as bad as Sandys and Hamor and some others in the Company," Sir Thomas said, "always reckoning up the pounds sterling."

"I just wanted to know. And now that I know, I think I shall retire to bed. Don't sit up late and let the fire go out." Lady Sara kissed her husband good night and turned to leave the room. Then, remembering her lap desk, she picked it up and said, "If you will not allow Strachey's wonderful letter to be printed, let me give it to Will Shakespeare to read. He is fond of Strachey, you know, and he asked me if there were any reports from him. If I tell Shakespeare to keep it to himself, he will. He does not want the Company to come to harm any more than you do." As an afterthought, she added, "And besides, Strachey's letter is addressed to me, not you."

"Oh, very well, do as you wish," Sir Thomas said, "but be sure you impress upon Shakespeare the need for circumspection."

"Trust me," Lady Sara said. "And trust him. Will Shakespeare is a good man to keep a secret."

JAMESTOWN
2 February 1611

"There are Englishmen living at Ritanoe."

As a mixed chorus of gasps and murmurs of disbelief rose from the assembled audience in the meetinghouse, Henry Spelman preened himself like a young turkey-cock. In all his fifteen years, he had never had so much attention. The moment he had set foot ashore with Captain Argall, he had been so besieged with questions that finally Lord de la Warr had decided to hold this special meeting. It was not everyone, after all, who stayed among the Indians for more than a year and lived to tell about it. A survivor of the Ratcliffe expedition at Powhatan Village in 1609, the boy had been adopted by the Paspaheghs. Samuel Argall, sailing upriver to trade for corn, had found him and brought him back.

"What do you mean, Englishmen?" Governor de la Warr leaned forward in his chair. Still suffering from the ague, he was swaddled in two cloaks and a blanket.

"Did you see them?" George Percy was skeptical.

"No, I never saw them, because they were five days' journey into the high country, but I believe they are there yet." Henry Spelman ran his fingers through his tow-colored hair and smoothed his beaded deerskin vest.

"How many? How did they get there?" Will Strachey, as the colony's secretary, was obviously thinking of details for a report to the Virginia Company.

"Hold off." John Martin raised his hand for silence. "How do we know there is any truth to this?"

Henry Spelman bristled. "Because the werowance Eyanoco himself told me. It was me—my light hair and skin—that made him think of the English in his village. He told the King of the Potomacs I was like them."

"Ah, but maybe this Eyanoco was jealous of your being with the Potomacs, and he made up a story about having some English of his own. These savages are famous liars. We all know that." Martin folded his arms across his chest.

"I'd not spend much time trying to find such Englishmen." Samuel Argall, who had spent the past fortnight in Henry Spelman's company, raised one eyebrow and gave Governor de la Warr a telling look.

"But Eyanoco did not lie!" Spelman quivered with excitement. "I know he spoke true, because—" The boy cast about for further proof. "Because—" His thin face lit up. "Because Eyanoco told the King of the Potomacs I could build a house like his English had built for him at Ritanoe! Now, I ask you, how would an Indian know about English houses, unless he had seen one? He said the English built houses with stones, and they put one room on top of another."

"Did he say how many of these English people are there?" William Strachey, patient and persistent, spoke quietly.

"Yes!" Young Spelman said triumphantly, looking from Argall to De la Warr to Strachey, and then out over the heads of the assembled audience. "Yes, he did. He said there were two boys and four men that came to Ritanoe after Powhatan burned their town and killed the others years ago in the land of the Chesepians. There was a woman, too, a young one, but she ran away upriver, and they never saw her again. But the rest—the men and the boys—are there yet, I tell you."

On a bench near the front, Meg Worley sat very still. She had not moved—in fact, she had barely breathed—since Henry Spelman had first said the words "English living at Ritanoe." Her eyes had not left the boy's face, and she leaned forward, her lips slightly parted, as if to drink in his every syllable and take nourishment from it.

"Well, Strachey, make note of this." Lord de la Warr leaned back in his chair with an air of finality. "Two years ago the Virginia Company issued instructions to search for the lost Roanoke settlers. If and when the Company chooses to send us the wherewithal to search, we might find out more about these so-called English."

"But might it not be worth it to us to seek them out?" Strachey asked.

"Seek them out?" De la Warr laughed scornfully. "With what, man? With whom? We've barely enough men to keep ourselves alive here, and to keep off the savages. We've no men to spare for some wild-goose chase! This Ritanoe is a long way off. Besides, if we found them, we'd have to feed them!" He slapped his thigh and laughed again, and a few people in the assembly laughed in dutiful response. "No, they will have to wait. If they are the Roanoke people, they have waited twenty years and more to be found, so a little longer won't hurt them. Perhaps, if all goes well, we can spare a few men to search for them before this year is out."

Meg Worley could not sleep that night. It was long past bedtime, but

she could not stop thinking of Anthony Gage. Inside the log walls of
Jamestown's palisade, all was darkness except for the lanterns at the watchtowers. To the west, the evening star shown diamond-bright in the clear
winter sky. Watching it from her window, Meg wondered if she ought to
make a wish, and then she wondered what that wish should be. What if
that brash young Spelman boy spoke the truth, and there were Englishmen
living among the Indians at Ritanoe? But more likely they were Dutch or
Spanish, from some passing ship, she told herself. She should go to bed.

It had been twenty-three years since Anthony Gage had kissed her
good-bye on the heights of Plymouth Hoe, and it was folly to think she
would ever see him again. What had made her so foolish? She had ruined
her looks and wasted her life in pursuit of a fairy tale. For the first time in
her life, she was feeling old. In the mornings, when she awoke, her joints
felt stiff, and the arrow wound in her right shoulder still pained her. When
she looked into a looking-glass, she could see that the tiny lines around her
eyes and mouth, which had once appeared only when she smiled or laughed,
were now permanent, like lines on a map. In a few days she would be forty.
That was old, she thought. Old, and yet she had never been a wife nor borne
a child.

Seeing Temperance and Will with their infant son gave her spells of
melancholy. Gabriel was now six months old. He and Will and Temperance
and Meg had been in Jamestown since October. They had come back
because George was no longer there: He had returned to England with
Thomas Gates. Temperance and Will had settled into their old house, and
Meg took the house that had once belonged to Peter and Martha Scott. "I
do want you to be close to us, but won't it trouble you, being alone in that
house?" Temperance had asked.

"No," Meg had said. But she had been wrong. Thinking of Peter and
Martha Scott, like thinking of Temperance and Will, made her think of
Anthony Gage, and she scolded herself. But somehow she could never
forget that Anthony had sent for her. It was not his fault that she never got
there, that the ship she sailed on in 1588 was attacked by a French privateer,
and that a Frenchman tried to rape her and slashed her cheek through with
his sword. What if Anthony were still alive somewhere, wondering why she
never came?

Too restless to sleep, she paced back and forth. When darkness fell
there was nothing to do but go to bed. Candles were too precious to waste,
and pitch-soaked torches were likely to cause fires, so Jamestown retired at
sunset and rose with the dawn. Meg had done that for most of her life. On
the farm, her aunt and uncle had kept rush lights for rare occasions, and

she could remember only a few times of evening light. Standing at her window, Meg began to slip the pins from her hair. Anthony had liked to watch her do that. He liked to wind tendrils of her hair around his fingers as they talked, after they had made love. In all the time they were together, they had made love in the nighttime, in the dark, only once. That was the last time, in an inn at Plymouth, the night before he sailed for Roanoke. All the other times had been furtive couplings in the daytime: in the farmhouse loft, or in the cow shed, on the days when Aunt Elizabeth went to market. At first, Meg had been afraid. "What if I should conceive a child, and us not man and wife?"

But Anthony had made light of her fears. "Dearest heart," he had said, "you and I are betrothed. There is no harm in what we are doing. Believe me." And so Meg had believed him, and because of him she was now three thousand miles from that farmhouse in Devon. Because Anthony Gage, only son of the dour-faced rector of St. Boniface's Church at Okehampton, did not want to study for the ministry and had left home; because Aunt Elizabeth needed help at the farm and had hired Anthony to work for bed and board, Meg's life was forever changed. Anthony had brought her not only love, but learning: He taught her to read, he told her the names of the oceans and the lands across the seas, he taught her the names of the stars in the heavens. That last night at Plymouth, she and Anthony had seen the evening star, just as she was seeing it tonight. Meg looked up at the sky, made a wish, and then, pulling a rug about her, lay down on her pallet to sleep.

JAMESTOWN
27 September 1611

 "The laws of England and the Church, Mistress Worley, are not made for casting off one's wife."

George Yardley smiled ruefully. With a twig he had picked up, he absentmindedly traced a circle in the soft earth floor of Meg's house as he spoke. Then, realizing what he had drawn, he brushed over the spot. A circle reminded him of a ring, and a ring reminded him of the one he had given Temperance when they married: a slender circlet of gold, with the words "Be true in heart" engraved inside. He snapped the twig in two, and threw it on the floor.

"Have you spoken to her yet?" Meg said.

"No." George leaned forward on the joint stool and put his head in his hands. He did not want to speak to Temperance; he did not even want to be in Jamestown. But when Gates had sailed back to the colony in July, George had had no choice but to sail with him, if he wanted to keep his position as captain of Gates's guards. After all, he had told himself, people died like flies at Jamestown, and it was possible that by the time he returned, neither Temperance nor Will would be alive. It would be folly to throw away his position for fear of seeing Temperance. But he had seen her. That he could not avoid, since everyone who was able was required by law to attend prayers twice a day. And on Sundays, when Reverend Buck, now assisted by a new young minister, Alexander Whitaker, read the service for morning prayer, George was required to sit with Gates at the front of the meetinghouse, and from that position he could see the entire congregation. That first Sunday, Temperance and Will had come late and sat in the very last row.

Temperance, her breasts rounded with the fullness of motherhood, her hair demurely bound under a matronly cap, still had the face that had enchanted George from that day he first saw her in the Globe Theatre. The luminous brown eyes, the mobile, petulant mouth, were still as easy to read as the pages of a book. With grudging satisfaction, he saw that she was as uneasy as he. Her eyes, when she entered and saw him there, immediately sought the wooden cross above the altar.

"We have erred, and strayed from thy ways like lost sheep. We have followed the devices and desires of our own hearts. . . ."

As the Reverend Whitaker's earnest young voice reverberated through the meetinghouse, Temperance kept her eyes fastened on the cross. When the General Confession was finished, she pressed her lips together in a grim, taut line. Then she bowed her head and did not raise her eyes again during the entire service. Neither, for that matter, did Will. But George had felt other eyes on him, and without looking, he had imagined that everyone present was watching him and Temperance and Will.

"Are you going to speak to her?"

Meg Worley's voice, gentle and insistent, brought him out of his reverie. She was a wise, kind woman. He had always sensed that. When he found out that she was still at Jamestown, he had sought her out immediately. She was one of the few people there who had known Temperance nearly as well as he had.

"Oh, I don't know! I don't know!" George put his head in his hands.

That was the honest truth. He had not spoken to Temperance since that awful day he first arrived at Point Comfort. "God knows, I don't want to."

"What will you do?"

"Sir Thomas has sworn to help me get our marriage dissolved. His cousin is the Bishop of Ely, and a bishop can obtain a decree of divorce. When it can be proven that the wife has borne a child by another man—" George's voice broke, and Meg put her hand on his shoulder. Hating himself for showing such weakness, he drew a deep breath and continued, "There have been such cases, and it is possible. But that, of course, will have to wait until I return to England. God knows when that will be."

"I think that you should speak with her," Meg said quietly. "You should know that this has come near to breaking her heart—and Will's, too."

"That is of no interest to me."

"Oh, Captain Yardley! How cruel a turn of fate this is! For all of you—for Will and Temperance and you!" Meg's voice was low and sad. "How could God let such a thing happen?"

"The same way He let you and your betrothed be parted, I trow. There is too much divine carelessness in this world," George said bitterly. "You can't think that was God's will, can you?"

"I must."

"Then you, Mistress Worley, are a saint." George smiled. Meg smiled back, and with one hand, she fingered a small gold cross on a chain around her neck.

"No, Captain Yardley, not a saint, by any means—but a fool, more likely."

"I wish I had some of your . . . foolishness, then. And I wish you would not call me Captain Yardley. We two have too much in common not to call each other by our given names. We are both alone, you and I, through no fault of our own."

"But we must not blame God. He never takes away our hope."

"For you, perhaps." George found the two pieces of the twig he had snapped, and began to break them into smaller and smaller pieces. "For you, but not for me."

"Not so, not so." Meg spoke with grave assurance. "God moves in mysterious ways, and despair is a sin. I kept hoping, and this summer I heard that there are Englishmen living at Ritanoe."

"Ritanoe is a long way off."

"Not when you've come three thousand miles."

"But I know of no plan to search for any English."

"Not yet. Lord de la Warr was too ill, and times here have been too hard. But now that we have Lieutenant Governor Gates to govern, and Marshal Thomas Dale to keep order, and all these new people and enough cattle and hogs, things will be put right again. Marshal Dale seems a hard man, but he will surely want to search. Maybe in the spring . . . who knows? I can wait. I have waited twenty years and more."

George was touched. "I leave tomorrow to take command of the new Fort Charles, where Kecoughtan used to be. Ritanoe is across the river and to the south, probably near threescore miles from there. If there is any way I can spare some men, I shall send them to Ritanoe as soon as warm weather comes."

Meg's smile seemed to light the dim room. "Ah, Captain Yardley— George!"

George took one of her hands in both of his.

"I promise. You have my word on it." He raised her hand to his lips. "Now I must be off, to make ready. Maybe—just maybe, mind you—I shall go and speak to Temperance."

"Do that, and . . . God be with you."

"And with you."

"Wait!"

As George turned to go, Meg unfastened the gold chain around her neck. She dropped it and the small cross in the palm of one hand and touched them lovingly. Then she closed her fingers over them and held out her fist. "Here. Take this with you. Send it with your men to Ritanoe. It will be a message from me to Anthony."

George did not go to see Temperance after he left Meg's house; instead, Sir Thomas Gates, looking troubled, waylaid him. "Dale has done it now!"

"What, sir?"

"The damned fool has ordered two women to be whipped, and there may be trouble over it. Get twelve of your best men and come to the front yard of the meetinghouse as soon as you can. The crowd is already there."

The crowd indeed, George thought. When he had left Jamestown last year, there had been near two hundred people living inside the palisade. Thomas Dale had brought 300 new colonists with him this past May, but summer's fever and bloody flux had carried off over 150 souls. In August, when Gates had arrived to take over as governor, he had brought three hundred more settlers with him, including his wife and three daughters. But his wife had died of ship's fever, and now the governor was planning to send his three young daughters, Mary, Margaret, and Elizabeth, back to England when Christopher Newport sailed at the end of the year. The governor was grief-stricken; the three-hundred-odd survivors already at Jamestown were weak and dispirited; the newcomers were angry and disappointed. Expecting to find a tidy little village of snug houses and tilled fields, they found instead a cluster of hastily built dwellings inside and outside a rude log palisade, a few acres growing corn amid dead tree stumps, and a graveyard abloom with new-made wooden crosses. The colony was weighed down with squalor and sickness, mud and mosquitoes, and fear of death. And as if that were not enough to keep order among the unseasoned and unruly, Sir Thomas Dale, now marshal of the colony, had decreed that Jamestown should be under martial law, with a code of punishment far harsher than any in England.

"What happened? What did the women do?" George had a premonition of disaster.

"I don't know," Gates said angrily. "Something about sewing shirts too short. All I know is people are not going to like this. One of the women—what's her name?—Laydon, the carpenter's wife—is with child." He shook his head grimly. "Don't stand there with your mouth agape, man! Do as I told you, and be quick about it!"

The whip was a small one, the kind used in England to drive a one-horse rig. Its lash was a thin braid of leather strips that would no more than sting a pony's flanks. But even a light touch of it would leave marks on a human's back, and twenty lashes well laid on would certainly draw blood. Lieutenant Andrew Buckler closed the fingers of his right hand around the whip handle, and at the same time clamped his lower lip firmly between his teeth.

"These two lazy wenches thought no one would notice they'd made four shirts a hand's breadth shorter than the rest, but *I* noticed!" Marshal Dale's deep bass rang out over the assembled crowd as Buckler raised his right arm.

"But, sir, I can't whip a woman!" Only an hour ago, Buckler had tried to reason with his commanding officer. "It's not right! Not for this!"

"Say no, and I'll have you before the martial court! I intend to show every man and woman in this place that rules must be obeyed!"

Buckler raised the whip high and brought his arm down smartly across his chest in a diagonal motion. As he did so, he closed his eyes, so that he only heard the snap of the rawhide as it hit Ann Laydon's back.

"One!" Sergeant Timothy Dowse called out in an anguished voice. The crowd, held back by George's soldiers, shifted and murmured uneasily.

Andrew Buckler opened his eyes. There was a thin red line across Ann

Laydon's white shoulders. Soon it would rise into a welt. He closed his eyes again and raised his arm.

"Two!"

Ann, who had not made a sound the first time, let her breath out in a loud gasp, as though the whip had forced the air from her lungs. Across the soft white skin of her back there was now an elongated X mark drawn in red. Just below the intersection of the lash marks was a large brown mole.

"Three!"

Now there was a red line across the mole, and a drop of blood oozed from it. Ann moved her shoulders slightly. She could not move much; her wrists, bound together above her head, were fastened to the branch of a young pine tree.

"She's a brave one, that one is."

"I hear they had to lock John Laydon in the guardhouse, he was so wild."

"Dale may have gone too far with this. Whipping's bad enough, but whipping a woman with child—"

"She's near five months along."

"She's got a little girl two years old. What will they tell that child?" George could hear the crowd's voices, but he did not take in their words. He had positioned his men to hold the crowd back about ten yards from the two bound, half-naked victims of Marshal Dale's wrath, and then he stood silent and sickened by what he saw.

The other woman was Jane Wright.

She stood up very straight, awaiting her turn at the whipping post with pathetic dignity.

The crowd had settled into a horrified quiet as Buckler's arm rose and fell, and the only sounds were the slap of the whip on Ann Laydon's flesh, and Sergeant Dowse's voice inexorably counting.

"Twelve!"

"Thirteen!"

The brown mole on Ann's back was now bleeding profusely. Buckler tried to avoid it with the lash, but no matter how hard he tried, he kept hitting it.

"Fourteen!"

Buckler's lower lip, clenched between his teeth, was bleeding.

At fifteen blows, Ann fainted. Her head, which she had turned from side to side in her agony, dropped forward between her upstretched arms, and her plump, bleeding body sagged against the slender trunk of the tree.

The crowd gasped. Buckler looked at Marshal Dale and fingered the whip. Dowse looked uncertainly from him to Dale.

"Go on!" Dale's voice rang out sharply over the audience. "I count fifteen; she's to have twenty! Get on with it!"

Buckler held the whip handle in his right hand, and with his left hand he held the lash, slippery with blood.

"I said, go on!" Dale folded his arms across his chest and waited.

Buckler raised his arm again. It was a cool September afternoon, but Andrew Buckler was drenched with sweat.

"Sixteen!"

"Seventeen!"

To one side, Lucy Forrest and a little knot of women were waiting to unfasten Ann Laydon, waiting to try to undo what the whip had done to her flesh.

"Eighteen!"

"Nineteen!"

"Twenty!"

As the women, cooing like mourning doves, rushed forward, Andrew Buckler walked slowly to a nearby tree and leaned his forehead against it. The crowd milled about angrily as Ann Laydon was carried away and Jane Wright brought forward. No one noticed Buckler there, leaning against the tree trunk; no one came to offer him a word of comfort. Then it was his turn to count, as Sergeant Dowse laid the whip to Jane Wright's back. When Buckler took his place near the whipping post, the crowd could see blood on the front of his jerkin. His lower lip was almost bitten through.

When it was all over, and Jane Wright, who did not faint, was untied, George tried to say some words of comfort to her, and then to Buckler and Dowse. But Andrew Buckler walked away without speaking to anyone.

Late that night, Ann Laydon, five months pregnant, began to hemorrhage. Then she went into premature labor. In the still night air, her anguished cries could be heard all across the palisade. Just before dawn, the cries ceased, and word went out that young Mistress Laydon had been delivered of a male fetus.

As the first rays of the sun gilded the treetops, Andrew Buckler, who had spent the night keeping vigil outside the Laydons' house, went back to his own quarters and shot himself.

Bone-weary and heartsick, Temperance walked slowly along the hard grassy path that passed for a street inside the palisade. Her own house was at the opposite corner of the triangle from the Laydon house. The early morning sun had just cleared the tops of the pine trees. Will would be anxious to hear the details of what had happened, and little Gabriel would be hungry. Soon she would think about weaning him, but not today. Today she wanted to clutch him to her, to feel his small, vigorous sucking at her breast, and to forget what she had seen at the Laydons'. The sound of Ann's exhausted weeping still rang in her ears, and she could still see John's face as he looked on the small, lifeless form, no bigger than a kitten, that should have been his firstborn son. Temperance and Lucy and Meg had wrapped the tiny body in a soft white handkerchief, and at noon there would be a burial.

They would bury Andrew Buckler, too, but not in the graveyard. Church law forbade the burial of a suicide in consecrated ground.

Alexander Whitaker, the young minister, had brought the news of Buckler's death to Ann and John Laydon, and asked them to say a prayer for him. "I don't hold Buckler at fault," John Laydon said wearily. "I don't even hold Marshal Dale at fault. I blame this godforsaken place for what happened here. The sight of blood, the smell of death—they mean nothing to us here, they are so common."

Shivering in the chill morning air, Temperance rapped lightly on the heavy oak door of her house and waited for Will to slide the bolt. She could hear him stirring, and she could hear Gabriel's small voice greeting the morning with his usual happy gibberish. Before long, he would be talking. He had walked a month before his first birthday. The iron bolt clanked; the door swung inward, and Will held out his arms to her.

"She miscarried. A little boy." Temperance spoke the words over Will's shoulder. "And Andrew Buckler shot himself."

"What?" Will pulled back from her so that he could see her face. He looked at her in disbelief. "I heard a shot, but I thought it was just the watch firing at some Indian."

"He was there all night, outside the door, and then he went home when it was over. We heard the shot, and then Reverend Whitaker came to tell us."

"Poor Andrew," Will said softly. "Poor Andrew."

"They are going to bury the Laydon baby at noon," Temperance said wearily. With one hand, she pulled off the knitted coif that bound her hair, and with the other she unfastened the laces of her bodice as she crossed the room to take up Gabriel. He had been noisily sucking his thumb, and now, greedily, he found her breast and began to suck almost before she had sat down.

"Little pig," she said, "you'll soon have to give this up. You're too big and too heavy." She settled herself on a stool with her back against the wall to let him nurse. Outside, a drum began to sound. It was the signal for the work parties.

"I must be off," Will said, bending to kiss his wife on the forehead. He kissed his son's forehead lightly, too, and turned toward the door. "We're repairing the south wall today. I'll come back here before the burial." Will, like every other able-bodied man at Jamestown, marched off to work to the beat of a drum every day but Sunday.

As the door closed, Temperance leaned back and closed her eyes. They felt gritty, heavy with fatigue. Gabriel suckled noisily, both chubby hands kneading her breast. If she let him have his fill, he might nap for a while. Then she could at least lie down, and maybe fall asleep. She tried to shut out the ugliness of the previous day and night, but she could not. Poor, poor Ann Laydon, with the flesh laid open on her back, with her womb empty and bleeding. Poor John Laydon, weeping, swearing, his thin frame trembling with helpless rage at the whipping; his pale face a mask of grief at the birthing. This might go harder with him than with Ann, Temperance thought. John was not strong. He had never really recovered his health after the Starving Time. If John Laydon had not come to Virginia, he could have lived out his life fashioning cupboards and building stairsteps in Bovey Tracey, the tiny Devon village of his birth.

And if she had not come to Virginia, her own life, Temperance mused, would have been as placid as her grandmother's had been: wedded, bedded, and buried in Norfolk, venturing once or twice to London, never setting foot on anything more dangerous than a Thames River boat, never knowing any passion stronger than a conjugal kiss. Neither, she supposed, had her mother. How long, she thought suddenly and guiltily, had it been since she had thought of her mother? And what, if she knew, was her mother thinking of her?

Of her youngest daughter, living in sin with a man not her lawful husband, and of her newest grandchild, by English law a bastard? Temperance had only received one letter from her parents in all the time she had been in Virginia. It came with Governor de la Warr's ship in the spring of 1610, and it proffered condolence for the loss of George and urged her to come home by the next ship. But since that spring, George had come and gone from Jamestown, and then come back again. Surely, Temperance thought, when he was in England he must have gone straight to Thickthorne to tell her parents. A month after Gabriel's birth, she and Will together had composed a single letter of announcement and apology to Anthony and Martha Flowerdew, but there had been no ship to send it by until nearly six months later, when the tiny *Blessing* had come and gone. Her master, a man named Adams, had promised to deliver the letter to Thickthorne. But letters often went astray, and there was no way to know whether it arrived safely. At any rate, there had been no answer.

Or perhaps they knew, and had nothing more to say to her. Temperance imagined her mother's pale oval face, the large dark eyes raised heavenward, the thin mouth shaping words of prayer for her wayward daughter. Her father, when he thought about it, would slap his knee and swear under his breath, the way he always did when something unpleasant occurred to him. Her sisters would make long faces and cluck their tongues, and then congratulate each other that their sinful sister was so far from them. Her brother, Stanley, would laugh and drink a toast to her, and raise a glass to his new nephew three thousand miles away. Paper was scarce at Jamestown, and ink as precious as wine; but maybe, Temperance thought, she should try to send another letter. Thickthorne these days was as far removed from her thoughts as the moon, and seemed more remote. At least she could see the moon.

Gabriel had nearly finished nursing. He was sucking drowsily and contentedly, his eyes tightly closed, their fine dark lashes resting against his cheeks. In a moment, she could ease him down on the pallet and stretch out beside him. She had not slept for twenty-four hours. It was blessedly quiet inside the house, and outside the only noise was the occasional twitter of a sparrow or a wren. With any luck, she could sleep until time for the burial service. But just as she closed her eyes, there were footsteps outside, and then a soft rapping at the door. "Who is it?" she said. She tried to speak quietly, but Gabriel's eyes flew open. Her heart sank. Now she would never get him back to sleep. As he began to wriggle happily, trying to get up, she spoke again, this time sharply. "I said, who is it?"

"It's George."

She scrambled to her feet, shaking out her skirts with one hand and pushing at her disheveled hair with the other. Dear God in heaven, she thought numbly. Her heart began to pound so fast that she could barely breathe. She had not spoken to George since the day he came ashore at Point Comfort, and since he had returned to Jamestown, she had only seen him from a distance. The two of them had not been alone together since that long-ago night in Plymouth before the ships sailed.

"Temperance, it's George," said the voice on the other side of the door. "May I come in?" It was a polite voice, the voice of a stranger.

"Yes," Temperance answered mechanically. "Yes, of course." She undid the latch, and the door swung inward. There he stood, ramrod-straight and in full military array, with the morning sun glinting off the burnished steel of his helmet. "Come in," she said stiffly, and stepped backward so he could enter. In two strides, he was in the center of the room, one hand resting lightly on the silver hilt of his sword. "You'll not need that," Temperance said. "I'm not armed."

His mouth, set in a grim straight line, softened, and his eyes, those familiar blue-black pools, met hers with the faintest flicker of amusement and embarrassment. Suddenly realizing he was indoors with his helmet on, he took it off and held it under one arm. "I am sorry," he said. "I . . . forgot my manners."

"Would you like to sit down?" Temperance pointed to the two joint stools in the corner.

"No, thank you. I'll not be long. I came to tell you—"

At that moment, Gabriel, who had crawled up behind Temperance and had been hiding shyly behind his mother's skirts, poked his head around and peered up at the visitor. George's mouth opened, but no sound came. His eyes widened as they studied the small, round face and the copper-gold curls. Gabriel, in turn, gazed upward in wonder at this stranger in shiny armor.

"This is . . . Gabriel," Temperance said.

George, still struggling with his emotions, said nothing. His mouth trembled, and he pressed his lips tightly together. There was a momentary look of such tenderness, such longing, on his face as he gazed at the child that Temperance was moved to pity. Aloud, she said, "I was hoping he would stay asleep so I could sleep." George did not answer, so she went on, feeling a desperate need to fill the silence, "I was up all night at the Laydons'."

"I apologize for disturbing you." He spoke stiffly. "That was a bad business, that whipping."

"Yes, it was. Ann had a miscarriage, you know."

"So I heard this morning. Dale acted unwisely, ordering those whippings," George said. "It went badly with Jane Wright, too." Still watching Gabriel, he shook his head.

"But Jane Wright did not lose a baby," Temperance said. "Poor John Laydon has to see his little son buried today."

George's right hand strayed to his sword hilt. His fingers closed around it, his thumb nervously caressing the smooth silver knob at its end. "At least he has the consolation of knowing that the child was his." He flung the words between them suddenly, sharply, without warning. Temperance recoiled as though he had pricked her with his sword.

"Oh, George—" she said softly. "We cannot undo what has been done, you and I, but—"

He cut her off. "I did not come here to discuss what has happened," he said coldly.

"But you made it happen!" She spat the words at him. "You were the one that made us sail on separate ships! That was your doing, not mine!" Just for an instant, his eyes met hers, and she saw that she had wounded him.

"I cannot change what is past," he said slowly. Then he turned his eyes on Gabriel, as though he dared not look into her eyes again. "I came here to tell you that I intend to get a decree of divorce. I thought you should know." He spoke slowly and precisely, shaping each word with icy formality.

"Won't that be difficult?" Temperance tried to match her tone to his. They were fencing now; their words glancing off each other. Thrust and parry, Temperance thought, thrust and parry, and see who drops his guard first. She was so tense that the back of her neck had begun to throb.

"Yes, but it can be done. Sir Thomas has friends at court, and a cousin who's a bishop."

"I see."

Gabriel, who had pulled himself upright and was holding on to his mother's skirt, let go and took a few unsteady steps toward George. Temperance reached for him, but she was not quick enough. George went down on one knee and stretched out an arm to keep him from falling. Gabriel crowed with delight and clutched at the shiny chain-mail sleeve.

"He has your hair," George said. "He's a handsome boy. Pity he's a bastard."

"Get out!" Temperance scooped Gabriel up and held him close. He, thinking they were playing a game, laughed and wriggled in her arms. "Go on! Get out!" Her voice, hoarse with fatigue and anger, broke on the last word.

George rose to his feet. "I only came to tell you about the divorce," he said defensively. "I also came to tell you I went to Thickthorne last winter, and I told your mother and father."

"Are they well?" Temperance would not give him the satisfaction of telling her what they had said about her and Will.

"Quite. But needless to say, not happy."

"I don't want to hear about it!" Temperance's voice rose with her temper.

"Then I shan't tell you." George looked disconcerted.

"Then why don't you go, if you have nothing more to tell me?"

"You—you're not fit to be told! There's a name for you, but I'll not say it in front of your son!" Now they were both shouting.

"Then leave! For God's sake, George! Just go!"

But he made no move to depart. "To think I gave you a ring that said 'Be true in heart.'"

"Then take it back!" Still holding Gabriel, Temperance began to rummage with her free hand in a small wooden box on the cupboard shelf. "Here!" She flung the ring at him. "Take it! Take it and be damned!" The slender gold circle bounced on the hard-packed earth floor and landed at George's feet. Slowly, silently, he bent over and picked it up.

"I'll not be damned, but you may be," he said quietly. Carefully, he unfastened the small metal tinder box on his belt, and dropped the ring inside. "Good-bye, Temperance." His eyes swept over her from head to foot, and then he glanced briefly at Gabriel, as though fixing them both in his memory. "I leave at noon for Fort Charles." His voice was flat now, emotionless. "God willing, we'll not see each other again in this life." With weary finality, he set his helmet firmly on his head, adjusted his sword, and, opening the door, strode off without once looking back.

Temperance stood in the doorway watching him until he reached the far end of the path and turned toward the main gate. Then her son, restless at being confined so long in her arms, began to fret and pull at her hair. Gabriel did not go back to sleep that morning, and Will did not come back in time for the burial of the Laydon infant. Numb with sorrow and stumbling from exhaustion, Temperance carried Gabriel with her to the burial service. She longed for Will to comfort her. It was not like him to be late, she thought, but the work gang's morning task must have taken longer than usual. Approaching the burial ground, she squared her shoulders and lifted her chin, and resolved to blot George Yardley from her memory.

But as Reverend Whitaker's clear young voice intoned the words of the service—"Man, that is born of woman, hath but a short time to live, and is full of misery"—Temperance's throat began to ache and her eyelids started to sting. "In the midst of life we are in death; of whom may we seek for succour, but of thee, O Lord, who for our sins art justly displeased?" As the minister's voice rose and fell, Temperance began to weep: first in small, hiccupping sobs; then louder ones, and finally she was crying so bitterly that Nathaniel Causey, standing next to her, took Gabriel from her arms, and Thomasine began to pat her shoulder ineffectually. "Poor thing! You are worn out from last night," Thomasine whispered. "Where is Will?"

Temperance, in her dazed state, had not noticed that the other men who had been working on the south wall with Will were there. After the service, the Causeys carried Gabriel and led her home, like a sleepwalker. She thanked them woodenly. Then she locked the door, gave Gabriel a piece of hard bread, and flung herself on a pallet, where she slept like a stone.

When she awoke, Gabriel was asleep, and the late afternoon sun was streaming in the windows. She rose hurriedly, smoothed her hair, and poked up the fire. Will would be coming home any moment. First they would eat, she thought, and then she would tell him about George. Dear Will, she thought gratefully. He was her rock, her mainstay. He would come and put his arms around her, and everything would be all right again. She wondered idly what had kept him from the burial service. Laying fresh wood on the fire, she set out strips of dried beef to boil. Beef and Indian bread with wild onions was one of Will's favorite meals. Jamestown now had cattle and hogs and chickens in abundance, and with the coming of autumn, the ducks and geese would be returning to the marshy lowlands near the river. This winter there would be no Starving Time. The worst that could happen to her and to Will had already happened, Temperance thought as she sat down to nurse Gabriel. George would eventually go back to England, and she and Will would make a life for themselves in Virginia. What had happened to the three of them could not be helped. Consoling herself by imagining the land she and Will would have some day, and the house they would build, and watching Gabriel, Temperance sat daydreaming until she heard Will's footsteps outside the door.

But before she could get to her feet and unbolt the door, he was pounding on it: three slow, heavy blows, without a word of greeting. That was not like him. Surprised, Temperance hesitated for a moment, thinking it might be someone else. "Will?"

The answer was three more knocks, as slow and heavy as the first ones.

"Will, don't tease me. Is that you?" Silence. But who else would it be? Temperance slid the bolt and opened the door.

"Just open it to anybody, do you?" Will said. He stepped inside, swaying slightly.

"Will, what on earth—"

"I know what went on here today." He seized her by the shoulders and looked down at her.

"What—"

"You can't play the innocent with me!"

"Will, what are you talking about?"

"Sit down." He let go her shoulders and, with an exaggerated sweep of his arm, indicated a stool by the fire. "Sit down, and tell me all about it." His voice was slurred.

"About what?" Temperance faced him angrily. "You are the one who ought to sit down. You've been drinking!"

"You're damn right I've been drinking, and if I had anything here to drink, I'd drink some more!"

Temperance had never seen him drunk. Tipsy once or twice, yes, from plum wine at Point Comfort, but drunk, never. She did not know whether to be angry or frightened. "Will, what is it? What's come over you?"

"What's come over you?" he mimicked her drunkenly. "I'll tell you what's come over me!" He swayed and gripped her by the shoulders. "You had George Yardley here today, in my house, and in front of my son!"

"Oh, for God's sake, Will!"

"Don't deny it! Richard Pace saw him here, and came to tell me." Will looked at her with red-rimmed eyes, and Temperance was frightened.

"Yes, George did come here, but only to tell me that he is going to get a decree of divorce," she said, trying to keep her voice steady. "I had no idea he would ever come."

Still holding her by the shoulders, Will shook her slightly.

"Nothing happened, Will! Nothing! I swear to God! How can you think that?"

"I can think it because I know it." He folded his arms across his chest and glared at her.

"Will, this is not like you. You must believe what I tell you."

He blinked slowly, and then looked at her with narrowed eyes. "No." His lips shaped the word with exaggerated precision. "Why else would George come here when I'm gone? If he just wanted to announce his divorce decree, he would have waited for me to be here, too, would he not?" Will rubbed a hand over his face and then shook his head, as if to clear it, to summon sobriety. "After all, I am his best friend." He paused. "And you don't bed your best friend's wife without his leave. No one would do that, would he?" Will's head dropped forward so that his chin touched his chest, and his broad shoulders shook with silent, drunken sobs. Temperance held out her arms to him, but he folded his arms again across his chest, fending her off. He rocked backward slightly, and she put out her hands to steady him. Her face was close to his, almost close enough to kiss.

"Will, dearest Will . . ."

He brought his folded arms up sharply, catching her under her chin, jerking her neck backward and driving her teeth into her tongue. "Don't 'dearest Will' me! You asked him here, didn't you? Didn't you?"

But there was blood in Temperance's mouth, and she was in such pain she could not answer.

POTOMAC
29 March 1613

 Just as Iapazeus had promised, she was there, sitting demurely beside the old King of the Potomacs and his two wives. Captain Samuel Argall breathed a jubilant but silent prayer of thanksgiving and bowed low before her. "The Princess Pocahontas, is it not?"

The wide dark eyes met his for an instant, and Argall imagined a faint glimmer of contempt. Then they swept downward and the sleek dark head inclined itself ever so slightly in his direction. She did not do him the honor of a reply.

"I am very glad to see you." Argall spoke slowly so that she could follow his words. John Smith had told him she knew some English, but that was in 1609. It had been four years since she had spoken with any Englishman. She raised her eyes, and her mouth arranged itself in the merest suggestion of a smile. Encouraged, Argall smiled back.

She was no beauty. A wide forehead, the high cheekbones of her race, the nose a bit large for the small face, the mouth sensuous and strong, with a willful expression. The eyes were her most striking feature. Wide-set, dark brown, under sweeping black brows, they were the eyes of a forest creature, at once intelligent, cunning, and gentle. By Argall's reckoning, she could be no more than eighteen, but she looked out upon the world with more wisdom, and bore herself with more grace, than any young woman he had ever seen. Winning her confidence would be no easy task.

"I have heard much about you from Captain John Smith," Argall said.

This time there was no mistaking her smile. "Ah!" she said. "You know Captain Smith?" Her voice was pleasant, something like the lower register of a flute or recorder. When she spoke, she revealed two rows of small, even teeth.

"Yes." Argall paused. Now his fish was about to take the bait. "Yes,

I saw him last year in London." Pocahontas was leaning forward now, listening eagerly.

"He was hurt when he left here," she said softly.

"But he is well now."

Joy and relief showed in her eyes. "Ah, I am—" She searched her memory for the right word. "Glad. Very glad."

"He sends you greetings." That calculated lie pleased her even more. "And your father, too. Captain Smith sends greetings to Powhatan, too." Pocahontas's face clouded, and she drew back slightly. That last remark obviously did not please her. Her reaction disturbed Argall. If she and her father were not on the best of terms, this plan might not work. He decided to take another tack. "I am here to trade for corn, as Captain Smith used to do," he said. "But your people have also given me three fine fat hares. Would you like to come aboard my ship and dine—eat—with me and my men? I could tell you more about John Smith."

She hesitated, and Argall held his breath. Then she shook her head, and his heart sank. "No," she said. "No, thank you." She glanced at King Powtowneck and his wives, who nodded in solemn agreement.

"I wish you would come," Argall said. If she would not rise to this bait, what was he to do next? "Perhaps you would like to think about it. If you change your mind, send word to the longboat, and we will wait for you."

"No, thank you," she said again.

"Well, then, I must say farewell. We sail at sunrise." To King Powtowneck, Argall said, "I must go now. I have business with Iapazeus." The crafty Iapazeus was a shrewd trader. With the right offer, he might be persuaded to lure the Princess Pocahontas aboard the *Treasurer.* Sure enough, when Argall explained what he wanted, Iapazeus's small beady eyes narrowed, and he smiled greedily.

"What you give me?"

"You bring her to my ship before sunset, and you shall have three strings of blue beads and a knife."

Iapazeus folded his fat arms and shook his head slowly, so that his greasy topknot waved back and forth. "No."

"White beads and a looking glass."

"No." Iapazeus looked him squarely in the eye. *"Mattassin."* Mattassin was the Indian word for copper. Argall tried desperately to recall what copper he had on board. They did not usually carry copper to trade, and this transaction might not be as easy as he had hoped. Then he remembered that in the ship's galley there was a large copper kettle they used for boiling peas and making porridge.

"Very well, then, a kettle." Argall made a circle of his arms to show the size. "A pot this big. Copper. *Mattassin.* "

Iapazeus grinned broadly. He raised his chin high, so that his beaklike nose pointed at the ceiling, and then lowered his head so that his chin touched his chest. "Ah, for *mattassin,* I come."

Argall was relieved. So far, so good, he thought. "What will you do?" he asked. "How will you get her?"

Iapazeus regarded him through half-shut eyes. They reminded Argall of a snake's eyes. "You go," he said, waving his arm in the direction of the ship. "You wait. I bring Pocahontas."

"By sundown?"

"By sundown."

Back aboard the *Treasurer,* Argall could do nothing but pace her deck from fo'c's'le to stern and back again, waiting, watching the shore. As the spring afternoon waned, the wind rose, and he pulled his cloak closer about him. The rows of bark houses in the Indian village looked snug, each issuing forth its plume of smoke. Inside, the occupants would be making ready their main meal, Indian bread made from ground corn, dried fruit, strips of dried venison or fish. In the *Treasurer*'s galley, a large pewter charger held neatly cut pieces of cold boiled hare. In the ship's great cabin, a jug of beer stood ready on the table. In the *Treasurer*'s gun room, the ship's only fully enclosed room besides the great cabin, a straw mat with two white blankets and a bolster had been laid out. The web was spun, Argall thought, but where was his prey? Squinting against the lowering sun, he leaned on the *Treasurer*'s forward gunwale and waited.

"Any sign of them yet?" John Rolfe, quiet, soft-spoken, and still melancholy from his wife's death, came and stood beside him.

"Nary a sign. I wonder."

"Wait and see. Maybe old Iapazeus will make good his promise yet." Rolfe, mourning for Gwendolyn, had especially asked to come on this trading journey. Argall had hoped the change of scene would do him good, but he had kept to himself much of the time, and so far had refused to take any Indian women the few times they had been offered. Pity, Argall thought. A bachelor himself, he took women wherever he found them, and congratulated himself for being single and unencumbered.

The sea was his real love. He had gone to sea at the age of fifteen, and had been a sailor ever since. He was now thirty-six, and had sailed the Atlantic Ocean five times—the last time in the unbelievably swift time of fifty-one days. This little voyage along the coast of the Bay of Chesapeake and up the wide Potomac River was child's play to him. But he had got the old werowance Potowneck to give him over a thousand bushels of corn, and now, if he could get Pocahontas, it would be a trip well worth the taking. With the Powhatan's favorite daughter as hostage, Thomas Dale, now deputy governor, could bring the river tribes to his own terms.

"Look!" Rolfe said. "There they come." Emerging from King Potowneck's house were Iapazeus and a short, fat woman who must be his wife, and with them was Pocahontas. The three were laughing and talking, and walking straight toward the pier. The sounds of their voices, the curiously musical blending of soft and guttural noises that made up the Algonquin dialect they spoke, were clearly audible, but unintelligible. They climbed into the waiting longboat, where four oarsmen were waiting to row them to the ship.

As the shrill notes of the bo'sun's pipe pierced the air, the longboat drew alongside the *Treasurer*'s port side, and the party prepared to come aboard. Iapazeus, grinning broadly and winking privately at Argall, was first up the rope boarding ladder. Argall shook his hand. Then Iapazeus's wife wallowed her way up, panting and smiling. The Princess Pocahontas, nimble as a cat, clambered swiftly and surefootedly up the ropes, gazing upward in awe at the ship's tall masts as she climbed. Argall and Iapazeus both held out their hands to her, and each took an arm as she reached the top of the gunwale.

"Ah, welcome aboard, Princess!" Argall was beaming. As Pocahontas leaped lightly to the deck, Iapazeus surreptitiously planted his large moccasined foot atop Argall's instep and winked at him. Argall acknowledged the pressure on his shoe with a barely perceptible inclination of his head, and then bowed to the royal visitor. "You do us honor," he said to Pocahontas. "You must see my ship, and then the three of you must dine with me."

On the small table in Argall's cabin, the ship's log and the navigational charts had been cleared away, and supper laid. Two wooden chests had been commandeered to make seats for the guests. Iapazeus and his wife sat on one, Pocahontas on the other. Argall, seated in his usual place, poured beer into four pewter goblets as the others took their places. On a stool next to him was young Thomas Savage, who had lived among the Indians during John Smith's time. Now, fluent in the Indian tongue, he served the colony as interpreter. Argall, who had trucked with Virginia Indians three times before and had an ear for languages, had mastered the essentials of Algonquin; but on such a delicate situation as this, he dared not trust himself to catch the nuances of their dialogue.

"We must have a toast," Argall said. "A toast to—peace between our people." He quaffed his beer in nervous haste and set his goblet down, not taking his eyes off Pocahontas. She sipped slowly, delicately, with shyly downcast eyes, placing her goblet carefully in front of her but not letting go of it. The slender brown fingers of one hand held fast to the pewter stem, and she sat up very straight. She reminded Argall of some wild creature poised for flight, a doe scenting danger. No, he told himself, he must be imagining that. How could she suspect anything? But how was Iapazeus planning to carry this off? Was he going to drug her? Catch her hands and tie her up? She would never submit to that without a struggle. She would cry out, and her cries for help would carry over the water. Argall did not let himself think what would happen then. Mechanically, with forced geniality, he performed his duty as host.

"You first, Princess Pocahontas. Help yourself. This hare was a gift from King Powtowneck."

The brown eyes met his as she took a piece of meat, and she smiled.

"You do us honor," Argall said. "We welcome you. Let us drink another toast, to your stay aboard the *Treasurer.*" He raised his goblet. As he did so, Iapazeus pressed his foot again.

At daylight the next morning, the *Treasurer*'s longboat went ashore. In it were a beaming Iapazeus and his wife, proudly clutching between them a large, shiny copper kettle. Watching them from the porthole of the gun room was Princess Pocahontas. She was too angry to weep. They had tricked her, old Iapazeus and his fat wife; they had trapped her like a vixen and bolted the door. Above her head, on the deck, she could hear footsteps and voices as the *Treasurer* prepared to get under way.

Captain Argall's deep voice rose above the hubbub of the others. "Free the mainsail lines! Check that foresail rigging! Stand ready at the capstan! We'll up anchor the moment the longboat gets back!"

Pocahontas did not understand all his words, but she understood the urgency in his voice. He was anxious to be off. He had played false with her, and she hated him for it. She hated all the English except John Smith.

The day she had said good-bye to John Smith—five years ago this winter—was as vivid as though it were yesterday.

"Up anchor!"

"Heave ho, for Jamestown!"

There was a great creaking noise as the sailors on the *Treasurer*'s foredeck turned the capstan, and then a clanking as the heavy anchor chain began to come up, but Pocahontas, the prisoner below decks, heard only the one word: *Jamestown.*

Jamestown. She knew every tree, every rock, every house, every corner. And Jamestown was only twelve miles from Werowocomoco. They thought to keep her there, these stupid Englishmen.

CHESAPEAKE BAY
30 March 1613

 Five days, Captain Argall had said. Five days by water, down the broad Potomac River, then along the shoreline of the Bay of Chesapeake, and up the river James to the fort at Jamestown. The first day, sailing downriver, watching the bluffs and rolling hills of the Potomac shoreline slip by, had been pleasant enough. The *Treasurer* was a large ship, larger than Powhatan's great house at Werowocomoco, which could hold a hundred and fifty warriors. Pocahontas was glad it was so large, since the river grew wider and wider. At Powtowneck's village, it was narrow enough to cross quickly in a canoe, but when they rounded the great bend and turned southward toward the bay, its banks spread farther apart and the river was swift.

By the evening of the second day, as they reached the place where the Potomac flowed into the Chesapeake, the *Treasurer* began to roll and pitch. Lying on her makeshift bed in the close quarters of the gun room, Pocahontas, who was unused to sea travel, listened to the creaking of the ship's timbers and feared the vessel might come apart. She tried to tell herself that this foreign way of travel was perfectly safe. Hadn't Captain Argall told her that this very ship had sailed many times across the great ocean, a journey that took as long as two moons? And this voyage was only five days. She tossed and turned, and when daylight came, she found that she did not want anything to eat. Captain Argall suggested that she come up on the main deck. A squall had blown in from the southeast, and it was raining, but the fresh salt air, he said, would do her good.

By noon, she went below again. Her stomach had begun to churn like the waters in the ship's wake, and she felt as if everything inside her wanted to come up. She tried lying down, but that did no good. She sat doubled up, hugging her knees, resting her forehead on them. Around her and above her she could hear the now-familiar voices of the crew, and occasional hurried footsteps as they went about their business. No one else seemed to mind this relentless rocking. She pressed her lips together and swallowed, but her mouth was unpleasantly dry.

"Pocahontas, are you unwell?" The voice belonged to Captain Argall.

He rapped lightly on the door of the gun room. "Pocahontas?"

"No," she lied. She did not want to talk; she needed all her concentration to keep from being sick.

"Pocahontas, don't you want something to eat? Some bread and cheese?"

"No." Even one-word answers were an effort. She hoped he would go away.

"Very well. Come out when you like."

She did not trust herself to speak again, and, after a moment, he left. After that, she lost track of time. Finally, exhausted, she dozed briefly. Late in the afternoon, she was awakened by another knock on her door. She did not answer, but the caller did not leave. Instead, he rapped again, insistently.

"Pocahontas? Pocahontas, please open the door." This time it was not Captain Argall's voice.

"No," she said weakly. "Go away." She did not care who it was. The gun room, designed to store weapons, did not lock from the inside. With a click, the heavy iron door handle moved, and slowly the door was eased open. Pocahontas looked up angrily.

"Forgive me for intruding, but we were afraid you were ill." It was John Rolfe, holding a tankard of beer and a piece of ship's biscuit. "We thought you should eat something."

"No. Go away!" Her stomach gave an ominous heave, and she put her head down on her knees.

Rolfe stood for a moment in the doorway, watching her. "I shall leave this here, in case you want it."

She did not look up again. Rolfe set the tankard and the biscuit on a chest near her. Then, without another word, he backed out of the room and gently closed the door. Just before dark, she crept over to the chest, nibbled on the ship's biscuit, took a sip of beer, and then fell sound asleep.

When she awoke the next morning, the sun was shining brightly and the *Treasurer* was sailing smoothly. The only uneven motion was a flock of gulls that swooped and screeched overhead. Pocahontas unbraided her hair, matted from the day before, and combed it. She was glad that no one but John Rolfe had seen her while she was seasick. She braided her hair, smoothed her dress, and hurried up on deck, feeling hungry. As she emerged from the gangway, half a dozen crewmen cheered.

"There she is!"

"Got your sea legs now, Princess?"

"Yesterday was only a piddling squall. Be glad you don't have to sail the Atlantic."

Pocahontas drew herself up, eyed them coldly, and turned her back on them without acknowledging their presence. Leaning on the foredeck gunwale, she peered eagerly at the shore. The *Treasurer* had left Chesapeake Bay, and was now making her way slowly against the currents at the wide mouth of a river.

"That's the river James." Captain Argall had come up behind her. "Wind and tide allowing, we could be at Jamestown by sundown tomorrow." He leaned on the gunwale beside her. "I am glad to see you are better."

He had treated her kindly enough, for one who had held her against her will. Pocahontas understood his motives, but she had doubts that he would get what he wanted from Powhatan. She and her father had not spoken to each other in four years, since the night she had betrayed him to John Smith. She had lived contentedly enough among the Potomacs, and she wondered if Powhatan, who had banished her, would be willing to bargain much to get her back. For her part, she cared little one way or the other. She would return to her people sooner or later. Until then, she would pass the time observing the English and their strange ways. Besides, Jamestown she knew as well as she knew Werowocomoco, or Orapakes, or any other Indian village, and Jamestown was where John Smith, if ever he did return, would come. That alone was enough to keep her contented.

The next day, as the *Treasurer* approached Jamestown, she asked Captain Argall where she was to stay. His brows drew together, and he pursed his lips.

"Princess Pocahontas, as you well know, before we left Powtowneck's village I sent a runner to tell your father of your . . . your being with us." Argall looked away, as though he would find the words he needed in the marsh grass of the distant shoreline. "My man should return to Jamestown soon. In the meantime, until we hear from Powhatan, we must keep you . . . safe." He rubbed his hands uneasily. "I would have you stay in the care of one of my men, Captain James Davis."

"I will stay where you say," she said amicably. As long as it was at Jamestown, any place would do. "Which is his house?"

Argall looked exceedingly uncomfortable. Still not looking at her, he answered tersely, "His house is not at Jamestown. It is upriver, at a place called Henrico."

At dawn the next morning, after a sleepless night at Jamestown, a furious, heavily guarded Pocahontas was put into a shallop for the two days' journey to the wilderness outpost of Henrico, forty miles upriver.

She vowed they would not keep her there long.

HENRICO
20 July 1613

"You can't keep her in irons! She's not a criminal!"

"Well, she's tried to run off twice, and the last time she got clear to the river. I have no choice but to confine her." Captain James Davis, now in charge of the fortifications at Henrico, took a large swig from the tankard on the table, and wiped his mouth with the back of his sleeve. "Governor Dale will have my head if she gets away!"

Across the table from him, John Rolfe frowned. "Dale won't like it if she pines away from being locked up, either," he said. "He sent word to Powhatan that Pocahontas would be well cared for, and from what I understand, you may have to care for her for some while. Old Powhatan does not seem very anxious to have his daughter back."

"You say he sent Richard Pace and the others back with seven muskets that are rusted out, and told them to tell Dale that all the other weapons were lost? How could he lose a dozen guns, each one near as tall as a man? And what of the swords? George Percy reckoned Powhatan had collected two or three score of those. You know he must be lying," Davis said.

"Of course he is. But he said he would give us five hundred bushels of corn to make up for the loss of the weapons, and to get Pocahontas back."

"But Thomas Dale won't settle for that."

"No."

Davis sighed. "Then I am to have Pocahontas on my hands for God knows how long, while Powhatan dickers with Dale. Damnation! I have to lock her up. I can't have a man watching her day and night."

"What about the women at Henrico? Could they not watch her?"

"You know how women are. I don't much trust them. They'd just as soon help her escape. The few I do trust have needs of their own to take care of. Ann Laydon is big with another child, and Lucy Forrest's husband is ailing, and Temperance Yardley—I mean Sterling—has a small boy and a husband who wants to run off to the Indians himself."

"Will Sterling? What do you mean?"

Davis offered Rolfe the tankard. "I mean he's gone near daft since they moved up here. Drinking too much, and always talking about how he could live so well among the savages, and be free like them, and such nonsense. He's certainly not the one to guard Pocahontas."

"Where are you keeping her?"

"In the main storehouse. It's the only place with a secure lock on the door."

"May I see her?"

Davis looked surprised. "What for?"

"I don't know, but I . . . should like to see her." Rolfe himself did not know why he wanted to see her.

Davis put both hands flat on the table and pushed himself up wearily. "Very well, then, if it pleases you, you may look at her. But she is not a pretty sight these days. Maybe having a visitor will sweeten her temper."

Rolfe was not prepared for what he saw. In the grain room of the storehouse, Pocahontas sat cross-legged on a pile of straw. On one slender ankle there was an iron cuff, and from it a long chain ran to a heavy ring fastened on the wall. Her hair, unbraided, hung around her shoulders in tangles; her dress, the beaded doeskin one she had worn when she was taken aboard the *Treasurer,* was badly stained and stiff with dirt. On the straw where she sat, there were dark stains and a smell of blood. Flies buzzed noisily around her.

"She's having her monthly time, just now," Davis said matter-of-factly. "Usually, she's cleaner."

Pocahontas, upon their sudden entry, had raised her head and straightened her shoulders. In the wide dark eyes, hatred and wounded pride looked out. Rolfe thought of a doe he had once seen caught in a bear trap. "My God, man!" He spoke to Davis in a low voice. "You can't treat her like an animal!"

"Come, now, Rolfe! She's only a savage wench, and a mean-tempered one at that," Davis said jovially. "If I took those chains off, she'd run away in a trice."

"But this—this is inhuman."

Davis laughed bitterly. "Inhuman! Have you ever seen a man with ten or twenty arrows in him? Or a man with the flesh scraped off his bones, the way her father's men killed John Ratcliffe? Look at her. She'd do the same to us right now, if she could." Pocahontas had recognized John Rolfe, and she looked at him with such fierce hatred he felt the back of his neck crawl.

He tried to smile at her. "Princess Pocahontas," he said, "I am sorry that they have to keep you like this. I—I must go now, but I'll come back."

She did not speak to him. He tugged at Davis's sleeve, and the two men turned to leave. When they were outside again, Rolfe spoke. "This will not do. Even Thomas Dale wouldn't like it."

"Then what am I supposed to do with her?" Davis's voice rose in exasperation. "God knows, I don't relish keeping her here any more than she likes being here. It's old Powhatan's fault, not sending for her."

"I have an idea," Rolfe said slowly. "When I crossed the river I passed near Mount Malado, and the place where young Reverend Whitaker has built his parsonage. He's got near a hundred acres enclosed there, with a log pale two feet higher than a man's head all around. What if you put Pocahontas there—in his keeping?"

Davis stroked his beard thoughtfully. "You know, that might work. He's got a boy or two about the place, and they could watch her, and maybe he'd like to try his hand at Christianizing her. That was the reason he wanted to come to Henrico in the first place, you know, to bring God to the Indians." He clapped John Rolfe on the back. "You're a good man to think of it. Why don't you stop at his place—Rock Hall, he calls it—and ask him, and then I'll go over in a day or two and arrange everything."

The young parson was delighted with the plan. He kept rubbing his hands together and saying, "God be praised!," as Rolfe explained the situation to him.

"It will be a perfect arrangement," Whitaker said. "I've plenty of room here, and plenty of time to instruct her in the faith. If I can succeed with her, then there will be others."

On his way back to Jamestown, John Rolfe tried to imagine Pocahontas in the parsonage at Rock Hall. When he thought of her there, in the care of Alexander Whitaker instead of in chains in the storehouse at Henrico, he felt a great satisfaction.

He also felt a slight but surprising twinge of jealousy.

HENRICO
27 November 1613

 "Lucy, that is your best cap! You don't mean for her to keep it, surely?"

"Why not? If it makes her happy to wear a lace-embroidered coif in this godforsaken wilderness, let her wear it. It does me no good lying there in the chest." Temperance and Lucy looked at each other, and then at Pocahontas, and smiled. They had transformed an Indian princess into an English lady. On her head was a linen coif worked with colored silk threads and edged with lace that almost hid the sleek black hair; on her shoulders, a green velvet cloak trimmed in gold, open down the front to reveal a bodice laced with gold cord, and a kirtle and petticoat of cream-colored satin and green grosgrain; on her feet were cream-colored stockings and black kid slippers; at her waist, a belt from which dangled a muff made of white rabbit fur.

It was the muff she liked best. They had tried to explain to her that muffs were for going out, not for wearing indoors, but she refused to be parted from it. Eyes shining, she stroked it lovingly with one hand, keeping the other inside it, as the three women sat before the fire in Alexander Whitaker's parsonage on a cold November afternoon.

"Now if only we had starch to starch you a ruff, Pocahontas, you'd be a proper English gentlewoman," Lucy said.

"That does not matter," Pocahontas said, smiling. Her English came easily now. "I have never looked on any clothes as fine as these. Our best clothes are only deerskins and fur and beads." Her fingers caressed the gold lace on the edge of her cloak. One of the first things that Reverend Alexander Whitaker had done for his new charge was to have the women at Henrico assemble a wardrobe for her: shifts, petticoats, stomachers and bodices, kirtles and gowns and cloaks. Most of her new wardrobe was of simple make and serviceable material, the kind of clothing a Sussex farm wife might wear, but to Pocahontas, accustomed to animal skin and braided grass, the feel of a Holland linen smock was luxurious, and a red stammel petticoat a thing of wondrous beauty. The shell-beaded doeskin garment that had been her only dress since the day she had been taken captive aboard the *Treasurer* had been carefully folded and laid in the wooden chest in her room.

Pocahontas seemed grateful to Whitaker for the kindness he had shown her, and, though she made no secret of her hatred for Argall and the others who had duped her into captivity, she bore the young parson no grudges. He, delighted with her, had begun to instruct her in the faith of the Church of England. He was also teaching her to read and to play simple tunes upon the lute. She did not see much point to reading, but she liked the sounds the lute strings made when she struck them, and she liked her English clothes.

"I say you may keep these clothes and wear them whenever you like," Lucy said cheerfully. "If there is one thing we have plenty of at present, it's clothes. We collected enough in that winter of the Starving Time to dress a score of women. They brought all their fine things, thinking to wear them at the court of Jamestown," she said wryly. "But the poor things died, almost before they found out they were in a wilderness." She shook her head. "I'll never forget how we had to bury Gwendolyn Rolfe while John was away at the Falls, and when he came back, he lay down upon her grave and wept."

"Rolfe?" Pocahontas's eyes had widened at the mention of the name. "Was she John Rolfe's woman?"

"Wife," Lucy corrected her gently. "Not *woman.* She was his *wife.* "

"Wife," Pocahontas repeated dutifully. "What happened to her?"

"She died of a fever," Lucy said softly. The three women were silent for a moment.

"That was a long time ago," Temperance said pensively. "Three years is a long time."

"But think how far we have come since then," Lucy said. "We may not eat well, but at least we eat now." She sighed. "But there are times when I'd sell my soul for a box of marchpane or some sugared plums."

"What is marchpane?" Pocahontas asked.

"It's a sweetmeat—a sweet made from almonds—nuts—pounded fine and mixed with sugar syrup and rosewater. We used to have it at Christmastime at home." Lucy sighed again, remembering.

"So did we," Temperance said. "And when company came, we used to eat our sweets on little trenchers—posy mats, my grandmother called them—with flowers and rhymes painted on them. And we had little silver forks, so our fingers would not get sticky from the fruits."

Pocahontas looked puzzled. "You like your home, and the ways of England," she said softly. "Why did you come here?"

Lucy and Temperance looked at each other, and then both began to laugh, but there was no humor in their laughter.

"We didn't come," Temperance said, "we were brought."

"We came because our husbands came," Lucy said.

Pocahontas nodded. That, she understood. "I would like to go to England," she said. "But I have no man to take me."

"It may be you will find someone," Temperance said.

"God knows, we have far too many men for the few women here now, and more coming." Lucy suddenly put her hand to her mouth and stared at Temperance. "May heaven strike me! I forgot! You have not heard the news, have you?"

The look in Lucy's eyes filled Temperance with foreboding. "No," she said, "what news?"

"Captain Davis came to our house yesterday to dine. He said Governor Dale is moving a company of men up to Henrico to settle at Bermuda Hundred, and he is moving Captain Yardley up here to command them." Lucy shook her head. "I thought of coming to tell you at once, but then I was afraid Will would be there. And then, so help me, Temperance, I forgot. Oh, dear heaven!" Lucy leaned forward impulsively and kissed Temperance on the cheek. "What will you do?"

"I don't know," Temperance said softly. "God help me, I don't know." She could not think. It had been two years since she had seen George. He had stayed at Fort Charles, nearly threescore miles from Jamestown, but the distance did not matter. With George on this side of the Atlantic, guilt gnawed at Will's vitals, and he continued to drink heavily. Last year Temperance had persuaded Will to leave Jamestown and move to Henrico, but his drinking and his despair had moved with him. "The fire is burning low," Temperance said abruptly. "I'll go tell the boy to bring in some more wood." She rose to her feet, pulled her shawl tightly about her, and left the room. Pulling the heavy door closed behind her, she leaned against it and put both hands up to her face. Though the room she had just left was drafty and the fire was low, her cheeks felt hot. Suddenly, Temperance wanted to rush blindly out into the cold winter afternoon. Instead, finding young Jeremy Mutton, Whitaker's servant boy, she told him to bring in more wood. Then she went back to Pocahontas and Lucy.

"Jeremy is coming with the wood, but I must go. I—I promised Gabriel I'd sew him a ball to play with, and he and his father will be back soon." She saw at once that Lucy understood. Had it been Thomasine

Causey or Joan Pierce, they would have asked a thousand well-meaning questions and insisted she stay and talk.

"Wait and I'll come with you," Lucy said. "It's a long, cold walk."

"No. There is no need for that."

Lucy's eyes sought Temperance's. "Are you certain?"

"Yes. I—I need a good long walk." Taking her cloak off the peg where she had hung it, Temperance flung it over her shoulders and pulled the hood over her hair. "Good-bye, Pocahontas. Enjoy your new clothes." Pocahontas smiled her thanks.

Lucy embraced Temperance. "God go with you."

Outside, a light snow had begun to fall. It had already covered most of the remnants of Indian summer's grass, so that only the tips of the blades were visible, poking up through the white like the stubble of a boy's first beard. Temperance picked her way lightly along the path, feeling the cold through her thin shoes. Will used to warm her feet when they had been out walking; stripping off her shoes and stockings, he would take one foot at a time in his big hands and rub it until it turned pink. Then he would kiss her bare insteps and ankles, and then sometimes his hands and his kisses would inch upward to her knees and thighs, and then they would make love by the fire, as they had done that first afternoon at Jamestown.

But that was long ago, before George had come back to Virginia.

The snow was falling thicker now, and Temperance quickened her steps. Ahead of her, the path was a faint indentation of sugary whiteness. No blades of grass now showed, and the trees had taken on a fairy-tale frosting. Except for the faint crunching of her own footsteps on the new-fallen snow, and the occasional crack of an overburdened twig, there was no sound. In the fading light of the winter afternoon, the unbroken stretches of snow were bathed in a blue-white radiance. In the distance lay the dark, curving ribbon of the river, and beyond it, the three rows of frame houses that formed the village of Henrico.

Temperance was glad Will had chosen not to live in the village. The houses seemed too close together, the palisade too confining. She had developed a liking for the wider spaces of the wilderness. Will had chosen instead the opposite side of the river, where two clusters of houses named Hope in Faith and Coxendale, about a mile apart, were protected by a string of five palisaded forts between them and the woods beyond.

Here, on higher, healthier ground than marshy Jamestown, and farther away from George at Fort Charles, she and Will and Gabriel had settled. But now George would be at Bermuda Hundred, less than five miles from their house. Until now, Temperance had nourished hopes that moving upriver would bring Will back to himself. Here he had farmed, fished, hunted, and served his watches at Fort Charity, the northernmost fortification. Here, in their tiny two-room house, Temperance cooked, washed, tended the garden, and cared for Gabriel, now nearly three. Will had wanted their house away from the inquisitive eyes and gossiping tongues of the other colonists at Henrico. He would rather be close to the Indians, he said, than to the English.

It seemed safe enough: Thomas Dale had ordered the forts constructed to protect the town of Henrico from Indian attacks, but since the abduction of Pocahontas the Indians had been ominously quiet. All in all, counting the people at Henrico and the various settlements around it, there were now some three hundred English colonists living upriver, with another five hundred or so at Jamestown, where Francis West had come back to serve as commander of the fort. The Indians had not killed anyone in a long time.

Why, then, did Governor Dale have to send George up to Bermuda Hundred?

Wearily, Temperance pushed open the door of her house. Expecting Will and Gabriel to be back any moment, she poked the smoldering ashes in the fireplace to life, threw more wood on it, and waited, shivering, for the logs to catch fire. She ought to be thankful, she thought, for small things: a fire and a snug house with two rooms and a planked floor and a loft, a winter's supply of apples and turnips and corn, a chest with warm clothes in it, a wood-and-rope bedstead with blankets and bolsters.

But the presence of George Yardley nearby, she knew, would make the house chilly, the food unsavory, and the bed uncomfortable, and God only knew what it would do to Will.

Rummaging in her workbasket, Temperance found a needle and thread, and took up the scraps of canvas she had saved from sewing a jerkin for Will. Sewed into a semblance of roundness and stuffed with straw, the scraps would make a passable ball for Gabriel, and the sewing would take her mind off George. As she sewed, she imagined Gabriel's small, round face under the tousled curls, and she thought how pleased he would be. Today Will had taken him hunting. The child was not afraid of the crack of a musket, and he had already learned how to open one of Will's bandolier cartridges and pour a charge of powder down the gun barrel.

Will had said he hoped to get a squirrel or two, but the main reason for his excursion was a small hunting party of friendly Pamunkeys just across the river. Will, whose laconic style was ideally suited to the subtleties of Indian trading, had become the area's principal Indian trader. Today he had gone to barter English knives and fishhooks for dressed deerskins.

Temperance, watching the steadily falling snow, worried that Gabriel would be getting cold. If Will did get skins, she was going to keep one to make a shirt for Gabriel, as there was no cloth as warm for the winter. At long last she heard the soft crunch of footsteps in the snow outside, and then Will, with Gabriel on his shoulders, pushed the door open.

"Ho, give us some supper! We're cold and starving!" Will swung his son down and gave Temperance a perfunctory kiss.

"'Tarving," Gabriel said solemnly.

"Did you do well with the Indians? Did you see any squirrels? Did you get any skins?" Amid this barrage of questions, Temperance was brushing snow off father and son, and pushing both toward the fireplace.

"A promise of four," Will said. "They'll bring them as soon as they're dressed and ready. We didn't get any squirrels, but look what I did get." Undoing his cloak, he revealed an Indian vest embroidered with shell beads and fringed at the bottom.

"Will! What on earth for?"

"For wearing. It makes a handsome doublet, does it not?"

"It makes you look like an Indian."

"Maybe I should be one," Will said lightly. "Or maybe I could get them to take me prisoner, and I could go and live among them the way Pocahontas lives among us. I should ask them to take you and Gabriel, too, and I would keep you as my number-one wife." Then he grew serious. "And if we had closer ties with the Indians, we might stand a better chance of keeping the peace."

"What do you mean? We have had peace, more or less, since Thomas Dale became governor, and now that he holds Pocahontas, they will not dare to harm any English."

"Perhaps so, and perhaps not so." Will stared thoughtfully at the fire. "I hear rumors of late. Dale has pushed the line of settlement far upriver into Powhatan's territory, and Powhatan does not like that. I say the longer the Indians are quiet, the more reason to fear."

"I hope you are wrong," Temperance said. "But at least Pocahontas likes us. You should have seen her when Lucy and I dressed her in our stored-up finery this afternoon."

"Well, if Pocahontas can wear English clothes, then I can wear Indian clothes. And so can Gabriel, if he chooses." Will opened his arms to his son, who was trying to climb into his lap.

"Hungry," Gabriel said, and began to suck his thumb.

"What shall we have for our supper?" said his father, rocking him back and forth.

"Turkey," Temperance said. "And beans, and baked apples." The beans were done with shallots and wild thyme; the turkey spit-roasted earlier in the day, and the apples had baked all afternoon in the ashes. They ate, and almost immediately afterward, Gabriel fell sound asleep at the table.

"He's had a long day," Will said softly. As Temperance rose to put the child to bed, Will put his hand on her arm. "Sit still. I can do it," he said. Gently, he slipped his arms under Gabriel, who did not stir, and then laid him in his trundle bed and drew a cover over him. Will stood looking down at his sleeping son for a moment, and then he looked at Temperance.

They made love that night, more passionately than in a long, long time. She had not the heart to tell him about George.

HENRICO
18 January 1614

 An icy wind was blowing off the river, and John Rolfe tried to pull his cloak closer about him as he rowed. Glancing anxiously at the pale winter sun, he paddled harder. He needed to get to Rock Hall before dark. All winter, he had told himself that the reason he had built a house downriver from Henrico was because he wanted to be close to his tobacco fields. The fact that Princess Pocahontas lived less than five miles away had nothing to do with it. He had enclosed fifteen acres on fine high land at the edge of a bend in the James River, and this year he would have four barrels of tobacco to show for his effort. He could not leave the tending of his land to his three company servants—Henry Tavin, Nicholas Ven, and Edwin Rose—as they knew nothing of tobacco-growing. He himself would not have known much, except for his chance meeting two years ago with the captain of the *Darling*, who brought some tobacco seeds from the Spanish settlements in the West Indies. Native Virginia tobacco was too harsh-tasting to be popular. Rolfe had reasoned that if he could grow the imported Spanish varieties successfully in Virginia, he stood to make a fortune, and so did his fellow colonists. All Europe seemed to have taken up smoking, and in England good Spanish tobacco was selling for as much as eighteen shillings the pound. Pipe-makers were prospering, and the demand for the fragrant Indian weed was growing almost faster than the plants themselves. And so Rolfe had moved up from Jamestown in the late summer, added a fair-sized room onto the small wattle-and-daub, thatch-roofed house Henry and Nicholas and Edwin had built, and settled in.

His being there had nothing to do with Pocahontas. He told himself that, but he knew in his heart he was lying. She had not been absent from his thoughts more than a few hours since the day he first saw her. He told himself she was a savage, a heathen, a member of a barbaric and ignorant race with ways far too different from his own to change, but in his mind's eye he saw only smooth tawny skin and lithe young limbs and sweet firm breasts and brown eyes of a startling intelligence. His fascination with this young Indian female surprised him: He had never been one to fancy dark-haired or olive-skinned women, and his Gwendolyn had been the fairest of the fair. Gwendolyn was plump, not lithe, and her breasts were soft and full. When he cupped them in his hands, he had to spread his fingers wide apart to hold them. He had sowed his seed in her body, and she had borne him a child so quickly. So quickly come, and so quickly gone, he thought sadly. Their tiny daughter had lived less than two months. Gwendolyn had wept bitterly to leave that little grave when they came to Virginia. It was grief that had weakened her, Rolfe thought, and when the fever swept through Jamestown that first summer, she had no strength to fight it. He had lost both child and wife in the space of six months in 1610.

For the past three years there had been a void inside him as empty as a gourd shell. Women were scarce in Virginia, and he could not have taken a wife again if he had wanted to. He was lonely, but at least he was not as badly off as George Yardley. Better a wife dead and gone than a wife living and unfaithful, he thought. Poor Yardley. And poor Sterling. It was common knowledge around Henrico that Captain Yardley's presence at nearby Bermuda Hundred had caused Will Sterling to drink even more heavily. He came into the main settlement now only to trade deerskins for wine and aqua vitae, and there were rumors that he made frequent visits to the house of a Pamunkey hermit priest on the far side of the river. The winds of the *Sea Venture* storm had wreaked more havoc than anyone knew, Rolfe thought as he rowed. He pitied Will and Temperance, and he pitied George marking time in bitter loneliness at Bermuda Hundred. And until recently, he had pitied himself. But that was before he saw Pocahontas.

He remembered that day on the *Treasurer* when he had leaned over the gunwales, curious to see a savage female close up, hoping to be amused.

What he saw first was a sleek dark head bent over, and two slender hands gripping the rope ladder. Then she looked up, her dark eyes wide with wonder, her red lips pressed firmly together, betraying the apprehension she felt at boarding this strange vessel. But there was animal courage here, too, and a self-possession he had seldom seen even among Englishwomen. Rolfe fancied he could read a slight touch of humor in the corners of her mouth. With each step she took on the ladder, her breasts, bare above the fringed deerskin garment she wore, bobbed ever so slightly. The dark aureoles around their nipples excited him, as did the swaying of her supple hips.

He had tried to stay away from her during the voyage back to James-town, keeping his distance and eating in silence when he sat at table with her in Argall's cabin. It was lust, pure and simple, he told himself, and lust was a sin—especially lust for a heathen. And besides that, she was a mere child. She could not be more than eighteen or nineteen, and he would turn twenty-eight come this September. He would pray, and these sinful feelings would pass. He felt guilty enough already for what he had done several times with Elizabeth Jones, a servant girl who belonged to Thomas Dunthorne, and who had come to Jamestown on the *Patience* in 1610. Elizabeth, rawboned and kindhearted, had made it a point to offer herself to him after Gwendolyn's death. With her jutting yellow teeth and brawny shoulders, Elizabeth was not likely to find a husband, even in Jamestown, where women were scarce. But she gave herself freely to the men who sought her out, and contented herself with the small favors—a string of beads here, a jug of wine there—that her customers bestowed on her. John Rolfe felt guilty about having her, but he took some satisfaction in knowing he was not the only man she raised her skirts for, and that what she did seemed to make her happy. And she, at least, was an Englishwoman and a Christian.

But try as he might, he could not get his mind off Princess Pocahontas. On that voyage back to Jamestown, he had once taken food to her in her quarters, hoping insanely that she would ask him to stay, or at least, that she would thank him. But she had done neither, and he went away, chas-tened. Then Argall had her spirited away to the isolation of Henrico, and Rolfe did not see her again until that July, when he went up to Henrico to inspect his tobacco plants and saw her chained like an animal in her own filth. At least Captain Davis had taken his advice, and she had been at Rock Hall with Reverend Whitaker since last August. On Sundays, when he went to Henrico to church, Rolfe could see her, dressed in English clothes, listening intently to Whitaker's sermon. To Rolfe's surprise, one Sunday she brought a basket she had woven, and presented it rather stiffly to him after the service.

"I give you this to make peace. You took me from my people, but I . . . forgive you," she had said. "Father Alexander says one must forgive wrongs."

"It was not I, Pocahontas. It was Captain Argall." Rolfe had tried to explain to her that he had had nothing to do with her capture, but his apology was met with a cool, impassive stare.

"Your Jesus says forgive," she said. "So I forgive you."

That was the only conversation he had had with her. But now Alexander Whitaker had asked him, as one university-trained man to another, to come to Rock Hall for a few days to assist with Pocahontas's instruction in the Christian faith. As he paddled swiftly against the river's erratic currents, his feelings swung from jubilation to trepidation and back again at the thought of being close to her, and he was profoundly grateful to Alexander Whitaker for making it possible. Thank God, he thought, for Whitaker's coming to Virginia.

Whitaker, Cambridge-educated, could have stayed all his life in some small secure living in a parish in the north of England, where his home was, but instead, at age twenty-five, he had volunteered to take up his ministry in the New World. Rolfe marveled at Whitaker's dedication. Unmarried, now twenty-eight, the same age as Rolfe, Whitaker seemed to live only to serve his God. But serving God in a wilderness was hard, even with a newly built frame church and the promise of a brick one soon to be raised, and with a congregation as hungry for the word of God as were the hundred-odd settlers in and around Henrico. It was lonely work at times, far from the civilized discourse of the clergy at home. Thomas Dale had built Whitaker a handsome two-story frame parsonage, but there was little social life to grace it. That was the main reason Whitaker had asked Rolfe, who had studied at Oxford himself, to visit this cold January day.

"Come Thursday and stay till the Sabbath," Whitaker had said at church last week. "I want to see what you think of Pocahontas's progress in the catechism. Besides, you'll be good company for her. She has little chance to talk to anyone with even a little learning, and she might well practice her manners."

John Rolfe had needed no urging.

Rounding the last bend of the river, he saw the parsonage on the south shore. Its rough-hewn oak clapboards had weathered this past year, giving it a soft grayish color. In the growing January dusk, he could see a cozy yellowish light through the small downstairs windows, and a plume of smoke from the wide stone chimney sent a signal of warmth and hospitality. But the house, with no trees to shelter it, stood by itself on a bare hill. Below it, at the bottom of the hill, a seven-foot log paling surrounded the house and garden grounds, offering protection from marauding animals and Indians. It was curious, Rolfe thought, that Alexander Whitaker should choose to live so isolated from his flock. When asked, he merely said the land was better here, and that soon the town would grow to meet him.

Carefully beaching the dugout canoe, Rolfe laid the paddles beside it and hurried to the gate. Whitaker had hung a bell on it, so that visitors could ring and be let in. Rolfe gave the bell rope a sharp pull and waited. In a moment, Jeremy Mutton, Whitaker's serving boy, drew the bolt and swung open the gate.

"Welcome, Master Rolfe." The boy's voice was soft. "The Reverend and Mistress Pocahontas have been waiting for you." *Mistress Pocahontas.* How strange that sounded. "May I carry that?" The boy held out his hand for the bundle Rolfe had brought: It contained a jug of persimmon wine for Whitaker and a change of linen for himself.

"Thank you," he said. He followed Jeremy's slender form up the sloping path to the house. When they reached the front door, Pocahontas opened it and curtsied gracefully, spreading her skirt wide.

"Come in, Master Rolfe," she said with a nod. "We have been expecting you." She smiled shyly, and Rolfe's heart melted.

Behind her, Alexander Whitaker waited to shake his hand and clap him on the back. "Glad you came, John, glad you came. We can use some company." To Pocahontas, he said, "That was well done, my dear. Now come and serve us a cup of wine."

Obediently, Pocahontas preceded the two men to a small table in front of the fire, where an earthenware jug and three goblets stood waiting. Seating herself on a joint stool, she motioned for Whitaker and Rolfe to take seats on a bench. "Will you have some of our wine, Master Rolfe?" She spoke softly, her manner a bit stilted, but Rolfe was mesmerized by the music in her voice.

"Yes," he stammered. "Yes, by all means." His eyes were on the strong, slender fingers and the fine-boned wrists that lifted jug and cup. Carefully, with just the slightest touch of awkwardness, she poured the wine into the heavy goblets, not spilling a drop.

"To your good health!" Whitaker raised his goblet high, and Rolfe and Pocahontas did likewise. "This is the first fruits of the grapes at Henrico—young, but drinkable, don't you think?" The pinkish liquid hardly deserved to be called wine, but they quaffed it in good cheer, all, for their own private and varied reasons, glad to see each other. "I thought we should have a drink of wine before we sup, since you've come all that way through the cold," Whitaker said. "Then, in a little while, we'll eat. Pocahontas has had a turkey aroasting all day for us, and we have Indian bread and squash and beans."

"A fine feast," Rolfe said. "I am honored."

"No, it is we who are honored that you would come and stay with us," Whitaker said.

"Yes," Pocahontas said softly, "we are glad." For a blessed moment, the wide brown eyes met Rolfe's, and he imagined he saw a gleam of genuine pleasure before the dark lashes swept downward and she looked demurely at her lap.

"Your English clothes become you, Pocahontas," he said. The white embroidered cap set off her dark sleek hair and the tawny rose of her cheeks; the tightly laced bodice above the full skirt made her waist as slender as a flower stem. Above her stays, the roundness of her breasts showed faintly through the white shift. Indeed, John Rolfe could not take his eyes off her.

"Yes, we've nearly made an English lass of her," Whitaker said proudly. "And she knows her catechism, and her letters, too. God be praised. That's why I asked you here—to see if you think she is ready for baptism." He leaned forward, his face suddenly serious. "I believe she is, and I want to send her back as a baptized Christian. The problem is, we haven't much time. Dale wants to leave next month, as soon as the weather turns warmer."

"Leave?" Rolfe was dumbfounded. More than that, he was dismayed by what he now read in Pocahontas's face. She obviously, desperately, did not want to leave. "What is Dale up to?" he asked. "I had not heard this."

"He sent word last week that he and Argall are planning to take Pocahontas and sail up the Pamunkey River to make contact with Powhatan, to bring him to terms. It will soon be a year we've had his daughter, and we've heard nothing from him since last July. Dale and Argall intend to force him to settle, and they want her with them when they bargain."

"Powhatan does not want me, and I do not want to go." Pocahontas's words hung in the air. Both men looked at her in amazement.

"What do you mean, he does not want you?"

"Pocahontas, you know you want to be among your own people, and if you are a baptized Christian, you can take the word of God to them. Don't you want that?"

She answered Rolfe's question first. "Powhatan sent me away from him. I have not spoken to him in nearly four years. That is why he sent only seven guns for me. He will not give much to have me back." There was bitterness in her voice. "I would rather stay with the English."

"Why? Why doesn't Powhatan want you? You must be mistaken. He is your father, and you are his favorite daughter." Whitaker was puzzled. Rolfe was silent, his eyes on Pocahontas.

"No," she said sadly. "For a while, he sent messengers to ask how I was, but I would not speak with them, and after a year, he sent no more." She sighed. "My sister Matachanna has my place now."

"But surely, Pocahontas, that was long ago—years ago. Your father will want you back. Even if he does not want you to live at Powhatan Village, he will not want a daughter of his to stay a captive among the English." Whitaker spoke confidently. "Don't you agree, John?"

"I don't know. I suppose so," Rolfe answered mechanically, not really hearing Whitaker. What he had heard was that Pocahontas was leaving, perhaps to live among her people again, and that prospect left him numb.

"Well, God will provide. We have only to trust Him," Whitaker said cheerfully. "Now, let us have some dinner."

The meal was excellent: The turkey that Pocahontas had roasted over hot stones was hot and juicy, the Indian bread cooked to a golden brown, the vegetables delicately seasoned with herbs. The conversation was pleasant: talk of gardening, tales of hunting, and much praise of Pocahontas's English. But Rolfe's head was spinning with thoughts of Pocahontas's leaving. How had he been so foolish as to think she would stay? All things considered, he would be better off if she left, but this one evening in her presence had made him unable to bear the thought of her absence.

After the meal had been cleared away, Whitaker catechized her so that Rolfe could hear her answers, but Rolfe, his eyes fastened on her face, had his own responses.

"First, I learn to believe in God the Father, who hath made me. . . ."
God knows, he seldom made better.

"My duty toward God is to believe in him, to fear him, and to love him with all my heart. . . ."
To keep from tempting a widower.

"What is thy duty toward thy neighbor?" Whitaker's voice prompted gently.

"My duty toward my neighbor is to love him. . . ."
To love him, to love me.

When the exercise was done, Whitaker said, "I think she is ready, don't you?" Rolfe did no more than nod absently, but the young parson went on, "Good. Then we will baptize her next Sabbath day. Her Christian name will be Rebecca. We have talked about it, and Pocahontas likes that name. It is my sister's."

Rebecca. Rebecca Rolfe.

The candles were burning low. Whitaker called to Jeremy, who had been dozing by the fire, and took him by the hand. "We always join hands, the three of us, for evening prayers," he said, reaching for Pocahontas's hand. "Will you join with us, John?"

Rolfe reached for Pocahontas's other hand quickly, so that Jeremy did not come between them.

"Our Father, who art in heaven . . ." Rolfe could swear that during "deliver us from evil," Pocahontas squeezed his hand.

"And now to bed," Whitaker said, immediately after the "Amen." "We'll leave our guest the warmest place." He pointed to a wood-and-ropework bedstead covered with skins in the corner. "I think you'll be comfortable there, John."

Pocahontas, without so much as a backward glance, had disappeared up the narrow, steep staircase at the end of the room.

"We have only two rooms upstairs," Whitaker said. "One for her, and one for Jeremy and me. Come, Jeremy. Sleep well, John." As Whitaker and Jeremy Mutton climbed the stairs, Whitaker tousled Jeremy's hair and let his hand come to rest on the boy's shoulder. John Rolfe, tired and bewildered by all he had seen and heard, rolled himself up in his cloak, lay down on the bed in the corner, and fell sound asleep.

Afterward, when he tried to remember that night, he could only recall that something—a sense of being watched, perhaps—had made him open his eyes in the darkness. There was no moon that night, and the room was nearly pitch-black except for a faint glow from the banked embers in the fireplace. He lay motionless, blinking, until he could just barely make out the outline of a form kneeling beside his bed. Startled, he raised his head.

"Who is it?" he said sharply, but even as he spoke the words, fingers touched his cheek and a voice silenced him with a soft "Shhh!"

He put his hand up and seized a slender wrist. He was convinced he must be dreaming. "Pocahontas! What are you doing here?"

"Shhh!" she said again. "Be quiet, John Rolfe!"

Just hearing her say his name made him feel that somehow they were intimates. He sat up and swung his legs off the low bed. "What is it, Pocahontas? What do you want?" A strained silence was her only answer. In the darkness, he groped for her hand and closed his fingers around it. "Tell me what it is," he whispered. He could hear her drawing a deep breath, like one about to swim under water.

"I want you to marry with me," she said. Now Rolfe knew for certain that he was dreaming.

"What?"

"I want you to marry with me," she said patiently. "Your woman and child are dead. You can marry with me."

On her lips, he found the incorrect preposition charming. "Pocahontas, what are you saying?"

With faint exasperation, she said, "I want you to marry with me so I do not have to go back to Powhatan. I want to stay with the English."

Rolfe, bewildered, sat silently clutching her hand, trying to realize what she was saying. "But, Pocahontas, you don't know me," he said hesitantly. It all seemed too precipitous. In his fantasies, it was he who he wooed and won her, not the other way round.

"I know you," she said resolutely. "I know you have no woman."

"Yes, but—"

"I will please you." In the dark, her free hand suddenly felt between his legs. He inhaled sharply and clamped his lips between his teeth. Unabashed, she caressed him and said, "It is not good for you, not to have a woman."

"You—you must not do that," he whispered. "English women don't do that."

"Then how do they make love?"

"They don't—I mean, they—oh, Pocahontas!" Holding both her hands, he kissed them ecstatically and pressed them against his cheek.

"I will make love so you like it, if you marry with me," she said. "If you marry with me, it will be a good"—she struggled for the right word—"marrying. Powhatan will be pleased to have an English son. No other werowance has that. He will be above all the others, and that will make him happy. And that," Pocahontas said, "that will be good for all the other English."

Rolfe marveled at her shrewdness.

"You are right," he said, "I had not thought of that."

"Then say yes."

Still Rolfe hesitated. After all, he thought, she is a savage. Her father skins people alive and scrapes off their flesh. She knows nothing of English ways but the catechism and the Lord's Prayer and how to curtsy.

Her hands felt warm and soft in his. She was so close to him that her breath blew against his face. "Yes," he said at last. "Yes!" Letting go her hands and taking hold of her wrists, he put her arms around his neck and slid his arms around her waist. "Yes, Pocahontas, I will marry you."

"Good."

They embraced a trifle awkwardly, since he was sitting on the edge of the bed and she was kneeling beside it. Then Pocahontas took his face between her hands and kissed him lightly. "I am glad," she said, and kissed him again, this time using her tongue. The pleasure was so exquisite that it made Rolfe slightly giddy. He gave in to it for a moment, pulling her against him, feeling her breasts through her thin smock, kissing her deeply and hungrily, and then he pulled back. "Pocahontas, we must not do this now." Another kiss, and he must take her, right there on that rickety bedstead. "We must wait until we are married," he said shakily.

"Why?"

"Because it would be . . . wrong." It was bad enough that he craved union with a pagan; he would not add fornication to his sins.

"When can we marry?"

The sooner the better, Rolfe thought, but he said, "We must think. After you are baptized, I shall write a letter to Governor Dale, and then I must go and ask your father. We must keep this secret until then." Then a happy thought struck him. "I know," he said suddenly. "When Governor Dale and Captain Argall sail upriver with you next month, I shall go along, too, and I shall ask Powhatan for your hand then. Dale can come with me to bargain with him, and settle his affairs with your father at the same time." It was too dark to see Pocahontas's face, but he knew she was smiling.

"That is good," she said. "I am happy." She kissed him—lightly this time—and rose to her feet. She turned to go, and then she stopped. "Will you take me to England?"

"Yes." Her guilelessness amused him, and he laughed. "Yes, Pocahontas, someday you shall go to England. I promise."

"Good. I must leave you now. Soon it will be light." As silently as she had come, she left. But at the foot of the stairs, she paused. "I am glad, John Rolfe," she whispered, and then she was gone. The only sound of her departure was a faint creak as the stairs gave under her footsteps. John Rolfe sank back on his bed, where he lay in a state of suspended rapture until dawn.

THE PAMUNKEY RIVER
6 March 1614

 From the high fo'c's'le of the *Treasurer,* Thomas Dale swept the shore with his spyglass and laughed scornfully. "Not a sign," he said. "Not a single, solitary sign all morning. Those savages yesterday were bluffing."

"I'd not be too sure yet, sir." Young Samuel Collier, recently promoted to lieutenant, stood at Dale's elbow. "Remember what they did to Captain Ratcliffe and his men on this same river five years ago."

"Ratcliffe was a fool," Dale said through his teeth. "He went ashore with forty men, unprotected, where he knew there were at least a hundred warriors."

"We'll not do that." Captain Samuel Argall joined them. "But we may run into trouble when the river narrows. By this afternoon, as I reckon it, we should be within an arrow's range of the banks on both sides." Argall squinted with a practiced eye at the heavily wooded shoreline of the Pamunkey River. The prospect looked peaceful enough: The only discernible movements were the dancing reflection of the morning sunlight on the water and the slight swaying of the distant treetops in the breeze. The Pamunkey was broad here, nearly a mile wide, but as it twisted and turned its way further north, it narrowed. Argall knew that, and he expected the Indians to take advantage of that fact. As long as he could keep the *Treasurer*'s bow heading straight into the current and not veering off to one side, they would be all right. His ship carried fourteen 9-pound guns, and most of Dale's men were wearing armor. Dale had brought more than two hundred breastplates and closed helmets with him when he came: Armor in England was becoming obsolete in a military dominated by muskets and artillery, but as protection against arrows and Indian spears, there was nothing better. The next best thing was a heavily quilted jack-coat, or a shirt of chain mail, and the men who did not have armor had those. But there were only 150 Englishmen against no one knew how many Indians, and Dale was determined to bring the savages to heel. In the gun room of the *Treasurer* were three stout wooden boxes full of long matchlock muskets. There was one for every man aboard.

There was also a bed for Princess Pocahontas in the gun room. It was crowded, but so far she had not complained. In fact, for one who had been held against her will for more than a year, Argall thought she seemed in remarkably good spirits. He had not been told of her secret betrothal to John Rolfe, and so he attributed her cheerfulness and docility to the fact that she had been Christianized: The young parson at Henrico had baptized her only last month, and now she was to be called Rebecca. Governor Dale was immensely proud that the first official conversion of a savage had taken place during his term of office, and he and John Rolfe made much of Pocahontas/Rebecca when the ship's company gathered for evening prayers. Argall thought that Rolfe in particular seemed very solicitous of her welfare, walking about the deck with her, finding her special dainties to eat.

That was all right for Rolfe; Argall himself had no taste for savage women, even one in English clothing. Before he left Jamestown, Elizabeth Jones had bestowed her heartiest favors upon him, and he had given her a Spanish pistole, with the understanding that the coin represented payment for some time in the future as well as the past. But his ship was woman enough to him: To keep her fittings polished, decks spotless, her crew in order, to stand on her poop deck when she was in full sail and feel her moving under him like a living thing, was all a man could wish for, he thought. But this sailing up and down rivers and around the edges of Chesapeake Bay was beginning to bore him. He would be glad of a chance to go to sea again.

Now they were moving into a narrower channel, and he gave the orders to take in sail. The river here was still deep, but he dared not go too fast and risk running aground on a hidden sandbar. Soon the *Treasurer,* using only her main and foresail and jib, was making her way slowly, almost lazily, between the narrow wooded banks of the Pamunkey. Dale, Collier, and two or three of the other officers were now on the fo'c's'le. The rest of them lounged about the main deck, enjoying the unseasonably warm air. It was early March, not yet spring, but it felt like May. Pocahontas and John Rolfe, their heads close together, were gazing at the shore on the port side. From all quarters there arose a peaceful hum of voices, punctuated now and then by idle laughter.

Then, without warning, came a sudden rain of arrows from the shore on the starboard side. Two or three struck the ship's gunwales and held fast, their feathered ends quivering. Most of the rest fell with a harmless clatter on the decks, but one of them struck Samuel Collier. He staggered and fell backward, an arrow protruding from his hairline. Around him, officers and men leaped into action.

"Take cover! Take cover!"

"Collier's hit!"

"They've hit us—now they'll run!"

"Wait and see!"

Although the Indians on the shore had disappeared into the forest, Argall prepared to fire one of the starboard guns. He could not bear to stand by without returning fire. He would teach those savages to fire on his ship.

"Gunners to your posts! Fire Number One when ready!"

In a few minutes, the nine-pounder belched forth its charge with a deafening report and a large puff of smoke. The cannonball seemed to disappear into the forest, doing no discernible damage. Then, around the next bend, they could see the rounded rooftops of an Indian village. It was just out of the gun's range. When Governor Dale saw it, he ground his teeth and swore. "Damnation! We'll show those bloody savages! We'll not leave one stick or straw standing!"

Meanwhile, John Pott, the surgeon, carrying bandages and his box of surgical instruments, had made his way to the fo'c's'le to minister to Samuel Collier. The lieutenant lay on his back, rigid with fear, a yard-long arrow shaft protruding from his hair just above his forehead, where the point of the arrow had stuck. Blood from the wound was running down his forehead and into his eyes. "Help me! For God's sake, somebody help me! I'm hurt bad. I can feel my brains oozing out!"

Pott knelt beside him, peered at the wound, and chuckled. Then he dipped his forefinger in the blood, held it up to examine it, and said, "Not a brain. Not a sign of one."

"For God's sake, man, don't jest! I'm hurting!"

Pott laughed again and leaned over the wounded man. "It hurts, Lieutenant Collier, but I assure you it's only a scrape. Only a scalp wound. The arrowhead went in just under the skin here."

"Look how I'm bleeding!"

"Head wounds always bleed like a stuck pig. Hold on, now, I'm going to work this arrow loose and then sew you up. You were lucky."

A few minutes later, Samuel Collier, his forehead neatly bandaged, was resting against a coil of rope on the main deck and listening to Thomas Dale's plans for retaliation. Dale had persuaded Argall to drop anchor, and now the *Treasurer* rode the current, straining at her cable in the middle of the river.

"We'll send a couple of shells into that village first, to scatter them."

Governor Dale began to pace back and forth. "Then, when I give the order, Dowse's company will take turns firing their muskets while the boats are lowered, and the rest of us will get ashore as fast as we can, and Dowse can follow us. Rolfe, you take Collier's company. I want half with muskets, half with pikes, and see that those with matchlocks have their matches well lit, so they can use them to start fires ashore. I want to see every house in that village in flames."

At this, there was some murmuring of disapproval among the men.

"What's the matter?" Dale looked around him angrily. "Do you think they wouldn't do the same to us, given half the chance? Let any man who has no stomach for this work stay aboard and answer to me after we are done." There was scorn in Dale's voice. He paused, challenging someone to protest. When no one responded, he continued, "Good. Now let us show these Indians they can't fire on an English ship and go unscathed! Savage bastards!"

It was then that Dale remembered Pocahontas. She was standing near the cabin door with both hands pressed to her mouth. From her pose, it was not clear whether she was trying to hold back a cry of rage or to send up a silent prayer. Above her hands, her eyes, wide with horror, searched the faces of the Englishmen around her.

"I am sorry, Princess," Dale said uncomfortably. "You had better go below."

Then he began to bark orders to others. To the wounded Samuel Collier, he said, "You go below with the Princess, and stay with her."

Rolfe whispered something in Pocahontas's ear, but she pushed him away angrily and turned to follow Samuel Collier below decks.

Meanwhile, muskets rattled, winches creaked, sailors shouted orders, soldiers called out encouragingly to one another. At Captain Argall's signal, the *Treasurer*'s gunners lobbed two shells at the Indian village, which was now within range, plainly visible through the trees. The first shell did not find a mark, but the second hit the largest of the long houses, making a hole in its straw roof and causing about a dozen Indian men to make a hasty exit, shaking their fists and shouting at the English. At that moment, Lieutenant Dowse's men discharged their muskets, and four of the Indians fell. The others dived for cover, and for an instant all was silence as both sides took stock of the damage.

"Have at it, men! Let's to it! Pace, have your company fire when ready!" Thomas Dale, ready to go over the starboard gunwale and down the boarding ladder, waved his sword above his head and shouted over his shoulder, "Keep these savage dogs on the run!" In a moment, he had clambered down, and was splashing through the shallows, urging his men onward. They followed him admiringly.

"Dale is not one to hang back, is he?"

"No one will ever accuse him of cowardice!"

"They may accuse him of cruelty, though. There are bound to be women and children here."

"Come on, we'll be left behind!"

Only John Rolfe was silent. Trying not to think of the look on Pocahontas's face, he clutched his pike and followed the others.

The Indians, frightened by the Englishmen's firepower, had swarmed out of their houses like ants whose hill had been disturbed, running this way and that in their panic. There were many women and children. This was a fairly large village, with forty houses, but most of its fighting men were obviously absent: A fact that boded ill when the English thought about it later. The few able-bodied men who were there, seeing the overpowering numbers of the English, were trying to flee into the woods with the others, dragging the bodies of their fallen comrades with them. One of a pair who had been lifting a dead Indian suddenly stiffened, hit in the chest by a musket ball, and then slowly crumpled, falling on top of the one already dead, making a sudden pool of fresh blood on the bare ground beneath him. The other Indian, panicked, disappeared behind one of the houses.

"Got him! That makes five!" It was Thomas Dale, who seemed to be everywhere, seeing everything at once. "Dowse! Laydon! Pace! Get your men into these houses! I want to see them burning! And get someone into that cornfield! We'll not leave them any corn, either!"

It had taken only a little while to empty the village of its inhabitants; now it was the work of a few minutes to set fire to a season's crop and forty-odd homes. Rolfe, assigned to fire one of the largest houses, could not help but pause and look inside before he held his makeshift torch to its straw walls. They built well, these Indians. The frame of bent saplings arched at least nine feet overhead; the walls of marsh grass and reeds sturdily constructed to keep out wind and rain; the center fireplace large and lined with smooth stones. To judge from the furnishings, this must have been the chief's house. There were two large platforms made of tree branches lashed together with vines, and these couches were luxuriously covered with piles of furs and deerskins with the hair left on. Other skins hung on the walls, providing both insulation and decoration, and several large baskets containing what looked like Indian bread and dried meat hung from the high ceiling. Against one wall was a sort of rack with shelves that held small stone tools for cooking and dressing skins, an assortment of baskets and clay pots, and a collection of arrowheads and stone ax-heads. The packed earth floor was freshly swept, and everything was in its place. On the fire, supported by four large stones, a pot of Indian corn and beans simmered, giving off an aroma of peaceful domesticity that was oddly incongruous with the chaos taking place outside.

Rolfe stood just inside the door, hesitating. He was about to put his torch to the house of a man he had never seen, one who very likely had never done him any harm. That in itself was reason enough to hesitate, and the thought of Pocahontas stayed his hand further. Pocahontas, who had begged him not to go ashore. He stepped into the center of the house's one large room, and as he glanced about him one last time, he saw several clay pots filled with small, exquisite white shells on the rude shelf next to the wall. Impulsively, he selected two tiny shells that were almost identical, and put them inside his shirt. When the time was right, he would give them to Pocahontas as a peace offering, and have them made into earrings for her. Then he heard Thomas Dale's voice calling to him and remembered the business at hand.

Resolutely, he held the flame of his torch to the thick straw above the doorway and watched it catch fire. It caught quickly. The weather had been unusually dry for February and March; there had been no rain for nearly three weeks. In a matter of minutes, the entire roof of the house was ablaze, the orange and yellow tongues of fire licking skyward and giving off a large spiral of thick blackish smoke. Rolfe backed quickly away from it, his nostrils burning from the heat and smoke; his ears suddenly assailed by a loud crackling noise. At first he thought it was just the fire he had set, but when he turned around, he realized that the sound of this one house burning was multiplied by thirty or more as the nearby structures went up in flames. All the houses were fairly close together, twenty feet apart at most, and the heat from them was intense, the smoke thick and choking.

Thomas Dale, his face blackened with smoke, was fairly dancing with pleasure. "Got them all! Look at them burn! And we got their corn, too! This will teach them not to fire on English ships!" Dale moved among his men, slapping them on their backs, congratulating one and all. "Now back to the ship. There'll be an extra ration of beer for every man tonight!"

By the time the last man climbed aboard the *Treasurer,* the sun was beginning to set. John Rolfe, oblivious to the shouts and laughter of men returned safe from a battle, made straight for the gun room. A worried Samuel Collier met him in the narrow gangway below decks. "She's not let up weeping since you left. I tried to talk to her, and reason with her, but she wouldn't—"

"Never mind. You did what you could." Rolfe pushed past him into the gun room. Pocahontas stood with her back to him, looking out the gun port toward the shore. "Pocahontas?" he whispered, but she did not turn around. "Rebecca." The Christian name drew no response, either. In three steps, he was across the narrow room and standing behind her. But her grief was so private he could not bring himself to touch her. She stood motionless, watching the smoke curling upward, black clouds sullying the blue sky. Rolfe kept his distance directly behind her, uncertain how to proceed. She was aware of his presence, but she chose not to acknowledge it. The only indication of her weeping was a slight jerk of her shoulders, accompanied by one small, heartrending sniffle. Hesitantly, ever so gently, Rolfe touched her shoulder.

She wheeled around to face him. "Don't touch me!" Her eyelids were puffy, her cheeks blotchy and smeared with tears. "Murderer! English dog! How could you do this?" She turned her back on him again.

"Pocahontas," Rolfe said softly. "I—I know how you feel. But I didn't kill anyone. Believe me. And I didn't want to go ashore. You must believe that. But Governor Dale is in command, and we all must do what he says."

There was no response.

"And they did shoot at us first," he said defensively. "They might have killed Samuel Collier, or me, or—or you."

"That was Namontack's village. His father lives there still. Now his house is burned to the ground, and he will go hungry when winter comes." Pocahontas crossed the room suddenly and knelt beside the wooden chest that contained her clothes. Flinging back its lid, she rummaged among its contents and pulled out her Indian dress, the fringed deerskin garment she had worn at the time of her capture. Then she began to undo the fastenings of her bodice.

"Pocahontas! What are you doing?"

"I cannot be English. I cannot marry with you." She raised her tear-stained face to his. "I will go back to my people, and they will drive your people into the sea." She began to undress herself with feverish haste.

Rolfe's heart sank. He saw his happiness and the security of the Virginia colony about to be thrown over like the clothes she flung on the floor. "Pocahontas!" He caught her roughly by the wrist, and when she tried to pull free, he seized her by both wrists and forced her to look at him. "Stop this! You can't go back to Indian clothes, and you can't go back to your people." He pointed to the deerskin dress. "You put that on, and bare your breasts, and every man aboard this ship will rape you. I won't be able to stop them."

Very slowly, like a flower wilting on its stem, the sleek black head drooped lower and lower, until he could no longer see her face. "You speak the truth, John Rolfe," she said, her voice so low he could hardly hear it. "I cannot go back, but I cannot stay, either." She began to weep again, this time in great wrenching sobs.

What had they put her through, he and Whitaker, with their bumbling efforts to take her from her people? Tenderly, as though begging forgiveness, he touched her cheek, and when she did not pull away, he put his arms around her. Still sobbing, she buried her face against his shoulder. He held her silently for a moment, stroking her hair. As her body relaxed a little, he picked her up and carried her, unprotesting, across the room to a gun box, where he sat down and held her on his lap like a child. "Dearest Pocahontas." He rocked her gently back and forth, and gradually her sobbing ceased. "I love you. And if you love me, all this will come right in the end." But he spoke with a confidence he was far from feeling.

MATCHCOT
11 March 1614

 From the smooth grassy promontory between the village of Matchcot and the river, Powhatan's 400 warriors watched the English ship; from the decks of the *Treasurer,* Thomas Dale's 150 Englishmen watched the Indians on the shore. They had been watching each other since yesterday, when messengers had been sent to Powhatan to announce Pocahontas's presence and demand a settlement from him. Dale had given the Indians until noon today to respond: If no message had come by then, the English would attack in full force. The Indian force outnumbered them, but the English had guns. English cannons aimed at Matchcot could easily demolish the town; English muskets, fired in volleys from the safety of the *Treasurer*'s decks, could dispatch most of the warriors before they had even had time to fit arrow to bow.

At dawn, Pocahontas demanded to be taken ashore. "I must speak to my people," was all she would say, and neither Rolfe's nor Dale's nor

Argall's entreaties could persuade her otherwise. Pale and drawn (she, like most of the others aboard and ashore, had not slept all night), she paced the main deck, wrapped in a heavy woolen cloak and shivering. "You must let me go," she said to Dale. To Rolfe, she said, "You tell him I must go. Make him see. There must be no more killing."

"Pocahontas, you cannot go ashore now." Dale spoke kindly but firmly. "The messengers are sure to be back before noon, with terms from Powhatan. Wait and see." Taking Rolfe aside, he whispered, "Come to my cabin," and then disappeared in the direction of his quarters.

Rolfe put his arm around Pocahontas. "Are you cold?"

"No." But she continued to shiver now and then. The strain of the past two days showed in her face, and since the burning of the Indian village she had hardly spoken. Rolfe had thought they were reconciled, but he could not be sure what she was thinking. He did not know what she might do if she saw her father, or what Powhatan might do when he heard she was here. What if Powhatan should suddenly appear and reclaim her, and declare war on the English?

"Stay here. I shall be back in a little while," Rolfe said, and slipped away to meet Dale in the great cabin. The governor was pacing nervously back and forth.

"She must not go ashore. The messengers are bound to be back before noon. I don't want to fight, and I don't think Powhatan wants to fight, but I don't know what terms he is willing to give for his daughter. What if she has been telling the truth all along, and he does not want her back on any terms? Then what?"

"I don't know," Rolfe said. "But if Powhatan were to let his eldest daughter be kept by the English and do nothing to get her back, he would lose face among the other tribes. He cannot afford that. On the other hand, a marriage and an alliance with the English would give him great power."

"I hope to God what you say is true. Are you still of a mind to go through with this?"

"Yes."

Dale stopped pacing. "Then when the messengers come, no matter what they say, suppose you—and I'll send Dowse with you—you go and ask Powhatan for her hand. The old devil is bound to be flattered, and you can tell him you want peace for a wedding gift. What do you think of that?"

"I think," Rolfe said slowly, "that it would please Pocahontas very much." When he told her, she smiled. It was the first time she had smiled in three days.

At midmorning, there was still no sign of the Indian messengers. The sun, climbing steadily higher and higher, shone on the gleaming, painted bodies and polished spear-tips of the Indians, and on the metal breastplates and muskets of the English. Governor Dale had resumed his pacing, this time on the main deck. From time to time, he surveyed the shore with his spyglass and shook his head in the negative. Then, all at once, there was a commotion on the shore. Some of the Indians were shouting and waving toward the ship; others were pointing to two newcomers, young boys who were standing at the water's edge, shading their eyes against the sun to look at the ship. When Pocahontas heard the noise and saw them, she, too, began to shout and wave. "Munto! Wintako! Munto! Wintako!" To the bewildered Rolfe, she said, "Those are my brothers! My little brothers! Oh, now I must go ashore! They have come to see me!"

"What a godsend!" Thomas Dale spoke in a conspiratorial tone to Rolfe and Argall. "Let us send a boat ashore and invite them to come aboard to see their sister. That will give us time. If the messengers don't come, the others won't dare attack as long as Powhatan's sons are with us. In the meantime, Rolfe, you and Dowse go ashore and announce that you have a matter of great import to discuss with Powhatan. Say you cannot wait for the messengers."

And so Munto and Wintako, their eyes wide with wonder at the English ship and at their sister dressed as an Englishwoman, were entertained aboard the *Treasurer,* and a nervous John Rolfe set off with Timothy Dowse to ask Powhatan for the hand of Princess Pocahontas in marriage.

Looking back on it later, Rolfe never ceased to wonder at Powhatan's behavior. At first the old chief had refused to see the English visitors. Then, just as they were leaving, Powhatan sent his brother, a tall, majestic-looking Indian called Opechancanough, to find out what they wanted. When their message was duly relayed to him, he sent word that he would allow the marriage to take place, and that he would be glad to live in peace with the English. Powhatan also gave notice that he himself would not attend the wedding ceremony, but that Opechancanough would come.

JAMESTOWN
5 April 1614

Opechancanough had seen many wedding ceremonies in his time. Long ago in Seville he had sometimes assisted Father Segura at nuptial masses in the great cathedral. And in his own land, among his own people, Opechancanough, as a werowance, had often bound the strand of polished marriage beads around a couple's clasped hands to signify their union. He had feasted and made merry many times when his warriors chose wives, and more than once he had attended his brother Wahunsonacock when he added another woman to his retinue. Great werowances such as Powhatan were entitled to as many women as they wished; ordinary men must content themselves with one.

Opechancanough himself had had only Nantea as a wife. She had given herself to him long ago, when they were both young, when the Jesuits had brought him back to his people at Uttamussack. As the brother of the Powhatan and a werowance in his own right, he could have taken other wives, but somehow Nantea was all he ever wanted.

Something about Pocahontas reminded him of Nantea: the delicate frame, small-boned but strong, the glossy black hair, the all-knowing eyes. Pocahontas, his brother's firstborn daughter, had been the delight of Opechancanough's heart since she was old enough to smile at him. Now she was about to be forever separated from her people. Wahunsonacock, knowing he could not keep Pocahontas from marrying John Rolfe, and not wanting the English to know that he could not control his own daughter, had grudgingly agreed to the marriage. He had tried to put a good face on it, hoping at least to reap some diplomatic benefits from this union. But such was his bitterness that he stubbornly refused to come to the wedding.

It was nearly time for the ceremony to begin. Inside the meetinghouse the roughhewn cedar pews were nearly filled. Opechancanough was pleased to see that so many of the English, near two hundred, by his count, had come to witness the nuptials. He only wished that this wedding of an Indian princess could have taken place in a grander setting. He thought longingly of the majestic soaring arches of Seville's cathedral, of stained-glass windows that let in daylight colored like emeralds and sapphires and rubies, of richly embroidered altar cloths and gold candlesticks, of fragrant incense. Here was only a cavernous box of a building with walls made of earth and sticks and a roof made of thatch, with a crude wooden altar and pulpit at one end and a hollowed-out tree stump for a baptismal font at the other. Here the windows were merely apertures with shutters, and the merciless daylight streamed in to expose the chinks and the patches and the splinters within.

But on this occasion the English had done their best to make it look festive. The chancel was a bower of creamy-white dogwood blossoms and dark, glossy leaves, and there was a small Turkish rug for the couple to stand on. Near one of the front pews that faced the congregation, three musicians stood ready to play. Two of them wore the buff jerkins of soldiers, and one held a tabor, the other a small wooden flute. It was the third musician who caught Opechancanough's eye. He was a head taller than the other two, and in his arms he cradled a lute. But it was neither his height nor his instrument that drew attention to him; it was his clothing. Over his plain English shirt he was wearing a magnificently beaded Indian vest. As Opechancanough puzzled over this, the unlikely-looking trio began to play, and the soft, sweet notes of reed and string filled the meetinghouse and silenced the murmuring crowd.

The music grew louder, signaling that it was time for the ceremony to commence. Pocahontas drew herself up nervously, awaiting the moment to walk down the aisle. Opechancanough stepped closer to her and offered his arm. Smiling, she put her arm through his. In her other hand, the white blossoms of her wedding bouquet trembled.

"I wish you happiness, Pocahontas," her uncle whispered in her ear.

Opechancanough was glad that he had worn the shirt made of turkey feathers that Nemattonow had designed. His son had showed the village women how to craft it so that none of the places it joined were visible, and it appeared to be a seamless garment of intricately patterned grays and blacks and whites. Opechancanough, too, drew himself up as the music continued.

At the front of the meetinghouse, John Rolfe stood ramrod-straight, his eyes on Pocahontas, and beside him, Ralph Hamor kept his eyes on John Rolfe. Two ministers wearing white chasubles and red-embroidered stoles took their places at the altar rail.

"Now, Pocahontas." Opechancanough did not wait for the English to tell him when to move. Pocahontas tightened her fingers in the crook of his arm, and the two of them stepped forward.

At the altar rail, the Reverends Alexander Whitaker and Richard Buck waited, smiling. With a wave of his hand the Reverend Buck indicated where Opechancanough and Pocahontas were to stand, and the music ceased. As the musicians moved to sit down in the front pew, the tall man in the Indian vest looked searchingly, directly into Opechancanough's eyes. It was not a long look, but it made the skin on the back of Opechancanough's neck tingle. Something about this Englishman's gray eyes struck him as the look of a kindred spirit—almost of an Indian. Then the ceremony began, and Opechancanough thought no more of the man.

"Dearly beloved, we are gathered together . . ." Reverend Buck began to read the service in his deep, mellifluous voice. ". . . I require and charge you both, as ye will answer at the dreadful day of judgment when the secrets of all hearts shall be disclosed, that if either of you know of any impediment, why ye may not be lawfully joined together in matrimony, ye do now confess it."

The minister paused.

Opechancanough raised his eyes to the cross above the altar and said a silent prayer to the Christian God he had nearly forgotten. The silence in the church was breathless; not a rustle, not a whisper, not even a breath could be heard. From his place before the altar, John Rolfe looked at Pocahontas and lifted his chin slightly, as though daring anyone to speak. Pocahontas kept her eyes fastened on the quivering blossoms of her bouquet. Reverend Buck went on with the service. "Who giveth this woman to be married to this man?"

"I do." Opechancanough's voice rang out strong and clear in the hushed atmosphere. His self-assurance caused a few scattered whispers in the crowd. There was even more whispering when Opechancanough, at the end of the Lord's Prayer, crossed himself with a practiced hand.

But during the festive celebration that followed, Opechancanough stood aloof and pretended he could not speak any English. Then the man in the Indian vest sought him out and spoke to him haltingly in his language.

"This was a pretty ceremony," the gray-eyed man said, "but do you think it will keep peace between our people and yours?"

"I do not speak for Powhatan," Opechancanough replied. "I cannot say." But when he watched Pocahontas and John Rolfe cut their wedding cake, Opechancanough felt a sadness come on him, stronger than anything he could remember since Nantea had died. He suddenly loathed himself for allowing this union to take place, and it seemed wrong to celebrate. He should have counseled his brother against this wedding at all costs. Now he could not even bring himself to say good-bye to Pocahontas. Bidding farewell to no one, he slipped away from the noisy throng, made his way to the palisade gate, and disappeared into the forest. He could not bear to watch Pocahontas's happiness, knowing what must come soon to the English in Virginia.

MATCHCOT
20 May 1614

 Thomas Dale gazed thoughtfully at the assortment of objects on the table in front of him: two large pieces of copper, five strings of blue and white glass beads, five wooden combs, ten fishhooks, and a pair of small horn-handled knives. "Offer him this stuff at first, and tell him he shall have a grindstone when he sends her."

Ralph Hamor, newly promoted to Indian ambassador, began packing the things carefully in a leather pouch.

"And if those are not enough, and he wants to bargain, ask him what he will take for her. I want her at any price." Dale grinned and rubbed his hands together. "Those Indian wenches—I want one to do for me what Pocahontas does for John Rolfe."

Ralph Hamor thought of Thomas Dale's young wife, Elizabeth, in London, waiting patiently these three years for her husband's return. They had been married less than two months when he set out for Virginia. "What will you do with an Indian wife when you leave here? What about—what about Lady Elizabeth?"

Dale pursed his lips thoughtfully. "We were man and wife for such a short time," he said, "I hardly feel married. And just between ourselves, Ralph, Elizabeth has some looks, but she—she is not very well versed in the art of love. I fear she never will be."

"But she is your wife," Hamor said. "You cannot very well take an Indian wife back to England, and you cannot sail off and leave such a one here. Powhatan would be furious, and that would make things worse than ever for the English."

Dale threw back his head and laughed boisterously. "Of course I'll take her with me! Set her up in a house in London, give her a few beads, tell her that is the English custom." Leaning forward with one foot on a bench, Dale laughed again, and slapped his knee. "She'll never know the difference! Now hie yourself to Powhatan and bring me back an answer."

And so, early in the morning of May 18, little more than a month after Pocahontas's wedding, Ralph Hamor, accompanied by seventeen-year-old Thomas Savage as official interpreter, set out on his mission. There were also two Indian guides George Yardley had sent from a village near Bermuda Hundred. All four set out on foot for Matchcot, Powhatan's summer lodge at the head of the Pamunkey River, some thirty miles distant. By dark on the second day, they had reached the bend of the river directly opposite Matchcot. The two Indian guides cupped their hands and shouted across the water. Almost immediately, through the dark, came an answering shout, and then a rapid exchange of Algonquin. In almost no time, two Indians paddling a long dugout arrived to ferry them across the river.

"Ah, look!" Savage said excitedly. On the opposite shore, attended by two men carrying torches, stood an imposing figure wearing a feather headdress. "Powhatan himself has come to meet us!" As soon as the canoe touched the shore, Savage leaped out.

"Thomas Savage!" Powhatan said joyfully, and held out his arms to the boy. The old man was genuinely moved. He embraced Savage, and then ran his hands over the boy's head, arms, torso, and legs admiringly, and showered him with a barrage of questions.

Savage answered him at length in Algonquin, and then turned to Hamor. "He says I have been a stranger to him these four years, since the day he gave me leave to visit my friends at Jamestown and I never came back. But he says I am still his child, because John Smith gave me to him years ago."

Then, suddenly, without a word, Powhatan stepped forward and grasped Hamor roughly around the throat. Hamor, thinking he was about to be strangled, tried to pull the old man's hands away. "What is he doing?" he gasped. Powhatan, wiry and surprisingly strong, continued to choke him, all the while pouring forth what sounded like a stream of curses.

Young Tom Savage chuckled. "He says you are not wearing the chain of pearls, and he wants to know what you have done with it."

"What chain of pearls? What is he talking about?" By this time, Hamor had forced Powhatan's hands away from his neck, and the werowance stood silently glaring at him. Savage asked him a brief question, and received a lengthy reply.

"He says he sent his brother Dale a chain of pearls for a present when he first arrived, and told him that if he sent any Englishman to him, he was to wear that chain around his neck as a sign. If any Englishman came without the chain, Powhatan would not receive him.

"Damn! I never heard of any such chain!" Hamor felt a surge of renewed anger at Governor Dale. "Tell him that since I came with two of his own people as guides, and you, who are nearly a son to him, I did not need to wear the chain."

All this was duly related to Powhatan, whose expression changed gradually from hostile suspicion to a grudging politeness. When he had greeted the Indian guides, one of whom was apparently well known to him, Powhatan invited Hamor's party to his house, where he seated them all on straw mats and offered around a small clay pipe of tobacco, growing more and more convivial. Well he might be at ease, thought Hamor. Outside, surrounding the house, were at least a hundred bowmen, their longbows at the ready, their quivers full of arrows, and inside, seated cross-legged on either side of Powhatan, were a dozen comely young women. As the pipe of tobacco passed from hand to hand, the old man, speaking through Tom Savage, inquired first how his "brother" Thomas Dale fared, and next he asked about his daughter Pocahontas and her marriage. Although he had undoubtedly heard all about the wedding from Opechancanough, Powhatan insisted on a detailed account, from Pocahontas's bridal headdress to the honey and walnut cakes of the wedding feast. Then he asked about John Rolfe, whom he referred to as his "unknown son"—where he lived, what he hunted, how tall he was.

"How do they . . . like and love together?" Powhatan asked his last question in a confidential tone, leaning forward to hear the answer.

"Tell him Pocahontas is very happy." Hamor could say that honestly. He had seen her playing hostess at her own fireside, with her beaming husband looking on; he had seen her planting herbs in the garden Rolfe had made just for her; he had seen contentment in her face as she sat beside Rolfe at church. "Tell him that she is so happy with us that she will never want to come back here." Hamor had meant that as a jest, but Powhatan's face clouded.

"It was not just to tell me of Pocahontas that you came all this way," he said. "I have given you my daughter. What is it you want of me now?" He folded his arms across his chest and waited for Hamor to speak.

"Your brother Dale has sent you presents." Reaching for the leather bag, Hamor began laying out the trinkets he had brought. Powhatan eyed each one—the copper pieces, the beads, the combs, the fishhooks, and the knives—with mounting approval. "And besides these," said Hamor, "your brother Dale wishes you to have a great grinding stone. If you will send some men to him, he will give it to them."

Powhatan, grinning broadly, leaned back slightly and said, "That is very good. Tell my brother that I am pleased with his gifts. When you go, I will give you gifts to take back to him." The grin suddenly became a look of cunning. "Now, what does my brother Dale want of me?"

Hamor took a deep breath. This was the crucial part, to get the message across with the proper mixture of delicacy and firmness. If Thomas Dale could marry Powhatan's youngest daughter, Indian-white relations in Virginia would be assured for at least a generation. "Your brother Dale," he began slowly, "has heard that your youngest daughter, Matachanna, is very beautiful. Her beauty is known throughout all your territories." At the mention of his daughter's name, Powhatan stiffened. Hamor hurried on, fearing he would interrupt. "Your brother Dale has sent me to entreat you, by the brotherly friendship that now exists between him and you, to allow Matachanna to return to Henrico with me—"

Here Powhatan whispered something to Thomas Savage, but Hamor shook his head at Savage and continued. "To return with me, so that he may see her beauty for himself, and may make her . . . his wife."

Powhatan's eyebrows drew together in a frown.

"The reason for that is, that now you are friendly and are firmly united with the English and made one people, your brother Dale desires to make a natural union between you with this marriage." Hamor had hoped to avoid saying what he was about to say, but he realized that now he must say it: "And your brother Dale has resolved to dwell in this country—your country—as long as he lives." Dale, Hamor knew, was planning to leave for England the year after next.

Powhatan listened gravely as all this was translated, and then, uncrossing his arms and placing his hands on his knees with deliberate slowness, he spoke.

"I am grateful for your brother Dale's salute of love and peace, and I value his presents." He paused. "But though he is a greater werowance than his brother Newport, his gifts are not so fine as the ones Captain Newport gave me when he came with John Smith." When Savage translated this, Hamor's heart sank.

Powhatan continued, "As for my daughter Matachanna, she is not here. She has gone to be wife to a great werowance who lives three days' journey from here. He gave me two bushels of roanoke beads for her."

Hamor tried not to let his disappointment show in his face. He would make one last effort. To Savage, he said, "Tell him that I know his power and greatness to be such that if he wishes to, he can call back his daughter and return the roanoke beads with no ill will. He can say to this werowance that his daughter is too young to marry. After all, she is barely twelve." The absurdity of Dale's marriage proposal struck Hamor anew, and he made this counterproposal without much enthusiasm.

"Tell him if he will do that, his brother Dale will give him three times the value of the roanoke in glass beads of all colors, and copper, and hatchets, and things that are much more useful than two bushels of oyster-shell beads." Hamor finished, and held his breath as he waited for the translation. If the answer was yes, how could he live with his conscience, taking a twelve-year-old girl to a thirty-two-year-old married man who would lie to her and separate her forever from her people? And if the answer was no, what would he tell Thomas Dale?

Powhatan's face was impassive as he spoke, and it was impossible to read his thoughts. His answer was not short. "I love Matachanna as dearly as I love my life. Though I have many children, I delight in none so much as her. If I could not look on her, I think I should not live, and if she went to live among the English, I could not look on her." The sadness in his voice betrayed his longing to see Pocahontas, and the reason why he had not come to her wedding. "Because I long ago resolved never to come among the English, never on any terms to place myself in their hands." He paused for a moment, gazing into the fire, and then he went on, "Tell my brother Dale he has one of my daughters already. I hold it not brotherly of him to desire to bereave me of two of my children at once. But tell him he need not fear any injury from me or my people. There have been too many of his men and mine killed. I am old, and would gladly end my days in peace. Now, you are weary and I am sleepy; let us have food and end this talk." Powhatan clapped his hands suddenly, summoning an attendant who brought two great wooden bowls filled with chunks of Indian bread. Another servant brought in a large bottle of sack that Captain Newport had presented to him years ago. It was still almost full. Powhatan's servant carefully measured out about about three spoonfuls each into giant white oyster shells, and the old chief and his guests ate and drank in amiable silence.

"Well, we have done what we came for," Hamor said to Savage as they lay down to sleep, "and I am not sorry for the way it turned out. We can get an early start back tomorrow."

As soon as it was light, Powhatan invited them to his house, where stood a huge steaming pot of Indian peas and beans cooked together, along with a basket of bread that could have fed a dozen men. While they were eating, two of Powhatan's women were boiling freshly caught trout for their second course. At midmorning, Powhatan served up roasted oysters, crabs, and crayfish; before noon, a party of his men returned from hunting with a doe, a fat buck, and two large turkeys, all of which were dressed and put to roast for the next meal. The remarkable thing about this hunting party, however, was not the quantity of game it brought back, but the fact that one of its members spoke to the Englishmen in their own tongue.

"You don't know me, do you, Ralph?" he said, grinning and holding out his hand to Hamor. The fellow's skin was bronzed by the sun; his head was shaved except for a strip of hair down the middle, from the center of his hairline to the nape of his neck, and at the back of this hair, a large turkey feather was attached. From one ear dangled two polished shells. Around his neck hung a shell necklace, around his waist was a fringed deerskin garment, on his feet were beaded moccasins. "It's Will Parker."

"Will Parker! Great God, man, we thought you were dead these three years!"

"No, just caught and kept." Parker shrugged. "Party of Nansemonds found me chopping wood outside Fort Henry, and they wanted my hatchet and took me with it. Made me chop wood for them for near a year, but then I got away from them and came up here. Been here ever since. Found I like living like the Indians. Always plenty to eat, not much work to do. But I reckon I'll go back with you, if you can get old Powhatan to give me leave." He squatted on his haunches in front of them, Indian-style. "Tell me how it goes at Jamestown."

When Hamor and Savage had finished trying, as best they could, to recount the uneven history of Dale's building of Henrico, the planting of two new settlements, Bermuda and Shirley Hundreds, upriver, and the Virginia Company's plan to apportion fifty-acre headrights to each of the colonists during the coming year, Parker stood up.

"I trow I'll be just in time to get myself a nice parcel of land and not have to work for it!" He laughed. "Yes, I will go back with you, and see how I like being landed gentry. And it does my heart good to look on English faces. You are the first I have seen in all this time—no, I take that back." Parker chewed thoughtfully on a twig. "I did see one, but he was dead."

"Who was it?" Savage asked.

"Don't know. Tall fellow, with yellowish-gray hair. Found him in the woods away to the south, near the place where the Nansemond River forks. He'd been dead a good while when I came across him. Don't know what he died of. Had no wounds on him, not that I could see, anyway. I did pick through his clothes, and a little bag he had with him, trying to see who he was, but all he had on him was a little gold cross. I kept that."

"We thought *you* were dead," Hamor said. "When Captain Davis went down to Fort Henry, the Indians told him you fell sick in the woods, and that they carried you to their village, and that you died there. He was sorry to lose you."

"Well, I was not sorry to lose him. He was a hard man to serve. And from what you say, Thomas Dale is no easy master, either. If I don't like him, I may run off to the Indians again." Parker laughed like a horse, showing all his yellow teeth.

At it happened, Hamor, who had never much liked William Parker, was not anxious to take him back, and Powhatan, who never liked giving things up, was not anxious to let Parker go. "You have my daughter, and I am content you should have her. I have an Englishman, but you are not content that I should have him," the old man said crossly.

"Very well then. When I return, I must tell Thomas Dale that William Parker is here, and when he hears that, he will come and take him." When Savage translated this, Powhatan glowered.

"Take him, then. He shall go with you, but I will send no guides with you. The ones you brought must remain here, and if anything evil happens to you along the way, you will have yourselves to thank."

Just as they were leaving, Powhatan presented them with two beautifully dressed white buckskins. "Give these to Pocahontas and my unknown son." There was great sadness in his voice. When the visitors had packed away these gifts, Powhatan went with them to the river's edge and stood for a long time on the shore, waving to them. As soon as they were safely on the opposite bank, he went back to his house, smiling to himself. To his wife Winganuske, he said, "Go to the other house and tell Matachanna the Englishmen are gone. She may come out now."

4

REUNIONS

■

1614–1619

Met you not with my true love
By the way as you came?

—*Sir Walter Raleigh,*
   "Pilgrim to Pilgrim" (1599)

HENRICO
1 June 1614

 At sunrise, Temperance slipped outside for a few moments. Seeing the sky turn pinkish-gray and knowing that daylight was close at hand, she felt comforted. Watching, weeping, praying beside Gabriel's trundle bed these past few nights, she had begun to cherish the dawns as signs of hope, however fragile they might be. Each one meant that her son had lived one more day, and the inexorable progress of the sun across the sky seemed to promise that time and nature would make him well again. But in all his three years, Gabriel had never been so sick. His little stomach heaved, and he begged for water, but when she gave him some, it came right back, blood-tinged. Each time that happened, fear gnawed inside Temperance until she felt she, too, would vomit blood. Now, wearily watching the sun's first rays glinting on the river, she pressed her aching back against a tree trunk and tried to pray: *Dear God, make my child well. And make his father quit drinking. And thank you for sending Meg.*

Meg had come upriver on the spring supply boat three weeks ago, to surprise them with a visit, and had stayed to help nurse Gabriel night and day. She was with him now, waiting for Temperance. Temperance pulled off her cap and let the breeze blow through her hair for a moment. The weather had been unseasonably warm, and the May flies, which were usually gone by the end of that month, were still swarming, making life miserable for livestock and humans alike. She and Meg had trouble keeping them away from Gabriel. Maybe today, with the wind from the river, the flies would not be so bad, and the weather would be a little cooler. With a sigh, Temperance put her cap back on and went inside.

Will was asleep at the table, his head in his arms. He was snoring loudly, his broad shoulders rising and falling with the deep, drugged sleep of exhaustion and half a bottle of aqua vitae. He had not been himself since the journey to Jamestown for Pocahontas's nuptials. Opechancanough had said something to him at the wedding feast that had disturbed him deeply, and hardly a day passed that he did not talk about danger from the river tribes. "They cannot live next to us in peace for long. Kalono says so, and I believe him." Kalono was the aged Pamunkey hermit who lived just across the river, less than a mile from their house. Will had taken to visiting him often. Will made dire predictions about an Indian attack, and yet he kept on going among them to trade, sometimes even staying overnight in their villages now that Powhatan had declared a truce in honor of his daughter's marriage to an Englishman.

Since his son had taken sick, Will had not left the house except to fetch wood and water. But today he was going to Henrico to get oatmeal and fishhooks. Temperance knew that he would also manage to get some sack or aqua vitae, or, failing that, some of the raw wine made from Virginia's wild plums and persimmons. He always brought back something to drink.

Temperance put her hand lightly on his shoulder. She hated to wake him, but he had a six-mile walk ahead of him. He did not move, and she gave his shoulder a gentle shake.

"Ah!" He raised his head with a jerk and stared at her with red-rimmed, panic-stricken eyes. "What is it? Is—" He looked toward the room where Gabriel lay.

"No, no. He is just the same. Meg is with him. I just thought you would want to set out soon if you're going to the storehouse today."

When Will left, Temperance went into the other room, where Gabriel slept and Meg watched. She looked up at Temperance and smiled. "How many bedsides have you and I kept watch at, I wonder?" she said softly.

"I don't know. I can't remember them all," Temperance said. And how many deathbeds, she thought. Dear God, don't let this be one. The two women sat beside the little bed Will had made, watching the sleeping child's chest rise and fall, rise and fall.

"You know, since I helped bring him into this world," Meg said wistfully, "I've always looked on this child as mine—as the child I never had. That's the thing I regret most, when I look back." She sighed. "I should have so loved to have Anthony's child. I used to wish I had conceived a child before he left for Roanoke. Then at least I'd have something—a part of him."

"Do you still hope, after all this time? Meg, you know, by now—Jamestown's been here seven years this spring—if anybody from Roanoke were still alive, would they not have been found, or found us?"

Meg nodded. "I reckon. But this is a big country, and not much of it settled, even by the Indians. Who can be sure?"

"Meg, do you never think of getting married? There are lots of men here. It is not too late, you know."

"No." The answer was simple and final. Later that evening, when Will came back, Temperance thought how curious it was that they had had this talk about Anthony, because of something Will had heard in Henrico.

When he came home, there was a faint smell of liquor on his breath, but he was not drunk. He went straight to Gabriel's bedside, where he sat for nearly an hour, not saying anything, not moving, just watching, waiting, Temperance knew, for his son to awaken and know he was there. But Gabriel lay in a deep sleep.

"He is better," Will said. "Oh, God, tell me he is better."

"It's too soon to say," Temperance said gently.

"Let us see how it goes with him in the night," Meg said.

After they had eaten, Will said, "You know, I met a curious fellow today at Henrico."

"Who?" Temperance said dutifully.

Meg yawned and said politely, "Who was it?"

"Never mind," Will said amiably, "I can see you're not anxious to hear."

"No, no."

"Go ahead."

"This morning, when I came to Henrico, there was a crowd of people in the marketplace by the storehouse, and in the midst of them there was an Indian who spoke English better than some Englishmen. They were all listening to him, so I tarried there to see what he was saying. The fellow was not an Indian at all, even though he had a feather headdress on, and he was wearing a fringed buckskin just like an Indian. He said he had been carried off by the Nansemonds, down near Fort Henry, more than three years ago, and finally got away. His name is Parker—William Parker."

"How did he get here—to Henrico?" Meg asked.

"He came back with Ralph Hamor, or so he said. Now he's on his way to Jamestown. He heard the seven-year terms are up, and he wants to claim his fifty-acre headright. But he said it pleasured him to live among the Indians." There was a wistfulness in Will's voice. "In all that time, he said, he never saw an Englishman—except one dead one—until he ran across Hamor and Savage at Matchcot. A strange fellow." Will shook his head.

Meg, who had been sitting with her back against the wall and was on the verge of dozing off, suddenly sat upright. "What do you mean, he never saw an Englishman except a dead one?"

The question reverberated in the small room. Temperance sat up, Will leaned forward, and the three of them stared at each other.

"Good God, Meg," Will said softly. "I never thought to ask. What a dunce I am." He put his head in his hands.

"No matter, Will," Meg said. "You had other things on your mind, after all, and it might be nothing. But do you remember anything he said?"

Will frowned thoughtfully. "Not much. I just remember he said something about how he had happened on a dead man once in the woods, and he was curious because the man was an Englishman, and all alone."

"Did he say where this man was?"

"If he did, I don't remember it. God strike me, Meg, I am a sorry one!"

"No matter," Meg said with a shrug. "If it was anything—if that man was Anthony, and he was dead, then what?" Silence hung in the room, as each of them, awestruck, pondered the question.

"After twenty years," Temperance whispered, "after all that time."

"You have got to know," Will said suddenly. "At least you can know all this Parker fellow knows. You must speak with him. I'll take you to Henrico tomorrow."

"Oh, Will! I don't even know if I want to know." She looked entreatingly from one to the other, as if she were begging them to decide for her. "After all," she said, twisting her hands in her lap and looking down at them, "if I don't know, I can still hope."

"No," Temperance said briskly. "No, Meg, after all this time, if there's a chance to find out something, you know you want to know. You must do as Will says. You can leave at first light tomorrow morning."

"But we cannot both be gone all day, and leave you by yourself with Gabriel," Meg said.

"Yes, you can. He will be better tomorrow, and you two will go to Henrico."

It was a warm morning, and the swarms of May flies buzzed around Meg's head and arms like so many Furies. Skipping a little, she tried to match her steps to Will's long stride.

"Sorry," he said. "I am going too fast for you." He slowed his pace.

"No," she said, slightly out of breath. "How far have we come?" she wanted to know.

"Oh, probably about two miles, as I reckon it. Noontime will see us there."

They lapsed into silence, the only sounds being the soft thudding of their footsteps on the hard grassy path and the sounds of bird calls: the shrill warble of an oriole, the chirp of a sparrow, the harsh caw of a crow. Far above their heads, the pine branches made a lacy canopy, partially shielding them from the June sun. Meg looked up sideways at Will, who kept his gaze on the path straight ahead. His mouth was set, and there was a look of unhappiness in his eyes—a restlessness and a sadness that troubled her.

"You—you are a good person, Will," she said. "And you're good to take me, with Gabriel sick and all."

"No, not good." He smiled down at her. "Not good, just curious. I want to see what you find out."

"It's like to be nothing," she said. "But if I didn't go and ask this man, I trow I'd spend the rest of my years wondering."

"I've wondered, too," Will said. "At first, years ago, there was such talk about hunting for the lost Roanoke people, and there were those stories the Indians told about English in clothes like ours, and George Percy's tale of the blond-haired boy in the woods, and Henry Spelman's claims about Englishmen living at Ritanoe—you cannot help but wonder."

"I think I want to know," Meg said slowly. "And then, sometimes, I think maybe I don't. But when you told about this William Parker and what he said, something told me I had to see him. You know—" She caught herself. She had been about to tell Will about the gold cross she had given to George Yardley two years ago.

"I know—what?" Will asked.

"Oh, nothing. We shall see what Master Parker has to say when we get there."

When they found him, he was sitting under a tree near the storehouse. He did not rise to greet them, but grinned at them with his yellow teeth and narrowed his small, piglike eyes suspiciously. What an unpleasant-looking creature, Meg thought. She extended her hand to Parker when Will presented him, but she hated to touch him. He was still dressed Indian-style in a single fringed buckskin garment that covered his greasy body from waist to knee.

"Bear grease," he said, seeing her distaste. "Best thing in the world to keep off flies and mosquitoes. Indians know that." Parker's head, which had once been shaved except for a strip of hair from forehead to nape, was now covered with a fine, scraggly fuzz, and the one long lock was matted and filthy. He had begun to grow a beard and had taken off his Indian beads, but the total effect of his attire and behavior was that of some strange hybrid, neither English nor Indian. "It's luck you caught me. I'm about to make for Jamestown, to put in for my Company share. With fifty acres of my own, I might even live like an Englishman again."

"An Englishman is why Mistress Worley wanted to see you," Will said. "To ask you about the one you found in the woods."

"What does she want to know for? And why does she want to know it? There are plenty of live Englishmen around here, if she's got a hankering for one." Parker cackled at his own wit.

Will grabbed him by his topknot. "I've got a hankering to show you some manners. Take care how you treat a lady!" Will was at least a head taller than Parker, and could easily have lifted him off the ground.

"Ow! You watch out yourself! I don't have to talk to her, or you, either, if I don't want to. What's in it for me, anyway?"

"Please!" Meg said. "I have no money, or I would give you some. But I just wanted to ask you about this man I hear you found—where he was, and . . . what he looked like."

"Didn't you ever hear of the lost Roanoke people?" Will asked, letting go Parker's topknot.

"Yes, I heard. Who hasn't? I even heard the Indians talking about them." Parker preened himself.

"What did they say?" Will and Meg spoke almost as one.

"Oh, not much. The story around Nansemond was that there used to be a whole village of English among the Chesepian Indians, down close to the bay, and that Powhatan made war on them—English and Chesepians— and burned all their towns and crops just before the first supply came to Jamestown. Some said a few English escaped and went to live at Ritanoe, but I never went there to see."

"The man you say you found in the woods—where was he?" Meg asked. Her heart was beginning to pound.

Parker stroked his scraggly chin and squinted at the sky, as though he could read some invisible map there. "Let's see now. That was when I had just got loose from the Nansemonds, and I was trying to follow the river, walking by night and hiding out in the daytime. That was when I found him. Must have been, oh, someplace between Point Comfort and Mulberry Island. He was all by himself. Must have been some loner, like me, running from the Indians. But 'twasn't an Indian that killed him, at least as near as I could tell. No marks on him, just lying there all peaceful under a big oak tree, dead as a fish out of water."

"What did this man look like?" Meg said softly.

"Oh, he was a good-sized fellow. I noticed that right off. Tall, about as tall as him." He pointed to Will. "Dressed in clothes made of buckskins, he was, with Indian shoes on his feet." The next words fell on Meg's ears like hammer blows, each one sharp and distinct. "His hair was gray, but yellowish-colored. He probably had light hair when he was young."

Meg held tight to Will's arm. He put his hand over hers, and neither of them spoke. Parker, pleased to be the object of such undivided attention, went on, "I looked around, to see if he had anything that would tell who he was, but all that was on him was a little bag around his neck with this in it." Rummaging in a pouch at his waist, Parker drew forth a thin gold chain. Attached to it, dangling from his hand, was a small gold cross. "Pretty, ain't it?" Parker said, holding it up to the light. Meg swayed; Will caught her as her knees buckled, and eased her down on a bench against the storehouse wall.

"It's mine, Will," she whispered. "That cross is mine!"

Parker, his mouth open in amazement, stared at her and then at the cross in his hand, as if he were trying to understand her meaning. Then he closed his mouth firmly and tucked the cross into one grimy palm. "Oh, no," he said craftily. "This here is a solid-gold cross, and I found it. You got no proof it's yours. This came off a dead man threescore miles from here. It don't belong to you, but if you want, I'll sell it to you." He folded his arms across his chest and grinned. "Name me a price."

"You bastard!"

Will's fist caught him off guard, and he fell backward against the wall of the storehouse. Before he could recover his footing, Will hit him again, knocking loose one of his front teeth. Spitting blood and clutching his chin, he watched speechlessly as Will searched in the grass for the cross, which had flown from Parker's hand in the assault.

"Here it is!" Will knelt to pick it up, to give it to Meg. Gently, he took her hand in one of his, and with the other he pressed the cross and chain on her upturned palm and closed her fingers around it. Then, for a moment, he held on to her hand tightly with both of his. Looking down, she saw that one of his hands was skinned and bleeding from his having hit Parker.

"You hurt yourself," she said numbly.

"No matter."

"What's the matter?"

"What happened?"

Captain James Davis and Lieutenant Samuel Collier were coming along the path in front of the storehouse.

"Nothing," Will said. "Master Parker"—he spat out the name—"Master Parker and I had a little disagreement, but we settled it." He cast a threatening look at Parker, who glowered at him but did not speak.

"You were just here yesterday, weren't you, Sterling?" Davis said, looking puzzled. "Is anything wrong? Your young one worse?"

"No," Will said. "But Mistress Worley here had reason to believe Parker might have seen . . . someone she knew, so she came to ask him. We had best be on our way back now."

All that time, Meg had sat on the bench as still as a stone, the hand with Anthony's gift to her lying in her lap. She had not opened her fingers to look at the cross. As William Parker took himself off, and Davis and

Collier went on about their business, she nodded mechanically to them as they passed by her. Then at last she opened her hand and looked at the cross. With one finger, she touched its four points; then she traced its width and length. She moved her hand so that its angles caught the noontime sun, and watched its burnished surface gleam.

"Do you want to put it on?" Leaning over her, Will took hold of the ends of the chain and brought them up slowly, like one performing a religious ceremony, and fastened them around her neck. "There," he said softly.

She stood up, turned to face him, and kissed him on the cheek. "Thank you," she said. She said no more, and he did not ask her.

"If you are rested enough, we had better start back," was all he said.

They had eaten their midday meal on the way, as they walked: chunks of bread and a small jug of cider. Now they retraced their steps along the wooded pathway, this time with the sun at their backs. At first they walked along in silence, and then Will spoke: "Just tell me one thing, and you can save the rest for Temperance when we get back. How in heaven's name did Will Parker come by your gold cross?"

"I gave it to . . . George Yardley to send to Ritanoe, two years ago, when he went down to Fort Charles."

"Then George's presence in Virginia has done some good after all," Will said bitterly.

"Oh, Will!" The two walked on in silence, the afternoon sun lengthening their shadows on the grassy path, the pine trees whispering over their heads. When they rounded the last curve in the path and came within sight of the house, Will stopped suddenly, stared at it, and then began to run toward it in long, loping strides.

"What is it, Will? Wait!"

Over his shoulder, as he ran, he shouted, "There's no fire! Something's wrong!" And then he kept on running. No fire. Nothing coming out of the chimney, though the air had grown chilly as dusk approached. Temperance had said she would have a hot supper waiting. And she had been planning to make more broth for Gabriel.

Gabriel. Meg, too, began to run, but by the time she reached the house, Will had long since disappeared inside the open door. Hearing no sound, she paused, feeling like an intruder. Then she stepped inside, blinking in the dimness. Temperance was sitting on a stool next to Gabriel's bed, and Will had flung himself on his knees beside her. Gabriel lay on the bed, his eyes closed, his small, thin wrists crossed over his heart in pitiful, final repose. Will had not spoken; Temperance made no sound. Moving like one in a trance, she leaned forward and carefully drew the white coverlet over the little face.

"I had to cover him up," she said in a small voice, to no one in particular. "The . . . flies." Then, hunching forward, hiding her face in her lap, she began to weep. She had not even acknowledged Will and Meg's presence. Her sorrow made no sound; her body shook with silent paroxysms of grief.

"Oh, God," Will said. "Oh, dear God. This is my doing—this is my punishment." He buried his face in his hands. "My punishment."

Meg, unable to keep her distance any longer, came and knelt between them. She put one arm on Will's shoulder and the other around Temperance's waist. "The Lord giveth, and the Lord taketh away," she said softly. "Blessed be the name of the Lord." But they refused to be comforted, and she did not know what to do. There were more things at work in this grief than the simple death of a child. Suddenly, she had an idea. "I am going out for a while. I'll be back later.' Rising, she shook out her skirts and straightened her cap.

"Where are you going?" Will asked.

"To get Reverend Whitaker. I'll be back before dark." She knew the way, and if she walked quickly, she could be at the parsonage in half an hour, and be back at the cottage with Whitaker in plenty of time before sunset. There were times when people needed the comforts only a man of God could give, she thought, and this was, without question, one of those times. Meg was tired, and confused thoughts swirled about in her head. She did not know if God had chosen to punish Temperance and Will by taking their only child, but somehow they must be made to accept His providence. They had not knowingly done wrong when they conceived this child, so how could God punish them for it? Alexander Whitaker, this kind young parson she had met when he first came to Jamestown, would know what to say to them.

This time she was glad he had chosen to live outside of Henrico, on the same side of the river as Temperance and Will. When she reached the log palisade that ran around the parsonage, she found the gate slightly ajar. Good, she thought, there was no need to ring the bell and wait for Jeremy Mutton to come down and let her in. There was plenty of daylight left, if she and Whitaker could leave immediately. She hurried up the hill and rapped on the heavy front door, but no one came. Wishing that Whitaker had installed a knocker on his door, she rapped again. Still no answer. Too exhausted to realize she had not thought to call out, she walked over to a window and peered in.

The Reverend Alexander Whitaker and Jeremy Mutton were on the floor, naked. They were lying chest to chest, embracing, but each had his head between the other's legs, so that they resembled some giant four-legged insect. What they appeared to be doing with their mouths, in silent, violent ecstasy, was something Meg had only the vaguest notion of, had never imagined, and never wanted to see again.

Breathless, speechless with revulsion, she fled. She ran as fast as she could down the slope of the lawn, terrified that they might have sensed her presence, that they might come after her. She reached the gate, taking care to leave it slightly ajar, just as she had found it, and ran on, not stopping until she was safely out of sight in a grove of laurel trees. She leaned against a tree and closed her eyes, panting for breath. Her knees felt weak, and there was a stitch in her side. Slowly, she let herself slide down the tree trunk until she was in a sitting position. Her heart was behaving strangely, and she had never felt so tired.

This can't be, she thought wildly. Am I going to be like Anthony, dying alone under a tree? Did he feel like this? But gradually, as she rested, she began to breathe easier, the pain in her side lessened, and the strength began to come back into her legs. It was just this day, she thought. Nobody could bear what has happened in this one day. The news of Anthony, after all these years. The child's death. And now this. Wearily, she gathered her skirts and got to her feet. Poor Will. Little Gabriel. Dearest Anthony. Temperance. Alexander Whitaker. Jeremy Mutton. What, she wondered, did God have in mind, when He sent them all into this wilderness?

JAMESTOWN
27 April 1616

As a sudden breeze rippled the wide waters of the James, the *Treasurer* strained at her moorings as if she were anxious to set sail. From her fo'c's'le, Captain Samuel Argall kept a watchful eye on last-minute preparations. On the pier, sailors had been working rope and winch all morning, hoisting supplies aboard: barrels of salted pork, casks of cheese, ship's biscuit, peas, and a special gift from Pocahontas's father—dried venison. In all this time, Powhatan, true to his word, had never visited Jamestown, nor had he ever journeyed to Varina, where Pocahontas and John Rolfe had made their home, not ten miles from Powhatan Village. But Powhatan had his own ways of knowing how they fared. He had known when their son was born, and had sent a pair of dressed doeskins; when he heard that they were going to England, he sent three baskets of smoked dried venison. He also sent his daughter Matachanna and her husband, Tomocomo, to accompany Pocahontas. Matachanna was to help care for little Thomas Rolfe, not yet two years old, and Tomocomo was to count the numbers of Englishmen on the other side of the ocean and bring Powhatan word of their strength.

They were all assembled at the edge of the pier, waiting to board. Samuel Argall watched this traveling party with great satisfaction, once again congratulating himself on having had the wit to abduct Pocahontas. Had it not been for him, he thought, this happy scene would not now be taking place. With the Rolfes was Thomas Dale, returning at last to England after serving five years as governor of Virginia. They were a joyful group, anxious to be off on this bright April morning. John Rolfe was as happy a man as could be found in all Virginia: Pocahontas had not ceased to delight him; moreover, she had borne him a strong, healthy son, and the Rolfe land at Varina was producing tobacco that was selling for three shillings the pound in England. Others had begun to grow the weed, too: Last year's crop was two thousand pounds; this year Virginia would ship out five times that. Tobacco fever was beginning to spread. A man could plant twenty-five acres in tobacco and reap seventy-five pounds sterling a year at current prices; the average wage earner in England was lucky to see fifteen pounds sterling a year. Virginia at last had a cash crop, thanks largely to Master John Rolfe.

Pocahontas, too, was happy. She was about to have a dream come true: she was at long last going to see England. Matachanna, childless after two years of marriage, welcomed the chance to go along and help mother little Thomas. She stood holding him and talking to him as they watched the ship making ready. Her husband Tomocomo walked bravely up and down the pier, trying not to show his fear of transatlantic travel.

All of Jamestown had gathered this morning to see the *Treasurer* off, and before that, to witness the transfer of authority at Dale's departure and the formal swearing-in of Deputy Governor George Yardley. The latter, resplendent in a red velvet cloak and a doublet with gold braid, surrounded by a half-dozen halberdiers in full armor, had already assumed a commanding air. He stood watching the activity on the pier with a benign and somewhat possessive look, as if the entire scene—pier, passengers, crew, ship, and cargo—belonged to him.

Well he might look pleased. The colony he was to govern had prospered in the last three years. Four new settlements—Henrico, some thirty miles upriver; five miles below that, Bermuda Hundred; then West and Shirley Hundred across the river from Bermuda Hundred, and Dale's Gift, on the Jamestown peninsula, were thriving. Jamestown itself was now a small, neat village that could boast some proper houses made of framed timber, not wattle and daub. In a row facing the riverbank stood eight large and commodious dwellings, three of them with two stories and a loft, and a large new storehouse. The two-story houses belonged to the Pierces and to Francis West, the military commander of Jamestown, with the remaining house, the largest, being reserved as the governor's residence. There were gardens with English flowers in them, and vegetable plots with tidy fences. The old palisade remained, as did some of the original houses within, but peaceful relations with the Indians had encouraged building outside the walls. Only about fifty people lived at Jamestown now, and Francis West, with little to occupy him, spent much of his time at his place upriver, which he called Westover. The rest of the Virginia colonists, numbering about three hundred, were scattered in the newer settlements as well as the older ones at Point Comfort and Kecoughtan. The terrible fevers had ceased to take their toll, and Jamestown was no longer a charnel house. The colony was beginning to do well in other ways, too: ships leaving for England were taking on cargoes of potash, charcoal, ships' masts, and tar as well as tobacco.

At last the loading of the *Treasurer* was done, the last barrel of drinking water swung aboard, and the passengers, shouting and laughing, clambered across the gangplank. At a signal from the deputy governor, Lieutenant Timothy Dowse began to beat a brisk tattoo upon his drum. Lines were cast off, and slowly, majestically, amid the noise of the drum and the huzzahs of the assembled spectators, the *Treasurer* began to drift away from the pier. As the great square sails unfurled and slowly filled with wind, the crew scrambled aloft to set the smaller topsails. The *Treasurer* was at last under way. Ashore, the crowd of spectators—they numbered no more than forty in all—began to disperse. There were fields to be plowed, fish to be caught, gardens to be weeded, houses to be cleaned, fences in need of mending.

Deputy Governor Yardley planned to inspect the fortifications of the palisade, take dinner with the Causeys, and depart for Bermuda Hundred. He would continue to make his residence there, especially since that, with over a hundred people, was the largest settlement in the colony. Bermuda Hundred did not really resemble Bermuda, but something about the gently rolling hills that stretched inland from the river had inspired Thomas Gates, before he left for England two years ago, to give the plantation that name. George found it a pleasant place, and as the commanding officer in charge of the Hundred, he was entitled to a large house with three rooms. It was wattle and daub, but it did have a plank floor and a chimney at each end. He lived there with Richard Pace, his lieutenant, and Tom Goodwyn, once ship's boy on the *Sea Venture,* now, at twenty, the age George had begun soldiering, a sergeant. They had two boys, John Philips and Samuel Garrett, to wait on them. Some of the survivors of the *Sea Venture* had now settled on land adjoining George's at Bermuda Hundred, and he could visit them when he felt lonely.

All in all, George's progress in Virginia had been more than he had hoped for: from captain of Thomas Gates's guards to commander of Fort Charles, to commander at Bermuda Hundred, and finally, to deputy governor. With advances in office had come increases in pay and prerogatives, and now, as deputy governor, he was in an excellent position to acquire land, and tenants from the Virginia Company to work it. All he had dreamed of doing in Virginia he had done—except to live there with Temperance. He had not seen Temperance since that day he had gone to speak with her at Jamestown, almost four years ago, and he did not intend to see her ever again, if he could help it. Without the decree of divorce, he was not free to remarry, but there would be time for that in a year or so, after he had made his fortune.

As he strolled back toward the palisade, he saw Meg Worley hurrying to catch up with him, and he stopped. He had not seen her, either, since the day he left for Fort Charles.

"Captain Yardley!" she called. "Or now I should say Deputy Governor Yardley." She held out her hand to him. She was still a handsome woman, or at least she would have been, were it not for the scar across her face. "Congratulations."

"Thank you," he said, clasping her hand. "So you still live here, inside the palisade?"

"Yes," she said. "I had been hoping you would come here these past two years, because I had something to tell you about this." Smiling, she put her hand to her throat and lifted the gold cross on its chain. Then she told him William Parker's story.

"So that is how I believe it happened," she said, and then she paused. "Unless—unless the man Master Parker saw was one of your men."

"No," George said. "The fellow Parker described to you could not have been one of my men."

"I was hoping you would say that."

"I am glad that makes you happy," George said. "You are very fortunate. Contentment comes to few in this life, I trow." Then he paused. "I suppose you hear from Temperance?" He tried his best to make the question sound idle, unimportant, but he choked ever so slightly on the name. No matter. Meg Worley was not easily deceived, and she looked at him with such pity that he felt his cheeks growing hot.

"Yes," she said softly. "I do." She did not say anything else, and George was annoyed. Did she want him to beg for information?

"Her child must be . . . what? Six years old by now." He spoke with studied casualness.

"Her child is dead."

George was surprised that four words could pain him so. "Dead? How?"

"Some sickness in his stomach. He died when I was there two years ago."

"I am sorry." Suddenly, he did not want to hear any more. "I really must be off now. I have some business with Dr. Pott." Bowing low to Meg, he swung his cloak about him and strode off.

Bermuda Hundred
20 October 1616

 "Mark my words, there will be trouble with the Indians this winter." The Reverend Alexander Whitaker's pale, slender fingers played with the stem of his wine goblet as he spoke. Across the table from him, Deputy Governor Yardley frowned.

"I know," he said angrily. "This refusal to pay the corn tribute is just the beginning. For two years, the Chickahominies have paid us five hundred bushels at the end of the summer, and the moment Dale leaves the country, they say they can't do it. And with Pocahontas in England, who knows what Powhatan may do?"

Whitaker nodded in solemn agreement. "One has to remember that savages—heathens—are no more than children, and they cannot be trusted."

"Well, I wish to God we had not trusted them to give us corn. I thought with tobacco prices going so well, we should plant all we possibly could, and let the Indians grow the corn. You know, and I know, how badly the Virginia Company wants to turn a profit here, and tobacco is the way to do it. Nobody in England wants corn," George said with a wry laugh. "It is hard to grind; it sticks in your teeth, and it runs right through your bowels."

"Well spoken," Whitaker said with a rueful laugh, "and we don't have enough of it to last the winter."

"More wine?" George sighed as he refilled their goblets. He was glad he had asked the Reverend Whitaker to stay the night with him. Now that there were so many people living at Bermuda Hundred, the young parson had begun to divide his time, preaching one Sunday at Henrico and one at Bermuda Hundred. The deputy governor was hungry for company, and in need of someone he could confide in. "I don't know what the proper course is," he said. "If we aim to make a success of this colony, we have to raise tobacco; if we raise tobacco, we cannot grow enough food; if we cannot grow enough food, we have to bargain with the Indians; if we bargain with the Indians, we end by fighting with them—and then where are we?"

The Reverend Whitaker took a sip of his wine and set it down slowly and thoughtfully. "That is why we must convert them. Bring them to Christ."

George looked at him skeptically. "And how would you do that? We've barely enough ministers for ourselves, let alone to send among the savages. And think how many of them there are. Powhatan himself commands near fifteen hundred warriors—not to mention their women and children. And then there are the other tribes."

"But with God, all things are possible," Whitaker said. "If we could start with their own priests—their medicine men, perhaps. If we could convert just one, think of the power he would have! The rest would come easily." His slender face glowed at the prospect.

"I don't know," George said doubtfully.

Whitaker was not to be discouraged. "Their priests live alone, some of them, like hermits in the forest. The other Indians come to see them, and they give advice and cure diseases. They have tremendous power over their people." He frowned slightly. "The trouble is, they are very unfriendly. Suspicious. There is one like that living not far from Rock Hall. Kalono, he calls himself. I have done my best, but he will not receive me. He refuses to speak with me, even though I can speak their tongue fairly well because of Pocahontas. But when I go to his house, he pretends not to understand me. He folds his arms and glares at me with a look sharper than knives. I believe he tells his people to hate the English, and I believe he is the one responsible for the killing of our people's hogs and chickens." Whitaker paused for a moment, and then he brightened. "As soon as cold weather comes, I shall visit this Kalono again, and this time I shall see if he likes presents. I shall take him a hat with an ostrich plume, and a velvet cloak with gold braid on it."

George laughed admiringly. "You are a clever fellow," he said. "If anyone can convert the savages, you can. But meanwhile, what are we to do this winter?"

Scarcely two weeks after George's conversation with Alexander Whitaker, the Pamunkeys and the Chickahominies began stealing livestock around Henrico and Bermuda Hundred. Almost every other day, an angry colonist appeared at the deputy governor's house to report losses:

"Two sows gone."

"My best setting hen stolen."

"Our one milk cow vanished."

And always the same question: "What are you going to do about it?"

The deputy governor, anxious to strike back, fearful of starting a war, ever mindful of the pitiful discrepancies between the number of Indians and the number of English, lay awake long into the night pondering that question, and when he fell asleep, he ground his teeth. At last he said to Lieutenant Richard Pace, "Go down to Jamestown, and tell Captain West I want a score of men. He has a dozen or more there, and he can send to Point Comfort and Fort Charles for the rest. Tell him I need them for a scouting expedition, but there could be trouble. Get back here with them as soon as you can."

To Sergeant Tom Goodwyn, he said, "I want every able-bodied man here to be ready at a moment's notice. We'll march as soon as the others arrive."

To his officers' protests that the deputy governor ought to send one of them in command and not risk himself, he replied, "John Smith did it, and Thomas Dale did it. I cannot govern unless I do it."

But twenty men cannot travel unnoticed, and long before the assembled force was ready to move, word of their coming had been swiftly and silently passed among the Indian villages at the fringes of the white men's settlements. War councils were held, strategies planned.

On the neck of land formed by a deep bend in the river between Henrico and Bermuda Hundred, all the tobacco-curing sheds were set on fire, and the three occupants of the house nearest the sheds had their throats cut, by Opechancanough's orders. Farther downriver, on the other side of Henrico, the Pamunkey Indians followed the instructions of Kalono, the old Pamunkey priest-hermit. On the last day of October, it was Kalono who told them to take vengeance on an English man and woman whose house was on the outskirts of the settlement.

On November 1, the deputy governor, who had decided to give the Indians one last chance to negotiate before attacking with his full force, set out early in the morning with a company of twelve carefully selected men. To impress the King of the Pamunkeys, they wore metal breastplates and closed helmets. Six of them carried muskets primed and ready; the others carried pikes. The deputy governor wore his sword in a garnet-encrusted sword belt and carried a pair of pistols inlaid with mother-of-pearl. Since the distance to Arrohattoc, the main Pamunkey village, was half by land what it was on the hairpin curves of the river at that point, and speed was crucial, they marched the four miles through the woods instead of depending on oars and capricious winds to transport them upriver.

Had they gone by water, they would have come upon the still-smoldering cornfields near the bend of the river, but instead they tramped in the opposite direction, unaware of the devastation behind them. Marching toward Henrico, they came upon a small house in a clearing bordered by tall pine trees, and they saw that the Indians had been there before them. The roof of the house was ablaze, and flames leaped skyward from the dry thatch. The gate hung ajar, and the neatly fenced field and garden were deserted.

"Damnation! Pray God there is no one still in there! Goodwyn, take your men and go see!" George could hardly contain his rage. "Godless savages! This is their answer! We'll not parley with them. We'll go back right now and gather our main force, and we'll attack them before the sun rises again!" Shading his eyes against the morning sun, the deputy governor watched as Tom Goodwyn and four of his men ran toward the house, about a hundred yards away.

"But where are the people? What's happened to them?"

"Run off, maybe? Or carried off?"

"Whose house is it?"

"Look! There was somebody in there! They're bringing somebody out!"

As the voices of his men jangled in his ears, George Yardley stopped and stood very still. The soldiers ran on ahead of him, but he did not move.

Whose house is it? No. It can't be.

Suddenly, he began to run, catching up with his men, shoving some aside as he ran. Just then, the wind changed, and clouds of acrid black smoke from the thatched roof engulfed the men running toward the house. Coughing, choking, and swearing, they paused in confusion, trying to escape the smoke. Only George, panting for air that seared his lungs, ran blindly on.

They had laid her on the grass. He had known who it was the moment he saw the hair, even from a distance.

"I—I think she may be dead, sir." Tom Goodwyn, who had carried her out, was crouching over her. The other men gathered about her in shocked silence. George knelt down. There was a great deal of blood, but he had seen worse-wounded men on a battlefield, and some of them had lived. Tenderly, with trembling fingers, he searched for a pulse in her neck. At first he could feel nothing, and he fancied her skin was already growing cold to his touch. Then he found it: a tiny flutter of a pulse, no stronger than a butterfly's wing.

"No," he said weakly, leaning back on his heels, "she is not dead."

"Who is it?"

"Where's her husband, if she had one?"

"Indians must have taken him."

The voices rang in George's ears. The men who had come up from Jamestown didn't know, and neither did his own men from Bermuda Hundred. None of them had been in Virginia six years ago. Only Tom Goodwyn knew.

"She is—she was—my wife," George said woodenly.

A chorus of puzzled and sympathetic murmurs came from the men crowded around him.

"What shall we do, sir?" Goodwyn touched him lightly on the shoulder, and George jumped as if he had been struck. "She's bleeding right badly, sir," Tom said.

With the energy of a madman, George began to undo his heavy quilted doublet. Underneath it, under the chain mail and next to his skin, he was wearing a linen shirt. It could serve for bandages. They would have to stop the bleeding, and then, somehow, they would have to take her back with them. He could not bring himself to think beyond that. "Here, Pace, help me tear this into pieces, and be quick." With one motion, George ripped his shirt in two and handed one piece of it to Richard Pace, who happened to be closest to him. There was a hideous gash at Temperance's hairline. When he touched it, a whole patch of her hair moved, and he caught a glimpse of bone. Good God, he thought, they've tried to cut off her scalp. He tied a strip of his shirt around her forehead, lifting her head as gently as he could. She did not stir. "We've got to have some way to carry her—something to carry her in." He glanced around him at his men. None of them had a cloak; they, like him, were all in battle dress. In a good heavy cloak, with a man at each corner, they could have carried her easily.

"It's three miles to Henrico," Tom Goodwyn said. "We could send for help."

Desperately, George tried to force his benumbed brain to function. If they sent for help, they would have to wait for a man to get there and for the help to get back. That would be six miles. Too long. Temperance was going to need a surgeon. If they started now, they could be at Bermuda Hundred with her before anyone could go to Henrico and back.

"No," he said.

Richard Pace spoke up: "Maybe we could carry her in our arms—three or four of us together."

"No," George said. "No, it's too far."

"You should put something on, sir," Goodwyn said gently. "You're cold." George, naked to the waist after stripping off his shirt, had not even realized that he was shivering. As he bent over to pick up his jerkin, his hand touched the heavy woolen fabric of Temperance's petticoat. It was coarse red stammel, and there was a good bit of it. In a flash of inspiration, he spread the hem to its full width.

"What are you doing, sir?"

"Making a litter."

Working with frenzied haste, George loosened the stays of Temperance's bodice so he could slip his hand underneath and undo the ties of her petticoat. Then, as gently as he possibly could, he slipped the petticoat off her waist and down over her hips. The white shift under the petticoat was horribly bloody, and he hated for the men to see it. He was seized with an overpowering, irrational urge to lie down with her, to cover that cold, still body with his own. Instead, he drew the edges of her kirtle over her legs as best he could and spread her petticoat on the ground. "We'll need a man on each corner," George said, "and one man at this end, to carry her feet. Pace, you take her feet, and you, Goodwyn, here, and Brinton, you and Waldo there. I'll take this side. We'll change over when we get tired."

But George did not change over. He walked at Temperance's head all the way back, and he did not get tired.

When they reached the path that led to Henrico, Tom Goodwyn said, "Sir, do you think maybe we should take her to Henrico?"

"No!" George spoke sharply, and they tramped on in silence. No one challenged him. In a little while, by way of explanation, he said, "She needs a surgeon. There's none at Henrico." There was no surgeon at Bermuda Hundred, either, but no one dared to point that out. When they were about half a mile from Bermuda Hundred, George told Tom Goodwyn to go on ahead. "Tell the boys to make sure there's a good fire going, and to put some water on to heat."

"Shall I send for Mistress Forrest or some of the other women?"

"No!" Again, George spoke sharply, and again no one said anything. He did not care. He had not wanted a gaggle of curious people at Henrico, and he did not want any of the women at Bermuda Hundred clucking around Temperance, either. She was probably going to die soon, if she were not dead already, and all he wanted was some time to be alone with her. At last they reached the house, and like some giant ten-legged insect, the makeshift litter and its bearers crept inside with their inert burden. Then George, remembering his other responsibilities, spoke to Lieutenant Pace: "See that these men get an extra ration of beer, and report to me in an hour."

"Do you need any help?" Tom Goodwyn, like the others, received a terse reply.

"No." Then George added, "Perhaps later." By the fireplace in the house's main room, John and Samuel, the two houseboys, were waiting, wide-eyed.

"We done like you said, sir."

"There's a fire in the other room, too, and some water on."

"Thank you," George said. Then he went into his room, closed the heavy oak door, and knelt beside Temperance. The wound on her head seemed to have clotted; at least as far as he could tell. The first thing to do now was to see if she was wounded anywhere else. If she lived the night, he thought, he must get her to Jamestown, to a surgeon. With his knife, he cut her blood-soaked shift at its hem and ripped it up the middle. He saw with horror that the dark auburn ringlets of her pubic hair and part of the skin there had been cut off. But the worst wound seemed to be the head. Something—their approach, perhaps—had caused her attackers to take flight before they took her scalp. But maybe they cracked her skull, George thought, and she would never wake up. *And if she does wake up, what then?* He would not let himself think of that, nor of what had become of Will Sterling.

"Captain Yardley, sir?" That would be Pace, reporting back as George had told him to.

"Yes. Come in."

Pace looked at the inert form on the bed and shook his head sadly. "What are you going to do, sir?"

"Have the longboat ready at daylight. I shall take her to Jamestown, to a surgeon. John Pott is there."

"But what about the men, sir? And the plans to march on Arrohattoc?"

"That will have to wait," George said curtly. His eyes were on the figure on the bed. "She must have a surgeon."

"But couldn't someone else take her?"

"No!" George drew a deep breath. "No, I will take her at first light in the morning. We should be there by late afternoon."

"What about the Indians at Arrohattoc?"

"God damn the Indians! Don't you think I can see what they've done to her?"

"But I thought—you said you would attack tomorrow. The Chickahominies and the Pamunkeys know you have sent for extra men, by now, and they'll be expecting—"

"Let them wait."

"But, sir, the men—"

"That will do, Lieutenant Pace! You forget who gives the orders here."

At dawn they carried Temperance to the longboat. The current downriver was swift, and a little before sunset they tied up at the Jamestown pier. By sunset, word had spread to every house in Jamestown that the deputy governor had arrived with a woman who had been nearly scalped by the Indians, that he had once been married to her and in the eyes of the Church she was still his wife, that Dr. Pott had seen her, and that she was likely to die. As the November dusk closed in, candles were lit, fires were stoked, and speculations swirled about the little settlement like the smoke from its chimneys.

In the governor's house, the deputy governor, refusing nourishment and fighting off sleep, sat in a chair beside a bed in a second-floor chamber. As the sky outside grew dark, he put his head in his hands and wept.

The next morning, as wood was chopped and water was drawn, there was only one topic of conversation in the palisade at Jamestown:

"He is just sitting there, they say, and he won't come out, and he won't let anybody come in."

"He cannot do this. What about our men he sent up to Bermuda Hundred? What about the Indians?"

"Well, she was his wife, you know. You've heard that story. . . ."

"Meg Worley knows them as well as anybody, and he would not even let *her* in."

"The man's gone daft! What if the savages upriver attack while he's swooning about over this woman?"

"A fine deputy governor he is! I wish we had Governor Dale back."

"And Captain West is gone to Westover."

"Yardley's left threescore men up at Bermuda Hundred without a commander."

The day passed, and night came again without the deputy governor's notice. All he knew was that Temperance was still unconscious, and if she did not awaken soon, she was going to die. He longed with all his being for her to open her eyes just once, and know that he was there. Bone-weary, he forced himself to sit upright on a joint stool so that he would not fall asleep. The room was warm; he had seen to that. A fire crackled cozily in the fireplace, and a large stack of wood lay nearby. Outside, the November wind blew in gusts and made the candle on the table flicker. Now he watched the candle's flame as he listened to Temperance's breathing. His eyelids drooped, and he dozed. So deep was his fatigue that he did not hear Temperance when she made a small whimpering noise and turned her head from side to side. George stirred, but he did not awaken. In a few minutes, Temperance moaned softly. This time he heard her.

Gently, hardly daring to touch her, he felt for her hand through the blankets that covered her and laid his hand over hers. She moved her hand under his, and love and pity and joy welled up within him. He would wait for her to speak first, lest he startle her. She did not open her eyes, but she moved her lips as though she were trying to shape a word.

"Will?"

Slowly, George withdrew his hand from hers.

"Will!"

This time it was a cry of warning. She began to gasp and writhe, as if she were struggling with some unseen assailant. George, afraid that she would harm herself, put both hands on her shoulders. "Be still!" he said, bending over her. "Temperance, you're hurt. You must be still."

Suddenly, the pale, contorted face relaxed, and the eyes flew open. At first it was a blank stare, and then it changed slowly to a look of puzzlement. "You?" she said. "Where is—?" She closed her eyes again, as if trying to remember what she wanted to ask.

"Yes," George said softly, "me."

NEAR THE CHICKAHOMINY RIVER
9 December 1616

 "Tell him we want two hundred bushels of corn."

Henry Spelman, the deputy governor's interpreter, dutifully relayed this message by shouting across the clearing in Algonquin to Kissanacomen, the King of the Chickahominies. Kissanacomen, wrapped in a long turkey-feather cloak, listened impassively, and then slowly moved his head from side to side. Viewing himself as the counterpart to Yardley, Kissanacomen followed the Englishman's protocol and did not deign to speak directly to him. Instead, he spoke briefly to a tall Indian next to him, who then shouted back in the Indian tongue to Spelman. Behind Kissanacomen, in a clearing on the banks of the Chickahominy River, two hundred warriors watched and waited.

Spelman translated, "He says that is not possible. He doesn't have any corn to give us. He needs it all for his own people, because the English have taken his land."

"The devil he says!" George Yardley said, trying to control his anger. "Tell him if he wants protection from the Pamunkeys, two hundred bushels of corn is hardly payment, but we are prepared to accept it."

This information was duly relayed, and coldly received. Kissanacomen folded his arms across his chest and uttered one word to his spokesman, who repeated it to Spelman, who did not need to translate it for George.

"Damn!" George said. "Very well, then. Tell him we have talked to his enemy—to Opechancanough—and that we will make war on him with Opechancanough if he does not come to our terms." Then, turning to Tom Goodwyn, George said, "Pass the word to the men at the rear to prime and load, and be ready to move to the front and fire when I give the word."

"But these Indians are not expecting an attack," Spelman said. "They have come in good faith to parley. You can't open fire on them."

"Captain Spelman, you are the interpreter, not the commander here," George said sharply. Behind him, he could hear the rattle of his men's matchlock muskets. "You'll do as you're told, Spelman! That's an order, in case you have forgotten your English!"

"Aye, sir. I'll remember that, sir." Spelman spoke with ill-concealed hostility.

"See that you do."

A brief dialogue between Spelman and Kissanacomen's man ensued. George stood to one side so that he could see out of the corner of his eye when the men in the rear had their muskets ready. But Henry Spelman's remarks had given him pause. It was true that these particular savages had come to the clearing to bargain, not to do battle. But then he thought of another clearing where savages had come, and of a limp and bloody form stretched on the grass, of a pale, thin face and wounds yet unhealed, and blind rage overcame him. "First company to the fore! Stand ready!" Twenty musketeers moved rapidly to the front, thrust their gun-holders into the soft earth, and placed the long muzzles of their weapons in the forked supports. "Fire! Fire at will!"

There was a sharp staccato burst of gunfire, followed by shouts of anguish and rage as a score of Indians crumpled to the ground. There were cheers from the English ranks. Miraculously, Kissanacomen was un-harmed, but his spokesman took a musket ball in the forehead and fell lifeless at his feet. The Indian chief stood his ground. He swore and shook his fist at the English. Through the clouds of smoke from the muskets, George could see him, and the deputy governor knew he had made an enemy for life. He thought about that on the way back to Jamestown.

But George did not spend much time thinking about Kissanacomen that December; he had other, more pressing, matters on his mind, and the most pressing of all lay on a bed in the governor's house in Jamestown. Temperance, weakened by the pneumonia she had contracted when she lay so long unconscious, was still unable to sit up for long. Her wounds had begun to heal, but her spirits had not.

"She has had a great shock, and she has lost so much in such a short time," Meg told George the evening he returned from the Chickahominy. "You must be patient." They had come downstairs after visiting Temper-ance's room, where she lay listlessly staring at the ceiling.

George sat down heavily and put his head in his hands. "If she would just—just smile at me once! But she only lies there, looking at me as though I'm a stranger."

"Perhaps you are, to her. Give her time."

"In God's name, how much time does she need? It's been three weeks!"

Meg leaned across the table and took hold of George's wrists, pulling his hands away from his face. "Three weeks, yes, but she has not seen you in five years, and she has not lived as your wife for six."

"Am I being a fool?"

"No. But so much has happened, George, and so much may yet happen. What if Will is not dead?"

"Then what in God's name must I do, Meg?" George asked wearily.

"Bide your time." Meg smiled at him. "Give her time to get well first. And remember, she has got to mourn for a while." No one knew what had become of Will. His body had not been found, and it was presumed that the Indians carried him off with them, most likely to torture and kill him at their leisure. Temperance could not or would not say; questions about what had happened sent her into fits of pitiful sobbing.

"You are a wise woman, Meg. I have always known that." George smiled. "I shall do as you say. That is all I can do."

"There is one other thing."

"What?"

"Pray."

George resolved to pray, but he also resolved to do some other things as well: Temperance should want for nothing within the deputy governor's power to give her. He traded a hundred acres of choice river land to Thomas Dunthorne for the service of his maidservant Elizabeth Jones, so that she could work out the remaining years of her indenture waiting on Temperance. He took two captive Indians from the prisoners he had taken at the Chickahominy and made them his huntsmen, so that Temperance would never want for fresh venison and turkey. In their spare time, he had them shoot rabbits to make her a fur cloak lined with the softest of doeskins. For the rest of her wardrobe, until he could send for things from London, he persuaded Thomasine Causey and Meg Worley to part with petticoats, kirtles, gowns, and caps from their own clothes chests, and to sew three new linen shifts; he cajoled John and Samuel, together with Elizabeth Jones, to prepare endless delicacies that might tempt a convalescent's palate: plum jelly, pigeon pie, boiled crabs. He saw to it that the governor's house was extravagantly stocked with firewood and rushlights and candles, so that Temperance would have warmth and light all around her.

Thank God, he thought, for the lucrative position he held. As deputy governor, he was entitled to fifteen hundred acres of land, and he had the use of the governor's hundred tenants to work it. With tobacco selling so well, he might clear as much as three hundred pounds sterling this year. Not bad for a man who had left England with little more than the sword at his side. If he played his hand right, and if these damned Indians behaved themselves, he stood an excellent chance to be appointed governor. And if, God willing, Temperance was at his side, what could he not accomplish? . . .

                 ✶ ✶ ✶

Temperance peered at the stranger's face in the looking glass and frowned.

"It's going to look better and better now, ma'am, you'll see. Every day now." Elizabeth Jones, a comb in her hand, stood behind Temperance. Elizabeth could not yet comb the top part of the hair where the wound was, but she had just finished combing the rest, and the long red-gold locks hung down Temperance's back. "You have such pretty hair, ma'am. Not many as have that color." Elizabeth's own hair was straw-colored and straight; her face broad-boned, coarse of feature, with eyes that seemed too small for it. But beneath their pale, stubby lashes, the hazel eyes looked on the world with good-natured tolerance. She did not expect much, either from herself or others, so she was seldom disappointed. Silently, deftly, she bound up Temperance's hair and fastened it at the back of her head with long ivory hairpins.

"Hand me my cap," Temperance said, still looking at her reflection in the glass. She was deathly pale, and there were bluish rings under her eyes. She bit her lips to give them color.

"If you put it on just so, you'll not know anything was there," Elizabeth said encouragingly, holding out the white embroidered cap. The wound on Temperance's head had begun to heal now, knit together by John Pott's surgeon's skills; its gaping red edges faded to a dark pink line, a sort of half-circle whose ends disappeared into the hairline. Her other wound, the wound between her legs, had been slower to heal, and still pained her every time she moved. It took a long time for skin to reconstruct itself over raw flesh, and she could not sit up long without discomfort. She was grateful for Elizabeth's nursing.

"There!" Elizabeth said. "You see? How fine you look. Shall I tell Master George you're ready?"

"Yes." Temperance sighed. Dressed in a cream-colored shift and a loose green velvet dressing gown, she was venturing downstairs for the first time. It was Christmas Day, and George had begged her to let him carry her downstairs to dinner. He was waiting, excited as a schoolboy, outside her door.

"Ah, look at you!" he said, his voice trembling. "I am so glad to see you up and dressed!" Holding out his hands to her, he crossed the room to where she stood, and she mechanically offered him her hands and a cheek to kiss. His lips brushed her skin lightly, carefully, as if she were a piece of fragile porcelain. "Now," he said, "if you put this arm around my neck, so—and then I can put my arms under you—like so—ah!" He lifted her suddenly, a bit awkwardly, and she grimaced with pain. "Can you bear it?

Is it hurting too much?" He was frantic with worry.

"No," she lied. All she could think of was how effortlessly Will used to swing her up in his arms. George, careful of his footing, did not look at her as he carried her down the stairs. She could feel his body trembling, either from the exertion or the emotion, or both, and she could see the pulse in his temple throbbing.

"There she is!" Meg, sitting by the fireplace, called out to them. She was the only dinner guest. George, fearing that too much company would tire Temperance, had invited no one else.

"Temperance, you look better every day." Meg kissed her cheek.

George settled her carefully in the only chair in the governor's house: a heavy wooden straight-backed affair that was, by its very nature, uncomfortable. But its high carved back at least gave her something to lean against. As George busied himself with tucking a fur rug around her knees, Temperance leaned back and closed her eyes. "What is it?" he said, alarmed.

"Nothing. Just let me rest." She wished he would stop fussing over her.

The big oak table was set with two pewter candlesticks and a pewter bowl full of apples, and the Christmas afternoon dinner was a veritable feast: crabs, roast turkey, venison, fresh pork, Indian bread, turnips, squash, beans, and for a sweet, candy made from ground chestnuts and wild honey.

"It's not quite marchpane," George said, "but it's as like as one can have it in Virginia." Marchpane. Her favorite sweet. God knew what he went through to get this substitute. Temperance was feeling surfeited already, but to please him she took another piece. It was the least she could do.

Beaming, he refilled her wine goblet. "I think a little more of this won't hurt you," he said. It was sack, brought from England and saved for a special occasion. "It's Christmas, after all."

Dinner was as festive as desperate small talk could make it. They spoke of the weather (it felt like snow, and it was time for some), about the tobacco crop (nearly ten thousand pounds for the whole colony this year), about the governor's house (a fine frame structure, nearly as good as an English house). Temperance felt like standing up and shouting, "My husband is missing and may have died a horrible death in some Indian village, and I have lost part of my scalp and all of the hair on my privates, and you sit here saying that it might snow!" Instead, she leaned back in her chair and drew a deep breath.

"Are you getting too tired?" George asked anxiously.

"No!" she snapped. In wounded silence, he turned his attention to the wine in his goblet. Meg, her eyes on the table, broke off another piece of bread.

They were saved by a knock at the door.

"Happy Christmas, my boy!" A booming voice reverberated in the hall when John answered the door.

"It's Master Brinton, sir." Temperance would have known that voice anywhere. How many hundred times had she heard Edward Brinton's bass rolling out the Lord's Prayer in the meetinghouse at Jamestown?

George leaped up from the table. "Come in, come in!" he said.

Edward Brinton's burly frame nearly filled the doorway. "I hope I've not come in your dinnertime," he said. "But I've brought a present for Mistress Temperance."

"You needn't call me 'Mistress,' Edward," Temperance said. "You've known me too long for that." Edward looked suddenly uncomfortable, and George and Meg exchanged nervous glances. "I am glad to see you," Temperance said, holding out her hand to him.

"And I am glad to see you looking well." He grasped her hand in both his huge paws. How did a stonecutter, a man so good with his hands, manage with such big, blunt fingers? she wondered.

"I've made you something," he said, fumbling in the pockets of his jerkin. One by one, he set them out on the table: first a tiny crèche, then a Joseph and a Mary, and last, the Infant Jesus, which he placed in the crèche.

"They're beautiful!" Temperance was overcome.

"Well, they're oak. Not carved as fine as I'd like, but I wanted you to have them." Edward Brinton smiled at her. It was a kind and knowing smile, a smile of remembrance, compassion, encouragement, and it moved Temperance to tears. But she swallowed hard and did not cry. She did not want to spoil his pleasure by weeping. "Thank you," she said softly. "Thank you very much."

Later that evening, after George had carried her back upstairs and Elizabeth had got her ready for bed, Temperance arranged the little wooden pieces on the chest next to her bed so she could see them. While she was looking at them, George came to say good night. At first, when she was so ill and before Elizabeth had come, he had slept on the floor beside her bed. Now he slept in the bedchamber on the other side of the stair hall, and Elizabeth slept on a daybed in Temperance's room.

"I hope today didn't tire you too much," George said.

"No."

"Those are lovely pieces."

"Yes."

Kneeling beside the chest, George picked up the tiny figure of the Christ Child and held it up to the light. "This is so small, and so perfectly formed," he said wonderingly. "It must have taken him hours and hours."

Temperance watched George's face as the candlelight played upon his features. She had not really looked at him up close in such a long time. He was not as boyish-looking as he used to be, and she fancied she could see the shadows of age lurking about his nose, sharpening the line of his mouth, etching small lines at the corners of his eyes. As he put the Infant Jesus back into the crèche, Temperance caught a brief look of sadness in his eyes. He had not meant for her to see it, but she did, and it opened some floodgate within her. Watching George fondle the carved wooden baby—George, with no son of his own—she thought of Will and his delight in Gabriel; seeing the empty crèche, she was reminded of a small empty trundle bed, and her eyes filled with tears. She blinked as she looked at George, and the tears trickled down her cheeks. Absorbed in examining the crèche, he did not notice that she was weeping. She turned her face away from him, but it did no good. Her throat contracted, her chest ached, and all at once she began to sob: violent, racking sobs that lifted her shoulders off the pillow as they came.

"Temperance!" The tenderness in George's voice only made her sobs louder. "Oh, Temperance! Temperance, my poor darling!" George's tone was oddly jubilant. He slipped his arms underneath her and gently raised her up, so that her head was cradled against his shoulder. Then he sat on the edge of the bed, rocking her silently back and forth.

"Oh, George, I miss them so!" She felt his body stiffen. He stroked her hair, but he did not answer.

"I can't help it!"

"I know," he said without emotion, "I know." But he continued to hold her, and after a while her sobs grew lighter. She had no more strength to cry.

"God has punished me," she said. "God has taken my son and my—and Will—for what I've done to you."

For a long time, George did not answer. At last he said slowly, wearily, "No, Temperance. You must not think that." There was silence between them again. Then, in a voice so low that it could barely be heard above the crackling of the fire, he said, "And I forgave you—long ago. I told you that."

Temperance pulled back from him so that she could look into his eyes. "When?"

"Over and over, when I first brought you here. Don't you remember?"

"No." At her bewilderment, George's mouth curved itself into a faint smile. It made Temperance think of happier times, when she had first seen that smile. "When did you forgive me?"

"Oh, I don't know," he said. "It happened without my knowing. But I knew when I saw you—" His eyes strayed to the wound at her hairline, and he could not finish. A log in the fireplace burned through and fell with a shower of sparks.

"You—you've been very good to me, George," Temperance said in a whisper. "So much has happened. I . . . don't know quite what to do."

George's chin was resting on her shoulder, and his voice came softly in her ear: "Just be here," he said.

BRENTFORD, MIDDLESEX, ENGLAND
20 January 1617

Pocahontas had never been so happy. The English treated her like a King's daughter: the Bishop of London himself celebrated her attendance at his great church, Lord and Lady de la Warr entertained her in their fine house, and the King himself sent an invitation to the grand Twelfth Night masque at Whitehall. She had seen sights enough to last her a lifetime: London Bridge, spanning the broad Thames River like a street over the water, its edges lined with dwellings and shops; the forbidding Tower of London, where traitors and other evildoers were locked up and put to death; Whitehall, where the King lived; the majestic spires of Westminister Abbey. Everywhere she went, people pointed at her, and made way for her, and whispered in awe. A Dutchman had come and made an engraving of her dressed in brocade and pearls like the finest English ladies.

Everyone had paid her homage except the one person she wanted to see most of all: John Smith. Every day for the past six months, Pocahontas had been hoping to see him. He must be in London, but London was a big place. There were so many people in it that Tomocomo, who had come along to report to Powhatan on the number of Englishmen there, had thrown away the stick he had begun to notch to count them. That was just as well, Pocahontas thought. She did not care if her father learned about the English or not. She did not care if she ever saw him again. Her husband had told her they must visit Powhatan when they returned to Virginia, but she did not want to return. She longed to stay here, in John Smith's country, where people bowed to her as if she were an English princess. Surely, by now, John Smith must know that she was here. But he did not come to see her, and no one seemed to know where he was.

Then, after Twelfth Night, George Percy had invited the Rolfes to visit him at Syon House, the home of his brother, the Earl of Northumberland, at Brentford. On the second afternoon of their stay, a footman came to her chamber with word that Master Rolfe wanted her: there were visitors in the hall who desired to see her. Pocahontas hesitated; she was not yet dressed. That was the custom in England, she had been told. Ladies of fashion wore loose-fitting gowns at home, and laced themselves into bodice and kirtle, stomacher and gorget and ruff, when they went out. Very well, then, she thought, she would receive these visitors in her gown. It was a dark red velvet robe, edged with bands of gold braid around the sleeves and the neck. Smoothing the silk net coif whose pearl clasps held her hair in place, she hurried down the broad staircase of Syon House to greet her husband and the visitors.

John was waiting for her at the foot of the stairs. Taking her by both hands, he brushed her cheek with a kiss and said, "I am glad you're wearing that gown. There is someone here who wants to see you." He never seemed to tire of showing her off. No other Englishmen she had seen treated their wives with the homage he paid to her, and his adoration at times embarrassed her. As John led her toward the great hall, she heard men's voices, and then a familiar laugh, a deep, throaty chuckle, made her pull back.

So he had come at last.

"What is it?" Her husband was looking at her in total bewilderment.

"I don't know," she said. How could she explain to him that she did not want to be in the same room with him and the man she had loved since she was thirteen? Just hearing that laughter made her knees weak. What would she feel when she saw him? Was this some kind of cruel game these Englishmen were playing with her, keeping her from seeing him for so long, and now, when it suited them, presenting her to him for their amusement?

"Then come on," John said cheerfully. "The company is waiting."

Her hands had grown suddenly ice-cold. If only I had a muff, she thought frantically, and then she remembered that muffs were only for outdoors, no matter how cold your hands were. Stupid, these English were, about some things. All stupid, except for John Smith. She lifted her chin, clutched her husband's arm, and swept into the cavernous, tapestry-hung hall, her red velvet gown trailing behind her. Three men were standing with their backs to her, facing the warmth of the huge fireplace.

"Here she is," Rolfe said proudly, and they all wheeled around. There was George Percy, much healthier-looking than when he had been at Jamestown. The second man was Thomas Dale, without the Indian mistress he had yearned to bring back, looking vaguely discontented.

The third was John Smith.

Percy and Dale bowed low to Pocahontas, but John Smith quickly crossed the room, went down on one knee before her, and kissed her hand. He will feel how cold it is, she thought. That was all she could think of. His fingers were warm in her palm; his beard prickly against the back of her hand.

Slowly, he raised his eyes to hers and said, "Welcome to England, Princess Pocahontas."

Pocahontas caught her breath and turned her head away. At the sound of his voice on the syllables of her name, she felt as if he had walked up to her and suddenly fondled her breasts. Blushing, she could feel her cheeks growing as hot as her hands had been cold. She could not speak with him here, before these other men.

"I am very glad to see you," he said loudly. "But I have business to talk before I can take pleasure in your company." The slight pressure of his hand on hers told her he had understood. "Do me the honor of waiting here." Somehow he persuaded the others to leave, on the pretext of inspecting Sir Henry's garden. People generally did what John Smith told them to, Pocahontas thought. It was a long time before he came back.

"I told them that we were going to speak in your language," he said in Algonquin, "and that if we were alone, you might speak more freely about your father and the Indians in Virginia." He winked, and then grew solemn. Taking her by both hands, he drew her closer to the fire. "Let me look at you." His gaze moved slowly from the ornamented coif that bound her hair, to the cambric ruffles at her throat, to the red velvet gown, to the small gold ring that was her wedding band. "What happened to that little girl in the doeskin apron?" he said softly. "The one who used to turn cartwheels round and round the palisade?" Without waiting for an answer, he said, "Ah, Pocahontas, you are truly a princess now, a king's daughter, indeed." He was still speaking in Algonquin, but Pocahontas spoke to him in English.

"I am not my father's daughter anymore," she said. "He does not love me, nor I him. But he loved you, and he told you that what was his, was yours." She looked into the fire.

"You were very young then, Pocahontas." Smith looked away. Was he thinking, as she was, of that November night at Werowocomoco when she had danced the love-dance for him?

"I am not so young now," she said. "And you have no woman." She did not know that for a fact; she was guessing.

"No, Pocahontas." There was a note of resignation, of sadness in his voice. "You are not young, and I have no woman. But you have a husband."

"He wants to go back to Virginia," she said. "But I want to stay in England. I want to be forever and ever English, like you."

John Smith laughed bitterly. "But I want to go back to Virginia. I would give my right arm to go back, and here you are, trying to stay."

"Then why don't you go?" she asked, and then she paused. "I would like to go back to Virginia, if you went."

"I can't go back." He sighed. "My wound kept me idle far too long, and others took my place. Now I cannot raise the money to go back as I'd like." Catching hold of her hand, he sat down on a settle by the fire, and drew her down beside him. He did not let go her hand, but put his other hand on top of it with an affectionate little slap. "Now, Pocahontas, I have no prospects, and I am getting old." He tried to speak lightly, but neither of them laughed.

Pocahontas touched his cheek, letting her finger trace the line where his beard began. The skin that she remembered as tanned and ruddy, almost as tawny as her own, was pale now, and two deep lines had etched themselves on his forehead between his eyes. The thick sandy hair was thinner on top now, though still full at the back and sides, and there was no gray in it.

"How old?" she said, smiling at him.

"Thirty-seven this past January."

"And I am twenty-two."

"Ah, Pocahontas, dearest Pocahontas!" With forced cheerfulness, he held her at arm's length, pretending to examine her. "You will be a good wife to John Rolfe." Tenderly, he put his hand under her chin and lifted it. "You are better off where you are, and I, where I am, even if it's where I don't want to be. God knows what's best for us on this earth. You know that, don't you?"

"I do not know much about your God," she said slowly. "Indian gods want people to be happy. Yours seems to want them to be sad. But if that is what you want, then I will be sad."

He leaned over and kissed her forehead. "No, you'll not be sad. Promise me—" There was a catch in his voice. "Promise me you'll not be sad, but that you'll think of me sometimes."

She rose to her feet, shivering slightly in the chill of the great hall. "Yes, she said softly, "Oh, yes, my John Smith, I'll think of you. I'll think of you as long as I live."

JAMESTOWN
30 May 1617

 "Borage, they say, is good for melancholy." Temperance knelt and fingered the broad rough leaves of the herb, and then rose wearily. "Pick some."

Behind her, Elizabeth Jones obeyed her mistress, breaking off several leaves, snapping the stems with her strong, knobby fingers. "Oh, ma'am, you oughtn't to be sad," she said.

Temperance turned on her angrily. "What do you mean, I oughtn't to be sad? I'll be sad if I damn well please to be, and you mind your tongue."

"I'm sorry, ma'am. I only meant that now you've got your health back, you might get to feeling better in your spirits."

"I don't know, Elizabeth, I don't know." Temperance heaved a sigh. Gathering her skirts, she sat down on a bench George had had made for her garden. This spring he had ordered three of his tenants to lay out a garden for her, as near to an English country house garden as it could be. Nearly all the houses at Jamestown had some sort of plot with a few flowers grown from the seeds and bulbs that came regularly on the supply ships. What else, for so little cargo space, could give so much pleasure and remind people of home? the captains said.

And so much profit, Temperance thought idly. God only knew what George had paid for the irises, the daffodils, the daisies, the pinks, the bluebells that blossomed in bright neat squares in her garden. Hers was far grander than any of the gardens inside the palisade, which were little more than a patch or two of flowers or herbs enclosed by crooked fences made of twigs and branches interlaced. Temperance's garden covered twice as much ground as the governor's house, and was enclosed by a stout log paling.

"That will not only keep out hogs; it will keep people from planting their tobacco in our yard," George had said. He had spoken in jest, but he was not far wrong. Ever since John Rolfe's successful experiment with tobacco, every man who could hold a hoe had set himself to copying his example. Growing tobacco was hard work: The plants had to be grown from seed, the thousands of tender seedlings transplanted, the young shoots hoed and weeded, the tall plants kept free of insects, and when they bloomed, their blossoms picked off to encourage larger leaves.

Then, in the heat of August, the plants had to be cut, bound in bunches, and put in curing sheds where they would hang to dry until November. But the profits made all the work well worth it, and since 1614, when the first group of seven-year indentures were up and fifty-acre headrights were given out to the Virginia Company's shareholders, the settlements at Jamestown, Henrico, and the Hundreds had seen a frenzy of tobacco-growing. George, as deputy governor, had set fifty of his allotted tenant-laborers to raising tobacco, and if all went well, he might reap two thousand pounds sterling from this one year's crop.

"Think of it," he had said, over and over again, "think of it! My father was a merchant-tailor, and he was not a poor man, but he never, ever, took in more than five hundred pounds in a year. If prices hold, and we can harvest that much—maybe even more—for the next few years, our fortune is made! Ours and the colony's!"

George had fallen into using "ours" in an unthinking way these days, as if he and Temperance had never been apart. But they were not exactly together. She still slept in the larger of the two upstairs chambers, and he still slept in the smaller room. He had never suggested any other arrangement, and he was as polite and formal as if they had never lived together as man and wife. He treated her as an honored guest, inquiring how she slept, what she would like to eat, where she would like to sit. Sometimes he took her hand; sometimes he kissed her cheek, but he was careful to take no liberties. Sometimes, however, when she turned her head suddenly, she caught him watching her the way a cat watches a mouse.

Well he might watch her, she thought. She herself did not know her own mind. Sitting on the bench in the garden this May morning, she felt as listless and mournful as ever. She did not even care that a ship had been sighted and was making its way up the James. People were beginning to gather at the pier.

"Oh, Mistress Temperance!" Elizabeth was wringing her hands, standing on one foot and then the other. "Would you give me leave to go down to the pier?"

"You may go, Elizabeth."

As Elizabeth hitched up her skirts and scurried down the path, Temperance rose from the bench and went into the house. There was not a ship in the whole world, she thought, whose passengers or cargo would be of any interest to her.

But she was wrong. In a little while, she heard the sound of men's voices outside the house, and above them she could distinguish George's voice.

"Temperance! Oh, Temperance!" His voice was vibrant with excitement.

She went downstairs and opened the door.

"Look what the *George* has brought us!"

The three of them were standing in the morning sunshine: George, Samuel Argall, and John Rolfe. George stood between them, his arms around their shoulders. "Welcome home," she said politely. "I am glad you had a safe voyage." To Rolfe, she said, "Where are Pocahontas and Thomas?"

A spasm of pain crossed his face. "Pocahontas is dead."

"What?" Temperance could not believe she had heard right.

"She died at Gravesend. She—" His voice broke.

"Oh, John! I am so sorry! Don't speak of it now, if you'd rather not. I can hear about it later. Where is Thomas?"

"In London. I left him—"

"You needn't tell me now," Temperance said gently. "But you know everyone is going to ask you."

"Perhaps we can talk about all that at dinner," George said. "They will take dinner with us." He looked anxiously at Temperance. "You will join us, won't you?"

"Yes," she said. "Yes, I will."

Not only did she say yes; she went to the kitchen, and directed an amazed Elizabeth, John, and Samuel in the boiling of fresh-caught rockfish and crabs, the baking of Indian bread, and the preparation of poke sallet leaves with vinegar and acorn oil. She especially wanted this dinner to comfort John Rolfe.

A decent dinner, she had discovered, could provide a momentary respite from grief.

George, seeing the extraordinary interest she had taken in the kitchen, was elated. "Let us enjoy this fine dinner, and not talk of business or serious matters until afterward," he said. And so they spoke of tobacco and its growing fashionableness in Europe, of the number of new-cleared acres in Virginia, and of the sweetness and abundance of rockfish in the James this spring. While the table was being cleared, George brought out a precious bottle of sack he had been saving and poured a generous quantity into each of four small silver cups. He also brought a box of crumbled tobacco leaves and three small white clay pipes.

"Gentlemen, let us smoke to Virginia's health. King James may call it a 'stinking weed' if he likes, but tobacco is going to make this colony rich." He smiled. Then, looking solemn, he said, "Before Temperance leaves us, John, if you will, tell us about Pocahontas."

"It was sudden—so unlooked for." Rolfe gazed long and thoughtfully into his cup of sack as the others waited in silence. "I still can't believe she has gone." He paused, struggling for control of his grief. "She took sick after we came back from Brentford, and it being such wet, chilly weather in London, she could not get warm, somehow. Even when she sat by the fire all day, she was cold. We gave her hot milk possets to drink, and a doctor came and bled her, but it did no good at all. It came time for us to sail." He glanced at Argall. "Samuel had the ship provisioned and ready, and Pocahontas was still not well, but she said she would go. She was so brave."

He looked at his three rapt listeners as if seeking confirmation of that fact, and then he went on, "She knew the Company was anxious for the ship to be off, with the supplies and all, and with Samuel and me to take up our duties here, and she would not hear of our delaying on her account. So we set sail on the twentieth of March. But by the time we had got to Gravesend, Pocahontas had to take to her bed. Breath came hard for her, and she was cold—so cold." He shook his head. "We tried to keep her warm with hot bricks and a little warming stove, but they did no good. At last she begged me to take her ashore, so she might get warm before she died."

Rolfe cleared his throat. "And she asked if there was any way we could bury her on English soil." He put his head in his hands and was silent for a moment.

"She need not have worried. I was not about to bury her at sea," Samuel Argall said softly. "Even if she hadn't asked, John, you know I'd have put in at Gravesend for her."

"We carried her to the rector's house near the church there," Rolfe went on. "He prayed with her, and she was very glad of that. She said she hoped to meet Jesus, and she thanked us all—" Here he broke down and sobbed.

Temperance leaned over and silently stroked his arm. You and I are partners in grief, she thought.

Recovering himself somewhat, Rolfe raised his head, and with a grateful glance at Temperance, went on, "She died some while before noon, and we buried her that same day. March the twenty-first, it was. We buried her in the chancel at St. George's Church." Leaning back, Rolfe took a drink from his silver cup. "I shall have to go and tell Powhatan. I dread that."

"And Thomas?" Temperance said after a pause. "Where is he?"

"I left him in England," Rolfe said sadly. "At the time, I thought Virginia would be no place for a two-year-old with no mother, so I sent Matachanna and Tomocomo to take him to my cousin in London." He sighed. "I also thought that if I brought him back here, Powhatan might want him raised as an Indian, and there might be trouble. So I left him, but I already wish I had kept him with me," he said ruefully.

"But at least you have him," George said wistfully.

"Yes," Argall said, "think on that. When he is just a little older, you can send for him."

But I can't send for Gabriel, Temperance thought. Wrapped in her own grief, she said nothing. Watching George's face as he talked of John Rolfe's son, another thought struck her. George was grieving, too, for the son he never had. She was suddenly aware that John Rolfe was looking at her with a vaguely puzzled expression. I can see it in his eyes, she thought. He is wondering why I am here, and if I am sharing George's bed. Rising from the table, she said, "I must go now. You men have other matters to attend to."

They rose, too, and bowed. She offered her hand to each of them in turn, treating George no differently from the others.

When dark came, Temperance undressed herself, sending Elizabeth away, wanting solitude. Barefoot in her loose white shift, she padded over to the window and leaned out. Downstairs, the men were talking, as they would probably do far into the night. She could see a faint yellowish glow of candlelight from the room where they were, directly below her. Beyond it was the dark expanse of the James River, and beyond that, although on this moonless night it was too dark to see, the opposite shore, three miles distant. Not that far, she thought, and yet no one lived over there. Jamestown was ten years old this spring, but it had only fifty-two people. Half the houses inside the palisade were empty; their original occupants had long since died or left to work tobacco fields upriver. The place had the appearance of a ghost town. But there were no other towns in Virginia, and there were no more than 450 English settlers in the whole colony. How many had come, how many had died, Temperance could not begin to count. Sarah Harison. Elias Crookdeck. Peter and Martha Scott. Anthony Gage. *Gabriel. Will.* And for what? So that England could possess a few miles of wilderness at the edge of a continent no one had even crossed? So that a few people might get rich from growing a weed for men to smoke?

Temperance sighed and lifted her hair so that the faint breeze from the river could cool her neck. It was a sultry night for so early in the summer, and she thought gloomily of all the hot nights to come. And the flies. And the mosquitoes. And the sickness. Below her, the men's voices rose and fell. How could they keep on scheming and scraping, plotting and planning, for the future of an enterprise that seemed so pointless, a place that was so dreary? And yet they came and went, came and went, braving the terrible Atlantic, carrying food and tools like an army of ants building a hill. Forswearing England, they scratched out clearings at the edge of a wilderness. Temperance was suddenly seized by a longing for home, for roads that went somewhere, for fields of oats and barley bounded by stone walls and neat green hedges, for thick-walled houses that had stood for hundreds of years, for high church steeples with bells in them, for wagons and coaches and horses.

She sighed and stared out at the starlit sky. Temperance's mother had always told her she must trust in the machinations of divine Providence. Surely God had some reason for bringing her here to George's house. She sank to her knees, leaning on the chest below the window, and, clasping her hands tightly, she closed her eyes and began to pray. She did not know how long she knelt there. The long day had tired her more than she knew, and she dozed as she prayed, her chin resting on her hands. So it was that when George tapped lightly on the door to her room, she did not hear him. But when he opened the door and whispered her name, she turned and held out her arms to him.

WEROWOCOMOCO
20 November 1617

 "You have hunted well today, my brother. Your aim is as true as it ever was." Wahunsonacock spoke in a low voice as he and Opechancanough moved stealthily toward a clearing near the river.

"The next buck will be yours," Opechancanough said. "Watch the clearing. You know many deer come this way to drink from the river." Bows held at the ready, with arrows nocked, the two men crept silently through the pine trees, Wahunsonacock in the lead. Suddenly, he stopped and flung out his left arm, palm flat, pushing the air backward, signaling to his brother to stop as well. At the edge of the clearing, picking her way daintily toward the riverbank, was a sleek white-tailed doe. Ears twitching, eyes bright with caution, she raised her head and sniffed the air, but Wahunsonacock and Opechancanough were downwind, and their scent did not reach her. Besides that, both were wearing the heads and skins of recently killed deer, so that at a glance through the trees the Indians appeared to be two young bucks out foraging for the last of the autumn leaves.

Wahunsonacock edged forward, every muscle taut, every nerve attuned to the doe's movements. Now she was ambling toward the water, and Wahunsonacock was closing the distance between him and his quarry. At fifty feet, he stopped, drew his long ash bow into a graceful arc, sighted down the slender hickory foreshaft to the bone tip of his arrow, and let go.

He caught the doe in her right side, and the force of the arrow drove it deep into her vitals. She dropped to her knees, and then, by the time Wahunsonacock and his brother reached her, she had rolled on her side, her legs thrashing helplessly as her lifeblood rushed out onto the dry grass beneath her.

"Well done! Well done!" Opechancanough said, clapping his brother on the back.

"She is a good fat one, too," Wahunsonacock said with satisfaction. "We shall dine well before the sun sets on this day. I told Winganuske to have the fire laid, and all in readiness for a feast."

"I am glad to see you smile, my brother," Opechancanough said gently. "You see, life is good, in spite of sorrow."

"But the pleasures of the hunt cannot take away the pain in my heart for Pocahontas, even so." Wahunsonacock sighed and slowly shook his head. The buck's head he wore moved, too, and the animal's dead eyes seemed to mirror his sadness. "If only I had seen her before she left for England. If only we had spoken, just once, after I banished her. That is what pains me the most."

"You did what you thought was right," Opechancanough said. "You must not grieve over it now."

"I should have gone to her wedding. You tried to tell me that I should go, and I would not listen to you. You should have forced me to go."

"I could not do that. You, after all, are the Powhatan."

"Fah!" With a practiced stroke of his knife, Wahunsonacock slit the doe's belly and began to gut the carcass.

"You can take comfort in her happiness," Opechancanough said. "They say she was happy, you know. She liked the English."

"The English! May the wrath of Okee and all the lesser gods strike them all!" Wahunsonacock flung part of the deer's intestines on the ground. Both his hands were covered with blood. "If it were not for the English, my daughter would not be dead!"

"You don't know that. Perhaps she would have taken ill just the same, had she stayed at home."

"No!" Wahunsonacock spoke savagely. "Not so! It was living among the English that killed her!"

"I lived among foreigners once," Opechancanough said thoughtfully, "and it did not kill me."

"That was different." Wahunsonacock wiped his forehead with the back of his hand, leaving a bloody smear across his face. "The worst part of it is, Pocahontas is buried across the ocean. I shall never see where she rests."

"Perhaps someday you can go and find where they have put her," Opechancanough said.

"No!" Wahunsonacock answered sharply. "I shall never, ever go among the English, neither in their settlements here nor in their country across the sea."

"What of your grandson, then?"

Wahunsonacock's expression grew suddenly tender. "He is with Matachanna and Tomocomo, and soon they will bring him here. He will not be brought up in an alien land. John Rolfe promised me that." Wahunsonacock smiled. "And when he is old enough, I shall make him a present of all the land between Powhatan Village and Arrohattoc."

"That land is very close to the English at Henrico."

"Not for long, my brother, not for long." With both hands, Wahunsonacock pulled out the rest of the deer's entrails. "Now that Pocahontas is gone, there is no need to play at peace with the English. I say it is time to move against them, to drive them out of the land once and for all."

"I am glad to hear those words from your lips." Opechancanough smiled. "I was afraid your grief had made you as soft as a woman."

"No, it has only filled my heart with more hate for the English." Wahunsonacock wiped his knife blade on the grass.

"We must plan our moves with care," Opechancanough said. "There are many more of them this time. They swarm and settle like bees in a field of flowers."

"And their stings are dangerous," Wahunsonacock said grimly. "Remember what George Yardley did to Kissanacomen and his warriors at the Chickahominy, pretending to come in peace and killing twenty in cold blood. That has never been avenged."

"But the Chickahominies are not our people."

"That is no matter. The English are our enemies."

Opechancanough squatted down beside his brother. "This time will not be as easy as before. There are more English, and that means more guns. We must outwit them. Surprise them. Take our time, and develop a plan. You and I cannot do this by ourselves, my brother. We shall need the werowances and the warriors of all the river tribes."

"Let us begin with our own sons," Wahunsonacock said. "Let us talk to Tanx-Powhatan and Nemattonow before this moon is full." He finished gutting the deer and sat back on his heels. "Go cut a sapling to carry this with. Then you and I shall have a fine dinner and talk of destroying the English." Wahunsonacock spoke cheerfully, his grief forgotten for the moment.

Opechancanough did as he was told, and in a few minutes the two brothers were on their way back to Werowocomoco, the ends of the sapling on their shoulders, the doe slung by her feet, swinging between them.

"Many years ago, when I was with the Jesuits, I had to choose a saint's name for the sacrament of Confirmation," Opechancanough said. "I chose to be called Henry, after a great king of that name. Saint Henry conquered many kingdoms in the name of his God, and his power spread far and wide. Now I am his namesake, and I feel his power. It may not be this year, or even next year, but in the end we shall triumph over the English in the name of our god Okee, and the rule of the river tribes will last forever."

LONDON
2I November I6I8

"A rocking horse? Oh, George!"

"Of course, a rocking horse. The eldest son of a knight needs to know how to ride, does he not?"

"Not when he's ten months old." Temperance laughed and shook her head.

"Isn't this a handsome horse? Those are real glass eyes. And look how richly it's caparisoned. The crimson and blue are almost the colors of my livery." George rubbed his hands together exultantly. "Elizabeth!" he shouted. "Elizabeth, bring Argall in here!"

"Don't shout, George. She can hear you quite well without it."

"I'll shout to the rooftops if I want to, today," George said. "I'll shout so loud they can hear me all the way down the river to Westminster, to Whitehall, and all the way to Newmarket, so His Majesty himself can hear me. For God's sake, Temperance, it's not every day a man gets a knighthood."

"Here he is, sir. I was just achanging him." Elizabeth Jones, her face aglow with excitement, brought Argall to his father. "When will you and Mistress Temperance be leaving, sir? I've laid out her things already."

"At twelve noon. With good horses and dry roads, we'll be at Newmarket in two days. The ceremony is Thursday at two o'clock." George swung his son high into the air above his head, and the baby crowed with delight. "And after that, Elizabeth, you'd better practice saying 'Lady Yardley' and 'Sir George.' "

"Yes, sir. I will, sir." Elizabeth curtsied as Temperance had taught her to, but the movement as executed by her large, bony frame left something to be desired. "I'll go and see to your things, ma'am."

George swung Argall up in the air twice more and then set him astride the large wooden rocking horse. "See here, Argall. This is the way a knight's son rides, a knight's son rides, a knight's son rides!" George pushed the rocking horse back and forth in as wide an arc as its rockers would make, while Argall laughed with glee.

"Look at that, Temperance! See how he likes it!"

"See how *you* like it, you mean." Temperance could not help but smile.

"When are you going to get this fellow out of these dresses and into some breeches?" George said teasingly, pulling down the hem of Argall's blue worsted smock.

"You'd have him in a little suit of armor, I suppose, if you had your way," Temperance said. "I'm surprised you haven't thought of having one made, with your coat of arms emblazoned on it."

"Temperance, don't mock me," George said, letting the motion of the rocking horse slow down. He did not look at her, but kept his eyes on his son. "The reason for this knighthood is the governorship. You know that. Sir Edwin Sandys thinks it wise, and he is going to replace Thomas Smythe as treasurer of the Company. And there are others in the Company who think the governor of Virginia ought to be a man with a title." George raised his head and looked at Temperance. "A knight must have a coat of arms, and a coat of arms belongs on his possessions. Don't begrudge me the use of mine."

"But on twelve liveries?" Temperance said. "What do we want with twelve liveried footmen? People will laugh."

"No, they won't," George said. "Dearest heart, I am about to draw a thousand pounds sterling a year as governor of Virginia, and I stand to make three thousand more from tobacco." He began to rock his son again. "Argall, you're a lucky fellow. My father was only a merchant-tailor in Southwark, but your father is Sir George Yardley, captain general and governor of Virginia!"

The journey to Newmarket and the ceremony of George's investiture were a blur in Temperance's memory: the jolting carriage, the crowded hall, the King's great jeweled sword, the wine in silver goblets. As she climbed the stairs to bed, she pondered the events of the past few days and tried to think what they meant. "Yardley is only a merchant-tailor's son, and all of London knows it!" someone in the street had shouted. "You really ought to persuade George to curb his extravagance. His enemies will have the more to criticize," said her cousin, John Pory. Pory, now secretary of the Virginia colony, had told her that Sir Thomas Smythe was bitterly opposed to George's knighthood and might work against him. But what could Sir Thomas do? Temperance wondered.

When Elizabeth had finished undressing her and closed the door, she nestled down in the softness of the feather bed and blankets, sliding her bare feet into the places where the warming pan had been. The room was cold, even with the fire still burning in the fireplace, and the linens on the high curtained bed were chillier than the air. It had been a long, tiring day, but she was oddly wide awake now. Downstairs, the men were still drinking and talking. It might be hours before George came to bed. Temperance stretched and yawned. The warmth of her own body heat had spread under the covers so that the bed was now a snug nest. The canopy overhead and the curtains on the sides kept out the drafts and gave the illusion of shelter. These were new ones, made of heavy crimson velvet, fringed in gold and embroidered with the crimson and blue of the new Yardley coat of arms. The bedstead itself was new; its heavy oak frame with the carved head and foot and the four square tester posts would be dismantled and packed for the voyage to Virginia sometime within the next few weeks.

She was drowsily trying to picture how the bed would look in the governor's house at Jamestown when George came upstairs. She heard the thump of boots on the stair steps, and then the familiar deep rumble of his voice as he dismissed Samuel Garrett, whom he had raised to the exalted post of head footman. The heavy iron latch clicked, and the door to the bedchamber slowly opened.

"Temp'r'nce?" Wine had thickened his tongue and erased the vowels from her name.

"Temp'r'nce?" He barely whispered, just loud enough so she could hear if she happened to be awake, and soft enough not to disturb her if she were already asleep.

"I'm not asleep."

In three steps, he was across the room. Pushing aside the bed curtains, he bent over her and kissed her, his breath warm and redolent with wine. Then he sat down on the edge of the bed and began to unfasten his doublet. But the doublet was new, and it fastened from neck to below the waist with a row of twenty velvet-covered buttons and loops. His fingers fumbled with them ineffectually. Even sober, Temperance thought with amusement, he would have trouble undoing those.

"Here. Let me." She sat up, and as she did so, the bedcovers fell away from her breasts.

"Let you? Oh, dear heaven, will I let you!" George caught both her hands as she reached for the row of buttons, and began to kiss them, first the palms, then the wrists, then the inside of the forearms, alternately and fervently, all the way to her breasts. Temperance laughed and kissed his forehead.

"How can I unbutton you this way?" she said.

He raised his face to hers, kissed her once lightly on the mouth, and cradled her face in his hands. "Oh, quick, Lady Yardley, be quick!" He was breathing heavily, and his chest rose and fell as Temperance undid the doublet's buttons. With passionate haste, he flung it off and kissed her again.

"Oh, dear God, Temp'r'nce, I love you! Temp'r'nce, oh, Temp'r'nce!"

She unfastened the wristbands of his shirt.

"I do love you, you know," he said thickly.

Temperance seized his shirt by its hem, and he, obedient as a child, lifted his arms so she could pull it over his head.

"You don't know how much I love you," he said.

"You'll have to do your boots yourself," Temperance told him.

At long last, and not without difficulty, he was fully undressed, his trunk hose and garters, his embroidered shirt, and his boots scattered like flotsam and jetsam on the bed and on the floor. He slid under the covers and lay on his back, snuggled down against Temperance so that their bodies touched from shoulder to toe.

"Ahhh!" he said, and closed his eyes. For a moment, Temperance thought he was going to fall fast asleep. Then he opened his eyes, turned on his side, and, propping himself on one elbow, began to caress her with his free hand.

" 'Member when I first did this?" he said, touching her privates. "I wasn't a knight then."

"I remember," Temperance said. She had seen George tipsy once or twice; drunk, never. But the exhaustion of the long day of travel and the amount of wine that evening had done their work. George was blissfully, unabashedly drunk. It amused and touched her to see him without his shell of sobriety. He was as defenseless and guileless as a child.

"I wasn't a knight then," he said, "but I loved you then, just as much." With a lurch, he got on his knees and began to kiss her breasts.

Temperance stroked his hair and whispered, "I know, George. I loved you then, too."

He lifted his head and looked at her, blinking as if to bring her face into focus. "What d'you mean, *then?* Don't you love me now?"

"Yes."

"Say it. Let me hear you say it."

"I love you."

"George."

"What?"

"Say, 'I love you, George.' " The words were slightly slurred, but he said them slowly and patiently.

"I love you, George."

"Aahh, that's better!" He began to kiss her again. He put his hand between her legs.

"Here is where the Indians hurt you," he said tenderly. "But I shot them."

"I know you did, George. I know." Temperance wished he would hurry up.

George took so long that his breath had begun to turn sour in her nostrils, and when at last they coupled, their passions were ill-matched. The wine had taken its toll, and George lay back, spent and gasping, long before Temperance had come.

"Sorry," he said. "So . . . tired."

Frustration, mingled with pity and guilt, kept Temperance silent. But after a moment she thought once more of his infinite kindness, his patience, his generosity. She snuggled against him and whispered, "Never you mind. I don't mind. Go to sleep now."

George turned on his back, so that they were side by side but still touching. The heat from the warming pan was long gone; the fire had gone out; the room was cold.

"I love you," he said with unexpected clarity, "but you don't love me."

On January 10, they sailed for Jamestown. They did not arrive there until April 19, ninety-nine days later. It was one of the worst crossings anyone could remember. It was the cold that was the worst. Gloves, scarves, caps, muffs, cloaks, fur robes, layer on layer of wool stockings and pet-ticoats—nothing availed against it. At sea, with the dangers of fire on a wooden ship, the only heat allowed was the small cook fire on a bed of sand in the galley, no matter what the weather was. There were hand stoves: small ceramic pots with holes in them and a place to burn a lump or two of charcoal, but they were really made to burn herbs and sweeten the air, not to give off heat. Besides that, the supply of fuel was needed for cooking: boiled beef while the supply lasted, hot pease porridge when it was gone. But the porridge was not really hot: Food cooled so quickly by the time it was carried from the galley to the passengers' quarters amidships that it was hardly worth the heating. Cheese and butter froze; ale and wine turned so cold they made one's teeth ache.

If food offered little comfort, sleep had even less to recommend it. Temperance, as the governor's lady, was entitled to share the ship's great cabin with George and the captain. The latter, a friend of Samuel Argall's, had offered to sleep elsewhere, but the great cabin, with windows port and starboard, was too cold. Its small square windows could not keep out the icy wind, and its door opened onto the main deck. It was also too small: two boxlike bunks, each so narrow that one person could barely squeeze into it, and no space for Argall. At first Temperance tried to sleep rolled in a rug on the floor with him beside her, but that arrangement proved too cold as well as too uncomfortable. At night, the only warmth was body heat—the heat of someone else's body next to one's own. Soldiers in the field in cold weather, George had told her, slept close together on their sides, nested like spoons in a box. But she and George could not sleep that way; the bunks were too narrow, the cabin floor too hard. So Temperance slept, when she could sleep at all, where she had slept on the *Falcon* long ago: in the cramped 'tween-decks space allotted to women passengers. She and Elizabeth made a sort of nest between them for Argall, and the three of them huddled or tossed there, night after wretched night.

There were ten other women besides Temperance and Elizabeth, most of them wives of men being sent out by the Virginia Company; none of them knowing what to expect of Virginia. Six of them never got there: four died of ship's fever; two died in childbirth, along with their newborn infants. It was the cold, everyone said, the unbearable, unrelenting cold. Eight of the male passengers and three of the sailors died as well. With the cold came dampness, and with the dampness came coughs, chills, and dripping noses by the score. There were not enough handkerchiefs in London, Temperance thought, to take care of the colds aboard the *George*. Nor was there enough soap to wash the handkerchiefs they had. Men used their sleeves, women their petticoat hems, and some merely snorted thick green mucous into their hands and flung it overboard. They also vomited overboard.

The *George* was 110 feet long from bow to stern, and she carried a crew of fifteen, and fifty passengers, all of whom were seasick at least part of the time. In the heavy seas of the Atlantic in winter, the *George* bobbed and danced like a cork in a tub, and there were days when even the captain looked queasy and kept to his cabin. Below decks, the stench became almost unbearable. Chamber pots could be emptied overboard, but the smells of vomit, urine, and the fetid odors of unwashed bodies and dirty clothing could not be washed away by the buckets of cold seawater the crew periodically sloshed across the rough oak planks. People who had colds joked about the benefits of being unable to smell.

When at last the ship reached the welcoming waters of the James River, spirits ran high, and the cheer that went up when the gangplank went down at Jamestown's wharf might have made the Indians in their distant villages stop and listen. To Temperance, the handful of frame houses and the log palisade on the riverbank looked like home. She could hardly wait to get ashore.

JAMESTOWN
25 August 1619

 They were shackled together, the twelve men in one coffle and the ten women in another. Their dark bodies glistened in the sweltering August sun.

"George! These are human beings, not cattle! Why are they chained together?" Temperance, Lady Yardley, whispered in her husband's ear.

"There is no need to whisper," the governor said. "They cannot understand a word you say. They know only their African tongues and the Spanish they got on Hispaniola. That is the reason they are chained together—it makes handling them easier. One cannot order them about in English, and unchained, they might run off in all directions."

"They are nearly naked, besides," Temperance said in a normal tone.

"No more so than the Indians," George said. The women wore nothing but short silk-grass skirts around their hips; the men, filthy-looking breechclouts of what looked like gray homespun. "They are a savage people, just like the Indians."

"Then why did you buy them?"

"Look at them, Temperance. They are all young and sound, every one of them. Probably not one over thirty, and not a sore, not a blemish, anywhere. Twenty-two good strong workers for a few score bushels of peas and meal and some fletches of bacon is not a bad trade, I say. The captain of that Dutch ship wants provisions, and Virginia wants servants. The Dutchman said these are good field workers from the West Indies. He got them off a Spanish trader bound for the Orinoco, but he wants to get rid of them before he sails for Amsterdam. Abraham Piersey and I intend to keep a dozen or so for ourselves, and sell the rest for fifteen hundred, maybe two thousand weight of tobacco apiece. People will buy them, just the way they buy English servants for a term of indenture. Piersey is this colony's merchant, and he says this is a sound trade." George took Temperance's arm and drew it through his. "I wanted you to have first choice of the women. Come now and choose which ones you want. Pick five."

"Five?" Temperance was dumbfounded. "Five is too many. One, maybe—or two at most, but not five, George!"

"Five. Two for the house here, and I'll put the other three with the men I take for the land at Hog Island."

Somewhat timidly, Temperance approached the row of black women.

"You can touch them, if you want to," George said. "Or make them open their mouths—wave their arms—anything to see how they are."

Temperance gave him a quizzical look from under the brim of her hat.

"Well, that is what you do when you buy any servant—white or black."

"No, thank you. I can look." But when Temperance got up close, she could hardly restrain herself from wanting to feel their hair. Coal-black and woolly, it stood out like a spiky lion's mane on some and a great fuzzy halo on others, while a few bound it on top of their heads with string or what looked like brass rings, and two had cropped it so close to their skulls that it looked like dusty black velvet.

Their eyes, in their dark faces, were startlingly white. But perhaps,

Temperance thought, her red hair and pale freckled skin seemed equally peculiar to them. All of them looked at her swollen belly, and some smiled. Temperance was eight months pregnant. Looking back on this day, she wondered what curious chemistry had governed her choices. She was drawn almost immediately to the regal bearing of a young woman on the end of the coffle. A close-cropped head, a long, slender neck, a back as straight as an arrow, a look of faint contempt for her coffle companions and her surroundings. Near the opposite end, the youngest-looking one of the lot stood twisting her hands, her eyes on the ground in front of her. Temperance walked slowly over to her and stopped. When the girl did not look up, Temperance gently placed a hand under her chin and raised her head so that the girl was forced to look at her. Sadness showed in those eyes, a sadness so deep it caught at Temperance's throat. The girl could not have been more than thirteen or fourteen. Well, she would make two. Temperance quickly chose three others to send eventually to the plantation at Hog Island.

George, who had been conferring with Abraham Piersey on the end of the wharf, came up beside Temperance. "Just point to the ones you want, and I'll have them unchained for you."

When she had done as he asked, Temperance was horrified to see that George's men were refastening the shackles around the ankles of the five women she had chosen.

"George! I don't want them chained together! Have him take those off!"

"Yes, you do," George said. "They do not speak your language, and they may want to run away from you. You must treat them like captives for a while, at least." He handed her a small iron key. "Keep this safe, and don't unlock them till I tell you."

Temperance dropped the key in her pocket. Then she gathered up her skirts, walked resolutely to the five black women, smiled at them, and touched each one lightly on the shoulder. Then, pointing to the governor's house and motioning for them to follow her, she set off down the wide path that led to the house, with the five trailing in single file behind her. Their chains clanked as they walked.

"Elizabeth!" Temperance did not need to call her. She had been watching from the garden, and she ran to open the gate.

"Here they are," Temperance said. "I think we ought to feed them first. They are bound to be hungry, but they don't speak a word of English."

Elizabeth rolled her eyes at that. Then she looked distastefully at the black women, inspecting each one in turn. "They're black as sin, aren't they?"

"Well, they're . . . different, Elizabeth. I'd not say black as *sin,* though."

"I'll set out some food in the kitchen. There's bread and some goat cheese. They can eat that," Elizabeth said grudgingly.

As she left, Temperance pointed to her and said, "Elizabeth." Then she pointed to herself and said, "Temperance—Lady Temperance." Faint smiles, glimmers of understanding appeared on five faces. Temperance pointed to the woman nearest her, with the halo of hair.

"Maria," the woman said, and pointed to her ample breast.

Smiling, Temperance repeated the name, and the woman nodded emphatically and smiled back. Then Temperance pointed to each of the others, who said their names, one by one:

"Antonia."

"Josefina."

"Francesca."

"Ata."

Of course, Temperance thought. They were from the West Indies; these were the names the Spanish gave them. Antonia, Maria, and Francesca would go to Hog Island; Josefina, the young sad one, and Ata, the one who held herself elegantly aloof, would stay in Jamestown.

The next day, Temperance, with George's permission, had unlocked the iron cuffs that shackled the black women to each other; in ten days, she had taught them a simple English vocabulary, mostly words of one syllable: *hot, cold, sweep, hoe, boil, eat, run, sleep, sun, night, day, go, stop, dig, wash, clothes.* Though they chattered among themselves in a strange mixture of African dialects and Spanish, they were for the most part quick and eager to learn English, and she wished they could learn even faster. She craved to know where they had come from; what sort of lives they had led. They were obviously used to, and expected nothing but, manual labor, and they did not try to run away.

Only Ata kept her distance. She did as she was told, but she ate little, said less, and took no joy in anything that happened around her.

"That one's a sullen wench if I ever saw one," George said. "I'll send her to Hog Island, if you like, and you take one of the others for your house servant."

But Temperance had refused. She was fascinated by this exquisite, melancholy creature, and she almost fancied there was some mysterious bond between them.

Temperance herself felt melancholy at times, and she did not quite know why.

5

THE

MASSACRE

∎

1622

These wilde naked natives . . . had all warning given them one from another in all their habitations, though farre asunder, to meet at the day and hour appointed for our destruction. . . .

—*John Smith,*
   Generall Historie (1624)

THE YORK RIVER, NEAR WEROWOCOMOCO
26 August 1619

 Harmon Harison looked at the sky and frowned. There was a bank of clouds to the south that held rain, for certain, and maybe a squall before the afternoon was over. That meant the shallop would have to put into shore and wait it out, and that meant they would not make Point Comfort by nightfall. He had told Jane they would be gone no more than three days, and when this day ended without his return, she would begin to worry. He was glad he had not taken Robert with him this time; the boy could be of some comfort to his mother. He had begged to come along, but a seven-year-old would have been too much in the way in a twenty-foot shallop with four men, and with the Indians so unpredictable, he might have been in danger as well.

The Indians were the other reason for Harison's frown. He had made this journey up the York River to truck with them for corn, but at each village he was met with contemptuous smiles and polite refusals. They had eaten all their corn during the winter, they said. They had none left to trade for English trinkets. The bag of glass beads, blue and white, and the shiny tin boxes lay untouched in the shallop's stern. Harison would return home emptyhanded as well as a day late. He could imagine Jane's face, drawn with worry and lack of sleep during his absence, bravely arranging itself in a forced smile when he told her he had no corn.

"We'll manage," she would say. "We can eat sallet, and catch more fish. We can do without bread for a while. We'll not go hungry." But they had themselves and Robert and four men to feed, and less than a bushel of corn left. It was his fault; he had put all but twenty-five acres of his three-hundred-acre tract into tobacco last year, and the little corn he did plant was stunted by a dry summer. Jane, he knew, would never complain. He had not known, when he married her, that he was getting a cheerful nature as well as a pretty face. He had first seen that face when it was contorted in pain on the day Thomas Dale ordered her whipped in the market square at Jamestown. It was Fate, he thought, that brought him there that day, and Fate that emboldened him to offer to take care of the servant girl Jane Wright when they cut her down from the whipping post. She had not belonged to anyone since her mistress, the widowed Margaret Whittingham, had died. Harison took her back to his house downriver, tended her wounds, and married her as soon as the welts on her back were healed. She had borne him a son the next year, and he thanked God for her every night in his prayers. Jane would never question his judgment or say that he was not a good provider, but his tenants might. They were good workers, and they needed bread.

So did John Martin, trying to feed fifty people at Martin's Brandon, his new settlement near Nansemond. Martin and his tenants, like Harison, had put too much land in tobacco and not enough in corn last year. It had been Martin's idea to take the shallop up the York River to visit the scattered Indian villages in search of grain to see them through until the harvest.

"Looks like heavy weather over there." Martin moved the tiller so that the shallop's bow nosed away from the cloud bank, closer in to shore. The York River was nearly two miles wide at its mouth, its heavily wooded banks broken here and there by the waters of small creeks that wound their way into the interior. "We'll do better to stay closer in, for now," Martin said. "We've not much cause to hurry, anyway, with no corn. Nobody's going to be very glad to see us come back emptyhanded, eh?" Well he might say that, Harison thought. Martin had no wife waiting for him, and his son had died the first summer at Jamestown.

"I reckon not," Harison said absently, letting his gaze wander along the riverbank off the shallop's starboard bow. All at once he caught his breath sharply and shouted, "John! Look to starboard! Am I seeing things?"

At the mouth of a small creek, just about to enter the river, was a large dugout canoe manned by two Indians. The craft was riding low and heavy-laden in the water.

"Well, I'll be damned!" Martin said. "What can they be carrying?"

"It's worth a look, I say," Harison said happily. "May be worth a trade." Under Martin's command, the shallop's crew took in sail and hove to, waiting for the canoe to draw closer. By that time the Indians paddling the dugout had spied the English boat, and they waved their paddles in cautious greeting. The shallop's crew responded with waves and shouts, and exaggerated motions of the arms to beckon them closer.

"It's bound to be corn they're carrying!" Harison said. "I know those baskets they put it in!"

"But will they part with it—that's the question," Martin said. As the two vessels bobbed gently near the riverbank, elaborately polite negotiations commenced, with Martin and Harison displaying handfuls of glass beads and holding up tin boxes, and the two Indians smiling and shaking their heads.

"No corn for the English," they said amiably in Algonquin. "Corn for Warraskoyack."

Harison's heart sank. There were three bushel-sized baskets of corn in that dugout, not nearly as much as he and Martin had hoped for, but enough to be worth the taking. "Offer them all the beads, and four tin boxes for those baskets," he whispered to Martin, who was serving as spokesman.

The offer was made; the answer was negative. In desperation, Martin offered them his entire stock-in-trade. The two Indians glanced at each other and then, smiling broadly, shook their heads. "No," one said.

"No truck," said the other. They put their paddles in the water and began to move away from the shallop.

Captain John Martin suddenly pulled a long French pistol from his belt and aimed it carefully at the Indian in the stern of the canoe. "Put ashore or I'll shoot."

Harmon Harison drew his own pistol and aimed at the other Indian. "Good," he said through his teeth. "Let's take them."

As the angry Indians beached their dugout, the shallop's crewmen leaped over the boat's gunwales under the protective barrels of the two pistols and splashed ashore. It was the work of a moment to heave the three baskets of corn into the larger vessel.

"Better leave them all the truck in return," Martin said. "We don't want them taking revenge."

"It's a fair trade," Harison said. "More than enough."

The Indians, however, did not share Harison's opinion. As the shallop trimmed its sails and headed downriver, they watched its occupants carefully, so that they would not forget the faces of the two Englishmen who had held the pistols.

JAMESTOWN
29 August 1619

Wahunsonacock, the Powhatan, was dead. He had not been well since Pocahontas's death. He had apparently died sometime the previous winter, but the news did not reach Jamestown until the summer, when Nemattonow, whom the English now called "Jack of the Feather" because of the swan's wings and headdress he wore, came to tell them. Opitchapan, the lame brother, had ruled briefly, but now Wahunsonacock's older brother, Opechancanough, was the Powhatan, and no one knew what that might mean. Now that both Pocahontas and her father were dead, Opechancanough blew hot and cold with the English, one day promising everlasting friendship, the next, demanding justice for some wrong, real or imagined. Governor Sir George Yardley's emissaries journeyed back and forth, back and forth between Jamestown and the Indian villages, often bearing contradictory messages. The perpetual uncertainty made George tense and irritable, and he ground his teeth when he slept.

Sleep was difficult enough as it was. The breezes from the river blew hotter than usual, and nightfall brought little relief. Even the birds were wakeful, and the drowsy twitter of a sparrow or a jay could be heard at odd hours during the night, as though they, like the humans, were complaining about the heat that hung over the Jamestown peninsula. The governor's house and half a dozen others outside the palisade were built with their broadest sides facing the James, so all their windows could catch the wind from the river, but the humid air that entered clung to skin and clothing like a damp blanket. Temperance, heavy and uncomfortable in the last month of her pregnancy, slept naked, with only a linen sheet for cover, and George did likewise. Nighttime was the only time they were alone these days. Two-year-old Argall and a houseful of servants created a constant commotion during the day, and a steady procession of visitors to see the governor often lasted into the evening.

Most of George's time had been taken up with the new colonial legislature: the General Assembly. This long-awaited body, provided for in the Virginia Company's Great Charter, was now to meet yearly and make laws for the colony, subject, of course, to Parliament's approval. On July 20, twenty-two elected representatives from the colony's plantations, along with the six-member Governor's Council and the governor, had convened for the first time. They gathered in the Jamestown meetinghouse, the only building large enough to hold them. There they met, day after day, in the sweltering heat. It was a historic occasion, everyone said, this first session of the first legislature in the New World. And for Governor Yardley, doing his best to keep order among the legislators and keep peace with the Indians, it was a trying time.

"George, if it weren't for me, those savages would be our friends," Temperance said one night as they were preparing for bed. "I am to blame."

"What do you mean?" George looked at her, puzzled. "What in the world are you talking about?"

"I am talking about that day when you fired on the Chickahominies— because of me."

"What?"

"Two years ago, you ordered your men to fire on Kissanacomen and his warriors because of what other Indians had done to me," Temperance said patiently. "Did you not?"

George stopped taking off his boots and gave her a long and searching look. "Yes."

"And that was the beginning of all the troubles, wasn't it?" Temperance sighed. "If you had not fired on them, they would not have attacked Richard Killingbeck and his four men, and they would not have killed William Fairfax's children. That is what I hear."

The two surprise attacks on unsuspecting households at the edge of the settlement the past winter had shocked the entire colony, and George was still trying to press the Indians to make reparations. Now he pulled off his boot and let it drop to the floor. "Damnation, Temperance! I don't know that to be true, and neither do you. We were not even in Virginia when all that happened." Frowning, he attacked the other boot for a moment, and then he stopped, leg in midair. "It was in Samuel Argall's time as governor, and he told me that Opechancanough said the Indians who attacked Killingbeck's party and Fairfax's house were outcasts—'fugitives,' Opechancanough called them, and he told Argall that the English must not take revenge on the river tribes for what a few renegades did." George went back to removing his boot.

"But you are going to take revenge," Temperance said. "Those are the very words of the Company's orders to you—to take a 'sharp revenge.' And if you don't, Sir Thomas Smythe and his faction will say you lack courage. You know they are looking to find fault with your governorship. You'll be forced to attack, and then the Indians will avenge that, and it will go on, and on, and it's all because of me." She climbed onto the big feather bed and sat cross-legged, pulling the sheet around her. "Things were peaceful with the Indians before that, with Pocahontas and all." She fingered the lace edge of a pillowcase. "It was me, wasn't it?"

George finished taking off his other boot and put his hands on his knees. "Who's to know, Temperance? Who knows what Opechancanough or any other savage has in mind?" He shook his head wearily. "I am doing my best not to cross him, and I am not planning any revenge. Smythe and Warwick and the others in the Virginia Company know nothing of the ways of the Indians, and they must believe what I tell them. I think Sandys believes me. God knows, there is not a man in Virginia who wants peace more than I do." He crossed the room to the cupboard, poured water into a silver basin, and splashed some on his face.

Temperance lay back on the pillows. "I'm sorry, George. I've caused you trouble, and I—I've not been a very good wife to you, either."

George, rubbing his face with a linen towel, did not answer immediately. Then he said, "Nonsense, Temperance." His tone was brisk, his manner was stiff; the effect was like the sudden closing of a door. It was obvious he did not wish any further discussion. Temperance sighed.

George did not mean to be rude; he came and kissed her lightly on the mouth to show that he did not. "You talk nonsense," he said gently as he climbed into bed. "You must not do that. I have enough people around me talking nonsense during the day." Without waiting for her to answer, he went on, "Henry Spelman came before the Assembly today and denied nearly everything."

"What?"

"He claimed that none of the charges against him was true—that he did not malign me before Opechancanough, and that Robert Poole, the fellow who said so under oath, was lying."

"Was he?"

"How do I know? Poole has lied before, you know. He lied about Opechancanough's wanting to come to Jamestown and pay me a state visit after Wahunsonacock's death, and then, when I sent word I would be glad to see him, Opechancanough sent back word he had never planned such a visit. He was offended, and if John Rolfe had not gone to Werowocomoco to explain the misunderstanding, Opechancanough would think me a fool." George pounded the bed pillows in frustration.

"That was clever of you to send John to talk with Opechancanough," Temperance said soothingly. "Perhaps you ought to make more use of John. Opechancanough is his uncle by marriage, after all."

"I know. But Poole and Spelman are the official interpreters, chosen by the Assembly." George raised himself on one elbow so he could look at Temperance. "And Poole is a crackbrain and Spelman is a . . . a snokehorn."

"You mean he lies? Deliberately?"

"I mean he would stab me in the back if he could. He has told Opechancanough I am a poor governor, and that a greater governor than I am will come to Jamestown by this time next year." George tried to pass this information off lightly, but Temperance could tell how deeply it had cut him. She thought of John Pory's warnings last year in London about opposition to George's knighthood, and she wondered if Henry Spelman was acting on instructions from George's enemies in the Virginia Company.

"What did the Assembly say to that?" she asked.

"Oh, they reprimanded him for spreading false rumors and trying to inflame the Indians. But the damage is done." Wearily, George lay back on his pillows. "Henry Spelman is a snot-nosed son of a bitch. He thinks he knows everything there is to know about the Indians because he lived among them for a year. He has hated me ever since—" George paused.

"Since when?"

"Since that day I fired on Kissanacomen and the Chickahominies."

JAMESTOWN
8 September 1619

 It was Ata who sat with Temperance all that long afternoon, as her labor pains grew stronger and stronger. Temperance did not want anyone else. Ata, with her quiet ways and her quick, skillful hands, was all Temperance wanted. Temperance had been right in her first impression. There was nothing ordinary about Ata. Her mother had been a king's daughter; her grandfather had been a powerful African chieftain with twenty villages paying him homage. He had also had powerful enemies, and one day, when he lost a battle, many of his people, including his wives and daughters, had been captured and sold to a visiting Spanish slaver. Ata's mother, pregnant at the time of her capture, had somehow survived the terrible ocean crossing, and had been bought at last by a sugar planter on the island of Hispaniola. Ata was born there, and until last year had lived all her life there until her master sold her, and the Dutch trader eventually brought her to Virginia. All this Temperance had learned bit by bit, as Ata learned English. As she and Temperance had come to know each other, the distance between servant and mistress had shrunk. Ata still grieved for her husband of one year, who had been sold with her, but the Dutch captain had sold him to a planter in Bermuda. She yearned to know what happened to him, and Temperance's heart went out to her. She thought of telling Ata about Will: that she, too, had loved someone and had lost him. But the intricacies of that relationship were more than Ata's still-limited knowledge of English could bear.

"I would like to have a baby," Ata said softly as she wrung out a linen cloth in cool water and laid it on Temperance's sweating forehead. "You are—" she groped for the word—"blessed."

Temperance gritted her teeth. At that moment, she felt anything but blessed: The pains were coming closer and harder, and she was trying not to cry out, so as not to frighten Argall. A two-year-old had no cause to know about birth, but she had told him there would be a baby soon. Before her labor began in earnest, she had kissed him and sent him off with Josefina, who had become his favorite playmate. But they might be inside the house, staying out of the afternoon sun, and she did not want him alarmed by the sound of his mother's voice in pain. "I think—I think it's coming!" she gasped. "Call Mistress Worley!"

Ata, serene and silent as a cat, slipped out of the room, and in an instant was back with Meg, who had been waiting downstairs.

"Come now," Meg said, "let's have this baby. Push!"

In a few minutes, Ata's strong, slender fingers were holding the baby's head, and then its body, and then, as Temperance, exhausted, lay back, Ata and Meg together held up a wriggling, squalling baby girl for her to see.

"She is so pretty," Ata said. "So . . . perfect."

"She is that," Meg said.

There was a touch of envy in each woman's voice.

"No newborn is pretty," Temperance said weakly. "But I am glad she is all there. Meg, you had better call George."

They named the baby Elizabeth, for no particular reason; they just liked the sound of it. But no one in the household could convince Elizabeth Jones that this new baby was not named after her. George was delighted to have a daughter as well as a son, and his birth gift to Temperance far surpassed the opal ring he had given her when Argall was born.

"It is not a present you can put in a box," he said mysteriously. "Guess."

"A horse?" Temperance said.

George laughed. "I know how much you'd like that! That will come in good time, but not yet."

"Well, I can't guess, then. Tell me." She smiled at him indulgently.

"It's land, Temperance—a place."

"A place?"

"A plantation upriver, away from the mosquitoes and the marshes of Jamestown." His voice trembled with excitement. "The Company has finally assigned me my two thousand acres as governor, and most of it is up at Queen's Creek near Tobacco Point, just below Charles City."

"George, you know I've not been there. Where is that?"

"Well, here is Henrico," he began, poking an indentation in the yellow silk coverlet on Temperance's bed, "and here is Bermuda Hundred, like this." His index finger traced a curving line that did not stay indented on the silk, so he put his finger down where Bermuda Hundred was supposed to be. "And down here, around a bend in the river they call Weyanoak Bend, is our land: a thousand acres on each side of the river." His finger drew a large circle on the bedcover, and then zigzagged across it a few inches toward Temperance. "And here is Jamestown, about twenty miles down this way." He leaned over and kissed her. "I'm going to build you a house on a rise overlooking the river—the most beautiful site, and finest house in Virginia!"

"Oh, George—" Temperance began, but he kissed her again.

"And the best thing about it will be its name," he said tenderly. "The name of our plantation will be . . . Flowerdew. Flowerdew Hundred, for Lady Temperance Flowerdew Yardley. And hundreds of years from now, people will say, this place was named by a governor of Virginia for his wife, whose family name was Flowerdew."

George had not been gone half an hour before the lying-in callers began to come. Thomasine Causey was the first. The Causeys lived in the house just east of the governor's mansion.

"Well, a girl at last!" she said in her soft, twittery voice. She bent low over the cradle where Elizabeth slept. "And she is precious! Just precious! I hope my next one is a girl, and it's soon: Thomas will be eight this September! How time flies!" Eight years ago, Thomasine's pregnancy had surprised everyone in Jamestown. Little Thomas Causey had been born,

Temperance remembered with a pang, just after Gabriel's second birthday. But Thomasine had reverted to her natural thinness after bearing a son, and the Causeys had had no more children. She brought a cream-colored bearing cloth edged with lace for the new baby. "I'd been keeping it so long, I was afraid it would get worn out with my looking at it," she said. "So I said to myself, Thomasine, you selfish thing! Temperance has more need of this than you do."

"Why, thank you, Thomasine," Temperance said. "It's lovely."

"Oh, you may have a dozen like it, I trow," Thomasine said with a nervous little laugh. There was envy in her tone, and envy in her look as she glanced around the room, at the big tester bed with its yellow silk canopy and covers, at the carved cupboard with its silver ewer and basin, at the two chests inlaid with holly and bog oak that George had brought from London. Thomasine finally took herself off, but a few minutes after Temperance heard her departing footsteps on the gravel walk below, another visitor arrived.

It was Joan Pierce, from next door. "I brought you this," she said. She was panting from her climb up the stairs. Unlike Thomasine, Joan had put on weight after the Starving Time. Now she took great pride in her cooking, and equal pleasure in her eating. Her plump hands held a pewter porringer with a custard baked in it. "Lots of eggs and milk," she said. "Good for nursing mothers." She set the porringer on the cupboard, and settled herself on a joint stool near the bed so that she could see into the cradle beside it.

"Temperance, she is adorable. So fair. I believe her hair's going to be red like yours."

LONDON, SOUTHAMPTON HOUSE
26 November 1619

 "Yardley is unhappy in the governorship. You can see that from his letters. But I think we must ignore his offer to resign. He is too good a man to lose, and the Company must reassure him of his value to the whole enterprise." Sir Edwin Sandys, the newly elected treasurer of the Virginia Company, paced up and down the spacious library at Southampton House as he spoke to his companion. "What say you?"

Near the fireplace, Henry Wriothesley, Earl of Southampton, laid aside a sheaf of papers on his writing table and frowned. "I'll warrant you this whole matter is Thomas Smythe's doing. He has never approved of Yardley's knighthood, and he is still grumbling about its being 'unduly procured.' And I trow Smythe has put Francis West and Samuel Argall and the others up to this petition to remove Yardley as governor." Sir Henry jabbed his index finger at a document on his desk. "Consider the signers: Francis West is jealous of Yardley's governorship; Samuel Argall is fearful Yardley will expose his privateering, and the two of them have somehow connived to turn Thomas Gates against Yardley, as well. Damnit, Yardley was Gates's own man, the best captain of guards he ever had, so he said. What reason would Gates have to turn against him now?" Sir Henry pushed back his chair and stood up. "I say we ignore these malcontents' petition, and I say we ignore Yardley's offer to resign."

"Done!" Sir Edwin grasped his friend's hand and clapped him on the shoulder. "I never wanted to remove Yardley, and if you are with me, I need not. Yardley is a good man, though he may be too soft on the savages. We can press him on that later." He gazed thoughtfully out the window. "Now all I have to do before the Michaelmas Quarter Court meets is to compose my speech about the future of the Company. On the morrow, I intend to tell the shareholders where the Virginia Company has been, and where I propose to lead it."

"Excellent." Henry Wriothesley leaned back in his chair. "You have done good work, Edwin. But you must be wary. Warwick and Rich will work with Smythe against us, now that you are treasurer, you can be sure. They will say we are expanding too quickly."

"I am not worried. Those popinjays do not frighten me." But Edwin Sandys resumed his pacing. "I aim to make the Virginia colony a success, and the Virginia Company solvent. Seventy-five thousand pounds sterling invested since 1607, and nothing except some tobacco and sassafras to show for it!" He shook his head. "All we have reaped from this entire venture, as far as the public knows, is the tale of the *Sea Venture*'s wreck on Bermuda that Will Shakespeare used to write *The Tempest.* It made a fine play, but it is not like to draw us any new investors."

Sir Henry laughed. "Perhaps we should have asked Shakespeare to put a speech in Ariel's mouth about our sore need of money," he said. "Some fine poetic lines about the Virginia Company, and all the audience would have rushed to buy shares, and saved us from financial ruin!"

"But if tobacco prices hold, and if the ironworks and the glassworks produce," Sir Edwin said, "we stand to do well this year."

"What of the Pilgrims and the Northern Virginia settlement? They are supposed to leave before long, are they not?"

Sir Edwin nodded. "Giving a charter to those pious Pilgrims won't cost us sixpence, but you know they're not likely to produce anything but Separatist-minded prayers and sermons when they plant their colony." Both men laughed, and then Sir Edwin continued, "But I swear by the end of my term as treasurer, there will not be one penn'orth of debt. We have to expand, if we want a return. Nothing ventured, nothing gained. We have to send out more tenants—I propose a hundred each for the governor's lands, and a hundred for the Indian college, and a hundred for the Company's lands—and then we'll send a hundred young boys for apprentices, and a hundred young women for wives." Sir Edwin paused. "We need more females there. You have read Pory's letter about the buggery cases."

Sir Henry slapped his knee and burst out laughing. "Damnedest thing I ever heard of! Two men buggering the sow was bad enough, but the *turkey*?"

He leaned back in his chair and laughed some more. "How in God's name did they hold it, I wonder?"

Sandys, who had joined in the laughter, shook his head. "I don't know. But we cannot let stories like that get abroad. We need more women in Virginia. Men don't work well when they are . . . ruttish. We want those planters to settle down, start families."

"And what is to be done with the Indians?"

Both men were silent, considering the answer to that question. Neither Edwin Sandys nor Henry Wriothesley had been to Virginia, and the only Indians they had ever seen were Pocahontas and her entourage when Rolfe brought them to London three years ago.

Sandys sighed. "I have doubts. You have read Yardley's letters. What do you make of them?"

"I don't know. He seems to think there is a need to fear the Indian king—what's his name?—Opechancanough. Yardley suspects the old chief may be plotting something. From what I read in Yardley's letters, Opechancanough, as the new Powhatan, wants a formal treaty granting us his land, and he wants some return for it."

"We have no call to deal with savages. We have claimed that land for England, and we shall occupy it as the need arises."

In due time, the treasurer of the Virginia Company and the Earl of Southampton would have good reason to regret their decision.

FLOWERDEW HUNDRED
10 March 1621

 "I wish to God Almighty the Council had accepted my offer to resign, but in little more than nine months, my term will be up, and I shall be quit of this damned governorship." Governor Yardley, seated on the porch of Flowerdew, his newly built house overlooking the wide shining ribbon of the James River, heaved a weary sigh and took another drink from the tankard at his elbow. "If I live—if we all live—that long."

"That is foolish talk. These Indians aren't going to attack us now." The man next to the governor drew thoughtfully on his pipe. "Not when they have made a league of peace with us, and not when we are about to give them a college. In faith, Opechancanough is now of a mind to have some English families live in his village to learn the language."

"Opechancanough is a wily old bastard."

"You have been here too long, and worked too hard. Have another drink." The newcomer, George Thorpe, poured a clear amber liquid into the governor's tankard and added some to his own.

"That stuff is not bad-tasting, when you get used to it," the governor said. "Sharp on the tongue, but it goes down well. Even if you never set up the college or convert the Indians, you have at least done one thing for Virginia. You have fermented corn and made a drinkable liquor."

Thorpe laughed. "That's what was wrong with Virginia," he said. "I could see it as soon as I came here. Too much water to drink, and not enough liquor. No wonder so many took sick."

"And so many died."

"That was not your fault."

"I tried, God knows, I tried! Two years ago, when I was first governor, I wrote to Sir Edwin and the Council not to send so many people in the summertime with so little provision." George shook his head. "But the ships just kept coming. That first summer I fed many newcomers out of my own supply, while it lasted, but many had to go hungry." He sighed. "Do you know that in these two years nigh onto two thousand people have come here, and near half of them have died? Fevers, fluxes, and their own discontents carried them off—and a good number of our settled planters, too." George paused. "Poor Alexander Whitaker."

Thorpe frowned. "Damned shame, a man of God drowning like that. Don't know what to make of it. What possessed him to try to ford the river at flood tide? He should have known better."

"Young Richard Mutton could not quit weeping after it happened. He kept saying it was his fault, that he had sinned, and he was the one who should have drowned. He would not go back in the house after the body was found, so I sent him to stay with the Forrests." George spoke wearily. "So many deaths. I reckon we have barely a thousand living souls in all of Virginia. I tried, but what could I do?"

"You did all you could, and you have been as good a governor as any man could be. Now drink up and don't talk about things you couldn't help. Your low spirits will sour my corn-mash liquor."

Governor Yardley leaned back and closed his eyes as the warmth of the drink spread through him. "There had better not be too much quaffing of this," he said, "or we'll have a whole colony in its cups."

"You've done well here," Thorpe said. "No one can fault your governorship. It was you, after all, who established the league of peace with Opechancanough, and you did try to reason with the Company about taking his land without giving him something in return."

The governor struck flint to steel and lit his pipe. The small yellow flame in the pipe's bowl made a brief glow, like a firefly, in the late spring dusk. He drew on the pipe contentedly and said, "It's this stuff that's going to give us all something in return. If tobacco prices hold, this whole colony will be rich. That is one other reason I want out of the governorship. I need to tend my land, and lay up something for my children."

"How old is Argall?"

"Three this past February." George drew thoughtfully on his pipe. "I wish to God we hadn't named him Argall, but to change his name now, with him not knowing why, would not do. When we christened him, I thought Samuel Argall and I would be friends for life." George spoke bitterly.

"What Argall—Samuel Argall, I mean—does now cannot hurt you." Thorpe spoke with conviction. "I doubt there was any man on the Council who took that petition to remove you—his work, I trow—as the truth. No one believes his tales about your cheating him out of land and tenants as governor. I'd forget all that, if I were you."

"How can I, with my only son named after such a knave as Samuel Argall?"

"You will, in time. All things are possible, given enough time," Thorpe said placidly. "That is what I say about the Indians: Anything is possible, given enough time. Give me a year, and I'll have them reading and writing and praying, all in the King's English."

"You do that," George said, stretching his legs out in front of him. He was glad he had made the twenty-mile trip upriver from Jamestown yesterday, and that he had invited George Thorpe to come over from Charles City to Flowerdew. He had taken an instant liking to the rotund, balding councillor, who had arrived in January to set up the Company's proposed college for the Indians.

They had had an excellent dinner—Temperance had made a baked custard for the sweet—and George found it pleasant to sit out on the porch and have a pipe and a drink in good company, overlooking his own land. For the first time in months, he was beginning to feel relaxed. "Give me a little more of that liquor," he said, "and then don't let me have another drop."

Thorpe laughed. "It'll do you good. When's the last time you were drunk?"

"I don't know. So long I can't remember." But George did remember. It was last year, after the Council's last meeting with the Assembly. He had come home so drunk that Temperance had forbidden him her bed that night. Thinking of Temperance lately had made him feel uncomfortable. He had built her the finest house in Virginia, up here at Flowerdew, and she still seemed dissatisfied about something. He did not quite know what it was. He had been so busy.

"Well, you'll have more time when you're no longer governor. This Virginia is not a bad place. Good hunting, good fishing, good sailing. I like it much more than I thought I would," Thorpe said lazily. "While I am teaching the Indians, I think I shall have them teach me how they catch fish, and how they hunt deer. That would be a fair trade. Then I'll just settle here, and see how it goes. I would not mind spending the rest of my life here."

"Have you ever been married?"

"No." It was a jovial-sounding answer.

"Why?"

"Never wanted to. I can get what I want without it." Thorpe did not think it politic to mention that he had more than breakfast from his host's serving maid, Elizabeth Jones, only this morning. "I'd make a poor husband, anyway. Drink too much, eat too much, snore too loud. No woman would have me for long."

"What about children?" George said. "What about passing on your name?"

"Ah, but what if they turned out just like me? Why would I want to leave the world more Thorpes? It'll be better off when I'm gone, and nothing of me left." Thorpe laughed a deep laugh that shook his middle, and underneath the waist of his doublet, his belly moved gently up and down.

On that same evening, thirty miles away in the village of Werowocomoco, Opechancanough laughed. He was thinking of the next new moon, when he would begin his yearly visits to all the tribes that paid him homage. He would travel in a wide half circle around the English settlements in a leisurely journey that would take two full moons to complete. He would hold court among the Weyanokes, the Pamunkeys, the Chiskiacks, the Chickahominies, and the rest, and he would lay out in loving detail the scheme he had conceived last year: a carefully timed, concerted attack by all the river tribes on all the English settlements.

FLOWERDEW
30 September 1621

 Temperance had begun keeping a journal. She wrote in it erratically, sometimes filling a page or two every day for several days; more often letting it go blank and then jotting only a line or two. Tonight she opened the black morocco-bound book, smoothed its gold-edged vellum pages to lie flat, dipped a sharpened goose quill into a silver inkwell, and carefully wrote:

> 30 September, 1621
> Gabriel's birthday

Then she laid the quill back in its stand, covered the inkwell, sprinkled sand on the wet ink to dry it, and sat looking at what she had written, chin in hand. Gabriel would have been eleven years old today.

In the chamber next to hers, Argall and Elizabeth shouted and laughed, as Josefina made a game of undressing them for bed. In a moment, they would call for her to come and say good night. Argall, at three, was his father in miniature: solidly built and sweet-tempered, with George's chestnut curls and blue-black eyes. Elizabeth, just turned two, had her mother's coloring, but her hair was thin and wispy and refused to curl. She had an impish sort of face, with close-set brown eyes. She would never be a beauty, Temperance thought, but she had already learned to charm her father. George called her Little Muffin, and Argall was Big Brother—"Bro" for short—anything to keep from calling him by the given name his father had come to despise.

George had had to spend so much time tending to his affairs as out-going governor and the lawsuit Samuel Argall had tried to bring against him that he had spent barely three weeks out of the entire summer at Flower-dew. The children, accustomed to seeing their father constantly in the governor's mansion at Jamestown, missed him. Temperance missed him, too, or at least she told herself that she did.

She also missed the company of people at Jamestown: Meg, the Causeys, the Pierces, the Laydons, John Rolfe, the Forrests. Thomas Forrest had died last winter, and Lucy had gone back to England. Temperance regretted not being there to bid her farewell. But it was Meg she missed the most. They had begged her to come and live with them at Flowerdew, but she had declined. "Next year I shall be fifty," she had said. "I aim to live out my days upon my own fifty acres, but I shall come and visit you as often as you please." So George saw to it that his own tenants worked Meg's land and kept her little house at Jamestown in good repair.

There was plenty to occupy Temperance at Flowerdew. The house, with its eight large rooms—hall, parlor, great chamber, and buttery, down-stairs, with a kitchen just outside, and four bedchambers upstairs—had been finished in February, but the oak paneling and wainscoting for the parlor and great chamber that George had ordered from England had not arrived until March. There was the moving and the arranging and rearrang-ing of an entire household of two children and eight house servants to see to, and, once in residence, Temperance had had the gardens to plan.

Best of all, there was a horse for her to ride. George, true to his promise last year, had written to his brother Ralph to select a stallion and a mare and have them sent, and two handsome bays arrived at Jamestown in January. Temperance had taken the mare to Flowerdew, and when the weather was good, she rode every day, cantering over the green meadows and down to the riverbank, her hair flying in the wind. It was safe enough; there were no Indian villages within five miles, and since the house stood on a hill overlooking the river, she could ride fairly far away without being out of sight from the front gallery. Nonetheless, George insisted that one of the servants keep watch from the house while she rode.

"Wait until November," he would say, "when Francis Wyatt takes over as governor, and then I can ride with you." But George was away tonight, as he had been all week, at the session of the General Court at Jamestown.

"Mistress Temperance, we go to bed now!" Josefina, carrying Elizabeth astride her hip and leading Argall by the hand, appeared in the doorway.

Argall asked his nightly question: "When is Father coming home?"

"I look for him tomorrow. Come, now, and let us say good night." As Temperance tucked the blankets around each of her children, they snuggled down, the straw-filled mattresses of the trundle beds crackling under their weight. There were no feather beds in the children's room; straw, when they wet their beds, was easy to throw out.

"Good night, Elizabeth. Good night, Argall." Temperance gave each of them a kiss and turned to leave. "Josefina, when you go downstairs, tell Ata I am ready to go to bed."

She went to bed early, almost as soon as the children, when George was away. There was nothing to stay up for. Temperance was not a reader, needlework bored her, and with no one to talk to, she might as well go to bed and not waste the candlelight. She pulled the high pearl comb out of her hair and began to undo the laces of her sleeves.

"Let me do that," Ata moved so quietly that she often took Temperance by surprise. "I am the one to do that, not you," Ata said with a smile. "You are the lady; I am the servant."

"You know you are more my friend than my servant, Ata," Temperance said. "Someday I should play the servant, and you could have my part."

Ata began to take the hairpins out of Temperance's hair. "But I would not know what to do," she said, "and my hair would not be like yours." They both laughed. Temperance shook her head and ran her fingers through her hair, which, undone, fell almost to her waist. Ata took up a hog-bristle brush and began to use it in long, caressing strokes. Temperance held a small square looking glass before her face and inspected it closely.

"And you don't have wrinkles the way white people do," Temperance said, peering again at her reflection. She saw no signs of wrinkles yet, but she knew that one day she would smile or frown, and the crease line would not quite go away, and there would be a wrinkle.

"You have no wrinkles," Ata said, looking over Temperance's shoulder into the glass. Her smooth black face, shiny as a piece of polished ebony, was reflected beside Temperance's.

"Soon I will. I will be thirty-one this year."

When Ata had left, Temperance sat in her shift by the fireplace for a long time, watching the flames caress the new-cut logs and thinking. She was no longer young, despite what Ata said. The course of her life was set; the voyage probably half over. The children would grow up; she and George would grow old, and someday death would part them. The inescapable fact that one of them would die first seemed to her a cruel lottery.

Feeling gloomy and restless, she opened the door to the gallery outside her bedchamber and stepped outside. She had wanted a second-floor gallery like the one at Thickthorne, a long, narrow room that ran the length of the house and opened onto the other upstairs chambers. George had had one built to please her, but he had suggested that it be open to the outside, to the pleasures of Virginia springtimes and autumns. She breathed deeply, and the spicy fragrance of the pines near the house filled her nostrils. George had had all but one grove of nearby trees cut down when they built the house. Too dangerous, he said; too easy for Indians to conceal themselves in the event of an attack. He wanted the house to stand free and clear, and he also, as Temperance well knew, wanted the house to be visible far up and down the river, so that everyone would know that this house belonged to the richest man in Virginia.

Temperance could see the river now, winding far in the distance, shimmering in the light of the newly risen moon. It must be well past nine o'clock, she thought. She would go in soon. But the cool air with its promise of autumn was refreshing, and she lingered, leaning over the wall of the gallery, looking out at the night. It was too dark to see anything clearly, but she knew what was there: in front, the broad green sweep of lawn stretching down to the river's edge; to the right, a split-log fence marking the meadow where her horse grazed; to the left, another fence keeping the flowers in the cutting garden safe from rooting hogs. On this same side, but closer to the house, was the grove of pine trees, some of them towering a hundred feet into the sky. And it was there, just as she was about to go inside, that she saw something move.

It was a dark shape, perhaps only a prowling deer, but what if it were something else? What if this were a marauding Indian? She blinked once or twice, as if that could sharpen her eyesight, and peered into the darkness. Then she heard the unmistakable sound of footsteps running across the dry grass. In the split second between hearing and reacting, while her brain was commanding her frozen muscles to move, she heard her name.

"Temperance!" The sibilant ending was a loud hiss in the darkness directly below her. Heart pounding, she held her breath.

"Don't go in! Wait!" A loud whisper, and then a rustling of leaves.

Someone was climbing up the vines on the gallery wall. She stepped backward. She knew she ought to call out, to scream for help, but somehow she could not make her voice obey. In terrified fascination, she watched as a head—it was too dark to see the face—appeared above the wall, and then a leg was thrust over. "Shhhh! Be quiet!" A man's figure, silhouetted against the faint moonlight, swung itself easily over the gallery wall. "Temperance, forgive me for coming to you like this." The familiar voice rang in her ears; her breath left her.

It was Will.

He took a step toward her. "I so wanted to see you, and I knew you were alone. I didn't mean to frighten you." He took another step, and the faint light from the bedchamber fell across his face. "You thought I was dead, didn't you?"

Temperance could only nod. Not taking her eyes off Will's face, she moved over to the bench against the wall and eased herself down onto it slowly, as if in a trance.

With easy grace, Will dropped on one knee in front of her so that their heads were on the same level. He folded his arms across his other knee, leaned on it, and looked at her all over, like a lookout scouting uncertain terrain. Then, in a gesture so familiar it made Temperance's heart turn over, he rubbed his hand over his face from forehead to chin. "I have imagined this so many times, and thought of what my first words to you would be, and now I cannot remember any of them." He shook his head as if to clear it. "Let me see, now," he said to himself, and then to her, with a smile, he said, "How are you? You look well."

"Will, for God's sake!" Temperance clenched her fists. She felt as if she were about to shatter into tiny fragments. "Where in God's holy name have you been? It's been five years!"

"All in good time, Temperance," he said. "All in good time. I know I ought not to have come here. I am living with the Indians down near Warraskoyack—among the Nansemonds. But when you moved up here to Weyanoak Bend, I vowed to come and see you just once, to let you know that I . . . wish you joy." His voice broke and caught again. "You are where you belong. It has all come right in the end, you see." He was silent for a moment, and then he stood up. "I must go now. God bless."

"No," Temperance said. "W-wait!" She had begun to shiver uncontrollably.

"You . . . can't go. You haven't told me . . . what happened! C- Come inside." Josefina and the children, the only ones upstairs, were asleep by now. Temperance stepped inside, and Will followed her hesitantly. She crossed over to the fireplace and stood by it, hugging herself, trying to stop shaking.

Will stopped at the corner of the bed, pointedly keeping his distance from her. He was dressed from head to foot in fringed buckskin, and around his neck he wore a string of shells and bears' claws. His blond hair, grown long, was tied at the back of his neck with a deerskin thong, and he was clean-shaven except for a small tuft of chin hair like the Indians sometimes wore. The fair skin was weathered and brown now, like lightly tanned leather, but the gray eyes had not changed. His clear, steady gaze held Temperance's eyes so long that she blinked and turned her head. "I've not seen you this close in a long time," he said softly.

"What do you mean, 'this close'? When have you seen me at all?"

He smiled. "Many times, from across the river at Jamestown. One can see the governor's house from there, you know. It was far away, but I knew it was you."

Temperance felt the skin on the back of her neck crawl. "You mean you spied on me," she said angrily, "like . . . an Indian. You watched me mourn for you. You let me think you dead, all this time. For God's sake, Will! Have you no pity?"

"I knew that you were with George." He spoke quietly. "I knew that was where you belonged." He looked at her with a strange tenderness: a curious mingling of affection and admiration, an utter absence of ill feeling. "You know that, too, Temperance."

She did not answer.

"After all," Will said with a trace of the dry laugh she knew so well, "look what George can give you." He glanced around the richly furnished bedchamber. "This is what you were meant for, Temperance, not a dirt-floored hovel in a forest."

Temperance began to weep.

"Don't cry, dear heart," he said. "I didn't come here to make you sad. I thought to comfort you, and to bid you a proper farewell."

"I don't want you to bid me farewell." Temperance spoke in a low voice through her tears. "I want you to tell me why you never came for me."

"The Indians held me captive for a long time, Temperance." Will spoke impassively. "I thought they had killed you. Old Kalono had a—a piece of skin with the hair from your . . . privates. He stretched it and hung it on his wall."

"God in heaven!"

"I expected he would kill me in his own good time, but instead he wanted me to make music for him. One of his men had brought my lute when they took me, and they thought it had magical powers." He paused and stared into the fire. "I waited until Kalono's men left, and then I killed him."

"Then why didn't you come back to Henrico?"

Will shrugged. "What was there to come back for? I took Kalono's bow and arrows, and his knife, and his bearskin cloak, and left. I walked for two days. Then I came upon a village of the Nansemonds, and they took me in. I'd not eaten nor slept since I killed Kalono. They gave me half a turkey to eat and a pile of furs for a bed, and they asked no questions." Will looked at Temperance and smiled. "I have lived among them ever since."

"Didn't you think to search for me?"

"I told you, I thought you were dead," he said patiently. "It was not until the spring that I heard from the Indians there was a red-haired woman living at the governor's house, so I came to see for myself. That was when I first watched you from across the river. I saw you sitting in your garden one day."

Temperance shook her head slowly. "Then why didn't you come for me?"

"I have told you why."

After a long silence, Temperance spoke again. "Will, you cannot live like that. Not among the savages."

"Yes, I can."

"It is not . . . fitting."

Will burst out laughing. "Ah, Temperance! What, pray tell, is 'fitting' in this place? You make me laugh!"

Temperance drew herself up coldly. "You know my meaning. An Englishman cannot live like a savage."

Will grew serious again. "Yes, he can, Temperance. In truth, I have all I need. I have plenty to eat, a stout roof over my head, a good fire in the winter, a cool river in the summer, and day after day to do as I please." His eyes sought Temperance's. "And it is better that George thinks I am dead and gone. You must promise me never to tell him, Temperance."

She nodded woodenly.

"I have good friends now among the Nansemonds, some of the truest and best I have ever had."

"Do you have . . . women?"

Will laughed. "What kind of question is that? Yes, my dear, I do . . . have women. Many, and often. They think it an honor." He smiled at her. "I cannot have you, Temperance. I have to have something."

Temperance did not answer, and silence fell between them once more.

A breeze caused the candle on the table to flicker and almost go out; the fire in the fireplace blazed up briefly in the draft.

"I must go," Will said.

"Where will you go?" Temperance asked. "How far is it?"

"Back to where I live, to my village, near thirty miles south of here. About two days' walk." Will smiled again. "They will miss me. I am their chief musician. They think my music is magic."

Once more, Temperance began to weep.

"Don't cry," Will said gently. "Please don't cry."

"But I cannot see you once, and know where you are, and never see you again!"

"Yes, you can. It is better than not knowing."

Temperance studied the ashes in the fireplace.

"No, it isn't," she said. "I . . . still love you."

He did not leave until just before daylight.

"May God have mercy on us for what we have done," he said. "I never should have come here."

"But God knows how I love you!" Temperance whispered.

"I'll come to you again. Don't worry." Will began to put on his clothes.

"But—"

He put his finger to his lips and smiled. "I shall know when it's safe," he said. "Every Indian in the Chesapeake knows the whereabouts of the governor."

POWHATAN VILLAGE
20 October 1621

 They were an unlikely pair: the rotund, jovial deputy in charge of the Indian college, and the lean, taciturn chief of all the tribes of the Powhatan Confederacy. George Thorpe and Opechancanough sat opposite each other in the latter's new house on a bright October morning.

"This is a good house," Thorpe said. "I knew that you would like an English house."

"A very good house," said Opechancanough.

"It is a house worthy of the chief of all the Powhatans."

"And the Pamunkeys and Chickahominies, and others to the east." Opechancanough drew on his pipe and smiled with narrowed eyes.

"Yes," Thorpe said. "This house will serve you well." He looked at the ceiling with its heavy square beams, the stone fireplace with the roasting spit and hooks for pots, the thick plastered walls, the two leaded-glass windows with their tiny, diamond-shaped panes. "The chimney seems to draw well enough," he said, looking at the crackling fire. "You have an oven for bread, too. Your women will like that."

"And the lock," Opechancanough said. "The lock and the key." He fingered the small brass key on a string of blue beads around his neck. "Locks are good things. We cannot make them ourselves, and I am grateful for this one. There are times when I want to lock my house."

"I am glad you like it," Thorpe said with a booming laugh. "You can lock your house up tight as a drum." Not that there was much to lock up, he thought. Deerskins and glass beads and a few knives taken from foreigners were all the treasures Opechancanough cherished. What Opechancanough loved best was power; he cared little for its trappings.

On his arrival in Virginia last year, Thorpe had set himself one goal: to win the friendship and the confidence of Opechancanough. If the chief be for us, he thought, who can be against us? And so he had offered, on his first visit to Powhatan Village, to have a proper English house built for the ruler of all the Powhatans. A small one-room house, but a real wattle-and-daub, thatch-roofed house, nonetheless. The lock for the door had been a stroke of genius. Thorpe had presented the key to the proud owner on completion of the house, and he had been unprepared for the effusive thanks and the profusion of smoked venison and dressed buckskins that came in return.

Thorpe had come to admire this shrewd old man. It was impossible to tell Opechancanough's age, but by the look of the wrinkled folds of skin that hung from his arms and drooped under his chin, Thorpe guessed him to be well past seventy. Threescore years and more had not dimmed his mind or dulled his desire to control the tribes of the Chesapeake. Thorpe found him surprisingly, uncannily intelligent. He knew, for example, the proper names of many of the fixed stars: He knew the North Star, and the constellation the English called the Great Bear he called Manguahaian, the Algonquin word meaning "Big Bear." And Opechancanough seemed to know geography, to grasp the vast distances of the Atlantic Ocean, and Virginia's relation to Europe and the West Indies. How, Thorpe wondered, had an Indian in Virginia come by such knowledge?

Moreover, the concept of a single all-powerful deity was not unknown to this pagan chieftain. In discussions with Thorpe, Opechancanough had even gone so far as to allow that the English God might be a better god than the gods of his own people.

"Your God," he said, "has given your people more good things than our gods have given us in this world. Ships. Guns. Locks with keys."

If God had given Opechancanough those things, Thorpe thought, this remarkable man might have taken over far more of the world. Even without them, Opechancanough had managed to forge alliances with neighboring tribes on the Rappahanoc, the Potomac, and the eastern shore of Chesapeake Bay, to create a buffer zone with the Chickahominies between his own people and the English at Jamestown, and to cement a "league of peace" between the Powhatans and the English in Virginia. And he had only been proclaimed the chief Powhatan a year and a half ago. His brother Wahunsonacock had tried for years to accomplish these things, but except for the fragile peace with the English that came about through John Rolfe's marriage with Pocahontas, the preceding Powhatan had not had many diplomatic successes. He had courted the powerful Chickahominies for years before the English came, to no avail. With five hundred warriors at the ready, the Chickahominies felt strong enough to act independently until the English encroachments made them uneasy. But it was Opechancanough, not his brother, who persuaded them it would be to their advantage to make friends with these English settlers, and in return for that advice they made Opechancanough their ruler, calling him "King of the Ozinies." Opechancanough now held the reins of power, and the allegiance of some five thousand Indians scattered over tidewater Virginia.

"The English have gunpowder," the old chief said wistfully. "What good are arrows against guns? It is much better for our people to be friends now, and live in peace, than to make war."

"You are a wise man, Opechancanough," said Thorpe.

But Opechancanough seemed not to hear him. He was staring thoughtfully out the window. "Then the prophecy will not come true," he said.

George Thorpe felt a sudden foreboding. "What prophecy?"

The old man looked at him with hooded eyes—the eyes of a snake. "The prophecy of the three invasions."

"What is that?"

"It has come down to us from many years, from priests who lived alone in the woods by the great Bay of Chesapeake and studied the signs. Three times foreigners would come here in their great ships from across the ocean, three times they would come ashore. Two times, our people would drive them away, but the third time, the foreigners would stay and take our land

and kill our people." Opechancanough took a long pull on his pipe.

"But that prophecy is already false," Thorpe said, "from its beginning. We came here, but your people have not driven us away."

"Ah, no, my friend. You are wrong." Opechancanough narrowed his eyes. "You are not the first strangers to come here."

"What do you mean, we are not the first?"

"The first ones we killed. That was long years ago. They were not from your country. They were Spanish, not English. They were Catholic priests, and they went among the Pamunkeys."

Thorpe was dumbfounded. How did this old Indian chief speak so knowledgeably about Europeans? "The Spanish would still like to plant a colony here," he said. "But these who came—you say you killed them?"

"They were killed."

"Well, all the same, that does not prove the prophecy true," Thorpe said uneasily, "unless there were others before us."

"There were."

George Thorpe felt the hairs on the back of his neck rise. "Who?"

"A whole village of English—living among the Chesepians near the great bay. We burned their town." Opechancanough spoke with quiet satisfaction.

"When was this? Did any live?" Thorpe was awestruck.

"Some, for a little while, maybe."

"But when was that?"

"It was the year that John Smith and the three English ships came to Jamestown. They never saw the other English."

"That 'whole village of English' would have been the people from Roanoke," Thorpe said slowly. He looked Opechancanough in the eye. "Why did you kill them? What harm had they done you?"

Opechancanough's eyes glittered. "They had come here. That was enough. They were the second invasion that the prophecy foretold." He folded his arms across his chest.

"I see." Thorpe, not to be outdone, folded his arms across his chest, too.

"And we—I mean the settlement at Jamestown and all the others that grew from it—we are the third invasion."

"Yes."

"Well, this time the prophecy is wrong," Thorpe said with a hollow-sounding chuckle. "The people who made that prophecy did not reckon on our becoming friends, did they?" He smiled, but Opechancanough, puffing solemnly on his pipe, did not smile back.

"You are not going to drive us out," Thorpe went on, "and we are certainly not going to drive you out. There is land enough here for all of us to live in friendship. Our children and your children will grow up together in peace." He rose from the table. "Let this house be a sign of our friendship." He smiled and held out his hand to Opechancanough. "I must get back. You must come and see the college land soon."

"I will."

Opechancanough, watching the Englishman go, puffed on his pipe. When George Thorpe had vanished among the trees on the path to Charles City, he laid down his pipe. Then he smiled, allowing a curl of smoke to escape his lips.

CHARLES CITY
16 November 1621

 "I am glad you came, George, but I hope you're wrong." Nathaniel Causey slapped Governor Yardley on the back. "Have you been to see the rest of the Council about this?"

"No, you are the first. But I aim to visit the others as soon as possible."

"Well, you can stay the night here, and we can talk. Besides, I want to show you my new tobacco sheds."

"Why, it's George Yardley! What a nice surprise!" Thomasine Causey, her sharp features softened by a smile, swept into the hall and held out both hands to the governor.

He bowed low and kissed both her hands. "You are looking well, Thomasine. I wish I had come on a pleasanter mission."

"What in the world—is something wrong with Temperance? The children?"

"No, no. They are quite well. I have come because I have reason to suspect an Indian attack."

"No!" Thomasine was incredulous.

"Yes," her husband said. "There are rumors, anyway, and enough of them to be taken seriously." He turned to George. "Come and sit by the fire and have something to warm you, and tell us about all this. I've a jug of corn liquor just waiting to be opened."

"This house is small," Thomasine said apologetically. "But Nathaniel wanted to move up here before the next planting season, so we are just making do. 'Causey's Care,' we call this place, and we've plenty to care for." She waved her thin hands around the room, which contained a table, three joint stools, a chair, and a court cupboard with a pewter charger on its top shelf.

"We've not even had any company to serve on that charger yet," she said. "I brought it from the house in Jamestown, and it has just sat up there unused."

"Well, get it down and polish it up, and load it with some victuals," Nathaniel said jovially. "George shall be our first guest." He motioned for George to take the only chair. "We intend to break ground for the real house in the spring, as soon as the weather warms up."

"It won't be as fine as Flowerdew, but it will do for us," Thomasine said. "Plenty of room for us and Thomas, and for any more of us that might come," she said wistfully. Thomas was nine, but the Causeys had not yet given up the hope of having another child.

"Have a drink, George." Nathaniel Causey poured from an earthenware jug into two pewter cups.

"I'll leave you two to talk while I see about our dinner." Thomasine, following her husband's suggestion, took the large round charger tray off the cupboard and departed for the kitchen.

"To your good health," Nathaniel said, lifting his cup to George.

"And to yours." George took a large swallow and closed his eyes appreciatively as the liquor went down. "That is good stuff," he said.

"Thanks. I made it the way George Thorpe told me." Causey grinned. "Corn mash. Now tell me what the devil these savages are up to." Nathaniel Causey was a peaceable man. Unlike George Yardley and some others, he was not in the least fond of soldiering. If the truth were known, he did not even relish hunting. The sight of blood made him sick. "What makes you think there will be trouble? The league of peace is still in effect, is it not?"

"Oh, yes. But it is mightily strained at present. There has been no progress in finding the bodies of those three men from Berkeley Hundred that Nemattonow—Jack of the Feather—is said to have killed. There are people at Berkeley Hundred who will swear that he was there, and that he took the three men out hunting, and neither he nor they came back. But I cannot find Jack of the Feather to question him, and Opechancanough refuses to speak with me. That makes me fear trouble's afoot. Opechancanough was to have his men search for the bodies."

"But Nemattonow's a renegade, is he not? What was it Opechan-canough said to the Council meeting—that Nemattonow was 'far out of his favor'?"

"Be that as it may, we cannot punish Nemattonow unless the bodies are found. Opechancanough claims that they will have bullet wounds, not arrow marks, which would mean that they were not killed by an Indian."

"And if they have arrow marks?"

"Then we can try Nemattonow—Jack of the Feather—for murder."

Nathaniel took a sip of corn liquor and frowned. "That is a serious matter, but I warrant Opechancanough will not break the treaty over one man's guilt or innocence."

George held his cup in both hands, swirling its contents round and round. "If he is planning to move against us, this would be the time, with my term ending and Wyatt taking over as governor. I don't like it, and I don't like Jack of the Feather, either." He stared into his cup. "I want you to be on your guard, Nat, in case anything happens. You are in a remote area, mind you. How many men are here on your place?"

"Four. Five, if you count me. But I'm a damned poor shot; you know that."

"I should keep a watch, if I were you, for the next few weeks, at least, until this Jack of the Feather matter is settled. Your men can take turns."

"That will upset Thomasine."

"Better upset than—surprised."

At that moment, Thomasine came in to announce that dinner was ready, and no more was said.

"Did you get the Indian affairs settled?" Thomasine's question was offhand; it was obvious that she was not much concerned about the answer.

"Yes," said her husband. "Yes, we did. Come and have some roast pork, George."

FLOWERDEW
20 November 1621

 "George, you're wet to the skin!" Temperance said, pulling off her husband's sodden cloak. She touched his cheek. "And cold as ice!"

"There was ice," he said hoarsely. "Sleet mixed in with the rain, but it melted when it hit the ground."

"Elizabeth, go and make a hot milk posset, and put plenty of wine in it. And tell Josefina to bring a basin of hot water in here by the fire as quick as she can. And a blanket." Temperance began to undo the fastenings of his quilted jerkin. "You should not have been out today with that cough, even if the weather had been good."

"I had to," George said. "You know that."

"No, I don't know that," Temperance said. "I know that you can come down with the ague if you don't watch out." She was unfastening the laces of his jerkin.

"Samuel!" She called over her shoulder. "Samuel! Come and take off Master Yardley's boots."

"You needn't make such a fuss," George said weakly, but he allowed her to push him down onto the big high-backed settle by the fire, and he allowed Samuel to pull off his boots. Samuel was a good boy, he thought, always quick and quiet. His term of service would be up next year, and George wondered how he would ever replace him.

"There you are, sir." Samuel pushed a lock of blond hair out of his eyes and stood up straight. "Anything else?"

"No, Samuel," Temperance said. "Thank you. Put those boots upstairs, not too close to the fire."

Blanket and basin appeared, followed close on by the posset, and George gave himself up gratefully to Temperance's ministrations. Stripped of his wet clothes, wrapped snugly in a blanket, with his feet in a basin of hot water, he sipped the posset and began to feel a creeping warmth. Temperance, of late, had become especially attentive to his needs, and that in itself made him feel better.

"How are the children?" he said. "I only see them when they are asleep nowadays."

"They are well," Temperance said, "and they miss you. That is what you get, traipsing all over the countryside day and night."

George sighed, and the sigh turned into a coughing fit.

"You see?" Temperance said, taking the posset out of his hands so he would not spill it.

"I'll be well enough, come morning," he said at last. "I wrote to the Company that I would go myself to every settlement, and I will. I have to."

"But someone else could tell them—some of the other Council members. John Pory, for instance. He'd go."

"No, I want the warning to come from me, and I want to see for myself that the settlements have enough supplies and powder in case of an attack. It will be my last act as governor. Then, when Francis Wyatt comes, I can tell him that I myself have inspected every settlement and can give him an accurate count of the people and weapons in it. And it will do no harm for the Indians to know that I have been to warn all our people."

Every Indian in the Chesapeake knows the whereabouts of the governor.

Temperance thought of Will's words to her. Since their first meeting four weeks ago she had seen him only once, but the guilt was making her a better wife, prompting her to run to the door when George came home. It even endowed her with a new tenderness and passion in their lovemaking. She almost wished that he would notice the change and remark on it.

But he was preoccupied with the transfer of power to the new governor, Sir Francis Wyatt, and with the building of their new house in Jamestown, and with the curing of some thirty thousand pounds of tobacco now drying in the sheds at Flowerdew, Hog Island, and his plantation across the river. If prices held, he stood to clear about four thousand pounds sterling this year. Nearly everyone was taking advantage of the profit margin, and while John Rolfe had sent four barrels of Virginia tobacco to England in 1614, this year the colony's planters would send close to sixty thousand pounds. Plantations were scattered all up and down the James River—isolated and unprotected.

"I'll go down to Jamestown on the morrow," George said, "and then to Martin's Hundred and across to Point Comfort." He coughed again, and Temperance frowned. "But if I'm no better, perhaps I shall do as you say, and send Pory to the Eastern Shore instead of going myself. That's a long, cold sail across the bay."

"Good," Temperance said cheerfully. "After all, John is your cousin by marriage, and you did get him the colony secretary's post. He ought to do most anything you say."

"Well, he can go to the Eastern Shore. There are not many people settled there yet. But there are nearly fourscore at Martin's Hundred, and all their houses are out in the open on that flat riverbank, with a rise in the land behind them and forest all around—I hate to think how easy it would be for Indians to surprise them. They are so mad to plant tobacco, they don't keep watches on that rise as they ought." George shrugged.

"They want what you have, George." Temperance smiled and looked around them at the trappings of wealth: a marble mantelpiece, oak paneling, velvet curtains, a cupboard full of silver and pewter. In the kitchen and buttery, a profusion of meat and cheese and ale, the finest claret and sack money could buy, marchpane candies and crystallized fruits from London; in the chests upstairs, silks and velvets and gold lace; damasks and satins and fine Holland linens. "Everybody wants a good house, and good food and drink, and good clothes," Temperance said.

Except Will, she thought. Except Will.

"But they should be growing enough food to last them through the winter, so they don't have to beg from the Indians," George said. "And too many of them are spending just as foolishly as they earn—buying fancy clothes that are far above their station. Look at Harmon Harison, with his three hundred acres. He has bought Jane a red silk gown and a pearl comb for her hair, and yet he and John Martin had to go and steal corn from the Warraskoyacks." George frowned. "That reminds me. I had near forgotten Harison. His place is all by itself, and all he has is four men and his son—a lad not turned ten yet. I shall stop there on the way to Point Comfort."

"You had better go to sleep right now, if you're aiming to do all that tomorrow," Temperance said. "I'll go and tell Elizabeth to warm the bed."

A moment later, when Temperance came back into the room, George caught her hand, kissed it, and drew her down on his lap. "You are so good to me," he said. "What would I do without you? How did I ever do without you?"

"Oh, you did well enough," she said lightly, ruffling his hair. "And you could do it again, if you had to."

George tucked his arm around her waist possessively. "Thank God I don't have to. Thank God I have you."

Temperance gave his hair an affectionate tug. Above his head, where he could not see it, her face had remorse in every line. "You had better have me upstairs," she said with forced gaiety. "Come along."

Upstairs, Elizabeth Jones moved the warming pan back and forth rapidly between the two feather beds in the big bedstead. In winter they used two feather ticks; one to sleep on, and one light one on the top for extra cover, with the blankets and silk coverlet on top of that. Elizabeth had the pan almost glowing hot, and she moved it in broad strokes. She was glad that Temperance had asked her, not Ata, to warm the bed tonight. If the truth were known, Elizabeth was violently jealous of Ata, and she was hurt that Temperance constantly asked that black woman to brush her hair and help her dress—things Elizabeth herself had always taken pride in doing. Now there was Ata, always at Temperance's elbow, and Josefina to see to the babies. Elizabeth felt left out.

Even in the kitchen, there was new help: A husband and wife named John and Margery Blewet, who had kept a cookshop in Eastcheap near Candlewick Street in London, had been brought over by Master George to take charge of the cooking at Flowerdew. Elizabeth was supposed to preside over all these servants as housekeeper, but she did not like that sort of work. She looked forward to next year, when she, like Samuel Garrett, would finish her seven-year term of service and could set out on her own. Maybe by then she would find a man who would marry her. Most of them just laughed when she mentioned marriage. But Master George never laughed at her, and was always kind to her. She slid the warming pan up and down a few extra times on his side of the bed. He had a bad cough, and he had been out in the cold all day. Elizabeth didn't care if Temperance's side of the bed was warm or not. Mistress Temperance had someone else to warm her bed when Master George was away. Elizabeth knew. She had suspected something when Temperance took to bolting the door to her bedchamber, and then one morning just before daylight, unable to sleep, Elizabeth had stood at her window downstairs and had seen something that made her heart stand still: Master Will Sterling, the one that was supposed to be dead, was climbing down the vines from the gallery wall.

Elizabeth thought that Master George ought to know, but then, she thought, it would make him so unhappy.

JAMESTOWN
14 March 1622

 David Sprat and Walter Watkins had not known each other before they were signed on by the Virginia Company as "duty boys," so named, ostensibly, because that was the name of the ship that would take them and forty-eight others like them to Jamestown in the summer of 1620. But the name carried multiple meanings: The *Duty* carried them to Virginia; the duty done by the well-meaning London constables who rounded them up and sent them there; the duty awaiting the boys when they got there. Homeless youths, wandering the streets and living by their wits, they were being sent to learn honest work, the promoters said. It was honest work, true enough, but it was hard work: bending over hundreds of straggly tobacco seedlings in huge wooden flats, watering them, weeding them, transplanting them, one by one, into the fields where they would then have to be weeded and tended some more, till they grew to be seven or eight feet tall, and then they had to be cut, one by one again, in the hot August sun, and carefully hung in bunches to dry in ovenlike sheds.

But for David and Walter, Gabriel Morgan made all this drudgery bearable. He paid ten pounds apiece for the two fifteen-year-olds on the pier at Jamestown, promptly put them in his dugout canoe, handed each a paddle, and told them to head upstream. When they reached his place, some eight miles above Jamestown, he took them in and fed them venison and pork ribs and ale—all they could hold. The next day he taught them how to fish; the day after that, he showed them how to shoot his musket. The day after that, he put them to work in his tobacco fields. He treated his duty boys like brothers, not servants, and they worshiped him.

That was why, on this windy March morning, they were overjoyed to see a lone figure in a gray woolen cap paddling a dugout downriver. Morgan had gone off a week ago with the tall Indian named Nemattonow, known as Jack of the Feather, to do some trading on the Pamunkey River. This time Jack of the Feather had left his elaborate headdress and swan-feather cape at home, and had come to take Morgan to a village up on the Pamunkey, where there were many beaver skins to be had. Gabriel had said he reckoned to be gone four days, and on the fifth day, when he had not returned, the boys had kept an anxious watch on the river.

"It's him, I trow!" David said.

"Yeah, that's his cap." Walter held his hand up to his eyes and squinted. But when the canoe drew nearer, they saw that it was not Gabriel Morgan who wore the cap.

"Damnation! That's not Gabriel, it's that Indian!"

"Something's amiss!"

"Why is he wearing Gabriel's cap?"

"Go get the pistol!" Walter said.

When Jack of the Feather reached the house, they were waiting for him. David was holding Gabriel's pistol cocked and ready.

"Where is Gabriel?"

The Indian looked solemn. "Dead. Bad sickness, two days." Under the gray wool cap, the dark face was impassive. He took a step toward David Sprat. Under the beaded vest he wore, the powerful muscles of his shoulders and biceps tensed, rippling under the smooth brown skin. His eyes, now fastened on the barrel of the pistol, glittered like the eyes of an adder about to strike. Suddenly, his hand shot out, and he grabbed the gun by the end of the barrel and forced it toward the floor.

"Watch out!" Walter lunged for him, but with little effect. Jack of the Feather held David's arm and was trying to wrest the pistol from his grasp. With his free hand, David tried to shove the Indian's head upward and backward, while Walter tried to pull him off from behind.

Then the gun went off.

Jack of the Feather, a look of surprise on his face, reeled backward and dropped his arms. There was a small hole about the size of a bean in his vest on the left side. Bewildered, he looked down and covered the hole with his hand. Below it, at the edge of his vest, a trickle of blood appeared. It was a thin red line at first, then a wide ribbon that ran down, staining the buckskin at his waist. He fell heavily on one knee. Then, without a sound, he toppled sideways and lay motionless, arms across his chest, legs drawn up, eyes open, staring straight ahead. In the silence, the only sounds were the sounds of the boys' panting from exertion and the wounded Indian's gasping.

"He's bleeding bad."

Nemattonow's eyes did not move, but his lips did.

"Help," he whispered. "Help me."

"We can't do nothing for him," David said. "He needs a surgeon."

"We best take him to Jamestown," Walter said suddenly.

He bled more as they dragged him to the canoe, leaving a line of dark red splotches on the path. With a good deal of difficulty, they got him into the dugout and laid him out full length, with his head on a wadded-up blanket. His eyes were closed now; he seemed to have lost consciousness. The boys took their places and began to paddle in uneasy silence. Under their now-expert handling, the canoe with its grisly burden rode the down-stream current swiftly.

The sun was high overhead when they reached the pier at Jamestown. Two ships rode at anchor there, and various sailors, some idling on the decks, some clambering about in the riggings, hailed the dugout as it approached.

"What, ho!"

"Hey, they've got somebody lying down—somebody sick or hurt!"

"Looks like an Indian!"

When they reached the bank, several pairs of willing hands steadied the canoe.

"Who is he?"

"Who shot him?"

"It's Nemattonow—Jack of the Feather!"

"What is going on here?"

The boys saw a dark-haired man in a long red cloak striding down the pier. Just behind him was a younger and taller man with a blond beard. Both were wearing morions and breastplates.

"Ah! Here's trouble! It's Jack of the Feather!" Captain General George Yardley, who had retained his military title upon relinquishing that of governor, spoke to Lieutenant Tom Goodwyn. Then, turning to David and Walter, George said tersely, "What happened?"

But before they could answer, Dr. John Pott arrived and began pushing his way through the crowd. "Let me through, let me through." Pott spoke briskly, and when he reached the water's edge, he took command. "Let's get him ashore. You—and you—" He pointed to two burly sailors nearby. "You take him by the shoulders, and you take his legs." With others steadying the canoe, Jack of the Feather was lifted out and stretched out on the grass. He lay there like some fallen Titan, his feather collar askew, his beaded buckskin garments stained in dark wet blotches, his lithe power-ful body limp and helpless. "He's bled too much." Pott spoke with finality.

The Indian's chest rose and fell with his labored breathing, and then jerked in a kind of spasm. His mouth opened, and he tried to speak, but no sound came. He opened his eyes and looked at Dr. Pott with silent anguish, his lips desperately trying to form words. Pott held up his hand, motioning to the crowd for silence, and bent low to hear.

"Don't tell—" Nemattonow began, but he lacked the strength to continue.

"Don't tell . . . what?" Dr. Pott spoke gently. "What is it?"

With great effort, Nemattonow uttered a single word: "Bullet." He moved his head slowly from side to side.

Pott looked up at George. "What does he mean?"

"I suspect he means don't tell anyone he was hit by a bullet," George said. "I have heard he has always boasted to his people that he could not be hit by an English bullet. Now he does not want them to know."

Then Jack of the Feather suddenly began to hemorrhage from his mouth. He gasped loudly and rolled his head from side to side in a futile struggle. He coughed, and more blood bubbled from his mouth. His eyes, imploring, beseeching, searched the faces of those around him, and then, the seizure over, he fell back and lay still. Summoning the last of his strength, he whispered, "Bury . . . here."

They buried him as he had requested, in a grave near the English he had so often visited, under a small oak tree at the edge of the palisade.

"Bullet or no bullet," said Captain General Yardley, "this is not the last we will hear of Jack of the Feather. When Opechancanough hears of his death, there will be trouble. Mark my words."

FLOWERDEW
19 March 1622

 Will was fast asleep. He lay beside Temperance, one arm flung across her hips so that she was afraid to move for fear of disturbing him. He always slept soundly when he came to her, a deep, satisfied sleep that somehow pleased her to watch. She liked to think it was because of their lovemaking, but she knew that the likelier explanation was that he had covered nearly thirty miles— fifteen by canoe and twelve on foot—to reach her. It took him from daybreak to sunset, and then he had to bide his time in the woods, waiting for dark. After dark he would slip closer to the house, concealing himself in a clump of holly bushes near the corner closest to Temperance's room, watching until the lights began to go out. Then he would imitate the soft, low call of a barn owl twice, and watch for Temperance to open the door of her room to the second-floor gallery. George was away from Flowerdew these days more often than he was at home, which made it easier. He was no longer governor, but as a Council member, he had to attend regular meetings in Jamestown. If the Council was sitting and the moon was in its first quarter, Temperance knew to listen for the owl after dark. They had managed three of these foolhardy trysts since Will's first visit last September.

Now it was almost time for him to leave. She remembered the first time she had looked at his face while he slept: the time she had nursed him when his leg was wounded, in the beginning of that terrible winter at Jamestown. Looking back, she could not quite remember when it was she knew that she loved Will, or if there had been a time when she had stopped loving him. All she knew was that she loved him now, and that she was beginning to love herself and everyone around her because of him. She was beginning to love George again because of him. That did not make sense, but it was true. Through Will's eyes, she saw George's steadfastness, his sweetness, his dogged determination to please her, his devotion to Argall and Elizabeth, and for the first time, she was grateful.

Gently, she touched Will's tousled hair. She knew she must wake him; it would be daylight soon. He snuggled deeper into the pillows, but his hand began moving up and down the curve of her hip.

"It's time," she whispered.

"Next time is your turn to come to me," he said drowsily. "I'll not turn you out. I'll let you stay as long as you want to."

Temperance laughed. "But I don't know the way."

"I can show you. I can tie a string from one of the holly bushes, and all you have to do is follow it." He continued to stroke her hip. For a while longer, they lay in contented silence. Then he spoke again. "Temperance." His tone had lost its lightness.

"What?"

"What are we to do?"

"About what?"

"Us."

"I don't know."

Will sighed. "All I know is that once I made George a cuckold unwittingly; now I do it deliberately, with malice aforethought. God will punish us, Temperance. You and I will pay for our sins one day."

They were both silent.

"You know," Temperance said, "if it hadn't been for that storm, and the *Sea Venture* getting wrecked, none of this would have happened. You would likely be married to someone else by now, and I would be with George. Perhaps we would all be friends. And you would never have loved me." She sighed. "It was God who sent that storm. Do you think God meant all this to happen?"

"I don't know, Temperance, I don't know." Will toyed with the ribbons of her shift.

Temperance went on. "I loved George, and then he was lost, and then I loved you, and he came back, and then—dear God, what were we supposed to do? It all happened because we loved each other. We never meant to do wrong, did we?"

"But now we do," Will said in a whisper, "now we do."

Temperance shook her head. "When I was a little girl, and my mother used to tell me about sin, I never thought I would commit any. It seemed so easy to be good. There were the Ten Commandments, all laid out in the Bible, and we learned to recite them, my sisters and my brother and I. But the Ten Commandments were things no one would want to do. I never had any desire to worship false idols, and I knew telling lies would catch me up sooner or later, and I certainly had no call to steal or kill. All of those things were bound to be unpleasant, so I could be a good little girl with no trouble at all." She sighed again, and with one finger, traced the line of Will's cheek and jaw. "What I didn't know then was that sin is . . . sweet." Temperance raised herself on one elbow so that she could look into his eyes. "Sin is something so sweet you cannot help doing it, and you keep on doing it even though you know you will burn in hell for it. You say to God, 'I know better than you what is good for me,' and then you hope to heaven the Scripture is wrong." She fell back on the pillows. "But you always know, deep down, that you are the one who is wrong."

Will leaned over and kissed her lightly. "And both of us know we cannot keep on doing this."

Half an hour later, Will swung his legs over the gallery wall, lowered himself by holding on to the vines that covered it, and then dropped to the ground. His moccasined feet landed lightly on the soft earth below, but not lightly enough.

Elizabeth Jones, lying half-awake in her bed, heard the soft thud and sat up with a start. It was what she had been hoping to hear. She had been watching and waiting ever since she had heard the bolt on Temperance's bedroom door slide home, some six hours earlier. Now, taking care not to stand too close to her window, she peered out. It was him, all right. Master Will. For a long time, Elizabeth had been trying to decide what she ought to do, knowing what she knew. Now she had decided, and the sweet revenge of it made her smile.

FLOWERDEW
20 March 1622

"It's Father coming!" Argall, playing with his building blocks on the front porch, was the first to see the bark's sails round Weyanoak Bend in the late afternoon sun. "Come, 'Fina! Come, Muffin! Father's here!" He shouted over his shoulder as he set off on his short, fat legs down the wide slope of lawn.

"Master George is home!" Josefina called in her soft voice in the direction of the house, without much assurance that anyone inside would hear. Temperance was in the kitchen, showing Ata the mysteries of jelly-making, while the Blewets tended a huge roast of beef; Elizabeth was upstairs counting linens; Samuel and John had gone across the river to inspect some repaired fences. But they all were expecting George. Temperance made certain that the entire household revolved around his homecomings. Josefina, picking up Elizabeth, hurried after Argall. He was jumping up and down at the edge of the pier, waiting for the *Temperance,* the small pinnace George had named for his wife after Elizabeth's birth, to come close enough to throw its line ashore and pull in.

"Ho, Bro!" George, standing on the foredeck as his crew dropped the sails, waved as the small ship neared its landing place. When it drew close enough, he climbed onto the bow gunwale, jumped down onto the pier, and scooped his son up in his arms. "What ho?" George said, and Argall, with a delighted giggle, echoed him: "What ho?"

"Now let's see Muffin," George said, setting Argall down and holding out his arms to take Elizabeth from Josefina. "Mmmmmm . . . Muffin!" George nuzzled his daughter, and, taking off his hat and handing it to Argall, he set his daughter on his shoulders. "Now let us go and see your mother."

Behind them, Tom Goodwyn and six sailors prepared to row the

Temperance across to the Weyanoak plantation on the other side of the river. She was usually moored at the Flowerdew pier, with the crew sleeping aboard her, but this time George was planning to remain at home at least a fortnight. It was springtime; the tender green buds of the dogwood trees were nearly ready to open; Temperance's daffodils showed pale yellow spears; the new-plowed furrows of the fields lay ready for seed. On the rise east of the house, his windmill, built as he had remembered the windmills he saw in the Netherlands in his youthful soldiering there, turned gently in the breeze, pumping water for the house. It was the only windmill in all Virginia, and he was immensely proud of it. Now, at last, he would be home long enough to enjoy it. The Council would not meet again for a fortnight, and Opechancanough, strange as it seemed, had said that the killing of Jack of the Feather, "being but one man, should be no occasion of the breach of the peace." George had long looked forward to this time at Flowerdew. He would have time to take Argall fishing, to play with Elizabeth, and best of all, to be with Temperance.

"You know," he said to her after dinner, "I think I shall send down to Jamestown for my horse. I used to ride him some there, but there is no point in leaving him there now. Then you and I can go riding together. We have never done that." He stretched his legs contentedly. "It is high time we did."

Temperance smiled at him. "You've hardly had the time."

"Ah, but now I'll make the time," he said. "Now that I am rid of the governorship, I can do many things I've not been able to. I intend to quit running down to Jamestown so often, and settle in here like a proper planter should."

Temperance smiled at him again, but a sinking sensation took hold of her insides, and the simulated hooting of a barn owl rang in her ears. She rose and, lightly kissing the top of his head, said, "Time for the children's prayers. I'll go and see to them, and then send for you."

Fondly, George watched her go, and then he leaned back against the settle in front of the fire and began to count his blessings. All a man could want, he had. He had never expected to be so happy in this world.

"Master George, I . . . have something to tell you."

It was Elizabeth Jones, looking agitated, twisting her hands in her apron. What now? George thought. Can it be she's found a husband—or carrying some man's child?

"Come in, Elizabeth," he said kindly. "What is it?"

Temperance knew something was wrong when he came upstairs. The children clung to him, shouting and laughing, but he responded to them absently, his eyes on her, searching her face, his mouth in a grim, taut line.

"Thank you, Josefina. I shall call you when we're done with prayers," Temperance said mechanically. When the children knelt beside their beds, she knelt, too, and held out her hand to George as was their wont. He did not take it. Instead, he clasped his hands in front of him on the bedcover. When Argall and Elizabeth bowed their heads, he buried his face in his hands. Temperance recited the prayers without knowing what she said, and George and the children repeated after her. A lump of fear, like a cold weight, was growing in her stomach. She went through the motions of saying good night to the children and calling Josefina.

As Temperance closed the door to the children's room, George took her by the elbow and steered her toward their bedchamber. She tried to tell herself that it could be something about the Indians that had upset him, perhaps a message he had received while she was upstairs. But she had not heard anyone come to the house.

"What is it, George?" She slid the bolt on the door and turned to face him. "Tell me what is wrong." The cold lump in her stomach had turned to ice, and breath was hard to come by.

"You use that bolt quite often when I am gone, don't you?" His voice was choked, but with pain, not anger. His eyes, fastened on Temperance's, had a look of sad resignation, not surprise, as though he had long been expecting this confrontation.

Temperance felt as if something deep inside her had suddenly melted and run into her veins, making her too weak to move. The secret had burst, bringing with it a dreadful sense of release. He had found out. The worst that could happen had happened. She bowed her head. She could not beg his forgiveness; what she and Will had done was beyond forgiveness. She could not pray; she could not cry. She could only stand there, struck dumb with guilt. Perhaps, she thought wildly, George might kill her. But he merely continued to look at her, inflicting a pain worse than that of a sword.

At last he said, "Elizabeth told me. Even *she* was shocked."

Temperance bowed her head even lower. She had never thought of it quite that way, but what he said was true. She was as bad—no, worse—than Elizabeth. Fornication was bad enough, but adultery was punishable by death. George walked over to the windows that opened onto the gallery and looked out. "Was this why you wanted me to build you a gallery?"

"No!" Temperance lifted her head. "No, George! You mustn't think that!"

"You've not given me much cause to think otherwise."

"I never meant it to happen. I swear it."

George laughed bitterly. "Spare me that, Temperance. Don't tell me that again. It was no good even the first time."

"This was my fault," she said. "Not Will's."

George leaned his head against the velvet curtains and closed his eyes. *My fault, George. My fault.*

"I don't want to speak of it, Temperance. There are no words for this." When he turned to face Temperance again, his eyes were cold and hard as slate. "I am going to Jamestown as soon as it's light," he said in a flat voice. "I intend to stay there a week." He paused and looked out the window again. "And when I come back, I expect you to have your belongings packed, and the children's things ready to travel. I want you gone from here." His voice quavered. "I don't care where you go; I just want you gone. You can take Ata with you, if you like."

"What about the children?" Temperance asked woodenly.

"I shall take them to live at Jamestown. Elizabeth and Josefina can look after them there as well as here." George crossed the room to where Temperance was standing. She had not moved from the spot near the door with the locked bolt. He stood in front of her, his face pale, drained of all emotion. His eyes met hers, but the look in them was curiously impersonal, like the expression of a fellow passenger in a coach. "Good-bye, Temperance." He slid the bolt to open the door, but stopped with his hand on the brass doorknob.

"Maybe you should go out there." He jerked his head in the direction of the gallery. "Maybe"—he spoke with a venom she had never expected in him—"maybe you'll hear an owl tonight."

Before Temperance could answer, he opened the door and left without looking back. His boots made a dismal tattoo on the polished oak stairs. Temperance stood very still. There was no feeling left in her. She stood by the door of her bedchamber, frozen in disbelief. She could neither move, nor cry, nor think. She stood there for a long time. Then, without undressing, she lay down on the bed and stared at the ceiling.

Downstairs, before a fire that had gone out, George sat by himself, drinking corn liquor out of a jug. When daybreak came, he got into a boat and rowed himself unsteadily across the river, where the *Temperance* rode at anchor.

POWHATAN VILLAGE
21 March 1622

It had taken twelve days, just as Opechancanough had predicted. Seven of his swiftest messengers had set out as soon as word of Nemattonow's murder reached him, and now the last of them had returned to Powhatan Village with the answer that all was in readiness. From the Pamunkeys and Potomacs to the far north and west, to the Chickahominies, the Paspaheghs, and Kecoughtans on the north side of the river, to the Nansemonds and Chesepians near the great bay itself, word came back that every werowance's warriors were prepared to move. The strategy and tactics had been carefully worked out half a year ago, when Opechancanough, as the Powhatan, had made his annual harvest time journey to receive tribute from the river tribes, the members of the Powhatan Confederacy. For months the werowances had been waiting eagerly for the sign from Opechancanough. Some were more eager than others: Kissanacomen, who would not forget George Yardley's slaughter of his unsuspecting Chickahominy braves; Wanaton, whose village John Martin and George Percy had seized long ago at Nansemond; Tanakato, ruler of the Warraskoyacks, whose men had been robbed of their corn by Harmon Harison, Tanx-Powhatan, whose people Thomas Gates had killed at Kecoughtan, had been waiting for a long time to rid the land of the English.

In the meantime, Opechancanough had continued to gull the colonists, humoring Councillor Thorpe with his plans for the Indian college, politely receiving emissaries from Sir Francis Wyatt, the new governor, assuring Captain General Yardley that the league of friendship was stronger than ever. At first Opechancanough had thought to move against the English when summer came, in order to let them do the work of plowing and planting the spring crops.

And then came Nemattonow's death.

Basamuck had brought the news, and for two days Opechancanough had neither eaten nor slept, mourning the loss of his only surviving son.

Nemattonow, the valiant warrior, the skillful hunter, the talented crafts-man, the cleverest, stealthiest observer of the English, was gone, shot by a pair of stupid boys in a freakish accident. Opechancanough could hardly believe it. And the worst of it all was that the English had buried Nematto-now, the son of the Powhatan, in a hole in the ground on their land.

But Opechancanough had never told them that Nemattonow was his son. Perhaps, had they known that, they might have sent his body back.

Perhaps Nemattonow had become overconfident, coming and going as he pleased among the English, wearing his elaborate swan-feather costume, reveling in being called Jack of the Feather, boasting that he was invincible, that no English bullet could harm him. But he had a right to boast, Ope-chancanough thought. Nemattonow had his father's magnificent physique and his mother's beauty of feature. If only he had taken a wife; if only he had left a child. Now there would be no sons to carry on the line. Even a girl-child would have been better than no issue at all, Opechancanough told himself. Now he was alone.

If it were not for the English, Opechancanough mused, his children might all be alive. And Pocahontas would be alive. Wahunsonacock, whose grief for her had hastened his death, might still be alive. Opossonoquonuske and her husband and her three children would be alive. Namontack would be alive. When he thought of all of his people who had died because of the English, Opechancanough's hatred of all these foreigners flamed hot within him, and he knew that the time had come.

On the third day after Nemattonow's murder, he had dispatched his messengers with their simple, deadly message to the river tribes; at mid-morning on the twenty-second day of the month, when the sun was halfway to its noontime meridian, the attack on the English would begin. Every English settlement for seventy-five miles along the river, from the Falls to the Bay of Chesapeake, would be destroyed; and neither man nor woman nor child spared. Surprise would work in the Indians' favor, and the slaugh-ter should be but the work of a moment.

JAMESTOWN
22 March 1622

Thank God for the moon, Richard Pace thought. Hanging high and full, it silvered the broad stretch of the James River in front of him, and gave him enough light to keep on course. If he let the current carry him too far to the south, he would overshoot Jamestown as he sometimes did even in daylight. But now there was no time to waste. He wished he had not asked for his land across the river from Jamestown; it was too isolated. Too far when trouble came. He pulled on the oars with all his strength, praying with each stroke: Please God, take care of Isabella, and let me be in time to warn the others. Chanco is a heathen savage, but he is a good boy. Help him to protect her, and keep my house safe. Please God, let me get to Jamestown and home again in time.

The current was swift, and the cold, dark water sucked at the oars with each pull he made. It was near three miles across the river between his hundred acres and Jamestown. Pace did not know what time it was. Judging from the moon, it could not be more than two or three hours until daybreak. There would be a little time, but not enough. Not time to get word downriver to Martin's Hundred, nor upriver to Charles City and Henrico. Damned treacherous Indians, he thought. Maybe Chanco's Indian friend was mistaken; maybe there was not going to be a surprise attack on all the English settlements at midmorning.

He pulled up at last to the high grassy bank near the Jamestown palisade and leaped out, splashing up to his knees in the cold water, to drag his boat ashore. No lights burned in the old watchtowers of the fort; with the Indians so friendly, no watches had been kept at night in over a year. Making sure that his oars were secure, he set off at a dead run past the palisade, down the path to the governor's house. There were no lights there, either. Panting, he seized the heavy brass knocker and let it fall once, twice, three times. The knocks sounded loud in the stillness, loud enough to wake the dead, he thought, and yet nobody came.

"Halloo!" he called, letting the knocker fall again. "Governor! Governor Wyatt!"

At last a disgruntled-looking servant boy opened the heavy oak door. He held up a candle and peered out at Pace. "What do you want with him this time of night? He's asleep, or trying to be."

"Indians!" Pace said, breathing hard. "Attacking in the morning—this morning!"

The boy blinked and gaped at him, owl-eyed.

Pace reached for the boy's shoulder and shook him. "Go . . . get . . . the governor! Hurry!" The boy skittered away, his shirt flapping about his thighs.

Soon the governor, moving with surprising speed for a heavyset man, came down the stairs, hastily pulling on a long, fur-edged robe, with the boy hurrying beside him, lighting his way.

"It's Pace, Governor—Richard Pace, from across the river. I've just got word of an Indian attack. They intend to strike this morning, all up and down the river."

"How do you know this?"

"My boy Chanco—he's an Indian boy—he told me. Another Indian at Perry's place told him. I came as quick as I could."

The governor and Richard Pace and the servant boy all looked at each other in flickering candlelight, their eyes shining with fear.

"God's blood!" The governor shook his head in disbelief.

"Now that you know," Pace said, "I need to get back. My wife has been ill, and there is no one with her but Chanco."

Governor Wyatt shook Pace's hand vigorously and clapped him on the shoulder. "Go, and Godspeed. You've done good service this day."

To the boy beside him, the governor said, "Go down and tell Captain General Yardley while I get dressed."

The boy looked down at his shirt and his bare legs. "What about me?" his adolescent voice made the last word a squeak.

"You can dress later!" Governor Wyatt gave him a shove. "Now, go and be quick!"

Two houses away, the captain general, who had not closed his eyes at all the night of his arrival in Jamestown, had finally sunk deep in the drugged sleep of exhaustion. He did not hear the governor's boy pounding on the door. He did not hear Lieutenant Goodwyn shouting as he raced up the stairs, and he did not stir when Goodwyn opened the door to his room. Not until Goodwyn shook him by the shoulder did he awaken.

"Captain Yardley, there's going to be an Indian attack." Like a bucket of cold water, the words brought George bolt upright, shaking his head.

"What?" his voice was thick with sleep.

"Someone came and told Governor Wyatt. He wants you."

George reached for his trunk hose and began pulling them on, tucking his shirt into their voluminous folds. "Who came? What did he say?" Boots, left by the bed, were hurriedly drawn on.

"Somebody from across the river. Some Indian gave it away." Goodwyn picked up the heavy quilted jerkin lying on a chest and held it for George, who stood up and thrust his arms through the armholes.

"I've been afraid of something like this," he said grimly. "Did he say where?"

"He said all up and down the river, sir."

All up and down the river.

"When—how soon?"

"This morning. Daybreak, I reckon."

There is not time to get to Flowerdew.

"We'll try to secure Jamestown, and get a boat out in each direction to warn as many as we can," George said. His mouth had gone dry, so dry he could hardly speak. "You can start with this house. Rouse the servants, and see that there is a musket and powder and shot for every man. Then meet me at Governor Wyatt's."

The governor, in full battle dress, breastplate gleaming, sword clanking at his side, was pacing up and down the length of his hall when George arrived.

"Damnation, Yardley! I never expected this! You said these savages were peaceful! Opechancanough said they were peaceful! What in hell has happened? Are they really going to attack?" The portly, peaceable Francis Wyatt was barely keeping panic at bay. He would not have accepted the governorship if he had known he would have to fight Indians. He had thought all that ended with the Indian Princess marrying Rolfe. "Damnation!" he said again, shaking his head so that his jowls flapped. He glared at George, as though it were all his fault. "Well, you're the captain general. What are we going to do?"

"Gather everyone inside the palisade," George said. "And give every man a gun. There are fifty muskets in the storehouse, and with the others already in people's hands, that should be enough."

"What about me?" Wyatt said nervously. "What do I do?"

George answered with faint scorn. "You get inside the palisade, too. You have a guard of twelve men, you know. They are supposed to protect you." As an afterthought, he added, "If you have any important papers in this house, take them with you, in case the Indians fire it."

"Where will you be?" Wyatt wanted to know. The governor had made no mention of trying to warn the other settlements.

"I shall be upriver," George said.

"What?"

"Upriver. I'll take my boat and try to get word to the plantations along the shore. And . . . my wife and children are at Flowerdew." In name at least, she was still his wife, he thought.

"Great God, man!" Wyatt bellowed. "You're the captain general! You ought to be here, protecting the seat of government! What am I to do, with Francis West up at Westover, and you gone to Flowerdew?"

"You can try me in a martial court later," George said evenly. "I'm going. And I'll send another boat downriver to get a warning to Martin's Hundred."

With that, he turned on his heel and left. Outside, the sun was already gilding the tops of the pine trees. The journey upriver, against the tide and current, would take at least three hours.

FLOWERDEW
22 March 1622

 The flock of whistling swans took off as Will's canoe approached them, rising into the pale dawn sky like so many kites, white wings spread wide, black feet tucked under. There were only about a dozen of them, but their loud "woo-howoo"—a baying sound, more than a whistling—had startled Will when they flew over him at dawn. They had passed him on the winding river, and had landed around a bend to feed, where he now startled them. These were the first of the season. The big white birds left the Chesapeake Bay every spring, flying north and west, to summer in some far-distant waters, and then they returned in the fall, usually just before the first frost. Uncanny how they knew when to come and go, he thought.

When he had heard the swans' first calls, he had thought they were the signals of Indian lookouts, and that the rumor of an attack was true after all. Now, relieved, he paddled steadily onward, praying that the story Wintako told was unfounded. Wahunsonacock's youngest son had come last night to the Nansemond village where Will lived with a chilling tale:

Opechancanough had long been planning a surprise attack on all the English settlements. He had sat in secret council with every werowance months ago, and the Indians of the village had kept it from Will, lest he betray this news to the English. But now the date was set, and the secret was out. As soon as he heard, Will had waited until dark and set out for Flowerdew.

He knew that George was at Jamestown: The *Temperance* had tied up at Jamestown pier two days ago. On hearing of the Indian plot, his first thought had been Temperance's safety, and whether his best course of action would be to head for Jamestown and tell George, or to go to Flowerdew and warn Temperance first. The latter plan had won. Temperance could alert the men on the plantation and the one across the river, and be as secure at Flowerdew as anywhere. And so, taking up his bow and tying a quiver full of arrows on his back, he had set out in the dark, trusting his knowledge of the river and the light of the moon to see him safe.

By midmorning, he would be at Flowerdew.

Ordinarily, Temperance awoke with the sun. But this morning she had slept so late that Ata had to rouse her.

"It's after nine of the clock," Ata said in her soft voice. "Are you well?"

"Yes, I feel better."

Ata knew. She had rubbed her mistress's back when Temperance, unable to sleep for two nights after George left, had asked her to spend the night in her room; she had held her mistress in her arms, cradling her like a child when the tears finally came.

"I am glad," Ata said. "I brought you some tea with honey." She set the steaming cup down on the chest beside the bed and straightened Temperance's pillows.

"Thank you, Ata. And . . . thank you for last night. You are a great comfort."

"I am glad," Ata said again. "I will do anything for you. You know that."

"Yes." Temperance sipped her tea and said, "Before you go, would you lay out my riding clothes? I'll see the children, and then I think a ride would do me good."

"I shall tell Samuel to watch."

"No. There is no need for that. I don't need anyone to watch me ride."

"But Master George—" Ata caught herself.

Temperance lifted her chin. "Master George," she said, "has no say in the matter. I have been riding horses since I was ten. I shall be perfectly safe. And anyway, the Indians are at peace with us."

Down in the kitchen, Margery Blewet had other ideas. "I don't care what the mistress says," she said to Ata. "She's not herself, and I intend to set myself out on that porch and watch after her."

The house servants knew something had happened between the master and the mistress of Flowerdew, and they had already taken sides: Ata, Margery, and Josefina were for Temperance; Samuel, John, and Elizabeth, of course, were on George's side. Margery wiped her meaty red hands on her apron. "I can peel some turnips while I watch," she said.

It was a fine spring morning, sunny and cool, with a light breeze that smelled of new-plowed earth and budding green things. The river sparkled blue-gray and silver in the sunlight, and on the other side, Temperance could see the men working in the fields, setting tobacco plants. Behind them, the woods showed bits of color: the delicate new green of barely unfurled leaves, and here and there the snowy white of dogwood blossoms. Temperance urged her horse into a canter. George had tried to persuade her to order riding clothes and sidesaddle in the new fashion for women, but she had adamantly refused. "I am not riding any horse sideways in a long, trailing skirt with my knee hooked over a knob," she had said. Now she wondered if George would let her keep her horse.

The past two days had gone by in a blur. A week, George had said. She had a week to arrange the rest of her life. Maybe he would have pity on her and let her live at Flowerdew, for the children's sake. But there was Will to consider, and she did not even know where he was, or how to contact him. When he knew, would he want her to come and live with him, among the Indians? He certainly could not live at Flowerdew. It was an impossible muddle, and the more she thought about it, the more confused she became. She had thought briefly of going back to England, to Thickthorne, where her parents were, but could not bear the thought of being so far from Argall and Elizabeth. Or she could go and live with Meg at Jamestown. And when she thought about it, she did not really want to leave Virginia, either. Too much of her life was here now.

At the river's edge, she slowed the mare to a walk and turned to look back at the house. With its tall stone chimneys at each end and its double front porches, it was a handsome house, not nearly so grand as Thickthorne, but impressive in its roughhewn way nonetheless. Shading her eyes against the morning sun, she looked to see if Margery was still peeling turnips on the porch. She saw Margery, but she was sitting in a peculiar position with her head to one side, as though she had fallen asleep. Temperance reined in the mare and stopped, squinting to see better, and then she saw it:

Protruding from Margery's breast, its long, thin shaft barely visible from a distance, was an Indian arrow.

"Hell's bells," she said unbelievingly. "Hell's bells!" Then, digging her spurs deep, she crouched low over the mare's neck and rode at full gallop toward the house.

BERKELEY HUNDRED
22 March 1622

 "That was an excellent breakfast, Arthur, the best you've ever done." George Thorpe wiped his mouth with a linen napkin, folded it carefully, and laid it on the table. "Good fresh hen's eggs, well cooked. Not bad at all," he said with a chuckle. "At home I used to have nothing but oatmeal and black bread at breakfast. Where did you learn to cook?"

"My mother, sir. She showed me when she was ill. I cooked for her."

"Ah, yes. Of course," Thorpe said quietly. Arthur Mouse's mother, his only relative, had died a lingering death in Colchester the year before last, and Arthur, alone in the world at twenty, had adventured his small capital to come to Virginia. He and Thorpe had crossed on the same ship, and Thorpe had enlisted him to help with the Indian college. Now the two men lived in a house at Berkeley Hundred, ten miles east of Henrico and about twelve miles from the lands for the proposed Indian college. Since there were as yet no buildings and no students at the college, Thorpe had settled temporarily near the forks of the James and the Appomattox rivers in order to travel easily to the various settlements. Next year he would move to Henrico. The James River at Berkeley Hundred was both straight and wide, well over a mile across, and one could see an approaching vessel for a good mile in either direction.

After his breakfast, Thorpe strolled outside to enjoy the fine spring morning. He felt good about what he had accomplished in a year's time among the Indians. He had won Opechancanough's trust and friendship by building him a house with a lock and key; he had marked off where the first buildings would be on the college lands, and he had actual promises that when Indian youths began to attend the college, an equal number of English boys would live among the Indians. He was eager for that experiment to begin. Both sides had so much to learn from the other. It was a pity, he thought, that the two races had not been friendly all along. All it took was a little kindness and understanding, such as he had given to Opechancanough.

As Thorpe walked down the path that led to the river, he saw three dugout canoes coming upriver. They appeared to be full of Indians. He could see their feather headdresses in the distance. They were probably going to Charles City, three miles beyond Berkeley Hundred, to trade. But they might stop at Berkeley, too. He hurried back to his house. Arthur was cutting up onions to put in a pot of soup.

"Finish that up and come outside," Thorpe said cheerily. "We may be having company. Three canoeloads of Indians are headed this way. Have we got any more of those tin whistles? We could give them some if we have enough." Cheap tin whistles from Fleet Street made more friends than glass beads among the Indians, Thorpe had found.

Sure enough, he had been right. The Indians, a dozen Pamunkey braves of varying ages and sizes, came ashore. Four of them Thorpe knew well. They were good friends of Opechancanough's, and he had tried to teach them the Lord's Prayer in their native tongue. He spoke to them now in his halting Algonquin, and they replied that they had fish to trade. A good catch of fresh rockfish, they said.

"Come in, come in." Thorpe beckoned them inside. When they looked inside and saw Arthur, they smiled broadly to each other. Opechancanough's four men went inside, and the others, as if by prearranged plan, headed toward the handful of houses that constituted the rest of Berkeley Hundred. As the Indians crowded into the small house, one of them, spying the knife Arthur had been using on the onions, seized it and slipped it under his buckskin vest. Another took a large carving knife and did likewise.

Arthur saw them. In the congenial-sounding hubbub of voices, he hissed in Thorpe's ear, "They took our knives. They're up to something. Get outside, quick!"

Thorpe frowned at him. "Nonsense. They just want to trade."

"You can stay if you want to, but I'm leaving." Arthur forced a smile in the direction of the Indians and backed out the door. As soon as he got outside, he turned and ran as fast as he could toward the distant houses of Berkeley Hundred.

Thorpe watched him go and then turned back to his Indian guests and shrugged. "He is in a hurry about something," he said with a smile. "Sit down and I'll show you these whistles. Then we'll go look at your fish." He seated himself at the table and motioned for them to do likewise. Two sat down across from him, but the other two, one on either side of him, did not sit down. As Thorpe began to take the tin whistles out of a box on the table, he did not see the four Indians grin and nod at each other.

When the tall Indian stabbed him in the back with his own carving knife, he did not even cry out, and when the other Indian grabbed him by the hair and cut his throat, his face wore a look of utter bewilderment. The bright blood spurted from his jugular vein onto the table when they let his head fall forward. The four Indians clasped hands over his dead body in a gesture of triumph. Taking the box of tin whistles, they were about to leave when the Indian who had wielded the carving knife spoke.

"This fat Englishman talked too much. Let us do to him what he wanted to do to the English dogs!" Last year, when two ferocious mastiffs at Henrico had frightened some visiting Indians, Thorpe had offered to have the dogs gelded to make them docile. The indignant owners refused, but the Indians, who had never heard of such a practice, were highly amused. The story of Master Thorpe and the English dogs had circulated all over the Chesapeake.

The other three laughed and slapped each other on the back. Now they would play a good joke on the English.

"Let us see what he has between his legs!"

"I'll bet it's no bigger than the dogs' parts."

"Look at that. Fat men are never well hung."

"His mouth was bigger. Put those in there."

"Let's take this to Opechancanough. He can dry it and hang it in his house!"

The four Indians left the body of George Thorpe lying face up on the blood-soaked earth floor of his house. One small part of him they had carried away with them, and another part they had stuffed into his mouth. His eyes, wide open, still wore their expression of surprise.

NEAR MULBERRY ISLAND
22 March 1622

 Harmon Harison was pleased with himself. He and his four men, with a little help from his son, had brought in a harvest of four thousand pounds of prime tobacco last year, and his profit was 375 pounds sterling. This year he had bought two more workers, good strong fellows with seven-year indentures, and he had increased his tobacco acreage by fifty more acres. With any luck, if prices held, he might get five hundred pounds sterling for this year's crop. He was already making plans to enlarge his house, to build a summer kitchen, and perhaps a new barn. His new tobacco shed, half again the size of the first one, was nearly finished. It would be ready long before time for the fall curing. Twenty thousand tobacco plants, the yield from his 250 acres, would need a lot of room to dry. And he was already scheming to get more land. Three hundred acres would have been a handsome estate in England, but in Virginia there were already men with acreages in the thousands. George Yardley, for instance. He must have close to four thousand acres now—two thousand at Flowerdew Hundred and Weyanoak Bend, a thousand at Jamestown and Hog Island, and another thousand near Smith's Isle on the Eastern Shore.

Harison did not aspire to that kind of wealth. He planned to content himself with a thousand. Then Jane could sleep in silk and lace, if she wanted to, and Robert would ride a fine-blooded stallion, and Harmon Harison would have the best guns that money could buy. Firearms were his passion. He already owned a matchlock musket with an inlaid walnut stock, but he coveted one with mother-of-pearl. And Virginia's Chesapeake, with its flocks of wild geese and ducks and turkeys and its herds of deer, was a huntsman's paradise.

Harison thought of that now, as he set out a cask of good English beer for his guests. Ralph Hamor, his brother, Thomas, who had come to Virginia two years ago, and a party of six other men were meeting at his house to go hunting with Tanakato, the chief of the nearby Warraskoyack Indians.

The old werowance had invited them to hunt deer today.

Upstairs, Jane and a dozen women—wives of the hunters, some neighboring planters' wives, and their servant girls—were planning to piece quilts all day. They had spread out their materials in the two bedchambers, and the whole second floor was a beehive of activity. There were eighteen people up there: seven wives, six servant women, three young children—two boys and a girl, Harison thought, but they all looked the same to him—and two infants.

Downstairs, nine-year-old Robert Harison was fairly dancing up and down with excitement. He knew how to shoot a gun, but this was his first real hunting expedition.

"I'll go look again and see if I can see them," he said. The hunting party was awaiting the arrival of Ralph Hamor and the Indians, and Robert had run out—it seemed a dozen times at least—to look down the grassy path that led through the woods to Hamor's property, and beyond that, to the village of the Warraskoyacks.

"That's a fine boy you've got there," Thomas Hamor said as Robert left. Hamor, a bachelor, craved a wife and children, but there was not a woman in Virginia who was not already spoken for. He had had an eye on William Pierce's comely black-haired daughter Jane, but before he got around to asking for her hand, John Rolfe had married her. Last year the Virginia Company, true to its promise, had sent a shipload of ninety marriageable women ("not maids, but at least single women," the announcement had said). For 150 pounds of tobacco, or about 15 pounds sterling, a man could buy one of them for a wife. But a dozen of them had died on the voyage, and the rest were so quickly spoken for that Thomas Hamor did not have time to make up his mind which one he wanted.

"Thanks." Harison peered out the window at his son, who was waving excitedly. "Someone is coming."

In a few minutes, Robert reappeared, followed by six well-muscled Warraskoyacks. They entered the house, smiling broadly, and presented their gifts: a half-bushel basket of oysters each for Harison and Thomas Hamor, and a dressed buckskin for Ralph Hamor, as the honored guests of Tanakato.

"Where is he?" they asked. "Where is Captain Hamor?"

"Not come yet, but on the way," Thomas said. "He knows we are here." The younger Hamor wondered what could be keeping his punctual brother.

"What a lot of arrows!" Robert was fascinated by the loaded quivers each Indian wore on his back. "You must think to kill a lot of deer!"

The Indians looked at each other and smiled.

Then one of them said, "I will watch for Captain Hamor and tell him to hurry. Tanakato is waiting." He disappeared, only to reappear in a few minutes in a great state of agitation. He was out of breath from running. "Fire!" he gasped. "Fire! Tobacco shed!"

The shed had been empty since January, when the crop was shipped off, but there was straw all over the floor, and it was dry as tinder. Harmon Harison dashed outside. The two tobacco sheds—one not yet finished—were about a hundred yards from the house. He could see a thin wisp of smoke rising from the door of the old one. The other men, neighboring planters who knew the value of a tobacco shed, ran outside, too.

"It's burning, all right! Damnation!" Harison started to run toward the shed, followed by the other planters and the Indians. Thomas Hamor and Robert Harison, who had run upstairs to tell the women what had happened, brought up the rear.

As Harmon and his neighbors raced toward the burning shed, the Indians following them slowed their pace, and the one in the lead suddenly raised his arm straight up in a signal, and almost in the same motion seized an arrow from the quiver at his back. In the space of a few seconds, his fellows did likewise: Six longbows swung into position, six arrows were fitted, six bowstrings drawn taut, and six arrows flew across the yard with deadly accuracy at fifty feet. The six men behind Harmon dropped almost at the same time. Three of them toppled slowly forward, falling like trees, and lay facedown on the grass. They did not move. The other three crumpled up in various positions, clutching their chests.

Young Robert thought at first the men were playing some kind of hunting game. He could not believe his eyes. Then Thomas Hamor grabbed him by the arm, shielded him with his own body, and shoved him toward the house.

"Get inside! Run!"

As he ran, pushing the boy in front of him, Thomas Hamor felt a blow, and a sharp pain between his ribs. He stumbled, but fear gave him a last surge of strength, and he and Robert threw themselves inside. There was an arrow in Hamor's back, but it had not gone deep.

Meanwhile, outside, one of the dying men had time to call out, "Harison, watch out! The Indians—"

But Harmon Harison did not have time to watch out. "What the hell—!" Hearing the cries of the men, he had stopped and turned around. But just as he turned, two arrows caught him full in the chest. He looked down at them and put his hands on their shafts, a hand on each one, as if to make certain they were real. Then he opened his mouth, perhaps to curse the Indians, perhaps to warn his wife and son, but a bright red fountain of blood came out instead.

While two of the Indians were aiming at Harison, the other four made sure the other Englishmen were dead. Every one of the warriors had a small tomahawk in his belt, and they used the blunt side of them to bludgeon the men's heads. They raised the hatchets high and swung down rhythmically and hard, like men chopping wood.

"Don't look." Hamor leaned against the door as Robert watched two Indians smashing his father's skull with alternate blows of their tomahawks. The boy was so pale, Hamor thought he might faint.

"Don't look, Robert. He . . . wouldn't want you to." The boy looked at him in blank horror.

"Get his gun, Robert. Go get his gun! Be quick!"

Hamor took up his own musket and began to load it as fast as he could. The arrow was in the fleshy part of his back, and it hardly hurt at all. Once those Indians finished outside, they would attack the house. He would see about the arrow later. Upstairs, the women, watching out their windows, had begun to scream, and the children and infants began to cry. Numbly, Robert picked up his father's musket.

"Can you shoot it?"

The boy nodded his head.

"Good. Rest your barrel on the windowsill and fire," Hamor ordered. "No need to aim, just fire."

At the sound of the guns, the Indians, who had finished their bloody work in the yard and were walking toward the house, scattered.

"Good," Hamor said. "We may be able to scare them off. Watch the windows, and keep down."

"Give me a gun. I can shoot." Jane Harison had seen the slaughter from upstairs, and there was cold hatred in her eyes. She put her arms around her son, and then she saw the arrow in Hamor's back. "You've got to get that out," she said calmly. "Let me see." To two of the other women who had followed her down the stairs, she said, "Bring me some pieces of that white linen, and be quick! And stay away from the windows!"

Hamor marveled at her coolness. In no time, she had the arrow out and a bandage tight around his middle.

Upstairs, pandemonium reigned. The women whose husbands had been killed were sobbing loudly, and so were the frightened children. Afraid of Indians entering downstairs, they cowered on the second floor and wailed.

Outside, the Indians who had fled at the sounds of the muskets reappeared, running at a trot toward the path through the woods, the way they had come. Inside, Thomas Hamor leaned against the wall. His wound was beginning to throb, and so was his head. What was he to do now, with this houseful of panic-stricken women and children? Harison's wife and son, their arms around each other, were looking at him, waiting for him to tell them what to do.

A shout from upstairs decided for him.

"Fire! The roof is on fire!"

The Indians, unwilling to storm a house defended by firearms, had left a parting gift. The dry thatched roof would burn fast, and there was no way to put it out, even if there had been men to do it.

"Get everybody down here—and tell them to be quiet." Hamor spoke as calmly as he could, and Jane and Robert Harison obeyed him. In a moment, Hamor stood before what looked like a sea of tear-streaked faces. "We cannot stay here," he said. "And we don't know what the Indians may do outside. How far is the closest house?"

"Baldwin's," Jane said quickly. "Near half a mile. They're there— she's sick or they'd have been here."

"We'll have to make a run for it, then." A gabble of protests, like the cooing of frightened doves, ensued. Hamor held up both hands for silence. "We can't stay here and burn," he said. "And those Indians may come back." He found Jane Harison's face and kept his eyes on it. He had never noticed how pretty she was, and until today, how brave. In the midst of all the confusion, he found it a comfort to look at her. "You lead the way," he said. To the others, he said, "Stay together, and keep running. Don't stop for anything, no matter what happens."

From a distance, they might have been playing tag or follow-the-leader, the slender black-haired woman in front; behind her, other women holding their skirts up and trying to catch her, and behind them, women running slower, carrying children in their arms, all running across the grassy clearing as fast as they could, chased by a man and a little boy carrying muskets.

When they reached the Baldwin house, the man put his arms around the black-haired woman and the little boy and held them close.

In the forest on the other side of the clearing, the Indians looked back at the flames from Harmon Harison's burning house and tobacco sheds with great satisfaction.

"That was the Englishman who stole the corn from the Warras-koyacks' canoe," one of them said.

"He won't do it again," said another.

CAUSEY'S CARE
22 March 1622

"Nathaniel, leave off that woodchopping and come here! We have company!" Thomasine Causey poked her head out the back door of her kitchen. In the parlor, standing around the table with their arms folded, were four Chickahominy braves. They had brought a pack of dressed deerskins to trade. Nathaniel, grateful for a chance to stop, wiped his perspiring face with his sleeve and came inside, laying his ax by the door. He had had to sharpen it again—servants could not be trusted to look after tools properly. James and Laurance, the new duty boys, could barely be trusted to set out tobacco plants right side up, much less to keep hoes and axes sharp. Nathaniel made a mental note to lecture them on that when they came in from the field.

At that moment, his two duty boys, along with his other four men, were lying facedown in the soft furrows of his tobacco field, with arrows in their backs.

"They've come to trade, Nathaniel, and just look at this buckskin! Not a blemish on it anywhere—and look how big it is. That must really have been an enormous buck." Thomasine Causey spread a dressed deerskin on the table and smoothed its soft folds lovingly. "I've never seen one so fine. I wish Thomas were here to see it. I could make him a whole pair of breeches out of it." She had been sewing shirts for the boy this morning. Her needle and thread and scissors lay on the end of the table amid the pieces of gray linsey-woolsey she had been cutting. Thomas was at Jamestown visiting the Laydons.

"If you want it, my dear, you shall have it." Nathaniel Causey took a small wooden box from the cupboard, opened it, and began to lay out blue glass beads.

"How many for that buckskin?" He addressed the tallest of the four Chickahominies around his parlor table.

The Indian eyed the contents of the box greedily and held up both hands, opening and closing them twice.

"Twenty?" Causey imitated the Indian's gesture and received a smiling nod of assent.

"That's a lot, but it is a handsome skin."

"Wait, Nathaniel." Thomasine put her hand on her husband's arm. "Would he like a shirt instead? You may need those beads for something else, and I have that new one I just finished for you upstairs. I could make you another one in no time."

This proposal drew a broad grin from the tall Indian. He said something to his companions in Algonquin and they all nodded and smiled.

"Yes," he said. "Very good. Skin for English shirt."

"I'll go get it." Thomasine hurried out of the room.

Nathaniel closed the box of beads. "You bring me some turkeys next time," he said, "and I'll give you five of these for each one." The Chickahominies smiled at each other. As Nathaniel turned to replace the box on the top shelf of the cupboard, the tall Indian seized Thomasine's scissors from the table and plunged them into her husband's back.

"Aaaah!" His cry had in it more rage than pain. He staggered against the wall, his arms spread out as though he would embrace the rough plaster. Behind him, two of the Chickahominies were unhurriedly rolling up the buckskin, while the one who had stabbed him picked up Thomasine's work basket, and the fourth took the wooden box of beads down from the cupboard. Upstairs, Thomasine's light, quick footsteps could be heard. In a moment, she would come down.

Out of the corner of his eye, Nathaniel Causey saw the newly sharpened ax, its handle leaning against the door frame. He lurched toward it, covering it with his body so that the Indians would not see it, and managed to make his arms move and his hands take hold of the ax handle. The pain in his back was shooting through his body in sharp flashes like lightning. Summoning all his strength, he turned around, raised the ax high above his head, and swung it.

It hit the tall Indian. He had been kneeling with his back to Nathaniel, trying to open the lower doors of the cupboard. The blade of the heavy ax caught him in the back of the head, cleaving the brown, clean-shaven skull like a melon, opening it to show blood and brain matter around the ax blade like the insides of some exotic fruit. The Indian toppled sideways, and Nathaniel Causey, who had been known to turn squeamish at the killing of a rabbit, put his foot on the fallen Indian's neck and pulled the ax blade out of his skull.

The other three Indians stood motionless, frozen with horror. What they saw was a man with scissors handles protruding from his back, a look of glittering hatred in his eyes, and a blood-dripping ax in his right hand. Thinking him possessed by some supernatural power, they turned tail and ran out the front door.

Thomasine saw them as she came down the stairs carrying a shirt.

"What's the matter?" she said. "I thought I heard—" She turned around to look for Nathaniel.

"Oh, my God!" She saw her husband, who had sat down heavily on a stool, leaning on the ax handle. She glanced briefly at the Indian's body beside him, and then at the scissors handles sticking out of his back. Picking up her skirts to avoid the blood, she stepped nimbly over the dead Indian and pressed the soft material of the shirt she was carrying around the scissors blades.

"Hold still," she said, and with one quick motion, she took hold of the scissors handles and pulled them out, stanching the sudden flow of blood with the shirt.

"Aaaah!" Nathaniel grimaced with the pain, and then suddenly the wound felt better. He felt weak and dizzy, but with the relief from pain came the sweet certainty that he was not going to die. Unable to speak, he clutched feebly, gratefully, at Thomasine's skirts, and she held him close and kissed the bald spot on the top of his head.

Near SOUTHAMPTON HUNDRED
22 March 1622

Gabriel Morgan's house needed a new roof, and Meg, looking up through the holes in the thatch at the morning sun, was thankful there had been no rain during her stay. She had come last week with his two duty boys, David and Walter, after they had delivered the dying Jack of the Feather to Jamestown. The youths, grief-stricken over Gabriel's sudden death, had seemed uncertain of what to do next, and David had taken sick of a fever the day they arrived. Meg had helped to nurse him, and had then volunteered to return with them to take stock of their deceased master's property. "Why should I not be the one to do it?" she had said. "I've no one but myself to look after anyway."

And so she had come and looked after David and Walter, had tried to comfort them with boiled venison stews and baked corn bread as they took a sad inventory of Gabriel's belongings. She had told them the story of how, years ago at Point Comfort, Gabriel Morgan had saved her life, along with Lady Yardley's (who was not Lady Yardley then) and Master Will Sterling (who was later killed by the Indians). "Had your master not kept a sharp watch that morning, he might not have seen us in the snow-storm, and I'd not be here now."

Now, on this sun-dappled spring morning, Meg was preparing to return to Jamestown. The boys had gone down to the river to ready the canoe for the journey, and Meg had come in to make certain she was not leaving anything behind. As she glanced about her, she heard the boys' shouts in the distance and smiled to herself. She was glad they were in good spirits. Ah, youth, she thought, that can so quickly forget its grief.

The Indian, his knife still red and dripping with the boys' blood, appeared suddenly in the doorway. Behind him was another, and both were grinning, their mouths half-open like gargoyles. Meg, too stunned to make a sound, put both hands to her throat. As the Indian moved toward her with the knife upraised, she thought fleetingly of the Frenchman who had slashed her cheek long ago aboard the *Brave*. This will be no worse, she told herself as the knife came down.

"She's an old ugly one, isn't she?" Manato, the eldest son of Kissanaco-men, shook his head as he wiped the blade of his knife.

"Someone's cut her before us. Look at that scar on her face," Manato's companion said.

"Let us make ashes of her bones," said Manato, reaching for his fire-sticks.

In a little while, as the morning sun rose higher, so did a column of smoke from the house on the north shore of the river, higher and higher, until at last it was only a haze against the cloudless blue of the sky.

FLOWERDEW
22 March 1622

 The sun, shining through the trees, cast spotted shadows on the forest path. Will's moccasins made soft, dry rustling noises as he walked. Overhead, blue jays and crows sounded their harsh calls above the steady twittering of the sparrows. Such a peaceful morning, Will thought. God willing, he would find things peaceful at Flowerdew. Through the pine trees he could see the newly plowed earth of a tobacco field on the south side of the house. George's men were clearing the land to make another field beside it, and some of the felled trees lay on the ground, their needles not yet dead. As he neared the clearing, Will saw the gleam of metal from a whipsaw lying on the ground. Someone must be at work there now. But as he drew closer, he heard no sound of men talking or working. That was odd, he thought. It was not yet midmorning. Then he saw the whipsaw, and he knew. For a moment, earth and sky swayed before him, and a premonition of disaster more terrible than anything he had ever known swept over him. The center of the whipsaw's shiny-toothed blade was covered with blood. A few feet away from it lay a man's decapitated body, and a few feet from that lay another. The earth around them was wet with their blood. Their heads were nowhere to be seen. Will bent over and touched the outstretched hand of one of the bodies. The flesh was still warm. As he raised his head, thinking to look heavenward and utter a silent prayer for these poor souls, his eyes fell on the adjacent tobacco field. There, at the far end of the long furrows, lay three more bodies. Though none was moving, Will ran toward them in the hope that life might not have left them all. But he need not have hurried. The bodies lay like rag dolls flung down by some careless child. They had been killed with the hoes that lay beside them.

With a terrible, heart-stopping dread, Will looked toward the house. In the morning sunshine, with the smoke of the midday dinner preparation wafting from the kitchen chimney, it was the picture of serenity. But he was about three hundred yards away from it and could not see the front porch or gallery. From where he stood, there was nothing but open ground between him and the house. If he approached it from here, he would be an easy mark for an arrow, but if he could get around on the opposite side of the house, he could take cover in the grove of pines nearest the building. He ran, his moccasions sinking into the soft, dry earth of the plowed field, his breath sounding loud in his ears. All around him was an eerie quiet. Even the birds, frightened witnesses to the carnage in the field, had fled.

As he rounded the back of the house, he saw Temperance's mare. The empty saddle with its dangling stirrups sent a chill through him. The mare, like the birds, had been witness to violent death, and at the sight of Will she bolted, walling her eyes in terror, and galloped off into the woods at the edge of the lawn. Dear God, he thought, I'm too late. Where is she? Sick with fear, he came upon the front view of the house, but there was no sign of Temperance. There was a plump servant woman dead on the porch with an arrow in her breast, but no one else. He reached the safety of the pine trees and stopped to reconnoiter. Were the attacking Indians at this moment in the house, or had they already visited there and left their work for him to find? Heart pounding, he tried to think what he should do. Hesitation might mean a life—Temperance's life—but impetuous action could mean his own life, and no one to help Temperance.

As he squinted at the house's windows, wishing he could see inside, two Indians emerged from the woods on the opposite side of the clearing from him. They did not seem the least bit hurried; they approached the front porch with easy familiarity, as if they had been there just recently. Hastily calculating the distance between him and them, Will fitted an arrow to his bow. He could certainly get one; he had a chance, albeit a small one, of getting both. Sighting down the long reed shaft, he let fly his arrow. It hit one of the Indians square in the chest, and he crumpled to the ground. His companion, startled, looked around, saw no one, and fled back into the woods before Will could draw and aim again. Will waited.

In a moment, the Indian reappeared, with two others. He pointed to the grove of pine trees where Will was hidden, and then the three Indians began to run toward the house. There was no more time to wait. Will fitted another arrow to his bow. If he got one, the other two would come looking for him, and he could draw them away from the house. Breathing a prayer for accuracy, he drew back his bowstring and released it. The Indian nearest him fell. The other two left their companion where he lay and, after a brief consultation, began to run in the direction from which the arrow had come. That consultation spelled the end of one, for those few seconds gave Will time to shoot another arrow. He dropped the taller Indian as he ran, but the other one, too close now to retreat, ran on toward the pine trees.

Will Sterling, who had once thought to spend his life in London making gloves, now prepared to defend it in a hand-to-hand battle with a savage at the edge of a forest in Virginia. He thought of the bodies he had just seen in the fields, he thought of poor George Cassen's long-ago torture, he thought of Temperance, and cold fury gave him strength. He flung his longbow and quiver on the ground, drew his hunting knife from his belt, and waited.

In the bow of the *Temperance,* George shielded his eyes against the sun with both hands and tried to see through the trees to Flowerdew. Strangely enough, there had been no sign of anything amiss on the way upriver. The scattered handful of single plantations between Jamestown and Weyanoak Bend had been warned to keep a sharp watch. He had remembered Meg was still at Morgan's place, but as he passed there, the boys had shouted to him that they were about to set out with her for Jamestown, so that was all right. In his desperate haste, he dared not stop to speak with her. As the boat neared the last curve of the river before Flowerdew, George began to hope that the alarm had been a false one, some cruel joke played on the English by a disgruntled Indian.

"We're nearly there, sir, and God willing, we'll find all well." Tom Goodwyn leaned on the gunwale beside him.

"Pray God, Tom, pray God we do." George began to pace the deck. "Drop the main," he called to the crew, "and take down the foresail as soon as we round the bend. Row her in—it's faster." He did not want to waste time tacking against the breeze to get to the pier. Now they were approaching the cleared fields of his Weyanoak land across the river from Flowerdew. George leaned on the forward gunwale to get a better view. Suddenly, his hands gripped the wooden rail so hard that their knuckles went white.

In the tobacco field nearest the river, the laborers lay across the furrows where they had fallen, their hoes beside them. There were four of them. George clapped Tom Goodwyn on the shoulder and pointed silently to the bodies in the field.

"God in heaven!" Goodwyn said.

As the boat rounded the bend, they could see Flowerdew at last, with its wide sweep of lawn. How many times George had come round that bend in the river, always with a surge of pride in the house and its grounds. But this time there was something wrong with the picture. Far to one side, near the woods, the body of an Indian was sprawled. Across the lawn on the opposite side, two more Indians had fallen, and another, fallen but not dead, was crawling toward the house.

"Look there, sir!" Tom Goodwyn pointed to the moving Indian with one hand, and drew his pistol with the other.

"No, wait," George said grimly. "I'll get him. See to the boat and meet me at the house. Be careful." With that, he swung himself over the side of the boat and leaped onto the pier.

"*You* be careful, sir," Goodwyn said.

But George, possessed by blind rage, had already set off in a dead run toward the Indian who was crawling on his lawn. Who had wounded this one, he wondered, and who had been there to put arrows into the others? Were there rival tribes involved in this horror? He would get this fellow to answer a question or two before he finished him off. He dared not think what he might find inside the house. This Indian was hell-bent on reaching the house, too, wounded as he was: The savage bastard could barely drag himself along the ground. What did he hope to do inside, in that condition? What had already been done inside? George felt as if his arms and legs belonged to someone else, and that, try as he might, he would run and run and never reach the house.

In his mind, he saw another house, the little house near Henrico, with its roof on fire, and his men carrying out a woman's form. *Not again, please God, not again. It can't happen again.* But worse could happen. This time he could be too late. And this time there were the children. He cursed himself for having left. But Temperance did not love him; he was already too late.

As he ran, he kept his hand on the hilt of his sword. His French pistols were in his belt, but he would not waste a bullet on this half-dead savage. There was something peculiar about this fellow, something that didn't look quite right. *His hair, under its beaded headband, was blond.* As George stared at the light hair, the man stopped crawling. His head dropped forward, his body gave a little shudder, and he collapsed on the grass near one of the dead Indians.

It can't be, George told himself. I'm seeing things. At last he knelt beside the still form. The man lay facedown. There was no sign of life. Gently, George turned him over. A man deserves a little gentleness when he's dying, no matter who he is, he thought. As the blond head rolled back against his arm, George caught his breath. The face under its tan was deathly pale, but the gray eyes flew open. They fixed upon George with the familiar gaze of their boyhood in Southwark.

"My fault, George. My fault." Then a sudden spasm shook him. The gray eyes grew blank, and the jaw slowly relaxed. The face wore the look of one listening in openmouthed anticipation, but George, cradling the lifeless form in his arms, could not speak. Tenderly, as though he were laying a sleeping child to rest, he laid Will down. With thumb and forefinger, he closed the eyes. He put his palm under the chin to close the mouth. As he crossed Will's arms, he clasped the hands and laid his forehead against them for a moment.

"Dear God, take him, and forgive him. Forgive us all our trespasses, and deliver us from evil. Amen."

Then, drawing his pistol, George continued his journey toward the house. He could see smoke now in the sky behind it. They must have fired the tobacco sheds. At least the house was not burning, but the wide front door was standing ominously ajar. As he reached the porch, he saw Margery Blewet's body in the chair, and he could hear the sounds of sobbing from inside—a soft, slow, exhausted sobbing that terrified him more than loud crying would have. Pistol at the ready, he shoved open the front door and called out:

"Temperance!"

There was no answer. Only the sobbing from upstairs. George took the steps two at a time. Ata and the two children were huddled on the floor of the big bedchamber, and all three were crying.

"Temperance—where is Temperance?" They could only weep and point to the gallery. In a hurried gesture of comfort, he put a hand on each of his children's heads and then ran across the bedchamber to the gallery door.

She was at the far end of the gallery, on her knees, with her back to him. All around her, the wide floorboards were covered with blood.

"Temperance!"

At the sound of her name, she turned around, and George could see that it was not she who was bleeding, but Samuel Garrett. Both the boy's hands had been cut off at the wrists, and he lay curled up with the bloody stumps in front of him. He had bled to death. Slowly, wearily, Temperance got to her feet, staring at George as though he were a stranger.

George stood transfixed, watching her. The blessed realization that both his children and his wife were alive and unharmed began to take hold.

Temperance took a halting step toward him. "Samuel is dead, George," she said woodenly. "They cut off his hands. He came to me, but I—I couldn't make the blood stop." George could see that she had tied strips of her white shift in tourniquets around the boy's wrists.

"I couldn't get the blood to stop," she said again, and her voice quavered. "They found him chopping wood, and they cut off his hands with his own hatchet. They shot Margery Blewet while she was shelling peas on the porch, and then they went into the kitchen and cut her husband's throat with his butcher knife. There were two of them in the house, and then John came in and shot one, and the other one ran off and set fire to the sheds." Temperance was staring straight ahead, looking not at George but through him, reciting the litany of horror in a flat voice. "One of them killed Elizabeth with a knife. She was in the buttery. I saw her. Then we came up here, and some more Indians came, but someone outside shot them with arrows." She looked puzzled. "Was that you?"

George took a step toward her. "No, Temperance. It was Will."

Temperance's eyes widened. "Will?"

George nodded silently.

"Where was he—where is he?"

"Out there. He was hurt, Temperance. He died in my arms."

My fault, George, my fault.

George looked out over the gallery wall. Whose fault was any of this? he wondered. But for him, Will Sterling would never have come to Virginia.

"I am sorry," he said. He did not know what else to say. Temperance turned away from him and leaned against the wall. Her shoulders sagged, and she bowed her head. Fearing to intrude upon her private grief, George stood back, watching her. There was such sorrow in that small, slender form that George ached to touch her, to comfort her, but he dared not. Instead, he walked over and looked out over the lawn, at the grassy slope where Will's body lay just out of sight from the house. "I didn't want to leave him out there, but I couldn't carry him," he said softly.

Temperance pressed her fist hard against her mouth for a moment, as if to stifle a cry, and then, slowly, hands at her sides, she walked toward George. Her face was tear-streaked, and there were smudges of Samuel Garrett's blood on her cheek and forehead. The thin red scar of that other Indian attack still showed in her hairline. The red-gold hair, which had long since lost its hairpins, hung down her back in tangled curls. The entire front of her light green riding habit was dark with bloodstains not yet dry.

"George," she said in a small sad voice, "I know I've no right to ask you, but could you—would you—hold me for just a minute?"

Without a word, he opened his arms. In the other room, the children had stopped crying, and he could hear Ata talking quietly to them. Outside, he could hear shouts. Goodwyn and his men were trying to put out the tobacco-shed fire. There were other fires up and down the river, he knew, and people lying dead and wounded. He must go soon, and do what could be done. But for now, he wanted only to hold Temperance, not just for a minute, but for as long as she would have him.

POWHATAN VILLAGE
22 March 1622

Twenty miles upriver from Flowerdew, Opechancanough, reclining on a raccoon fur rug, received messengers bearing news of the day's victory. From the first war councils at dawn, to the surprising of the English in their houses, to the indiscriminate slaughter at midmorning, everything had gone exactly according to plan. One by one, fleet-footed runners arrived with their triumphant reports.

"Near Appamatuck, twenty killed."

"At Weyanoak, fifteen dead."

"Paspahegh, twenty-four."

"Above Nansemond, seventy-three in one place."

"Eighteen killed at Kecoughtan."

Next to Opechancanough, Basamuck, cutting notches on a stick to tally the dead, could barely keep up. "This has been a good day's work," he said dryly.

"And there will be a good day's feast to celebrate it," Opechancanough said. "There is nothing to fear from our 'friends,' the English. The only ones left are at Jamestown, and they will soon be gone." He filled his pipe with fragrant tobacco leaves and lighted it with a firebrand.

"We have made certain that the prophecy will never come true," he said jubilantly. "The seers were wrong. It is we who have put an end to their empire. Our people have driven the strangers from this land not twice, but three times, and this time they will not return."

Opechancanough thought of Wahunsonacock, whose body now rested in the tomb of the werowances. His spirit would rejoice at the end of the English. Opechancanough congratulated himself. On this day, 347 English men, women, and children had died in Virginia.

"See that the women start preparing the food," he said to Basamuck. "And tell them to make enough for not one, but three feast days."

After all, Opechancanough thought, he had waited long for this moment. It was fifty years ago that he had killed the Jesuits on the banks of the Pamunkey and vowed to drive the strangers from his land.

Along the river below Powhatan Village, while the Indians prepared to celebrate their victory, the English prepared to bury their dead. But even as the graves were being dug, the plans for revenge were being laid. Most of Jamestown, forewarned, had escaped harm, and across Chesapeake Bay, the new settlements on the Eastern Shore were untouched.

As he notched his sticks, the Indian Basamuck thought about the English who still lived, and in his heart, though he dared not tell Opechancanough, he felt the power of the ancient prophecy.

THE HISTORY OF VIRGINIA
1607–1622

From the wreck of the *Sea Venture* to the massacre of the James River settlers, most of the events in this novel are true. In the following pages John Smith, George Percy, William Strachey, and others recount in their own words what happened in Virginia and Bermuda from 1607 to 1622.

JOHN SMITH: His Rescue by Pocahontas, 1607

At last they brought him [Smith] to Meronocomoco, where was Powhatan their Emperor. . . . Before a fire upon a seat like a bedsted, he sat covered with a great robe, made of Rarowcun skinnes, and all the tayles hanging by. On either hand did sit a young wench of 16 or 18 yeares, and along on each side the house, two rowes of men, and behind them as many women, with all their heads and shoulders painted red; many of their heads bedecked with the white downe of Birds; but every one with something: and a great chayne of white beads about their necks. At his entrance . . . all the people gave a great shout. The Queene of Appamatuck was appointed to bring him water to wash his hands, and . . . having feasted him after their best barbarous manner they could, a long consultation was held, but the conclusion was, two great stones were brought before Powhatan: then as many as could layd hands on him, dragged him to them, and thereon laid his head, and being ready with their clubs, to beate out his braines, Pocahontas the Kings dearest daughter, when no intreaty could prevaile, got his head in her armes, and laid her owne upon his to save him from death: whereat the Emperour was contented he should live.

—Smith, "The Generall Historie of Virginia, New-England, and the Summer Isles" (1624), from THE COMPLETE WORKS OF CAPTAIN JOHN SMITH, Vols. 1–3, edited by Philip Barbour. Copyright © 1986 The University of North Carolina Press. Published for the Institute of Early American History and Culture, Williamsburg, Va. Reprinted with permission. Vol. II, 150–151.

JOHN SMITH: Pocahontas, 1608

Powhatan . . . sent his Daughter, a child of tenne yeares old, which not only for feature, countenance, and proportion, much exceedeth any of the rest of his people, but for wit, and spirit, the only Nonpariel of his Country. . . .

—Smith, "A True Relation of such occurences and accidents of noate as hath hapned in Virginia since the first planting of that Collony" (London: 1608), in WORKS, I, 93.

WILLIAM STRACHEY: Pocahontas, 1608

A well-featured but wanton young girle . . . sometymes resorting to our Fort, of the age then of 11. or 12. yeares, [she would] gett the boyes forth with her into the markett place and make them wheele, falling on their hands, turning their heeles upwardes, whome she would follow, and wheel so herself naked as she was all the Fort over. . . .

—Strachey, *The Historie of Travaill into Virginia Britannia.* Strachey's manuscript, completed in 1612, was not published in his lifetime. Quotations are from the edition by R. H. Major (London: Hakluyt Society, 1849), 72.

JOHN SMITH: The Love Dance, 1608

In a fayre plain . . . thirtie young women came naked out of the woods, onely covered behind and before with a few greene leaves, their bodies all painted, some of one colour, some of another, but all differing, their leader had a fayre payre of Bucks hornes on her head, and an Otters skinne at her girdle, and another at her arme, a quiver of arrowes at her backe, a bow and arrowes in her hand; the next had in her hand a sword, another a club, another a pot-sticke; all horned alike: the rest every one with their severall devises. These fiends with most hellish shouts and cryes, rushing from among the trees, cast themselves in a ring about the fire, singing and dauncing with most excellent ill varietie, oft falling into their infernall passions, and solemnly againe to sing and daunce. . . .

Having reaccommodated themselves, they solemnly invited him to their lodgings, where he was no sooner within the house, but all these Nymphes more tormented him then ever, with crowding, pressing, and hanging about him, most tediously crying, Love you not me? love you not me? This salutation ended, the feast was set, consisting of all the Salvage dainties they could devise: some attending, others singing and dauncing about them; which mirth being ended, with fire-brands in stead of Torches they conducted him to his lodging. . . .

—WORKS, II, 182–183.

WILLIAM STRACHEY: The Storm, July 1609

When on S. James his day, July 24. being Monday . . . the cloudes gathering thicke upon us and the windes singing and whistling most unusually . . . a dreadful storm and hideous began to blow from out the North-east, which swelling, and roaring as it were by fits, some houres with more violence then others, at length did beate all light from Heaven; which, like an hell of darknesse turned blacke upon us. . . .

East and by South we steered away as much as we could to beare upright, which was no small carefulnesse or paine to do, albeit we much unrigged our ship, threw over-boord much luggage, many a Trunke and Chest . . . and staved many a butt of Beer, Hogsheads of oyle, Syder, Wine, and Vinegar, and heaved away all our Ordnance on the Starboard side . . . for we were much spent and our men so weary as their strengths together failed them, with their hearts, having travailed now from Tuesday till Friday morning, day and night, without either sleepe or foode . . . and carefulnesse, griefe, and our turne at the pumpe or bucket, were sufficient to hold sleep from our eyes.
    —Strachey, "A True Reportory of the Wracke, and redemption of Sir Thomas Gates Knight . . ." (1610), in Samuel Purchas, *Hakluytus Posthumus or Purchas His Pilgrimes,* 20 vols. (Glasgow: J. MacLehose & Sons, 1905–7), XIX, 6–12.

JOHN SMITH: The Survivors of the Gates Expedition, 1609

Some lost their Masts, some their Sayles blowne frm their Yards; the Seas so over-raking our Ships, much of our provision was spoyled, our Fleet separated, and our men sicke, and many dyed, and in this miserable estate we arrived in Virginia.
    —WORKS, II, 220.

THE VIRGINIA COMPANY: The Success of the Gates Expedition, 1609

. . . and now seven of our fleet being in, they landed in health neer four hundred persons. . . .
    —*A True and Sincere declaration of the purpose and ends of the Plantation begun in Virginia . . .* (London: 1610). Reprinted in Alexander Brown, *The Genesis of the United States,* 2 vols. (New York: Houghton, Mifflin, 1890), I, 347.

JOHN SMITH: Factions at Jamestown, 1609

It would be too tedious, too strange, and almost incredible; should I particularly relate the infinite dangers, plots, and practices he [Smith] daily escaped amongst this factious crew. . . .
    —WORKS, II, 220.

GEORGE PERCY: The Gunpowder Accident, 1609

A greate devisyon did growe amongste them Capte: Smithe . . . incensed and Animated the Salvages ageinste Capte: West and his company. . . . And so Capte:

Smithe Retouringe to James Towne ageine [was] fownd to have too mutche powder aboutt him The whch beinge in his pockett where the sparke of A Matche Lighted very shrewdly burned him.

—Percy, "A Trewe Relacyon of the Proceedings . . . in Virginia," *Tyler's Quarterly Historical and Genealogical Magazine,* III, No. 4 (April 1922), 264.

JOHN SMITH: The Assassination Plot, 1609

Arriving at James towne . . . Ratliffe, Archere, and the rest of their Confederates, being come to their trials; their guiltie consciences, fearing a just reward for their deserts, seeing the President [Smith], unable to stand, and neere bereft of his senses by reason of his torment, they had plotted to have him murdered in his bed. But his heart did faile him that should have given fire to that mercilesse Pistoll. . . . The President . . . sent for the Masters of the ships, and tooke order with them for his returne for England. Seeing there was neither Chururgian, nor Chirurgery in the Fort to cure his hurt . . . so grievous were his wounds, and so cruell his torments (few expecting he could live) nor was hee able to follow his busines to regaine what they had lost, suppresse those factions, and range the countries for provisions as he intended; and well he knew in those affaires his owne actions and presence was as requisit as his directions, which now could not be, he went presently abroad. . . .

—WORKS, II, 223–224.

JOHN SMITH: Supplies at Jamestown, October 1609

Leaving us thus with three ships, seaven boats, commodities readie to trade, the harvest newly gathered, ten weeks provision in store, foure hundred nintie and od persons, twentie-foure Peeces of Ordnance, three hundred Muskets, Snaphances, and Firelockes, Shot, Powder, and Match sufficient, Curats, Pikes, Swords, and Morrions, more then men; the Salvages, their language, and habitations well knowne to an hundred well trayned and expert Souldiers; Nets for fishing; Tooles of all sorts to worke; apparell to supply our wants; six Mares and a Horse; five or sixe hundred Swine; as many Hennes and Chickens; some Goats, some sheepe; what was brought or bred there remained. But they regarding nothing but from hand to mouth, did consume that wee had. . . .

—WORKS, II, 225.

WILLIAM STRACHEY: Bermuda, 1609

We found . . . the dangerous and dreaded Iland, or rather Ilands of the Bermuda. . . . And that the rather, because they be so terrible to all that ever touched on them, and such tempests, thunders, and other fearefull objects are seene and heard about them, that they be called commonly, The Devils Ilands and are feared and avoyded of all sea travelers alive, above any other place in the world.

—"Reportory," 13.

GEORGE PERCY: The Starving Time, 1609–1610

Leftenantt Sicklemore and dyvrs others weare fownd also slayne wth their mowthes stopped full of Breade beinge donn as it seamethe in Contempte and skorne thatt others mighte expecte the Lyke when they shold come to seeke for breade and reliefe amongst them. . . .

Butt haveinge no expectacyon of Reliefe to come in so short A Tyme I sentt Capteyne Ratliefe to Powhatan to pcure victewalls and corne by the way of comerce and trade the whch the subtell owlde foxe att firste made good semblanse of Althoughe his intente was otherwayes onely wayteinge A fitteinge tyme for their destruction As after planely appered. The whch was pbly ocasyoned by Capte: Ratliefes credulitie for Haveinge Powhatans sonne and dowghter Aboard his pinesse freely suffred them to depte ageine on shoare whome if he had deteyned mighte have bene A Sufficyentt pledge for his saffety . . . suffreinge his men by towe and thre and small Numbers in a Company to straggle into the Salvages howses when the Slye owlde kinge espyed A fitteinge Tyme Cutt them all of onely surprysed Capte: Ratleife Alyve who he caused to be bownd unto a tree naked with a fyer before And by woemen his fleshe was skraped from his bones wth mussell shelles and befre his face throwne into the fyer. And so for want of circumspection miserably perished. . . .

Now all of us att James Towne beginneinge to feele that sharpe pricke of hunger whch noe man trewly descrybe butt he whch hath Tasted the bitternesse thereof A worlde of miseries ensewed . . . so mutche thatt some to satisfye their hunger have robbed the store for the whch I caused them to be executed. Then haveinge fedd uponn horses and other beastes as long as they Lasted we weare gladd to make shifte wth vermine as doggs Catts Ratts and myce All was fishe thatt came to Nett to satisfye Crewell hunger as to eate Bootes shoes or any other leather. . . . And those being Spente and devoured some weare inforced to searche the woodes and to feede upon Serpents and snakes and to digge the earthe for wylde and unknowne Rootes where many of our men weare Cutt off of and slayne by the Salvages. And now famin begineinge to Looke gastely and pale in every face thatt notheinge was spared to mainteyne Lyfe and to doe those things whch seame incredible As to digge up dead corpses outt of graves and to eate them. . . . And amongste the reste this was moste Lamentable Thatt one of our Colline murdered his wyfe Ripped the childe outt of her woambe and threw itt into the River and after chopped the Mother in pieces and salted her for his foode . . . for which crewell and inhumane factt I judged him to be executed the acknowledgment of the dede being inforced from him by torture haveinge hunge by the Thumbes with weights att his feet a quarter of an howere before he wolde confesse the same.

—"Trewe Relacyon," 265–267.

GEORGE PERCY: His Journey to Point Comfort, 1610

By this Tyme being Reasonable well recovered of my sicknes I did undertake A Jorney. . . . Our people I fownd in good case and well lykeinge haveinge concealed their plenty from us above att James Towne Beinge so well stored thatt the Crabb

fishes where wth they had fede their hoggs wold have bene a greate relefe unto us and saved many of our Lyves. . . .
—"Trewe Relacyon," 268.

WILLIAM STRACHEY: Arrival of the *Sea Venture* Survivors, May 1610

From hence in two dayes (only by the helpe of tydes, no winde stirring) wee plyed it sadly up the River. . . . Viewing the fort, we found the Pallisadoes torne downe, the ports open, the Gates from off the hinges, and emptie houses (which Owners death had taken from them) rent up and burnt, rather then the dwellers would step into the Woods a stones cast off from them, to fetch other fire-wood: and it is true, the Indians killed as fast without . . . as famine and pestilence did within. . . .
—"Reportory," 44–45.

THE VIRGINIA COMPANY: The Condition of the Colony, 1610

. . . in a few moneths, Ambition, sloth and idlenes had devoured the fruits of former labours, planting and sowing were cleane given over, the houses decaied, the Church fell to ruine, the store was spent, the cattell consumed, our people starved, and the poore Indians by wrongs and injuries were made our enemies. . . .
—Council of the Virginia Company, *The New Life of Virginea: Declaring the former successe and present estate of that plantation* (London: 1612), reprinted in Peter Force, ed., *Tracts and Other Papers . . . to the Year 1776,* 4 vols. (Washington, D.C.: Peter Force, 1836–46), I, No. 7, p. 10.

GEORGE PERCY: The Condition of the Settlers, June 1610

And those whch weare Liveinge weare so maugre and Leane thatt itt was Lamentable to behowlde them for many throwe extreme hunger have Runne outt of their naked bedds beinge so Leane thatt they Looked like Anotamies Cryeinge owtt we are starved We are starved. . . .
—"Trewe Relacyon," 269.

WILLIAM STRACHEY: The Decision to Abandon Jamestown, June 1610

In this desolation and misery our Governour [Gates] found the condition and state of the Colonie, and (which added more to his griefe) no hope how to amend it or save his owne company, and those yet remaynng alive, from falling into the like necessities. For we had brought from the Bermudas no greater store of provision (fearing no such accidents possible to befall the Colony here) then might well serve one hundred and fiftie for a Sea Voyage: and it was not possible, at this time of the yeare to amend it, by any helpe from the Indians. For besides that they (at their best) have little more then from hand to mouth, it was now likewise but their

Seed-time, and all their Corne scarce put into the grounde: nor was there at the Fort, (as they whom we found related unto us) any meanes to take fish, neither sufficient Seine, nor other convenient Net, and yet if there had, there was not one eye of Sturgeon yet come into the River. All which considered, it pleased our Governor to make a speech unto the Company, giving them to understand what provision he had they should equally share with him, and if he should find it not possible, and easie to supply them with some thing from the countrey, by the endevours of his able men, hee would make readie, and transport them all into their Native Countrey (accommodating them the best that he could); at which there was a generall acclamation, and shoute of joy on both sides, for even our owne men began to be disheartened and faint, when they saw this misery amongst the others, and no lesse threatned unto themselves. . . .

—"Reportory," 45–46.

JOHN SMITH: Arrival of De la Warr's Fleet, June 1610

. . . never had any people more just cause, to cast themselves at the very foot-stoole of God, and to reverence his mercie, than this distressed Colonie; . . . If they had set saile sooner, and had lanched into the vast Ocean, who would have promised they should have incountered the Fleet of the Lord la Ware. . . .

—WORKS, II, 234.

WILLIAM STRACHEY: The Return to Jamestown, June 1610

. . . our governour bore up the helme, with the winde comming Easterly, and that night (the winde so favourable) relanded all his men at the Fort againe. . . .

—"Reportory," 54.

WILLIAM STRACHEY: The Killing of Humphrey Blunt, July 1610

The sixth of July Sir Thomas Gates Lieutenant Generall, comming downe to Point Comfort, the north wind (blowing rough) he found had forced the long Boate . . . to the other shoare upon Nansamund side, somewhat short of Weroscoick: which to recover againe one of the Lieutenant Generals men Humphrey Blunt, in an old Canow made over, but the wind driving him upon the Strand, certaine Indians (watching the occasion) seised the poore fellow, and led him up into the Woods, and sacrificed him.

—"Reportory," 62.

GEORGE PERCY: Revenge upon the Indians at Kecoughtan, July 1610

Then Sr Tho: Gates beinge desyreous for to be Revendged upon the Indyans att Kekowhatan did goe thither by water wth a certeine number of men and amongste the reste A Taborer wth him being Landed he cawsed the Taborer to play and dawnse thereby to Allure the Indyans to come unto him . . . And then . . . a fitteinge opportunety fell in upon them putt fyve to the sworde wownded many others some of them beinge after fownde in the woods wth Sutche extreordinary Lardge and mortall wownds that itt seamed strange they Cold flye so far. . . .

—"Trewe Relacyon," 270.

GEORGE PERCY: The Killing of Oposonoquonuske's Children, 1610

. . . my Lorde . . . apointed me Chiefe Comawnder over Seaventie men and sentt me to take Revendge. . . . And after we marched wth the quene And her Children to our boates ageine . . . my sowldiers did begin to murmur becawse the quene and her Children weare spared. So upon the same A Cowncell beinge called itt was Agreed upon to putt the Children to deathe the wch was effected by Throweinge them overboard and shoteinge owtt their Braynes in the water yett for all this Crewellty the Sowldiers weare nott well pleased And I had mutche to doe To save the quenes lyfe for thatt Tyme.

—"Trewe Relacyon," 272.

HENRY SPELMAN: His Indian Captivity, 1609–1610

I was caried By Capt Smith our President to ye Fales, to ye litell Powhatan wher unknowne to me he sould me to him. . . . Powhatan . . . made very much of me givinge me such thinges as he had to winn me to live with him. . . .

I . . . ran away from amonge the cumpany . . . till I shifted for myself and gott to the Patomeckes cuntry. With this King Patomecke I lived a year and more . . . untill such time as an worthy gentleman named Capt: Argall arived. . . . Capt: Argall gave the Kinge copper for me which he receyved. Thus was I sett at libertye. . . .

—Spelman, "Relation" (1612?) reprinted in Brown, *Genesis,* I, 484–488.

THE VIRGINIA COMPANY: Rumors of Roanoke Survivors, 1609

. . . besides you are neere to Riche Copper mines of Ritanoc and may passe them by one braunche of this River, and by another Peccarecamicke where you shall finde foure of the englishe alive, left by Sr Walter Rawely whch escaped from the slaughter of Powhaton of Roanocke, uppon the first arrival of our Colonie, and live under the proteccon of a wiroane called Gepanocon enemy to Powhaton, by whose consent you shall never recover them. . . .

—Council of the Virginia Company, Instructions to the Colony (1609), *Records of the Virginia Company,* Susan M. Kingsbury, ed., 4 vols. (Washington, D.C.: Government Printing Office, 1906–35), III, 17.

WILLIAM STRACHEY: Rumors of Roanoke Survivors, 1610

At *Peccarecanick* and *Ochanahoen* . . . the People have howses built with stone walles, and one story above another, so taught them by those Englishe who escaped the slaughter at *Roanoak.* . . . at . . . Ritanoe, the Weroance *Eyanoco* preserved 7. of the English alive, fower men, twoo Boyes, and one younge Maid (who escaped and fled up the river of Chaonoke). . . .
   —*Travaill,* 34.

GEORGE PERCY: The Regime of Sir Thomas Dale, 1610–1611

Sr Tho: Gates Apointed Sr Tho: Dale their Marshall of the Collonie . . . dyvrs of his men . . . did Runne Away unto the Indyans many of them beinge taken agaeine Sr Thomas in A most severe mannor cawsed to be executed. Some he apointed to be hanged Some burned Some to be broken upon wheles, others to be staked and some to be shott to deathe all theis extreme and crewell tortures he used and inflicted upon them To terrefy the rest for Attempteinge the Lyke and some whch Robbed the store he cawsed them to be bownd faste unto Trees and so sterved them to deathe.
   —"Trewe Relacyon," 279–280.

JOHN SMITH: The Regime of Sir Thomas Dale, 1610–1611

So as Sir Thomas Dale hath not beene so tyrannous nor severe by the halfe, as there was occasion, and just cause for it, and though the manner was not usuall, wee were rather to have regard to those, whom we would have terrified and made fearefull to commit the like offences, than to the offenders justly condemned, for amongst them so hardned in evill, the feare of a cruell, painfull and unusuall death more restraines them, than death it selfe.
   —WORKS, II, 240.

RALPH HAMOR: Samuel Argall's Rapport with the Indians, 1613

. . . the everworthy gentleman Capt. Argall . . . by his best experience of the disposition of those people, partly by gentle usage & partly by the composition & mixture of threats hath ever kept faire & friendly quarter with our neighbours bordering . . . such is his well knowne temper and discretion . . . that they assuredly trust upon what he promiseth. . . .
   —Hamor, *A True Discourse of the Present Estate of Virginia* (London: 1615, repr. Richmond, Va.: Virginia State Library, 1957), 3.

SAMUEL ARGALL: His Plans to Kidnap Pocahontas, 1613

... I was told by certaine Indians, my friends, that the Great Powhatans daughter Pokahuntis was with the great King Patowomeck, whether I presently repaired, resolving to possess my selfe of her by any stratagem that I could use. . . .
   —Letter of Sir Samuel Argall to Nicholas Hawes, June 1613, in Purchas, XIX, 92.

RALPH HAMOR: The Abduction of Pocahontas, 1613

Iapazeus. . . making his wife an instrument (which sex have ever bin most powerfull in beguiling inticements) to effect his plot which hee had thus laid, he agreed that .. his wife should faine a great and longing desire to goe aboorde and see the shippe . . . so that it would please *Pocahuntas* to accompany her . . . so forthwith aboord they went, the best cheere that could be made was seasonably provided, to supper they went, merry on all hands especially *Iapazeus* and his wife, who to expres their joy would ere be treading upon Capt. *Argals* foot, as who should say tis don, she is your own.
   —*True Discourse,* 4–5.

JOHN SMITH: The Abduction of Pocahontas, 1613

... thus they betraied the poor innocent Pocahontas aboord, where they were all kindly feasted in the Cabbin. . . . The Captaine . . . told her before her friends, she must goe with him, and compound peace betwixt her Countrie and us, before she ever should see Powhatan. . . .
   —WORKS, II, 243–244.

RALPH HAMOR: The Abduction of Pocahontas, 1613

Pocahuntas . . . being most possessed with feare, and desire of returne, was first up . . . whereas she began to be exceeding pensive, and discontented. . . .
   —*True Discourse,* 6.

JOHN ROLFE: His Love for Pocahontas, 1614?

Let therefore this my will advised protestation, which I make betweene God and my owne conscience . . . no way led (so farre forth as mans weaknessse may permit) with the unbridled desire of carnall affection: but for the good of this plantation . . . and for the converting to the true knowledge of God and Jesus Christ, an unbeleeving creature, namely *Pokahuntas.* To whom my hartie and best thoughts are, and have a long time bin so intangled, and inthralled in so intricate a laborinth, that I was even awearied to unwinde my selfe thereout. . . .

* * *

Nor was I ignorant of . . . the inconveniences which may thereby arise . . . to be in love with one whose education hath bin rude, her manners barbarous, her generation accursed, and so discrepant in all nurtriture from my selfe. . . .

Thus when I had thought I had obtained my peace and quietnesse, beholde, another, but more gracious tentation hath made breaches into my holiest and strongest meditations . . . besides the many passions and sufferings, which I have daily, hourely, yea and in my sleepe indured, even awaking mee to astonishment . . . pulling mee by the eare, and crying: why dost not thou endeavour to make her a Christian? And these have happened to my greater wonder, even when she hath bin furthest separated from me. . . .

What should I doe?

—Letter of John Rolfe to Sir Thomas Dale, undated, ca. 1614, in Hamor, 63–66.

RALPH HAMOR: Negotiating with Powhatan for Pocahontas, 1614

. . . higher up the river we went, and ancored neere unto the chiefest residencie *Powhatan* had, at a towne called *Matchcot* where were assembled (which we saw) about 400 men. . . . *Powhatan*'s sonnes being very desirous to see their sister who was there present ashore with us, came unto us, at the sight of whom, and her well fare, whom they suspected to be worse intreated, though they had often heard to the contrary, they much rejoyced, and promised that they would undoubtedly perswade their father to redeeme her, and to conclude a firme peace forever with us, and upon this resolution the two brothers with us retired aboarde, we having first dispatched . . . Master John *Rolfe* . . . to acquaint their Father with the businesse at hand. . . .

Long before this time a gentleman of approved behaviour and honest cariage, master John *Rolfe* had bin in love with *Pocahontas* and she with him. . . .

—*True Discourse*, 10.

JOHN SMITH: Yardley's Return, The Rolfes' Departure from Jamestown, 1616

Whilst those things were effecting, Sir Thomas Dale, having setled to his thinking all things in good order, made choice of one Master George Yearley, to be Deputy Governour in his absence, and so returned for England, accompanied with Pocahontas the Kings Daughter, and Master Rolfe her husband, and arrived at Plimmoth the 12. of June. 1616.

—WORKS, II, 255.

ALEXANDER WHITAKER: Indian Priests, 1613–1616

Their Priests (whom they call Quiokosoughs) are no other but such as our English Witches are. They live naked in body, as if their shame of their sinne deserved no covering: Their names are as naked as their body: they esteeme it a vertue to lye, deceive, and steale, as their Master the Divell teacheth them. . . .

. . . I suppose the world hath no better marke-men with their Bowes and Arrowes then they be; they will kill Birds flying, Fishes swimming, and Beasts running: they shoote also with mervailous strength, they shot one of our men being unharmed quite through the body, and nailed both his armes to his body with one Arrow. . . .

They stand in great awe of the Quiokosoughs or Priests, which are a generation of Vipers . . . they live alone in the woods, in houses sequestred from the common course of men, neither may any man be suffered to come into their house or to speake with them, but when this Priest doth call him. . . . At his command they make warre and peace, neither doe they any thing of moment without him.

—Whitaker, "Tractate" (1613), in Purchas, XIX, III.

JOHN SMITH: Yardley's Attack on the Chickahominies, 1616

Master George Yearly . . . drew together one hundred of his best shot, with whom he went to Chickhamania. . . . Yearly seeing their insolencies . . . caused us all to make ready, and upon the word, to let flie among them, where he appointed: others also he commanded to seize on them they could for prisoners; all which being done according to our direction, the Captaine gave the word, and wee presently discharged, where twelve lay, some dead, the rest for life sprawling on the ground.

—WORKS, II, 256–257.

JOHN SMITH: His Reunion with Pocahontas, 1616

. . . Lady Pocahontas . . . was maried to an English Gentleman, with whom at this present she is in England; the first Christian ever of that Nation, the first Virginian ever spake English, or had a childe in mariage by an Englishman. . . .

. . . hearing she was at Branford with divers of my friends, I went to see her: After a modest salutation, without any words, she turned about, obscured her face, as not seeming well contented; and in that humour her husband, with divers others, we all left her two or three hours, repenting my selfe to have writ she could speake English. But not long after, she began to talke, and remembred mee well what courtesies shee had done: saying, You did promise Powhatan what was yours should bee his, and he the like to you. . . .

—WORKS, II, 260–261.

JOHN SMITH: Pocahontas's Death at Gravesend, Argall's Arrival at Jamestown, 1617

The Treasurer, Councell and Companie, having well furnished Captaine Samuel Argall, the Lady Pocahontas alias Rebecca, with her husband and others, in the good ship called the *George,* it pleased God at Gravesend to take this young Lady to his mercie, where shee made not more sorrow for her unexpected death, than joy to the beholders, to heare and see her make so religious and godly an end. Her little childe Thomas Rolfe therefore was left at Plimoth with Sir Lewis Stukly, that desired the keeping of it. . . . In March they set saile 1617. and in May he [Argall] arrived at James towne, where hee was kindly entertained by Captaine Yearley and his Companie in a martiall order, whose right hand file was led by an Indian. In James towne he found but five or six houses, the Church downe, the Palizado's broken, the Bridge in pieces, the Well of fresh water spoiled; the Store-house they used for the Church, the market-place, and streets, and all other spare places planted with Tobacco, the Salvages as frequent in their houses as themselves, whereby they were become expert in our armes, and had a great many in their custodie and possession, the Colonie dispersed all about, planting Tobacco.

—WORKS, II, 262.

JOHN CHAMBERLAIN: George Yardley, Knight, 1618

Here be two or three ships ready for Virginia, and one Captain Yardley a mean fellow. . . . Captain Yardley goes as governor and to grace him the more the King knighted him this last weeke at Newmarket, which hath set him up so high that he flaunts yt up and downe the streets in extraordinarie braverie, with fowreteen or fifteen fayre liveries after him.

—John Chamberlain to Dudley Carleton, November 28, 1618, *The Letters of John Chamberlain,* 2 vols. (Philadelphia: American Philosophical Society, 1939), II, 188.

JOHN PORY: Sir George Yardley, Governor, 1619

. . . the Governor here, who at his first coming, besides a great deale of worth in his person, brought onely his sword with him; was at his late being in London, together with his lady, out of his mere gettings here able to disburse very near three thousand pounde to furnishe himselfe for his return voiage.

—Letter of John Pory, September 30, 1619, in *Records of the Virginia Company,* III, 221.

EDWIN SANDYS: George Yardley's Knighthood, 1619

Sir Th Smyth was highly offended with Sr George Yeardleys being knighted: aleging that it beeing doon contrarie to his pleasure . . . for upon occasion of a motion made against Sr G. Yeardley by a noble person in contemplation as seemed of Captain Argall, Sr Thomas . . . not long after upbraiding again in open coort his unduely procured Knighthood . . . & this Against a man to whom they had professed frendship, who was chosen by themselves, & sent by them (in great part at his own private charges) to so difficult a service.

—Sir Edwin Sandys to the Earl of Southampton, September 29, 1619, *Records of the Virginia Company,* III, 217.

JOHN SMITH: The House of Burgesses, the Arrival of the Blacks, 1619

The 25. of June came in the *Triall* with Corne and Cattell all in safety, which tooke from us cleerely all feare of famine; then our governour and councell caused Burgesses to be chosen in all places, and met at a generall Assembly, where all matters were debated thought expedient for the good of the Colony. . . . About the last of August came in a dutch man of warre that sold us twenty Negars. . . .
—WORKS, II, 267.

JOHN SMITH: The Chickahominies' Revenge on the English, 1618

. . . the Salvages . . . partly for their trucke, partly for revenge of some friends they pretended should have beene slaine by Captaine Yearley, one of them with an English peece shot Killingbeck dead, the other Salvages assaulted the rest and slew them, stripped them, and tooke what they had. . . . On Sunday following, one Farfax that dwelt a mile from the towne, going to Church, left his wife and three small children safe at home . . . and a young youth: she . . . left the children, and went to meet her husband; presently after came three or foure of those fugitive Salvages, entered the house, and slew a boy and three children. . . .
—WORKS, II, 265.

THE VIRGINIA COMPANY: The English Revenge on the Chickahominies, 1619

The outrage don by the Chekohomini deserveth a sharpe revenge . . . not only to the psonall destruction of the murtherers, but the removing of that people further of from our Territories by all lawfull meanes if the same be not allready don by Captain Argall, as he seemeth to in sinuate. But for the rest mainteyne amity with the natives, soe much as may be, and pcure their Children in good multitude to be brought upp and to worke amongst us.
—Letter to Sir George Yeardley, June 21, 1619, *Records of the Virginia Company*, III, 147–148.

EDWIN SANDYS: George Yardley's Governorship, 1619

Only one thing dooth much perplex me. . . . The Governor Sir George Yeardley, having taken exceeding pains for the setting of matters in order in Virginia, & for laying the foundations of a regular State, according to his Instructions & other Directions; hath sodainly fallen into a violent resolution of quitting his Place, (grounding upon an error) & ceaseth not by all his letters publick & private to importune it. . . . But touching Sir George Yeardley, the assurance which I gave of his faithfulnes, experience & industrie, dooth cause me much to desire that . . . the woork . . . may passe on to his hands to be there established. . . . My humble suit to your Lordship is, if it shall seem good for the service of Virginia no advantage be taken of Sir Georges rash offer. . . .
—Sir Edwin Sandys to the Earl of Southampton, September 29, 1619, *Records of the Virginia Company*, III, 217.

GEORGE YARDLEY: Sickness at Jamestown, 1620

And had they arived at a seasonable tyme of the yeare I would not have doubted of theire lives and healths, but this season is most unfitt for people to arive here, and to tell you the very truth I doubt of much sicknes for many of them to the number of 100 least come some very weake and sick some Crasey and taynted a shore, and now this great heate of weather striketh many more. . . .
—Sir George Yeardley, Letter to Sir Edwin Sandys, June 7, 1620, *Records of the Virginia Company*, III, 298.

GEORGE THORPE: Sickness at Jamestown, 1620

I am persuaded that more do die here of the disease of their minds then of their body. . . .
—George Thorpe to John Smith, December 29, 1620, in Alexander Brown, *The First Republic in America* (New York: Houghton, Mifflin, 1898), 409.

GEORGE THORPE: Indian Relations, 1621

. . . there [is] scarce any man amongest us that doth soe much as affoorde them a good thought in his hart and most men with theire mouthes give them nothinge but maledictions. . . . If there bee wrong on any Side it is on ors who are not so charitable to them as Christians ought to bee. . . .
—George Thorpe, Letter to Sir Edwin Sandys, May 1621, *Records of the Virginia Company*, III, 446.

JONAS STOCKHAM: Indian Relations, 1621

Though many have endevoured by all the meanes they could by kindnesse to convert them, they finde nothing from them but derision and ridiculous answers. We have sent boies amongst them to learne their Language, but they returne worse than they went; but I am no States-man, nor love I to meddle with any thing but my Bookes, but I can finde no probability by this course to draw them to goodnesse; and I am perswaded if Mars and Minerva goe hand in hand, they will effect more good in an houre, then those verball Mercurians in their lives, and till their Priests and Ancients have their throats cut, there is no hope to bring them to conversion.
—Jonas Stockham, "Relation," May 28, 1621, in WORKS, II, 285.

THE VIRGINIA COMPANY: Indian Relations, 1621

. . . No injurie or oppression bee wrought by the English against any of the Natives . . . whereby the peace may be disturbed and ancient quarrells (now buried) bee revived, *Provided nevertheless* that the honour of our Nation and safety of our people be still preserved and all manner of Insolence committed by the natives be severely and sharpelie punished.

—Virginia Company Council, Instructions to Sir George Yeardley, July 1621, *Records of the Virginia Company,* III, 469.

JOHN SMITH: Prologue to the Massacre: The Death of Nemattonow, 1622

The Prologue to this Tragedy, is supposed was occasioned by Nemattanow, otherwise called Jack of the Feather, because hee commonly was most strangely adorned with them; and for his courage and policy, was accounted amongst the Salvages their chiefe Captaine, and immortall from any hurt could bee done him by the English. This Captaine comming to one Morgans house, knowing hee had many commodities that hee desired, perswaded Morgan to goe with him to Pamaunke to trucke, but the Salvage murdered him by the way; and after two or three daies returned againe to Morgans house, where he found two youths his Servants, who asked for their Master: Jack replied directly he was dead; the Boyes suspecting as it was, by seeing him weare his Cap, would have had him to Master Thorp. But Jack so moved their patience, they shot him, so he fell to the ground, put him in a Boat to have him before the Governor, then seven or eight miles from them. But by the way Jack finding the pangs of death upon him, desired . . . two things; the one was, that they would not make it knowne hee was slain with a bullet; the other, to bury him amongst the English. At the losse of this Salvage Opechankanough much grieved and repined, with great threats of revenge; but the English returned him such terrible answers, that he cunningly dissembled his intent, with the greatest signes he could of love and peace, yet within fourteen daies after he acted what followeth. . . .

—WORKS, II, 293.

JOHN SMITH: The Massacre, March 22, 1622

. . . on the Friday morning that fatall day, being the two and twentieth of March . . . as at other times they came unarmed into our houses, with Deere, Turkies, Fish, Fruits, and other provisions to sell us, yea in some places sat downe at breakfast with our people, whom immediatly with their owne tooles they slew most barbarously, not sparing either age or sex, man woman or childe, so sudden in their execution, that few or none discerned the weapon or blow that brought them to destruction . . . and by this meanes fell that fatall morning under the bloudy and barbarous hands of that perfidious and inhumane people, three hundred forty seven men, women and children, most by their owne weapons, and not being content with their lives, they fell again upon the dead bodies, making as well as they could a fresh murder, defacing, dragging, and mangling their dead carkases into many peeces, and carying some parts away in derision, with base and brutish triumph.

—WORKS, II, 294.

JOHN SMITH: The Indian Informer

. . . the slaughter had beene universall, if God had not put it into the heart of an Indian, who lying in the house of one Pace, was urged by another Indian his Brother, that lay with him the night before to kill Pace, as he should doe Perry which was his friend, being so commanded from their King; telling him also how the next day the execution should be finished: Perrys Indian presently arose and reveales it to Pace, that used him as his sonne; and thus them that escaped was saved by this one converted Infidell. . . .

Pace, upon this, securing his house, before day rowed to James Towne, and told the Governor of it. . . .

—WORKS, II, 297–298.

JOHN SMITH: The Death of George Thorpe, March 22, 1622

That worthy religious Gentleman Master George Thorp. . . . thought nothing too deare for them, he never denied them any thing. . . . yet this viperous brood did . . . not onely murder him, but with such spight and scorne abused his dead corps as is unfitting to be heard with civill eares.

—WORKS, II, 295.

JOHN SMITH: The Death of Harmon Harison, March 22, 1622

At the same time they came to one Master Harisons house, neere halfe a mile from Baldwines, where was Master Thomas Hamer with six men, and eighteene or nineteene women and children. Here the Salvages with many presents and faire perswasions, fained they came for Captaine Ralfe Hamer to go to their King, then hunting in the woods, . . . presently they set fire of a Tobacco-House, and then came to tell them in the dwelling house of it to quench it; all the men ran towards it . . . not suspecting any thing, whom the Salvages pursued, shot them full of arrowes, then beat out their braines. Hamer . . . followed after . . . but quickly they shot an arrow in his back, which caused him to returne and barricado up the doores, whereupon the Salvages set fire on the house. . . . Master Hamer with two and twentie persons thereby got to his house, leaving their owne burning.

Captaine Hamer . . . found his brother and the rest at Baldwins. . . .

—WORKS, II, 296.

JOHN SMITH: The Attack on Nathaniel Causey, March 22, 1622

Another of the old company of Captaine Smith, called Nathaniel Causie, being cruelly wounded, and the Salvages about him, with an axe did cleave one of their heads, whereby the rest fled and he escaped: for they hurt not any that did either fight or stand upon their guard.

—WORKS, II, 295.

JOHN SMITH: List of the Dead, 1622

The numbers that were slaine in those severall Plantations.

At Captaine Berkleys Plantation, himselfe and 21. others, seated at the Falling-Crick, 66. miles from James City.	22
Master Thomas Shefflds Plantation, some three miles from the Falling-Crick, himselfe and 12. others.	13
At Henrico Iland, about two miles from Shefflds Plantation.	6
Slaine of the College people, two miles from Henrico.	17
At Charles City, and of Captaine Smiths men.	5
At the next adjoyning Plantation.	8
At William Farrars house.	10
At Berkley Hundred, five miles from Charles City, Master Thorp and	10
At Westover, a mile from Berkley.	2
At Master John Wests Plantation.	2
At Captaine Nathaniel Wests Plantation.	2
At Lieutenant Gibs his Plantation.	12
At Richard Owens house, himselfe and	6
At Master Owen Macars house, himselfe and	3
At Martins Hundred, seven miles from James City.	73
At another place.	7
At Edward Bennets Plantation.	50
At Master Waters his house, himselfe and	4
At Apamatucks River, at Master Peirce his Plantation, five miles from the College.	4
At Master Macocks Divident, Captain Samuel Macock, and	4
At Flowerdieu Hundred, Sir George Yearleys Plantation.	6
On the other side opposite to it.	7
At Master Swinhows house, himselfe and	7
At Master William Bickars house, himselfe and	4
At Weanock, of Sir George Yearleys people	21
At Powel Brooke, Captain Nathaniel Powel, and	12
At Southampton Hundred.	7
At Martin Brandons Hundred.	7
At Captaine Henry Spilmans house.	2
At Ensigne Spences house.	5
At Master Thomas Peirce his house by Mulbery Ile, himselfe and	4

The whole number	347

—WORKS, II, 301–302.